Let the

A Novel by

Nick Alexander

BIGfib

Nick Alexander

Nick Alexander was born in 1964 in the UK. He has travelled widely and has lived and worked both in the UK, the USA and France where he resides today. *Let the Light Shine* is his thirteenth fictional work. His 2015 novel, *The Other Son*, was named by Amazon as one of the best fiction titles of the year; *The Photographer's Wife* published in 2014 was a number 1 hit in both the UK and France, while *The Half-Life of Hannah* is the 4th bestselling independently published Kindle title of all time. Nick lives in the southern French Alps with his partner, two ageing cats (Typhus & Leon-Pedro) and seven (nameless) trout.

Acknowledgements

Thanks to Fay Weldon for encouraging me when it most counted. Thanks to Allan and Sue for their proofing skills and to Rosemary and Lolo for being the most important people on my planet. Thanks to Karen, Jenny, Tina, Annie, Sylvie and everyone else who gave me feedback on this novel. It wouldn't have happened without you. Thanks to Amazon for turning the writing of novels back into something one can actually earn a living from.

Prologue

Christmas Eve, 1975, Margate.

Penny descends the staircase, banging the feet of her doll against the bannisters as she does so. They make a series of satisfying, almost musical, twangs.

The sun is shining through the stained glass window above the front door, casting colourful geometric patterns across the floor tiles.

At the base of the stairs she swings for a moment on the large final bannister. The lounge door is ajar and peering in she can see one edge of the television screen, her mother's slippered foot, and a single branch of the Christmas tree.

Penny *loves* the Christmas tree, loves the layers of greenery and the glittering coloured lights. She sometimes gets up during the night and comes downstairs so that she can lie down beneath the tree just to breathe in the pine smell and stare up into the twinkling forest of branches.

She loves the piled up gifts beneath the tree too of course – wonderful gifts from uncle Cecil who, like an early Father Christmas, turned up yesterday.

At midnight even more gifts will arrive when the real Father Christmas brings his own contribution down the chimney.

Her mother says something which she doesn't quite catch, and Cecil laughs in response and, drawn by the laughter, these sounds of happiness, she takes one step towards the lounge door, but then hesitates and continues on her way through to the kitchen where she walks as far as the dresser. Glancing back towards the lounge, she crouches down and opens the lowest cupboard.

Inside is the cake tin, and inside the tin is the Christmas cake her mother has been "feeding" with brandy for weeks now.

Penny considers opening the lid and touching her finger to the damp surface of the cake, then to her lips. She's done this a few times now and she remembers the spicy odour of the cake and the tang of the alcohol. But then, conscious of the danger of being caught, she closes the door and stands again. "You'll just have to wait until tomorrow, I'm afraid," she tells Lucy, her doll.

She walks the doll along the ledge of the dresser as far as the sugar bowl and then dips her finger into the sugar. When it comes up dry, she licks her finger and repeats the process.

She thinks about the packages beneath the tree and wonders if the *Operation* game she asked for is there. Ed, who has dared to squeeze the un-named packages (squeezing is strictly forbidden) says that it's not there, but, as it's the only thing she has asked for and as it's not even particularly expensive, Penny thinks he's wrong, or lying. Jennifer from number eleven got *Operation* for her birthday, and Penny, who it would seem has steady hands, has beaten her every time. She may well, she thinks, end up being a proper nurse when she grows up.

Vicky has asked for a cassette player so she can record ABBA from the television. She has promised Penny a proper party in her bedroom if her wish gets fulfilled. And Ed has asked for a train set, which Mum says is too expensive, though Vicky says he'll probably (being Cecil's favourite) get it anyway. Penny thinks a train set sounds boring.

"I don't know," Penny says, lifting the doll to face her and answering a conversation inside her head. "You'll have to see what Father Christmas brings, won't you?" The doll, with her one droopy eye, looks half-drunk, half-surprised.

Dangling Lucy by one arm, Penny returns to the hallway. Upstairs she can hear Vicky and Ed arguing (nothing unusual there), and when uncle Cecil laughs again, she pushes the door to the lounge open. Both Cecil and her mother turn and smile at her.

"Here she is," Cecil says. "My favourite youngest niece. Come and have a cuddle with your uncle Cecil."

Penny smiles shyly at him and sidles instead towards her mother, who is knitting, but Cecil stands and sweeps her up in his arms and then sits back down with Penny on his knee, his ample stomach pressing against her back. She looks down at his brogues and wonders how he gets them so shiny.

"So, the *Ning Nang Nong*?" Cecil asks. The *Ning Nang Nong* is Penny's favourite Spike Milligan poem.

"Yes!" she says.

"I'm not sure I remember how it starts," Cecil mugs.

"In the Ning Nang Nong," Penny prompts, and Cecil begins to recite the poem, speaking faster and faster and jigging Penny up and down more and more energetically as the poem progresses.

As soon as the poem is finished, Penny, though still giggling, wriggles free and moves to the far side of her mother's armchair. "What are you making?" she asks.

"The same thing I was making the last time you asked," her mother replies.

"A jumper for Ed?"

"Very good," Marge says.

"Is it lunch time?" Penny asks. "Because Lucy says she's hungry."

Her mother glances at the clock on the mantlepiece. "Not yet," she says, "but you were up early – there are sandwiches in the kitchen. If you're hungry take one."

Penny heads through to the kitchen and takes two of the tiny triangular sandwiches (which disappointingly contain fish paste) then returns to her bedroom where she eats them on her bed while forcing Bungle and Lucy to make up (they argued yesterday). The argument solved, she falls asleep.

When she wakes up, something has changed. She can't put her finger on it, but it's as if the air within the house has changed shape or tint or temperature.

She lies for a moment listening to the wind whistling past the leaky windows, to a gull squawking from a chimney pot, to a car driving past, to the silence of the house around her.

Her first thought is that everyone is sleeping, but the stillness somehow exceeds even that and she starts to feel panicky that everyone might have gone out without her.

She grabs Lucy's hand and, frowning deeply, steps from her bedroom.

She walks past the junk room and silently pads down to the first floor.

She tries the handle of Vicky's door first but it is locked, so she calls out, "Vicky? VICKY?"

"Go away!" Vicky replies, apparently through tears.

Next she climbs to the top floor and tries Ed's door which swings open to reveal uncle Cecil leaning over his camp-bed re-packing his suitcase. "Not now, Penny," he says, freezing but not looking up.

"Are you leaving?" Penny asks.

"Not now!" Cecil shouts, then as Penny steps backwards onto the landing, he adds, more softly, "Sorry. Yes. I have to get the three-thirty train."

Downstairs, things are no less strange.

The television is playing to an empty room, and Penny finds her mother swigging from the brandy bottle in the kitchen.

"Is that nice?" Penny asks, and her mother lowers the bottle, hides it behind her back and spins to face her youngest, all in a single movement.

"Spying on me now, are you?" she asks, her eyes red, her voice sniffy.

Penny stares at her mother wide-eyed and slowly shakes her head. "No," she says. "Where's Ed?"

"I don't know," Marge says sharply, "Now, go and play or something, OK?"

Penny stomps her way to the back door, then lets herself out into the garden. "I don't know what's wrong with them either," she tells Lucy.

But the wind out here is bracing and, despite the strip of sunlight, it's impossible to remain here, so she peers in through the kitchen window and seeing that Marge has vanished, she lets herself back in, creeps past the closed lounge door, and back upstairs to Vicky's room.

This time Vicky wrenches open the door and pulls her inside before locking it again.

"What's happened?" Penny asks, her voice wobbling. "Why are you crying? Where's Ed?"

"It's nothing," Vicky says. "It's grown-up stuff, that's all."

Penny huffs. She hates it when Vicky pulls rank on her. She's only two years older, after all. Well, three years older at this time of year.

"Where's Ed?" she asks again.

"I don't know," Vicky says, blowing her nose on a tatty tissue.

"Why is uncle Cecil leaving?" she asks, and suddenly she has Vicky's interest.

Vicky brushes her hair from her face and looks up at Penny. "Is he?" she asks. She sounds surprised. She sounds relieved, too.

"On the three-thirty o'clock train," Penny says. "He's putting his things in his case."

"Good," Vicky says. "I hate him."

"Why?" Penny asks.

"I... I can't tell you," Vicky says.

"Why not?"

"Look. If you want to stay, you have to stop asking questions, OK?"

Penny bites her bottom lip and nods. "He won't take the presents with him, will he?"

"How should I know?" Vicky asks angrily, then, "But no, Sis. I doubt it."

"Do you think you'll still get your music player?" Penny asks.

"I had better," Vicky says, suddenly sounding terribly grown up. "Otherwise..."

"Otherwise what?" Penny asks.

"Nothing," Vicky says. "Otherwise nothing."

Part One

Two Sisters.

Penny glances at her buzzing mobile then, continuing to stir the soup, she leans over to study the screen on which a single word is flashing: Vicky.

She sighs. She probably has about eight buzzes left before she has to decide what to do. She loves her sister – forty-five years of shared history makes that a given. But it doesn't mean that Victoria is an easy person to love, and it doesn't make their relationship an effortless one, either. So Penny generally attempts, at least, to choose the most fortuitous moment in which to speak to her sister. She tries to wait until a positive outcome seems feasible.

She gives the soup another stir as she glances back at her husband, Sander, seated behind her. He raises one eyebrow. She returns her gaze to the phone, now vibrating gently across the worktop, slowly making its way towards the abyss.

On the *for* side of the equation it is a beautiful October day. The sun is shining, the gulls are squawking and Penny is feeling relatively optimistic – energised, even.

On the *against* side, she needs to leave in – she glances at the kitchen clock – forty minutes, and she's just about to have lunch with her husband, a fairly rare occurrence these days. Plus she has already spoken to her mother this morning, which in some way makes her feel that her family obligations have perhaps already been fulfilled, at least for the current twenty-four hour period.

The phone is still buzzing like a wasp in a box, and it has almost reached the edge of the countertop now, so it's decision time and, realising that if she doesn't pick up it will be the third time in a row that she has failed to do so, she reaches out and snatches it.

"Hello you," she says in her best chipper voice, simultaneously turning off the gas. The soup, and lunch, will have to wait.

She walks past Sander – he rolls his eyes in commentary – then opens the back door and steps out into the garden. A robin is tweeting from a branch on the apple tree.

"Finally," Victoria says on the other end of the line. "I was beginning to think I'd been banished or something."

"It's a gorgeous day here," Penny says, powering through the negativity. "It's like summer almost. What's it like up in London?"

"It's sunny here, too," Victoria says. "Though less pretty than Whitstable, I expect."

"I can't talk for long I'm afraid," Penny warns. "I have to be in Ashford by three. We've got two unaccompanied juveniles arriving."

"Right," Victoria says. "It's just that I had Mum on the phone."

"She phoned me too," Penny says, pulling a weed from the base of the wall and unthinkingly chucking it into the garden of the uninhabited neighbouring house then feeling a little guilty about it. "Was it about Christmas?"

"Exactly," Victoria says.

"I told her we hadn't thought about it yet. Which is the truth, actually. We haven't."

"I know that. But we're going to have to think about it at some point. What do you think?"

"*I* think it's October," Penny says.

"I know it's October."

Penny grimaces. Irony is so often wasted on Victoria. "So I think that there's no hurry," she expounds. "I think we have plenty of time to think about Christmas."

"I know but–"

"Look, I'll chat to Sander," Penny interrupts, deciding that answering was a bad idea after all. The conversation is spoiling her relatively Zen start to the week and it's still a beautiful day. She wants to continue to enjoy it. "And I'll call you back at the weekend, OK? But I really do have to go. I'm sorry."

"Only we won't be here at the weekend. We're off to Venice," Victoria says, showing no signs of hanging up.

"Venice?"

"Yeah, you know. In Italy. The one with all the canals."

Penny pulls her phone from her ear and frowns at it briefly before continuing. "Yes, I do know where Venice is, dear."

"Oh, have you been there?" Victoria asks.

"Have *I* been to Venice? Hum. Let me see."

"There's no need to be like that," Victoria says. "Anyway... it's just a mini break. Just two nights, actually. It's a perk, from Bower and Watson, that's all. Bertie's staying at Aaron's place for the weekend."

"Right," Penny says. "Great. Well, you know, have a nice time and we can talk about it next week, OK?"

"Talk about Venice?"

"About *Christmas*."

"Oh, OK," Victoria says. "Are you all right? You sound funny."

"Yeah... I'm just... I don't know. I'm tired, I guess," Penny says. "I'm suddenly *very* tired."

When she steps back into the kitchen, Sander is pouring the soup. "Posh, I take it?" he asks. Sander has nicknamed Victoria, "Posh" and her husband Martin, "Becks." The kids have even started calling their cousin Bertie "Brooklyn" behind his back.

Penny pulls a face and nods. "Just popping off to Venice for the weekend, *darling*," she says in a mocking, pompous voice.

"With Becks?"

Penny nods. "Yep. It's a perk from his job, apparently."

"The hard lives people live, huh?"

"She wanted to talk about Christmas."

"Christmas? Already?"

"She just wants to decide where it's going to be, I think. You know how stressed she gets about Christmas."

"I know how stressed she gets about *everything*," Sander says under his breath.

"Yes. Well..."

"Is something up, love?" Sander asks, softening his tone. He has noticed an infinitesimal and unusual droop to his wife's shoulders.

Penny shakes her head gently and shrugs. "She just... you know what she's like. She said we should get away more. She said it would do us *good*."

"Right," Sander says. "Cheers, Vicky. Thanks for that."

"When was it, anyway?" Penny asks. "I was trying to remember."

"Bournemouth?"

"Yeah."

"Twenty-twelve, maybe?"

"That's what I thought. Twenty-twelve. It's been over two years, Sander. We haven't been anywhere for over two years. Not even a mini-break. Can you believe that?"

"Bournemouth was enough to put me off mini-breaks for life," Sander laughs. He pushes a bowl of soup across the table towards his wife. "Here," he says.

Penny sits down and raises a spoonful to her mouth. It's not really as hot as she would like it to be, but she won't say anything. She's trying to encourage Sander to help more around the house, and has decided that criticising what little he *does* do probably isn't the best way to achieve that end. Husbands, she has decided, need to be managed more like children. Reinforce the good behaviour, dissuade the bad.

As she tastes the soup – tomato, Heinz, lukewarm – she thinks back to that weekend in Bournemouth. It had been a raffle prize – a weekend in a hotel. It had been the *first* prize, supposedly.

Even now, she struggles to understand why they had gone. Something to do with not "wasting" the prize, no doubt. That and some misplaced idea that it would be, *could* be, "fun".

The hotel had been horrible, "shit brown" walls, as Sander always describes them, and questionable levels of cleanliness, too. It had rained all weekend (they'd gone out and got soaked only once) and their room – which looked out not at the sea as advertised but onto a graffitied red-brick wall – had been depressing and, when contrasted with the sea-views of their own draughty windows back home, slightly worse than disappointing.

The meals – not included – had been poor and overpriced, and to top it all, Sander had picked up a stomach bug and had spent the entire drive home asking her to pull into service stations so that he could throw up. Seeing as they had eaten the same meals, they had never been able to blame that one squarely on the hotel's restaurant, but they had their suspicions all the same.

Her sister's weekend in Venice will be nothing like that, of course. Penny imagines them now, in evening dress in a candle-lit restaurant eating lobster. She grimaces. No, it won't be like Bournemouth at all.

"So, Christmas," Sander is saying between sips of tinned soup. "I thought you just alternated, in which case it's their turn, isn't it? What's to think about?"

"Max says it's boring at their place," Penny says. "He wants us to do it here."

Sander sighs. "He's not wrong," he says. "But you know how much it cost last year. We were paying for it till March."

"I know," Penny agrees. "But last year was silly. If we do it here again, we'll just have to ask them to chip in or something. We can do that, can't we?"

"Hum," Sander says, remembering the pre-arrival cleaning regime and the post departure economy drive of the previous year.

"Hum?"

"I was just thinking," Sander says. "I mean, seeing as you always argue anyway, you could perhaps – shock – horror – even consider Christmas *apart* for once?"

"Christmas *apart*?"

"Yeah. What do you think?"

Penny smiles sadly at her husband. "You *know* that's not an option," she says.

Sander shrugs. "Just, you know, throwing it out there for discussion."

"You *know* how difficult Christmas is for us, Sander. For both of us. *And* for Mum."

"Maybe it wouldn't be so hard if you weren't together," Sander offers doubtfully. "Maybe you'd think about it less if you weren't there to remind each other–"

"*Sander,*" Penny pleads.

"This was, what, thirty years ago?"

"Forty," Penny says, "Your point being?"

"You're a shrink. Isn't your speciality helping people get over shit like that?"

Penny looks at him disdainfully, then bows her head and studies her soup, driving the spoon through the thick redness of it. "I'm a psychologist, Sander, not a *shrink*," she says, quietly. "And to my knowledge nobody *ever* gets over..." She clears her throat. She swallows. She's suddenly angry. It's bubbling up in her like a rush of boiling water from a geyser. She raises two fingers to form the quotes around the final three words. "Nobody ever gets over *'shit like that'*," she says.

"I didn't mean anything," Sander offers softly after a moment's pause.

Penny blinks at him slowly. "I know," she replies.

For a few minutes, they eat their soup in silence. Sander thinks about Victoria in Venice and the fact that he mentioned the cost of Christmas and wrestles with his sense of guilt. For they both know that he hasn't contributed financially for years.

Yes, he still sells the occasional painting, but he hasn't made any serious money from his work since the noughties.

He would love to make more money, of course. He would love, once again, to surf the buzz of success that he (briefly) experienced in 2000 and 2001. He would love to be able to whisk Penny off to Venice for a weekend break. The views might even inspire him to do some more work, some new work, some different work... But he can't take Penny to Venice, can he? They're overdrawn on every account.

Still, the house is paid for, he reminds himself. And these days that single achievement makes them millionaires, on paper at least. Yes, he, Sander, with an inheritance from his estranged Danish parents and one big sell-out show in Cork Street, had paid for this house, cash. Perhaps they need to sell the house and move somewhere cheaper. If they moved inland or even better, up north, the equity in the house would leave them well-off for years, perhaps even until retirement. But he's loath to lose this house. They have sea views from almost every window. He can hear the sea, even now, in the kitchen. And the pride he felt at being able to buy the place – a house! – with the proceeds from his paintings, is the biggest buzz he has ever felt, topping, in pride terms, even the births of Max and Chloe. Of course Max and Chloe are more important to him than the house, but he never felt that he'd done that much to make them happen. That always felt like Penny's miracle more than it was ever his.

So the house, no, he can't bear to think of leaving it. "I'd get a job if I thought there was anything else I could do," he says, finally, those thoughts leading to this one.

And because they've been married for almost sixteen years, and in love, on and off, for at least fifteen of those, Penny effortlessly deduces Sander's entire train of thought.

"I don't want to go to Venice," she says. "I really *don't*. And I hate all those posh restaurants they go to. All that crumb-brushing and putting the wine out of reach so you can only get a refill when the snooty waiter deigns to fill your glass. Yuck."

"Thanks," Sander says, "but..."

"And I'm *glad* you're a painter, not a lawyer, really I am."

Sander nods.

"Plus we're not doing so badly," Penny continues, glancing around the room as if to encompass the house, the furniture, the car outside and the soup on the table.

No, she thinks. *We're not being bombed and we're not hungry or homeless, and we're not worried about our son who was picked up by government security forces a few months ago and never heard from again.* Three quarters of the world would consider Penny and Sander obscenely rich just for owning a working tap out of which gushes safe drinking water. She knows this and she tries to remind herself of it often.

She glances at the clock again and then starts to spoon her soup at double speed. "I have to be in Ashford by three," she says.

"New arrivals?"

Penny nods. "Two kids. More Syrians, I think."

"Alone?"

"Yep. Unaccompanied minors."

"Related?"

"Not that I know of."

"The poor wee fuckers," Sander says.

"Yes," Penny agrees. "Yes, they're the hardest ones." The unaccompanied minors' backstories are always by far the most heartbreaking. "And you, are you staying in?"

"I might try to paint," Sander says.

"Good. Well, check the washing machine in half an hour, would you? I'll put it on, but just check it's not leaking again."

"I fixed it."

"I know. But just do me a favour and check it, OK?"

Sander shrugs. "Sure," he says.

Sander watches from his studio window as Penny drives away, then turns and stares out to sea. It's such a beautiful view from this room, an ever changing vista of blues and greens and greys. Today, the sky is a light, almost cerulean blue. Beneath it, the sea blurs from a grimy cobalt green at the horizon down to deep green-blue, perhaps indigo mixed with chromite, where it meets the shore. A touch of charcoal grey, too, Sander thinks, imagining himself trying to mix that exact colour.

Perhaps he'll paint another seascape. He sighs. He has an entire shelf of seascapes painted from this very spot. He enjoys the challenge of mixing the colours, of attempting to reproduce the myriad shades that light and nature and the laws of physics throw up every day, but in commercial terms, it's worse than pointless – the materials cost money, after all. And in personal terms, it's little more than laziness, the easiest route he has found to avoid doing nothing at all.

His big idea in the noughties, the one idea that paid for the house in fact, had been a series of Hopperesque interiors, all emerald greens and cadmium reds, all geometric shadows and visible rectangles of leaking light. His twist, his one great idea, had been to replace the figures in his paintings with depictions of blow-up dolls, their mouths rounded and plump, their busts pointy and over-inflated.

It had been this juxtaposition of artistry – for these had been painterly paintings – with the plastic disposable artifice of the modern world that had got everyone so excited. *Hopper's skill mixed with Warhol's barefaced cheek, The Times* had said of him. *The Times!* That's how big he had been.

He can still paint just as well, of course. He has lost none of his skills at mixing colour, depicting perspective or applying texture. It's just the idea that's missing, it's just that twist. But without a fresh flash of humour, he knows that he'll never be hip again. The art world changed in the sixties, and it's no longer enough to be a good craftsman. You have to be clever, witty, and hip as well.

He turns back to face the room and looks at the racks of paintings on the left hand wall. *Hundreds* of paintings and, including those upstairs, thousands perhaps. He needs to have a clear-out. He needs to make fresh space for new work otherwise he won't even have anywhere to put it. He needs to have a bonfire, perhaps this November the fifth? But how to admit the necessity of destroying unsold work to make space without admitting the futility of ever painting anything again?

He looks to the right, to the steel shelves containing his materials. He keeps them ready, organised and clean, just in case. He stares at them and waits, yet again, for an idea.

His eye drifts to the wooden box in the corner. Perhaps if he doesn't smoke today, that will help. Perhaps if he picks up his brushes and squeezes out pigments and leaves the box alone just this once. But then the doll idea had come to him when stoned, hadn't it? Or is that just a story he has told himself? He can't really remember anymore, if the truth be told.

He strokes his beard with his left hand, then exhales slowly and crosses to the box. He picks it up, caresses the lid and feels a tugging sensation deep in his gut. "Maybe just one," he mutters, already lifting the lid and breathing in the rich odour of the "blue dream" buds within.

He rolls the joint, then sits in his threadbare spoon back armchair and stares back out at the horizon. He flicks open the lid of his beloved Zippo lighter – a whiff of lighter fluid reaches his nostrils. Clouds are forming to the east, casting deep violet shadows onto the surface of the sea. Violet, ultramarine, and a tiny touch of indigo, perhaps, he thinks, blowing smoke towards the ceiling.

Seascapes with blow-up dolls, he thinks. Greek life-rafts with blow-up dolls. Dead blow-up dolls on a beach. Clothes store dummies. Robots. Actually robots could be funny. Expensive robots on life-rafts. No one would ever let *those* sink to the bottom of the sea – they'd have hundreds of boats out in a jiffy. But no, it would be seen as political comment, not art – too literal.

He stares into the middle distance and feels the dope wash over him, feels it spread out warming and soothing and relaxing his muscles. And when the first joint is finished, he rolls another one. After that, he promises himself that he'll work.

Or perhaps he should accept that it's over, the dope seems to tell him. Perhaps that's where true peace lies. He had his Warholian fifteen minutes of fame in 2001 so maybe he just needs to accept the nature of his own mediocrity from here on in. Perhaps accepting that it's over is where happiness lies.

At some point he sees Chloe come home, her face so buried in her Samsung that she doesn't even notice him looking down at her. And then, perhaps half an hour later, Max on his pushbike, his torch projecting a wobbling, yellow Hockneyesque triangle in the evening mist.

It's only when he sees car headlights come around the corner, only when he hears the Ford's clattering diesel engine that he realises how late it is.

Shit, he thinks. *The washing machine.*

And at that precise moment he hears Max calling up the stairs. "Dad? Dad?" he says. "Are you in? Only, the basement's all flooded again! DAAAD?!"

• • •

Victoria peers into the oven and then straightens and looks around the kitchen. The dinner, a tray of Delia's oven-cooked ratatouille and an organic chicken, should be ready right on time, she reckons.

She crosses to the kitchen sink and pulls the squirty bleach out of the cupboard. She particularly likes oven-based meals because once the food's cooking she can tidy the kitchen entirely and eat without her eyes straying to the pots and pans waiting to be dealt with. There's something reassuring, she finds, about the cold surfaces of a clean kitchen. She squirts bleach onto the sponge and begins to wipe the worktop.

The strange fluttering in her chest has returned and if she can just distract herself for ten minutes it might pass of its own accord. Sometimes she can avoid taking that second Valium tab.

She rubs at a stain on the worktop and then reaches for the nailbrush and starts rubbing at the joints between the tiles. Whatever possessed her to have a tiled worktop fitted? she wonders. She had thought it would be cleaner and more hygienic than the old wooden one. But she hadn't counted on these joints between the tiles, these little once-white spaces that just suck everything up like a sponge.

23

She forces herself to breathe deeply and the chlorine smell of the bleach calms her a little. She scans her body, senses the dryness of her lips (a new thing), the fluttering in her chest (an old one) and the aching knees and the vague headache (today's specials).

She snorts at the thought that if women ruled the world rather than men then people would be allowed to talk about the menopause, and women like her would be better prepared.

As it is, other than an occasional snide joke about hot flushes (if only that's all it was!) she was entirely unprepared for the grandeur of the coming change. Not a hot flush in sight, but instead, a buggering-up of almost every bodily process, a sensation that she's drying out like those fish they sell in the markets in Asia, yes, freeze dried and out-of-order in every way that counts, getting ready, it seems in her more pessimistic moments, for nothing other than death. She certainly wasn't expecting anything like *this* at forty-eight.

She crosses to the bookshelf and, glancing at the hallway to check she's truly alone, she reaches to the rear of the top shelf and pulls the blister pack into view. She breaks out a pill, snaps it in half and returns the remainder to the pack, and the pack to the rear of the shelf.

She crosses to the sink and, thinking *thank God for chemistry, thank God for bleach and Diazepam*, she downs it with a glass of water.

Victoria's relationship with Valium predated the first hints of menopause by at least ten years. But it had been under control until last year, hadn't it? A single doctor had been enough to keep her supplied back then, so at least she hadn't had to lie or cheat to get supplies.

But the fluttering, the anxiety, has got so much worse this year – another perimenopausal bonus. She sits at the kitchen table and attempts to concentrate on her breath – meditation style – as she waits for the Valium to work its magic. And when finally, ten minutes later, her breathing has returned to normal, she stands, checks the oven once again, and walks through to the lounge.

Marge, her mother, over for a visit, is seated on the new white sofa in front of a too-loud television game-show. Her head has fallen backwards and she's snoring loudly. She snoozes a lot since her stroke last summer.

Victoria takes the remote from the coffee table and lowers the sound which inexplicably wakes her mother instantly. "I'm watching that," Marge says through a yawn.

"I'm only turning it down a bit," Victoria says. "And you were snoring actually."

"I don't snore," Marge tells her. "I've never snored in my life. When did you ever hear me snore?"

"OK," Victoria says with a laugh. "Well, you were asleep at any rate."

"I just closed my eyes for a second. That's not a crime, is it?"

"No, Mum. That's not a crime."

"Is it dinner time yet?"

"In about half an hour," Victoria says, glancing at the time on the broadband box. "When Martin gets home."

"And Bertie?"

"He's in his room, doing his homework."

"That's what he tells you," Marge says. "I expect he's on that computer again. He's always on that computer."

"Well, he does his homework on *that computer*," Victoria says, "so you're probably right."

She has changed her mind about sitting in the lounge after all. She hands her mother the remote and turns and walks back to the kitchen. She's only just starting to float – she's not ready to be dragged back to earth by her mother.

It's seven thirty by the time Martin gets home, and by eight, when he has removed his tie and swapped his pin-stripe trousers for jeans, the dinner is, Victoria fears, slightly past its best.

But by then, her Valium bubble, augmented with a hefty glass of Prosecco, is fully formed and gorgeously impregnable. She feels as if she's wearing some kind of inflatable Michelin Man costume. Nothing can reach her now.

She serves up the ratatouille and watches as Martin massacres the bird with a carving knife. Amazingly, he thinks he can do it better than she can. It's a man thing.

"Breast or thigh?" he asks.

Victoria sits and stares at him for a few seconds before she realises that he was talking to her. "Oh, yes, sorry," she says. "Breast if there's enough."

"Well, I'm not hungry anymore," Marge says, a dig at the late mealtime. They'd all eat at six if Marge had her way. "I think I've gone past it to be honest, so you can have mine."

"There's plenty, Mum," Victoria says. "And you know what time we eat around here."

"Yes," Marge says, her downward-turned mouth momentarily evening-up the post-stroke lopsidedness of her face. "Silly o'clock, that's when you eat. It's not good for the digestion."

"You've stained your shirt," Victoria says, mesmerised by a red dot on Martin's double cuff as it moves up and down. His cufflinks are blue and pretty, but she can't remember if she bought them for him or not. Is her failing memory yet another side effect of the menopause, or is it instead the result of all the Valium she's been popping? She thinks she read something about Valium affecting your memory, though she can't, for the life of her, remember where.

Martin follows her gaze to his cuff and says, "Oh. Yeah. That'll come out, won't it?"

Victoria takes her plate from his outstretched hand and uses the occasion to study the stain close to. "What is that, anyway?" she asks, wondering if she has any Vanish left, and then wondering if one of those Stain Devil things mightn't work better.

"Dunno," Martin says. "Food?"

"It's very red for food," Victoria says.

"It *looks* like lipstick," Marge offers.

"Oh, yeah," Martin mugs. "That'll be it. The female clients all insist on doing this kneeling cuff-kissing thing these days. Ever since *Fifty Shades of Grey*. It's getting to be a real bore."

"Really?" Victoria asks. There is humour in Martin's voice, she can hear that. And there's a wry smile on his lips too. It's just that time stretches strangely when dragged through Valium. It takes her longer to react to things, which is, after all, probably the point.

"No, Mum," Bertie says. "*Not* really. Dad's joking."

"It's ketchup, dear," Martin says, finishing serving himself and sitting down. "Bon appétit!"

"It's a bit dried out, I'm afraid," Victoria says, poking at her chicken breast with a fork.

"I'm sure it'll be lovely."

"So, did you talk to your sister about Christmas?" Marge asks, her slurred voice making her sound slightly drunk. "I called her yesterday morning and she said she needed to speak to you first."

"I did. We spoke yesterday too. But she hasn't asked Sander about it yet."

"About what?" Martin asks.

"Whether we go there or they come here this year."

"It's only October," Martin says, then, "Hum, this aubergine is lovely."

"You said we could go *there*," Bertie says, looking concernedly at his father.

"I *said*, we'll see."

"Oh come on. It's much better there. There's nothing to do here."

"We'll all be together, wherever it is," Martin tells his son. "So, I can't see that it matters much, does it?"

"Except that they, like, live on a beach!" Bertie says. "And they have a proper tree and they've got animals, and an X-Box and a Wii, and that drone thing you can fly on the beach."

"I suppose it is more fun for the youngsters," Martin concedes.

"Plus, other people always drop in there," Bertie adds. "Like those Polish people last year, and the mad gypsies the year before."

"Penny's waifs and strays," Marge says. "You know what I think about that. Christmas should be for family."

"Do you think Will will be there?" Bertie asks.

"I expect Will has his own family to go to at Christmas," Martin says. "Why?"

Bertie looks down at his plate. "Dunno," he says, with a shrug. "He's a laugh. That's all."

"Anyway, I'll talk to her next week when we get back," Victoria says. "And we'll try to get a decision made."

"We could go down before Christmas," Bertie suggests hopefully. "We could have, like, a meeting to plan it properly and everything." He knows how his mother likes the idea of planning things properly.

"Actually that could be good," Victoria says. She hasn't been seeing as much of Penny as she'd like.

"I don't have anything against a weekend at the seaside either," Martin says, picturing himself casting-off from the jetty. He might even buy himself a new fishing rod.

"I just hope she's cleaned since I was there," Marge says. "That bathroom was like one big mould factory the last time I was down. Honestly, the ceiling was green."

Victoria imagines this and shudders. She decides she needs to remember to take her own bleach with her this time. She had been horrified to discover on her last visit that they "didn't use bleach anymore." Something to do with it being bad for the environment. Personally, Victoria prefers that her environment smell of bleach rather than feet and mould and guinea-pig poo, but hey... Momentarily she feels the tiniest flush of pride. At least she's better at *something* than her sister is. But then Marge says, "Still, I suppose it is harder for her, being a working mother and all," and the feeling vanishes.

Once she has digested the comment, Victoria says, "It's actually *our* turn to have them here." The mould is still in her mind's eye. "We went to Penny's last year, after all."

"*Mum*," Bertie pleads, dropping his fork and putting his hands together in prayer. "Please don't do this to me."

"There's nothing wrong with Christmas here," Victoria says. "But I'll talk to her. When we get back from Venice, I'll talk to her and we can decide, OK?"

"And you'll see if we can go down before?" Bertie asks.

"Yes," Victoria says with a vague smile. She's glad that Bertie likes his aunt and she's glad he enjoys hanging out with his cousins. Their ability to spend time as a big, happy family is one of the rare areas of her life where reality just occasionally meets her expectations. "Yes, I'll see if that's possible."

• • •

The sun is setting as Penny swings into Wave Crest, the sky lit up like one of Sander's colour charts. She has rarely, if ever, seen such a spectacular eruption of colour and once she has parked and turned the engine off she sits and stares and allows herself a couple of minutes, a brief, magical pause in what so far has been a horrendous day.

When the rapidly falling temperature within the car makes her shiver, she reaches for her bag from the passenger seat and climbs out.

Indoors, the house is dark and unusually silent. Even the cat, who generally keeps watch, ever hopeful for extra food, is absent.

"Hello?" she calls out, wondering if a lack of reply would make her feel concern or joy. Her life these days provides so few opportunities (with the exception of driving) for actually being alone. So these moments are rare enough to be treasured yet unusual enough to be unsettling too.

As she hangs her coat in the hallway, a door upstairs opens. "Hello?" Sander calls. "Up here."

Penny climbs the stairs and enters his studio. She finds him sitting facing the window. The room smells sweet with marijuana. "What are you doing in the dark?" she asks, thinking *like I don't know.*

"Looking at that," Sander replies. "Have you seen the state of the sky out there?"

"Hard to miss it," Penny replies, crossing to the window. "It's beautiful."

"So how was your day?" Sander asks, reaching for an unfinished joint in the ashtray and then crossing to stand at Penny's side.

"Don't ask."

"That bad?"

"Uh huh."

"D'you want to talk about it, or do you just want a puff of this to help you forget?" Sander asks, proffering the joint.

Penny shrugs. She rarely smokes these days, but tonight she feels she needs *something* to help her through, otherwise she might just cry. "Go on, then," she says, taking the joint from Sander's fingers and then leaning in towards the flame of his lighter.

She inhales, coughs, then takes another drag before saying, through smoke, "The rules are so stupid, that's the thing. It's like they've been designed to make the whole process fail."

"Asylum rules?" Sander asks. He's heard this rant before.

"Right. So, I'm supposed to be counselling this woman for trauma, OK?"

Sander almost imperceptibly nods.

"They're Syrians. Two daughters plus the parents. Dad got tortured by Assad. He's missing three fingers if that gives you some idea. And all three women got raped, the mother in Syria, and the daughters during the trip to Greece."

"God, how old are they?"

"Twelve and fourteen."

31

"Jesus."

"The son's missing, presumed dead, but possibly just rotting in a jail somewhere." Penny clears her throat before continuing. "So that's what I'm supposed to be helping her with, right? All of that. But we couldn't even get near the subject because what they *need* is someone to help them *now*. They're living in a single room, a horrible bedsit. Unhygienic doesn't even begin to cover it, believe me. Four people in two beds in a single room with one of those 1920 Belling cookers in the corner. They're officially not allowed to work, which is absurd, but they have to because no one can possibly live on five pounds a day seeker's allowance. And if the father gets caught – so this is an ex college professor painting people's bloody ceilings for three pounds an hour, yeah? – and if he gets caught, they get thrown out."

"Wow."

"I mean... Ugh..." Penny shakes her head. "How can I possibly be expected to help her with her trauma when it's ongoing? When we – the social services, the government, the system – are still causing it? And then on the way home, this ugly bloody skinhead – who I'm betting never worked a day in his life – gave me this." Penny pulls an English Defence League leaflet from her pocket, unfolds it and hands it to Sander.

Sander scans the bright red headlines of the various sections of text. "English Benefits for English people." "Time the Muslins went back home." "English pensioners MUST come first."

"*Muslins*," Sander says. "Are they people who wear muslin?"

"I know. It's *full* of spelling mistakes. And it's horrible. And there are way more of these hateful skinhead types scrounging benefits than there are immigrants, I'm telling you. I mean, if you met these Syrians – who just happen to be Christian, by the way – you'd swap them for baldy skinhead man in an instant. And all *they* really want to do, unlike Mister EDL, is get a bloody job."

"Sure," Sander says.

"And they're banging on about wanting to quit the EU, but they wouldn't have the foggiest what to do if we did leave."

"Right. It's stupid."

Penny can tell from his tone of voice that he has reached the limits of his capacity to listen to her. It's tough living with a partner who complains almost every day about her job – Penny gets that. "Anyway," she says. "Rant over."

"You do a tough job, Pen," Sander says, sliding one arm around her waist. "Some days it's going to get to you."

"Thanks."

Downstairs, the landline rings and then a few seconds later the mobile handset perched on Sander's easel starts to chirrup. "Don't, babe," Sander says, as Penny breaks free and picks it up. "It'll only be your mother."

Penny casts him a dirty look. "Yes," she says. "And?" She clicks on the answer button and then raises it to her ear. "Hi Mum," she says. "How are you?"

"D'you want tea?" Sander asks as he leaves the room.

Penny nods at him and says, "Uh-uh," perhaps to him or perhaps to her mother, he's not sure.

By the time Sander returns, the conversation is over and Penny is seated in his armchair watching as the last of the redness fades from the sky. "They all want to come down for the weekend," she announces.

"I thought they were in Venice."

Penny nods. "*After* Venice. Maybe the last week in October or perhaps for bonfire night? It's a Saturday apparently."

"Why?"

"Officially to plan Christmas," Penny says. "But Mum reckons they just fancy a trip to the seaside. And a bonfire on the beach, no doubt."

"It's nice to feel useful," Sander says sarcastically.

"I know. Do you think that's true? I mean, I was happy at first – I haven't seen Vicky for weeks – but when Mum said that... Well, I'm not so sure now."

"Who knows. And Christmas. Is that gonna be here then?"

"Still to be decided. But I was thinking, we'll need to sort the spare room out. All those boxes need to come back into our room, too. They've been there since the roof leak."

"I'll handle that during the week."

"Right, well, in that case, I might try to get a lick of paint on that back bedroom. You know what Vicky's like about stains and stuff."

"You're tired," Sander says. "You don't want to spend your weekend painting walls."

"Do we have any white paint left?" Penny asks, ignoring the comment because if she engages that train of thought they will inevitably end up discussing why she has to paint the room, why Sander doesn't do it. He doesn't seem to paint anything else these days, after all.

"There's some in the basement. If it hasn't dried out. But I really don't..."

"And we need to do something about the mould in the bathroom. Mum asked if we'd dealt with it and I said yes."

Sander laughs. "You liar! So, you realise that preparing for the Christmas planning weekend is going to be exactly the same amount of work as preparing for Christmas itself, yeah?"

"She's my sister," Penny says. "I have to see my sister. Even if she does just want to visit the seaside. And even if she does require hospital cleanliness wherever she goes."

"You get that no matter how much you do, it won't be enough," Sander says. "I mean, it's fine. I'm totally happy for them to come. But as long as you're ready for the fact that it won't be enough."

"She's a maniac and I'm a slattern. She'll just have to put up or shut up. Or go home."

"Slattern?"

Penny laughs. Sander's English is so perfect that most of the time she forgets it's not his first language. But then he'll say *loose* instead of *lose*, or slap an S on the end of pasta or accommodation to express the plural, and she'll remember. "Slattern? It's a dirty, untidy woman. It's a pretty old-fashioned word."

"OK," Sander says. "Slattern, huh?"

"You *could* bother to contradict me. You could say, 'Oh no, Penny, you're not a slattern.'"

Sander smiles. "I'm assuming you know the word better than I do. And yourself," he says. "Anyway, as far as Vicky is concerned, it sounds like you're ready for an argument. And they haven't even confirmed that they're coming yet."

"Only if she starts complaining."

"Which, of course, she will."

Penny wrinkles her nose and rolls her eyes. Her expression reminds Sander of their daughter Chloe who generally considers anything anyone over twenty says to be automatically idiotic. "Relax," Penny says. "We won't argue. I promise."

Sander laughs again. "How come I know you so much better than you know yourself?" he asks. "You're the shri... the psychologist. So, go on. Explain *that* to me."

Inexplicably, from Penny's point of view at least, it takes Sander a full eight days to move the twenty-two boxes of random junk and clothing back from the spare room to the walk-in wardrobe of their bedroom. Eight days, at – she works it out on her iPhone – two point seven five boxes per day.

Though the evidence – random items from the boxes appearing around the house – would appear to suggest that the principal reason is Sander's capacity to become distracted by the contents of said boxes, he denies this. He has fixed the washing machine (again), he points out. He did the food shop (undeniable, but why does it take Penny thirty minutes, and Sander seemingly a whole day?). Plus his favourite excuse of the last fifteen years: he has, of course, been thinking about ideas for a painting.

Whatever the reasons, by the time the room has been emptied, only three days remain for Penny to paint it.

Max, bless him, offers to help, but Penny prefers that he work on his physics project. Thirteen-year-old Chloe could be pressed into service, it's true, but Penny knows that sorting out the half-hearted adolescent mess she would leave behind would take longer than doing it herself. And as for Sander, well, three days has never been enough for him to do anything.

So between working full time and mopping up cat sick (and how can it be that no-one *else* ever comes across the cat vom' first?), between taking the car for its MOT and hunting for the lost guinea-pig (Beethoven is found alive and well and living beneath the kitchen sink), and between braiding Chloe's hair and then un-braiding it again when she changes her mind, Penny somehow finds the time to paint the spare room.

Yes, it looks a little uneven in the daylight, but well, that's just what happens when you finish up at midnight and when ten litres of emulsion paint on special costs seven pounds ninety-nine from Lidl. But Sander says he'll put pictures up in carefully selected positions to hide the brush strokes. And Penny just about believes that he might.

* * *

"Can we turn the heating up?" Chloe asks.

It's a cold, windy night outside, and they are eating Lidl pizzas in front of a film that no one is really watching. Penny's too tired to cook tonight, plus she's saving herself for the hosting marathon which begins tomorrow.

"It's on full blast I'm afraid," she replies. "It's because of the window upstairs. I'm trying to get rid of the smell of that paint."

Chloe rolls her eyes. "*Maybe* you shouldn't have painted it the night before they arrive," she says – an indisputable truth.

"Just... eat your pizza, OK?" Sander, who is feeling guilty about the paint thing, says.

"So is Christmas going to be here?" Max asks.

"I don't know. We'll be able to talk about it tomorrow won't we? But I expect so."

"Cool," Max says, through a mouthful of pizza.

"You'd rather it was here?"

Max nods. "It's all about how little mess we can make at auntie Vicky's. And those airbed things are rubbish to sleep on. Mine kept going down."

"How come they live in a flat if uncle Martin's so loaded?" Chloe asks.

"Houses are very expensive in London. Their flat is probably worth twice what this place is."

"How much?"

"Almost three million, I should think," Penny says, glancing at Sander who shrugs.

"They should sell it," Chloe says, "and go shopping."

"Wow," Max says. "That's a brilliant idea Chlo. They could buy a tent and live in that."

"Oh, shut up," Chloe says.

"Anyway, Christmas is boring in London," Max says.

"Christmas is boring everywhere," Chloe offers, picking the olives and slices of red pepper disdainfully from her slice of pizza.

Sander laughs. "Wow, you've added *Christmas* to the list of things you don't like?" He winks at Penny. "You won't be wanting gifts, then. That's a few quid saved, huh?"

"It is," Penny agrees, grinning. "I might even be able to buy *myself* something for once."

"Oh, Mum," Chloe says, her face suddenly lighting up. "I was thinking, if I, like, only have one thing for Christmas, could I, like, have a makeup box subscription?"

"How about we try that phrase without all the 'likes', huh?" Sander says, but it's too late to force a more elegant repetition because at the same time, Penny is asking, "A makeup subscription? Is that even a thing?"

Chloe nods. "Siobhan gets a really good one from Glossybox. It's only ten quid a month."

"Ten pounds *a month*?" Sander says. "For makeups? You must be joking."

"And they send you *what* for ten quid? A box of random makeup you don't even want?" Penny asks.

"No, it's really good, Mum," Chloe says, earnestly. "And the stuff's worth way more than a tenner. And if there's something I don't want – because some of it is going to be old... I mean, *grown-up* kind of stuff. Well, then *you* can have it, can't you."

"Wow," Penny says. "My generous daughter. Thanks!"

"I don't get it," Sander says. "What's the point of that?"

"Anyway, it's not going to happen," Penny says. "That's one hundred and twenty pounds a year. It's way too expensive, Chloe."

"But Siobhan–"

"I don't care about Siobhan," Penny interrupts. "That's a no. But if you're pleasant from now until then (Max raises his eyebrows at this – he doesn't believe in miracles) we might see about putting together some makeup that you're going to use and that I actually approve of. But you'll need to make a detailed list for Father Christmas. So we can see what kind of thing you want."

"What she *wants*," Max says, "is to look like a chav."

Chloe punches her brother in the arm. It apparently doesn't hurt much because Max just grins. "It's emo, you dork, not chav," Chloe says. "Tell him, Mum."

"What's emo? Wearing makeup?"

"Black nail polish," Chloe says. "Dork thinks it's chavvy."

"Ah," Penny says. "Well, I thought black makeup was goth, so..."

"Goth?" Chloe says. "Like, that doesn't even exist anymore."

"Chav does, though," Max says under his breath.

"Max!" Sander admonishes. "Stop!"

"At least I don't want to look like a *suit,*" Chloe says.

"Shut it."

"Maxey boy wants a suit for Christmas," Chloe says in a childish, taunting voice.

Penny and Sander turn to face their son. Penny looks confused yet hopeful while Sander simply looks horrified. "A *suit?*" he says. "Why would you want a *suit?*"

"I don't," Max says. "She just saw me looking at a website where–"

"He *does,*" Chloe insists. "He wants a tie and stuff. And a suit. He wants to look like those twats on *Suits.*"

"Oh, shut it, Chloe," Max says, now punching his sister back.

She rubs her arm and pushes her bottom lip out. "It doesn't matter what you wear," she says. "You'll still look like a dork."

The next morning, Penny has barely stepped out of the shower when she hears Sander call out, "They're here! They've arrived."

She gasps – she's way behind schedule – then wraps a towel around her middle, and runs up the three stairs that separate their bedroom from the main bathroom. As she passes Sander's studio, she ducks in and joins him as he looks out of the window. Below them, Martin's BMW is shuffling back and forth into a seemingly impossible parking space.

"Kiss?" Sander asks, turning to face her.

Penny pecks him on the lips, then comments, "You've been smoking? Already?"

Sander shrugs. "Just a little one to take the edge off things."

Penny rolls her eyes. "How can they even be here?" she says. "It's not ten yet, is it?"

"It's ten to eleven actually."

"Jees…" Penny says. "Can you do me a favour and go stack the breakfast things in the dishwasher? Vicky will have apoplexy if she sees the kitchen as it is. It looks like a Ramsay kitchen nightmare down there."

"Sure," Sander replies.

In their bedroom, next door, Penny dresses quickly, towels dry her hair and applies her minimum level of emergency makeup before running downstairs to find Victoria, Martin and Bertie watching Sander stack the dishwasher.

"Hello, hello!" she gushes, performing an actual double take at Martin and Bertie. Martin is wearing a blue sharkskin suit with a white shirt and a pale blue tie. Even Bertie is wearing, for some reason, an ironed shirt and a blazer. "You two are looking very swish."

Martin grins amicably and nods in the direction of his wife. "Ask her," he says, simply. "We resisted at first, but…"

"You know how Mum is," Bertie says, completing his father's sentence.

"I just wanted to see him in his new suit," Victoria says. "I had to go and pick it up from Savile Row for him, so the least he can do is let me actually see him wearing the damned thing. Don't you think he looks gorgeous, though?"

Penny nods. "I do," she says, honestly. She actually thinks Martin is looking almost embarrassingly sexy in the sheer new suit.

"That doesn't explain why *I* had to dress up," Bertie complains. "I feel stupid in this blazer."

"You look fine," Victoria says, then turning to Penny for confirmation, "doesn't he?"

"Yes, you look lovely, Bertie," Penny agrees even though she thinks that they all, Victoria included, look a *little* overdressed for a trip to the seaside.

"You'll need to rinse those off, first," Victoria tells Sander. He's in the process of loading the eggy breakfast dishes into the dishwasher.

"We don't rinse *anything* off first," Sander replies, carrying on regardless.

"But don't you get—"

"*Vicky*," Martin interrupts, fiddling nervously with his tie and grimacing as if he has toothache.

"Hang on," she tells him. "So, Sander, surely you must get loads of food stuck in the..."

"*Vicky!*" Martin repeats, more forcefully. "Let the man stack his own dishwasher however he wants, OK?"

"Sorry, I just... Of course. You're right," Victoria says, emulating Martin's gesture and fiddling with her bead necklace.

"Actually, *you're* right," Penny says, trying to defuse the tension. "But you know how lazy we are around here. And they seem to come out cleanish anyway."

"I think you must just have a better dishwasher than I do," Victoria comments.

"We don't, believe me. So where's Mum?"

"We left Gran in the car," Bertie says. "She's fast asleep. Shall I go check on her?"

"Yes," Victoria says. "And try to wake her up maybe? Gently, though."

"So can I change now?" Martin asks. "Now you've seen the suit. Honestly, I have to dress like this every day of the week."

"No," Victoria says, matter-of-factly. "No, you can't. I'm enjoying seeing you dressed smartly."

Martin grins at Penny and shrugs again. "See?" he says. "Shall I take our bags upstairs?"

"Yes," Penny replies. "You're in the top back bedroom. It might smell a bit of paint still. Mum's in ours. We're in the studio. And Bertie's in with Max."

"Bertie?" Victoria calls out. "Are you OK going in with Max?"

"Sure!" Bertie calls back from the hallway. He's already imagining the late night Xbox session that this will facilitate.

Penny, a little surprised that Victoria even asked him the question, frowns. She's not sure where they would have put him had he said that it *wasn't* all right. "I'll, um, go wake Max and Chloe up then," she says.

Upstairs, Penny has to shake Chloe repeatedly to wake her up. She gags at the smell coming from the guinea-pig's cage. "Wake up, get up, and clean Beethoven's cage," Penny says. "It stinks to high heaven in here."

"Oh, do I have to?" Chloe groans, "I'm so tired, Mum."

Max, on the other hand, she finds awake and typing messages into Facebook. "Can you get washed and dressed?" she says. "And wear something nice, please. They're dressed up like the royal family down there."

"Who is?"

"Martin's in a work suit and Bertie looks like he's just about to start public school or something."

"He *will* be soon. And then he'll be in the Bullingdon Club I expect. And after that he'll be PM or mayor of London or something."

Penny laughs. She enjoys these little moments of complicity with her son. "He's not *that* bad," she says.

"Why are they all dressed up anyway? Is something happening?"

"No, I don't think so. I think it's just because Vicky said so. You should consider yourself lucky I let you slob about in your trackies."

"I wouldn't mind a change," Max says, "But you'd have to actually *buy* me some nice clothes."

"You have nice clothes! Why don't you wear that blue shirt you got for Christmas?"

"Um, maybe because it doesn't fit me anymore," Max says.

Penny twists her mouth at this. Max, who has grown at least twenty centimetres since Christmas, is almost certainly telling the truth.

"OK, what about the flowery one then? Your James May shirt. I'll bet that still fits."

"It needs ironing. It's all crumpled up."

"Oh, just wear anything then," Penny says, caving in to the inevitable. "But try to choose something reasonable, please. Try not to let the side down, OK?"

Max looks at his mother strangely, and she hesitates and then glances down at her own slacks and jumper. "What? This is OK, isn't it?"

"Sure," Max says. "You look nice. But, you know, talking of not letting the side down..."

"Yes?"

"Do you think you can get Dad out of his favourite jumper for once?"

Penny sighs and nods. Sander's favourite jumper has become so permanent a fixture that she barely even sees it anymore. But Max is right. "Yes, Max," she says. "I'll see what I can do."

She leaves Max to shower and dress and then climbs to the top floor where she can hear Victoria and Martin settling in. Preparing to bask in the warm glow of praise for her decorating skills, she pushes the door open and asks, "Is everything all right for you, then?" But her smile fades almost immediately.

Victoria has frozen in mid gesture, caught in the act. In her right hand she has a small square of tissue and in her left, a package of moist, Dettol antibacterial wipes. She's been caught in the process of cleaning, or more precisely, *disinfecting*, the bedroom light switch.

Martin, who has removed his jacket and is busy unpacking his suitcase, grins amusedly. "Yes," he says. "It's lovely up here now, isn't it Vicky?"

Victoria bites her bottom lip and nods nervously. "Yes, lovely... So much, um, brighter than before," she splutters.

Penny looks her sister in the eye for a moment. She considers saying, "I have just spent the *entire week* painting this room. And the first thing you do when you arrive is *disinfect* it?" But then her eyes drift to the light switch in question and she sees that it truly is disgusting. It is grey and sticky and smudged and paint splattered, and has probably never been cleaned since the house was built, whenever that was. So her anger vanishes and is replaced, instead, by a hot flush of immature shame. "Great," she says crisply. "I'll, um, leave you to it then. See you downstairs."

They are walking along the seafront, restricted to a gentle amble by Marge's presence. It's a bracing October day, sunny and bright, but with icy gusts of wind that bring tears to their eyes. Because Penny is so behind schedule, and because Martin and Victoria are concerned about inconveniencing everyone with their visit, Martin has insisted on taking everyone out for lunch.

The seafront seems timeless and the light somehow cinematographic. Penny is repeatedly experiencing a strange sensation, part déjà vu, part time travel, every time she glances over at Martin, so stiff and upstanding and 1960s in his suit and his long overcoat.

Though she has managed to extricate Sander from The Jumper, she can't help but notice, following Max's remarks, the shocking contrast between the two families' wardrobes. And despite her best efforts, she can't help but feel an unwelcome pique of resentment that they can't afford nicer things. Martin's suit alone must have cost five-hundred pounds – perhaps a lot more – and Vicky's Comme des Garçons brogues have got to have cost another four.

Bertie and Max, as always when together, have regressed to childhood and are racing around and running along walls, and after the first half a mile, even Chloe forgets to sulk and joins in.

Sander and Martin, discussing the rugby, stride ahead, while the sisters walk either side of their mother, grabbing her arms whenever a gust of wind threatens to sweep her away.

"It's good to see the children getting on," Marge says.

"It is," Penny agrees, smiling at the sight.

"Chloe so rarely smiles these days," Marge adds.

"Oh, she's not so bad. She's a bit of a sulker maybe," Penny admits. "But she'll grow out of it."

"You put up with too much of her nonsense," Marge says. "Don't you think, Vicky?"

"I don't know," Victoria says, diplomatically. "Girls are different, I think."

"She's thirteen, Mum," Penny says. "That's just what thirteen-year-old girls are like, I'm afraid."

"Only if you *let* them be like that."

"Nope," Penny says, definitively. "They're exactly like that whether you let them or not."

By the time they reach V.C. Jones, an unassuming little fish and chip restaurant with Formica tables and piled-up cans of Fanta, Marge, who insisted on walking, is exhausted, and everyone is suffering from the cold.

"Ooh, this'll be lovely," Penny says as they push into the steamy interior. "I haven't had fish and chips for months."

"We'd have fish and chips every day if we lived here," Bertie says.

"I'm not sure about *every* day," Victoria replies. "We might get a bit fat otherwise."

"We never eat out," Penny confides to her sister as they shuck their coats.

Once the orders have been placed and everyone is seated, Martin claps his hands together. "Well, this is great, isn't it?" he enthuses. "I love these traditional places. So real!"

Penny sees that Marge, seated opposite, rolls her eyes and has to restrain a smirk.

"So, Sander and I were talking," Martin continues. "How do you feel about us all going to Spain next summer?"

47

"Spain?" Penny says, shooting a frown in Sander's direction. "I don't think we can afford to go to Spain."

"It wouldn't need to be expensive, apparently," Sander says sounding vaguely apologetic.

"I've been wanting to do a bit of the Santiago de Compostela route for years," Martin explains. "It would be fun if we could all do it together, don't you think?"

"Yes, that could be fun," Penny says, thinking that going anywhere is a financial impossibility, yet understanding Sander's need to play along. This not-being-able-to-keep-up with the Joneses thing can get embarrassing.

"You and I haven't been on holiday together since Paris," Victoria says, smiling at her sister.

"Wow!" Penny replies. "Paris!"

"Surely you've been away since then," Marge says. "You were in your twenties, weren't you?"

"Not together, we haven't," Victoria says. "And yes, I was twenty three, I think." Addressing Penny, she adds, "We had fun in Paris, didn't we?"

"Um!" Penny replies, nodding, even as she remembers Victoria's Gestapo-like grip on the holiday and their constant arguments about whom to trust and whom (according to Victoria) to run away from. It is not mere accident that they haven't holidayed together since.

"I think it's a lovely idea," Marge declares.

"Sounds lame to me," Chloe murmurs.

"Oh well, that's that then," Max jibes. "Call everything off. Chloe's not keen."

"I love a bit of proper sunshine," Marge says.

Martin pulls a face. He runs a finger inside his shirt collar. He suddenly looks uncomfortable. "Actually, Marge," he says,

"I think you might want to sit this one out. Camino de Santiago is a pilgrims' route. It's, well, it's a *walking* holiday."

"So?"

"So, fit as you undoubtedly are, I'm not sure you'll be up to it, I'm afraid. We're talking between fifty and a hundred miles in a week."

"A hundred miles *walking*?" Victoria says.

"A hundred *miles*?" Bertie repeats.

Penny, the only other person present who truly *loves* to walk, is suddenly wondering if there isn't some way by which they *could* afford this holiday after all. "Where do you stay, then?" she asks.

"In the *albergues*," Martin says. "They're like youth hostels."

"So they're pretty cheap, then?"

"Oh absolutely. A fiver a night or something. Per person, of course. Some of them you actually pay whatever you want. You just make a donation."

"Hostels?" Victoria says. "This is sounding less and less like my kind of holiday, dear."

"It'll be fun," Martin insists. "You'll see. And we'll all come back as fit as fiddles."

"I don't see why you have to choose the only holiday that I can't come on," Marge says.

"There are quite a few holidays you couldn't go on, Gran," Max tells her. "Paragliding, mountain climbing..."

"Bungee jumping," Bertie contributes. "Crossing a desert on a motorbike?"

"Now you're just being silly. What I mean is..." Marge starts. But then, thankfully, the waitress arrives with the first of their meals, interrupting that thought.

After lunch, as they are walking home, Bertie, Max and Chloe detour via the amusement arcade – Martin has slipped them a tenner – and Victoria and Martin, complaining about the cold while looking like an advert for a rom-com, stride ahead, leaving Penny and Sander to coax Marge homewards.

"I wish we'd taken them somewhere nicer," Victoria says, once they're out of earshot. "When Pen got all excited about eating out, it made me feel a bit stingy."

"I know," Martin says. "Me too. Perhaps we could all go out again this evening?"

"It's difficult," Victoria says. "You have to be careful not to put Penny's nose out of joint."

"I know," Martin says. "But, it'll be fine. Leave it to me."

"And I expect Penny's got stuff in," Victoria adds. "The fridge looked pretty full, though most of that is probably past the sell-by date knowing my sister."

"We'll find somewhere nice," Martin says. "Treat them. It'll be lovely."

"If only Sander would get a job," Victoria says glancing back to check that they are a good distance away. "It's really not fair on Pen."

"No," Martin agrees. "No, it's tough for her, isn't it. And what do you think about the holiday? Will they come? Sander seemed keen."

"I think you should have asked me first, is what I think."

"Because *you're* not keen?"

"Me? In a youth hostel? Come on."

"But..."

"Plus, Penny and Sander will *never* go. Firstly they can't afford it and secondly they can't organise a visit to the corner shop without drama, let alone a trip along some pilgrims' path in Spain."

"I can organise it," Martin says. "It'll be fun. And we'll all come back fit and tanned."

"I don't think you're listening to me," Victoria says, squeezing Martin's arm. "It's not happening."

Martin pulls a face.

"You can go," Victoria says. "I'm not stopping you. I'm just speaking for myself."

"Maybe I'll just go with Bertie then," Martin says. "It might do us good to do something together. Just the two of us. He's getting distant. And sulky. Like Chloe, really."

"Bertie's not like Chloe at all!"

"He barely gives me the time of day these days," Martin says.

"I think it's like Penny said, dear. He's just that age."

Almost half a mile behind them, Penny, Sander and Marge have had to pause to rest on a wooden bench. "You're not really going on this silly holiday, are you?" Marge, who doesn't like to be left out, asks.

"Unless there's some kind of miracle or we win the lottery we won't be going anywhere," Penny says.

"Winning the lottery *would* be a miracle," Sander comments, "seeing as we don't play."

"You don't want to be going on holiday with them, anyway," Marge says. "You two would fight like cat and dog on holiday, just the same as you did in Paris."

"That was years ago, Mum."

"But it's still probably true," Sander agrees.

"I thought it was insensitive," Marge comments. "I mean, they know that I can't go on a walking holiday, and they know that you can't afford it. So it's a bit rude, really."

"I think Martin genuinely thinks it will be pretty cheap," Sander says. "I think he was just trying to be nice."

"Cheap?" Marge sniffs. "They don't even know what cheap means. They just like to rub everyone's noses in it, is the truth of the matter. It's like Martin dressing up as Cary Grant and your sister wearing that Agnes B thing. They just want everyone to know who's top dog, that's all."

Penny wrinkles her nose. "You think?"

"She always was a show-off, your sister," Marge says. "Still, forgive and forget, eh?"

"I don't think they're like that," Sander insists. "They're just lucky enough to make more money than we do, that's all. You can't begrudge them that."

"Really?" Marge says doubtfully. "And luck, you say? Oh well... So, what about you, Sander? How's your *luck* these days? Have you sold any work?"

Sander clears his throat. "Um... No, Marge," he stammers. "No, I haven't."

"Well, I'd sub you if I could," Marge says. "For the holiday, I mean. But I'm afraid I'm probably even more broke than you are."

When eventually they get back to the house – after having grabbed a passing mini-cab, so cold were they from shuffling along the seafront – Martin and Victoria are seated in the lounge.

Martin has loosened his tie and removed his jacket, but in his crisp white shirt, he still, Penny thinks, seems to ooze wealth and well-being.

As she makes everyone cups of tea, she remembers when she first met Sander. For he had not always been such a scruff, either.

She had been invited to the private view by Sheena, the girl she shared her flat with. There would, Sheena had promised, be free Champagne, and who was Penny to refuse free Champagne?

On arriving in the gallery, she had been blown away by the beauty of Sander's huge paintings, and had giggled at the incongruous faces of the blow-up dolls he had painted, situated in business meetings, or dressed as waitresses or bus conductors.

When a short, Woody Allen-type guy came into the room she had asked Sheena if this, finally, was the artist. "No, it's that guy over there," Sheena had said, pointing to a man with long hair and big glasses, wearing a grey heavy-check suit and a pink bow-tie.

"I'll introduce you," Sheena had offered, but there had been no need, because Sander, who had locked eyes with Penny already (he had the bluest eyes she had ever seen) was already making his excuses and heading their way.

The suit still hangs in the closet upstairs, but even if Sander could get into it, which he can't, it would look horribly outdated nowadays. No one has been able to get away with lapels like that, or a pink bow-tie, for that matter, since the noughties, and even back then, you probably had to be an in-vogue Danish artist to do so. Sander later admitted that his publicist, who was gay, had chosen the suit for him. And that, Penny thought, sounded about right.

Still, men are so daft, Penny reckons. Because, just like women, all they really want is to be attractive, to be fancied, to catch the eye of the other sex. And there's really no easier way for a man to achieve that end than to wear a nice suit and an ironed shirt. It's the male equivalent of walking around in your lingerie, for God's sake, and yet most men, like Sander, spend their entire lives attempting to dress down. It's incomprehensible.

"Can I help you with those?" Martin asks from the doorway, and Penny jumps and blushes as if he has perhaps stumbled into her thoughts.

"Sure, you can carry two of these through," she says, taking two of the mugs of tea from the counter and holding them out. "Nice cufflinks," she comments, as he takes the teas from her grasp.

"Thanks," Martin says. "Vicky got them for me in Venice. They're supposedly Venetian glass, but I reckon most of the stuff they sell there comes from China. Though don't tell her that."

As he turns and walks away, she glances at his buttocks, pert and hugged by the material of his suit trousers, and tells herself, *"Stop it, Penny, you love Sander."* And it's true. She does. It's just that love isn't incompatible with wishing he dressed better.

And then in her mind's eye, or ear, she hears Martin saying, *"Vicky got them for me in Venice,"* and wonders whether her mother isn't right about him, after all. "Ooh, Vicky got them for me in Venice," she repeats quietly, in a silly nasal voice.

As Penny joins the others in the lounge, Victoria is saying, "Apparently, they all come over here for the benefits, and that's what's really got to change if we don't want them *all* coming over. Either that, or we need to get the control of our borders back."

"Um," Martin says, in a non-committal manner.

Despite Sander catching her eye and vaguely shaking his head, Penny asks, "So, who's this then?"

"I'm sorry?" Victoria replies in a mock-disinterested voice. "Oh, it was just something I read."

"Where's Mum?" Penny asks looking around the room.

"Gone for a kip," Sander replies, hoping that Marge's absence has diverted Penny from the subject at hand.

"Right," Penny says. "So, who exactly is supposed to be coming over here for our wonderful benefits system?"

"You know full well," Victoria says. "The refugees. The Syrians and what-have-you."

"I know full well that they're coming here because their country's at war," Penny says.

"Oh, come on. The whole place can't be a war zone. Syria's huge."

"Actually, it can," Penny tells her. "They're being bombed by their own government, by the rebels, the Americans, Qatar, the Saudis, and the Iranians. In fact it would be easier to list who *isn't* currently bombing Syria."

"But..."

"And when they're not being bombed, they're being decapitated or raped or thrown off buildings by ISIS. It's not the five pounds a day asylum seeker's allowance that's causing them to leave."

"So how come they're all men?" Victoria asks. "Answer me that."

"Penny," Sander whines, shaking his head, but she batts the intervention away with one hand.

"Who are all men?" she asks.

"In the newsreels. They're all men. You never see women or children, do you?" Victoria says, glancing at Martin for support. He gives her a *"search me"* shrug as his only reply. It's meant to convey, *"You're on your own here,"* but Victoria misreads it as a far more complex, *"You know I agree with you, but you also know that it's against rules to argue with my sister-in-law,"* shrug. She decides she's going to have to defend what she believes to be their shared point of view single handed.

"That's absolute rubbish," Penny says. "I'm dealing with a total of nine Syrian families at the moment and they're nearly all women and children."

"Nine!" Victoria says, sarcastically. "Wow!"

"How dare you!" Penny spits. "Plus, the United Nations – who collect *actual* data on these things instead of the gossipy hearsay you listen to – say that fifty-one percent of them are women, and fifty something percent are children, so…"

"That's not what *I* read," Victoria insists.

"This *is* kind of Penny's job," Sander mutters, half-heartedly offering a smidgen of support to his wife.

"Well, it is kind of the job of the journalist who wrote the article I read in the *Telegraph* too, I expect," Victoria retorts.

"Show me the article."

"I don't have it here. Obviously."

"You're impossible to argue with," Penny says. "I don't know why I bother."

"I just think that if all these fit young men…" Victoria says.

"And women and children…" Penny interjects.

"…stayed at home and *fought* for their country instead of running away, then we wouldn't have to risk British lives to save them, would we? I mean why do we…"

"*Who* would you like them to stay and fight?" Penny interrupts. "Assad? Al Qaida. ISIS? The Saudis? *All* of them, maybe?"

"Well, ISIS, obviously, to start with," Victoria says. "I don't know what sort of country we'd have if all our boys had run away during the Second World War. We'd probably be living under Hitler or something."

"Oh, for Christ's sake, Vicky," Penny says. "How can you be so bloody ignorant about everything? It's a totally different situation."

"Ignorant?" Victoria repeats, looking outraged. "Me?"

"What you're saying *is* ignorant. It's a statement of fact, dear sister."

"Oh, you've always thought you're so clever," Victoria says. "Ever since you got your bloody degree you think you know everything. Well I've a surprise for you, Penny. Going to college doesn't actually make you better than everyone else after all. And there *are* other sources of information out there beyond what your social worker mates tell you."

"Oh here we go!" Penny says. "You're the one who thinks you're above everyone. You're the one swanning around in your Agnes B trouser suit and quoting the *Torygraph* to everyone."

"How about you show me that studio of yours, eh?" Martin says, addressing Sander in an exaggeratedly calm tone of voice. "Maybe show me what you're working on at the moment?"

"Great idea," Sander says, even though he's not working on anything *at the moment*. He wonders if he can smoke a joint in front of Martin or if he'd be shocked.

"Sander!" Penny protests. "Don't leave me."

"This is sister stuff, babe," Sander replies. "See ya."

The two men carry their mugs of tea up to Sander's studio. The sunshine is streaming in, falling across the armchair. "Have the magic seat," Sander offers, propping himself up on a

57

pile of pillows against the wall and glancing in the direction of his dope box. "I'm fine down here."

"You're *sleeping* in here tonight?" Martin asks, looking around the room and noting the absence of a bed.

"We've got one of those blow-up things," Sander says. "It'll be fine – if I can find the pump. Do you mind if I smoke?"

Martin shrugs. "It is your studio. And your house."

"I mean.. you know..." Sander says, emphasising the word. "*Smoke.*"

"Yeah, I guessed," Martin laughs. "I don't, but please, knock yourself out."

"I certainly intend to try," Sander replies.

Downstairs, the argument rages on. But other than an occasional grimace when an intelligible shriek reaches their ears (generally Penny's voice), and other than Sander's comment that, "I knew they'd argue," to which Martin replies, "Well, of course," the men manage to avoid even the vaguest of references to the war being waged below.

"So, who do you reckon between Wigan and Salford?" Martin asks.

"Well, without McIlorum, Wigan are going to struggle," Sander replies.

When, twenty minutes later, the children get home, the argument is still ongoing.

"What's all that about?" Max asks, peeping in through Sander's door as he makes his way to the sanctuary of his own room.

"Refugees, I think," Sander says.

"Oh, I think we can safely say they've moved onto more personal issues by now," Martin says, winking at Sander. "Just lie low until tea-time, mate," he tells Max. "It will all be over by then."

The words, "Bloody bitch" rise up the stairwell, and Max says, "They're not going to kill each other, are they?"

Sander shakes his head. "It's just sibling stuff," he says. "It's just like you and Chloe, really."

"We never argue like *that*, though," Max says.

"You probably will," Martin tells him with a laugh. "One day. If you're lucky."

"*You* have a brother, right?" Max asks.

Martin nods. "And we argue *just* like that," he says. "But only at weddings. Weddings and funerals are best for that kind of thing. That's what we reckon in our family, anyway."

"Right," Max laughs. "I'll, um, remember that advice, uncle Martin."

By the time Marge comes downstairs at four, the house is in almost complete silence.

Max and Bertie are playing on the Xbox, and Chloe, in her own bedroom, is chatting to a friend via unlimited text messages.

Martin and Sander are watching the football with the sound turned low, and Penny and Victoria are gliding around each other doing their best to avoid any further interaction.

Penny looks red and angry still, while Victoria looks puffy and stoned, which, having taken an extra Valium, she pretty much is.

"Have you two stopped fighting?" Marge asks as she enters the room. "Is it safe to come in?"

Victoria and Penny half-glance at each other. "*I* have," Penny says, which provokes a groan from Victoria.

"I'll make tea," Victoria says, standing. "Anyone want a cup?" Everyone replies except Penny. "I'm assuming you don't, then?" Victoria asks, still not looking directly at her sister.

"Assume what you want," Penny says. "You always do anyway. Why let facts get in the way?"

"Ugh," Victoria groans, already leaving the room.

"Look, there's nothing wrong with a good fight to clear the air," Marge tells her youngest daughter, "But you're a bit old for all this sulking business."

"I'm not sulking," Penny says. "I'm angry. She said some very hurtful things."

"And I'm sure you said some back."

"She called me a liar and a snob and a–"

"Stop it. You sound like a five-year-old," Marge says. "Now go and make up before you ruin the weekend for everyone."

"No," Penny says. "Not until she apologises."

"Don't think you're too old for me to take you over my knee," Marge threatens.

"I think you'll find I *am* a bit old for that," Penny replies.

"Penelope!" Marge says. "Stop sulking and go and make up with your sister. Now!"

Both Sander and Martin look up at this unusual use of Penny's full name. For the most part everyone forgets that Penny even has a full name.

"No, Marjorie," Penny says, taking her revenge. "You go and make up with her if you want to." She can hear that she is indeed sounding like a five-year-old, but that realisation doesn't seem to help her stop. In fact it makes her angrier.

Why *does* the presence of her sister make her regress forty years, she wonders? What's that about?

"You're being silly," Marge says.

"Oh, mind your own business will you, Mum?" Penny says, exasperated.

"And you're being *rude*, now, as well. This *is* my business. You're my daughter and all this sulking is utterly ridiculous."

Penny's anger bubbles over again. It wasn't so far below the surface after all. "You know what's ridiculous?" she says. "*You* lecturing me. You telling me that I'm ridiculous when you're the biggest sulker of any of us."

"Me?" Marge says. "I never sulk. When did you ever see me sulk?"

Penny stands to leave, but as she storms from the room, crossing paths with Victoria in the hallway, she lobs her passing shot back into the room like a hand grenade. "Well, to start with," she says, "you haven't spoken to *your* brother for forty years. So I'd call that a pretty epic sulk, yeah?" She then pulls a truly childish grimace at her sister's shocked face and strides to the coat stand.

Once the front door has slammed behind her, Marge covers her mouth with one hand. "Well!" she breathes.

Sander clears his throat and Martin raises one eyebrow. Then they both turn back to face the TV screen.

"Jesus, Bellerín's fast," Martin says as the footballer streaks diagonally across the screen.

"Yes, he is," Sander replies. "He's *really* bloody fast."

The evening does not go to anybody's plan.

Penny refuses Martin's offer to eat out again, so he and Victoria go alone. Marge, now refusing to speak to Penny, announces that she's not hungry and retires to their bedroom the second they arrive in the lounge with bowls of pesto and pasta. Chloe escapes the tense ambience to a sleepover at her friend's house, and Max and Bertie make jam and peanut butter sandwiches (which Bertie has apparently seen on some American TV show) then return immediately to Max's room.

Sander waits until they're in bed that night, bouncing on the inflatable mattress in the studio, before he makes any attempt to intervene. "You'll have to speak to her eventually, you know," he says, once Penny has laid her head across his outstretched arm.

"Who?" she asks, already pulling away. "Mum? Or Vicky?"

"Well, both, I suppose," he replies. "But I meant Vicky."

"Oh, we never sulk for long," Penny says. "It'll all be forgotten in the morning. She does talk some rubbish, though."

"I think it's because you make her feel inferior," Sander says.

"I don't *make* her feel anything."

"Sorry, not what I meant," Sander replies. "I just think that, well... because she didn't get to go to college and she hasn't had a career and everything... you know? She feels like she has to fight to the death to prove something every time."

"Then she should choose a subject she knows more about than I do," Penny says.

"Which would be?"

Penny shrugs. "Search me," she says. "Shopping maybe?"

"Yeah," Sander says with meaning. "So, maybe you can see why she feels so insecure."

Penny sighs. "You're quite good at this when you try," she says.

"At what?"

"The psychology business. But like I said, it'll all be forgotten in the morning. Don't worry."

"Sure," Sander says. "But maybe you could just let her score a point from time to time?"

"I do," Penny replies. "Just not when she's slagging off war-torn refugees."

"Right."

"Mum's not gonna be so easy though."

"No. You might have to apologise for that one."

"Yes. Because as we have already demonstrated, Mum can sulk for forty years without coming up for breath."

"I didn't know he was still alive to be honest. You never talk about him."

"Mum's brother? Cecil?"

"Yeah."

"I'm not sure if he is. I'm not sure if Mum would even know. He'd be, um, seventy or so. So I suppose he probably is still chugging along somewhere."

"What did they fall out about?"

Penny rolls to her side and props herself up on one elbow. "I've no idea," she says. "I was only six. Well, five, really. *Nearly* six."

"Oh! So it was...?" Sander says, nodding, not wanting to say the words.

"Um," Penny says seriously. "Yes. It was that Christmas."

"He didn't have anything to do with what happened, did he?"

Penny pulls a face. "Cecil? No," she says. "But there was definitely some kind of falling out. I always assumed that it was because he didn't come back. I mean, after something that horrific, well, you'd have expected him to want to be there. For Mum. To support her."

63

"When did your dad die again?"

"When I was two. I don't remember *him* at all. Cecil sort of replaced him. For a while."

"You must have talked to Vicky about it at some point. I mean, she'd know, wouldn't she? She was older."

"Oh, no. I'm not sure she knows either. And she wasn't *that* much older. But no, we could never talk about Cecil. Or Ed. They're both strictly taboo subjects. Which is why not only will I have to apologise to Mum for mentioning him, but I'll have to find a way of apologising without mentioning him all over again."

Sander nods thoughtfully. He reaches out and strokes Penny's forearm gently with the back of his knuckles. "So why *didn't* he come back?" he asks. "You must have a theory."

Penny shrugs. "Who knows. People deal with trauma in weird and wonderful ways; they develop coping mechanisms. Everyone reacts differently. Maybe Cecil's solution was just never to come back. He loved Ed lots. He was kind of his favourite. Maybe he just needed to pretend that none of it had ever happened. That none of us had ever existed."

"That must have been pretty upsetting for your mum," Sander says. "I mean, she'd already lost her husband – to then be blanked by her brother..."

"It..." At the sound of the front door, Penny pauses just long enough to ascertain that it's her sister and Martin who have returned, then continues, speaking more quietly. "It was tough for us, too. I mean, he was like a father, and Father Christmas, and The Good Fairy all rolled into one. Things got really tough once Cecil vanished. There were no piles of gifts under the tree after that. Half the time there was no money for the bloody meter."

"And Vicky never said *anything* about Cecil disappearing?" Sander murmurs. "Not one comment?"

"She was probably suffering from PTSD," Penny whispers. "I mean, she saw everything. She was with Ed when it happened. But she hardly even cried. And she never said a word about any of it."

"Not *ever*?"

"Nope. She just went really quiet after that. It was like she'd taken a vow of silence or something. She used to be the funny one if you can believe that."

"Funny?" Sander asks. He pauses to listen, then whispers, "They're in the kitchen."

Penny nods and bites her bottom lip before continuing softly, "Yes, Ed was the serious one... Geeky, you'd call him nowadays, I suppose. And I was the little tearaway always getting into trouble. But Vicky was the funny one who made all the adults laugh."

"Which is something I'm truly struggling to imagine," Sander says.

Penny nods. "I know. I suppose... what happened... well, it changed her."

"You really couldn't talk to her about it? Not even now?"

Penny snorts. "No! It's a family taboo. And family taboos have to be respected."

"But..."

"Plus – and this is the psychologist talking, not your wife – there's no telling what would happen if someone *forced* her to talk about it. There's no telling how she would react. She may even have blocked the whole thing out. She might not remember. So it could actually be dangerous for her."

"Dangerous?"

"Yeah. She could have a breakdown or something if she wasn't ready."

"It was forty years ago," Sander says. "If she's not ready now..."

"Maybe she'll never be ready," Penny says with a sigh. "But if she does want to work on it one day, it will have to come from her, and it would have to be with a disinterested party, not me. Someone outside the family. A professional."

"How do you know she *hasn't* told someone?" Sander asks, rolling onto his back. The light from the streetlamp falls across his face giving him a strange orange glow – there are no curtains in the studio. "How do you know she hasn't been seeing a shrink for the last thirty years?"

Penny shrugs. "I don't. But she doesn't really strike me as someone who's been in therapy for thirty years. She strikes *me* as someone who's blanked everything out and done everything she can to forget."

"Hum," Sander says with a yawn. "Your family's weird."

"Yours wasn't much better from what I've heard."

"No," Sander agrees with a laugh. "You're right. God, this mattress is awful."

"Yes," Penny replies. "Yes, between the mattress and the streetlamp, I think it's going to be a long night."

"I could put a sheet up, maybe."

"Nah," Penny says, now rolling over and spooning her body against Sander's back. "It's fine."

Victoria wakes up with a gasp. She has beads of perspiration on her forehead and an unusual asthmatic whistle in her throat. Beside her, Martin is snoring gently, but she's confused about where she is. This doesn't feel like their bed, and the room, unlike home, is pitch black.

She reaches to the bedside table and fumbles for her phone. When the screen lights up the room with its dim green glow, she remembers.

She attempts to breathe deeply but it feels like someone is sitting on her chest. It feels like someone has stolen all of the oxygen from the room. Perhaps it's the fumes from the paint, clogging her lungs or something.

She had been dreaming about Ed, she realises. She tries to remember the context of the dream but only Ed's ghostly face and her sense of terror remain.

There's still no air in the room. She needs to escape.

Still wheezing and vaguely hopeful that Martin will wake up (he doesn't) she bounces from the bed and, still by the light of her phone, dresses in the first items of clothing she finds – her slacks and Martin's white shirt. Then, after stubbing her toe on Martin's suitcase (Penny's closets are full of boxes), and grabbing her handbag from the back of the chair, she leaves the room.

Downstairs, in the cold messy kitchen, she fiddles in the bag for a Valium tablet which she crunches up. It tastes horrible, but it's supposed to work faster that way.

She leans over the kitchen sink and attempts to open the window, but it is secured with some devilish anti-burglary lock which appears to require an absent key, so she pads to the back door instead.

Just as she places one hand on the door-handle, Solomon, Max's ageing tabby, bursts in through the cat-flap startling her.

She heaves the door open, then stands on the threshold and lets the icy air rush in through the open door but it doesn't seem to contain any more oxygen than the rest of the house, in fact the chilled air seems to be making her breathing even more difficult, so she shuts it again and slumps at the kitchen table. She will just have to wait for the Valium to do its stuff. She knows what this is. She has had panic attacks before.

Solomon jumps onto the table and though she's never been that keen on cats – they generally strike her as selfish and unpredictable – she begins to stroke him; she begins to speak to him. It's at least a distraction from thinking about Cecil, from thinking about Ed.

"So what were you doing outside?" she asks the cat, then, "I don't know what you want. Food I expect. Only, I don't know where they keep it." But the cat, it seems, wants nothing more than company and as she strokes his ears and then tickles his offered tummy, the tightness in her chest begins to ease.

By four thirty she's feeling almost normal. OK, not *normal* – she's feeling spacey and floaty from the combined effects of Valium and lack of sleep – but that, at least, is a relatively familiar sensation.

She boils the kettle; she makes, and sips, tea. And then she sets about the final phase of her four-am-panic-attack ritual: she starts to clean the kitchen.

Penny is awoken just after seven by the daylight. "I should have let you put the sheet up," she says to Sander, who she believes is already awake. But Sander just groans, rolls away, and pulls a pillow over his head. Her pillow.

"That's romance," Penny murmurs, sensing a new pain in her lower back and rolling from the air-bed onto her knees.

When she reaches the kitchen, she is stunned. She can't remember ever having seen it this clean.

She sniffs at the air. There's an unfamiliar odour of bleach, which is strange as she hasn't bought the stuff for months. They say it's bad for the environment.

She looks around at the emptied surfaces, at the shiny floor. The cat bowl is spotless, she notices. She feels a pang of guilt that they wash it so rarely, but thinks that placing it on folded sheets of kitchen roll is, all the same, overkill.

She grabs the kettle (shiny, descaled) and crosses to the sink (completely bleached) to refill it. She glances out at the back garden. The window has been cleaned too. It smells of ammonia.

The kettle plugged in, she leans back against the worktop and scans the room again, sees the shiny spice jars, the tea, coffee and cocoa pots ranged from large to small.

"Wow, Vicky!" she says. "You can come and stay *anytime.*"

As the kettle heats up, she checks the lounge and the dining room, but the miracle-worker is nowhere to be seen. Victoria must, she realises, have gone back to bed. She can thank her later.

The next person up – at ten to eight – is Marge. "Gosh," she says. "Who did this?"

"Who do you think?" Penny replies.

"Well, not you," Marge says. "That's for sure."

"It's nice, isn't it?" Penny replies, ignoring, for the moment, the barb. "I suppose it's her way of making up."

"Yes," Marge says. "Yes it's much better than the usual chaos you live in. But I expect she was just worried about the lack of hygiene. You know what she's like about germs."

Instantly, Penny's joy at her spotless kitchen begins to morph into an entirely different emotion.

"I know how busy you are," Marge says. "But you should try to keep it looking like this once they've gone. It would do you good to have a nice clean kitchen for a change."

One by one the residents of the house wake up and wander into the kitchen, and one by one their comments sharpen Penny's sense of injustice.

"Wow," Martin says. "Someone's been busy." And Penny has to explain that it wasn't her.

"Gosh," Sander says, when he walks in. "This is nice. Very nice!" And Penny has to restrain herself from pointing out that it could be this nice every day if only Sander cleaned it too.

Bertie's comment sends Penny over the edge into the beginnings of actual rage. "It smells like home," he says. "Has Mum been zapping all the germs with Dettol?"

"Only ninety-nine point nine percent of them," Max replies.

"There *are* no bloody germs," Penny gasps. "For Christ's sake, don't you two start!"

"Actually germs are everywhere, Mum," Max informs her.

"In fact germs are good for you, I think," Bertie offers. "Our biology teacher says it's bad for your immune system or something. If there aren't any, I mean."

Penny closes her eyes and pinches the bridge of her nose. "Just get your breakfast and get out, will you?" she says. "I've got Sunday lunch for eight to prepare."

Once the boys have smudged their jam, scattered breadcrumbs and retired to the dining room, Penny pulls the lunch ingredients from the suddenly half-empty refrigerator. She is unable to restrain herself from checking in the bin to see which items Victoria has dared to throw out. Her annoyance only increases at the realisation that it truly was all rubbish. She can't find a single item within its sell-by date with which she can accuse her sister of wastage.

She chops onions and puts minced beef out to defrost. She grates cheese and makes béchamel sauce. And by the time Victoria gets back up, the kitchen is looking perfectly ordinary, which in a way, Penny realises, she is glad about.

"Oh!" Victoria says on entering. "Gosh, that didn't last long!"

Penny glances over at her and shrugs. "It's called life, dear sister. It's called cookery."

"I cook," Victoria says, perceiving the dig even before Penny herself has realised what she meant to imply. "I'll, um, just have a cup of tea and I'll give you a hand getting it back under control."

"No thanks. I'm fine. Everything *is* under control," Penny says.

"It doesn't *look* it," Victoria retorts. "Anyway, every top chef needs a cleaner-upper."

"I don't," Penny insists. "It's just lasagne. And I'm *fine*."

Victoria crosses to the sink and returns with a sponge. "Just let me help you a bit," she says, already wiping down a worktop.

"Leave it!" Penny says, more sharply than she intended. She's realising that yesterday's argument isn't forgotten after all. She's still primed to react badly. "Leave it until I've finished, please," she adds, more softly.

"But if I keep things tidy, it'll make it easier for you," Victoria says, glancing over at the packaging from the mince, dribbling its red blood cells onto the kitchen table.

"Stop!" Penny shrieks, crossing the kitchen and snatching the sponge from Victoria's grasp, then lobbing it over her head at the sink. She misses and it bounces off the window leaving a soapy stain in the middle of the pane. "I can't stand people fussing around me while I'm cooking, OK?"

Victoria is just about to admit defeat when Marge's voice comes from the doorway. "You just can't stand that your sister's better at something than you are," she says. "You just don't like that she's shown you up by cleaning the place properly for once."

Penny and Victoria turn to face their mother.

"What?" Penny whistles incredulously.

"I think Mum's right, to be honest," Victoria says.

Penny opens her mouth to speak and then closes it again when words fail to materialise. "Right, that's it," she finally says, physically bustling Victoria towards the doorway. She can almost convince herself that she's joking.

"I wish you could just make a bit more effort to get on with everyone, Penny," Marge says. "You're so *brittle* these days."

"Both of you, out!" Penny shouts, tremblingly pushing them out of the kitchen and then squeezing the door closed behind them. "Out! Now! Before I scream."

The door closed, Penny takes a deep breath and tries to calm herself. As she turns back to the kitchen, she sees that the onions are burning, their grey acrid smoke rising into the air.

Only two people dare to enter the kitchen that morning.

Sander, looking confused, stoned, and inappropriately amused, informs her that, "They're leaving."

"Leaving?" Penny replies, wiping her hands on her apron.

"Uh-huh," Sander confirms. "I don't know what happened, but I think if you spoke to her, she'd stay."

"Nothing happened," Penny says, struggling to disguise the lie, deciding as she speaks to admit nothing.

"Vicky seems to think something happened."

"Oh, she's just being silly," Penny says. "She can't take a joke, that's all."

"They're really leaving," Sander tells her.

"But I'm cooking for eight, here," Penny says, running her fingers through her hair then regretting it. They smell of onions.

"I know. That's why you need to go talk to them. They're putting their bags in the car right now."

Penny looks up at the ceiling for a moment, then declares in a falsely casual voice, "Oh, you know what, Sander? If they want to leave, then just let them bloody leave. I'm done with grovelling."

Sander clears his throat and backs out of the room. "Right," he says. "If you're sure. I'll, um, leave you to it then. It's a shame though."

Ten minutes later, it's Bertie who opens the door. "I just wanted to say goodbye," he says.

"Bye Bertie," Penny replies flatly. She's busy peering inside the oven. She's wondering if she can freeze half of the lasagne despite having cooked the mince from frozen.

"Um, aunt Penny," Bertie says. "I wanted to ask you something."

Penny frowns at the lasagne then straightens. "Yes?" she asks briskly.

"I was wondering if I could come and live here," Bertie says. His expression is strange, almost theatrically earnest.

"What?"

"I was wondering if I could come and live here with you," he says. "It's so much nicer here."

Penny furrows her brow. She feels like he's speaking a foreign language to her. Considering the context, his words don't seem to make any sense. "What?" she says again.

But then Bertie looks around the room and Penny follows his gaze and sees what he's seeing: the renewed griminess of the kitchen, the empty tomato tins in the sink, the grated cheese on the worktop, the bloody wrapper on the table; a desolation that Penny has, she admits to herself, quite wilfully recreated.

"You cheeky little sod," she says, waving her hands at him in a shooing gesture. "Get out, go on! Bugger off back to your hygienic little flat in London the lot of you. I'm sick to death of you all."

Bertie looks soulfully at his aunt and then, with drooping shoulders, he turns and leaves.

Martin drives in silence. He tries to concentrate on his driving, on the physical sensations within his body, on the reflections of the countryside as they sweep across the polished bonnet of the BMW, on the luxurious smell of leather that drifts from the oh-so-comfortable seats of the new car. He is furious with Penny for ruining the weekend and knows that if he allowed his mind to stray that way – which he won't – he could be furious with his wife as well.

Victoria, for her part, is on the edge of tears. She stares from the side window at the occupants of the cars they overtake, at the trees streaking past, and she waits, like a scared child, for someone to pass comment.

Bertie, feeling shaken and inexplicably scared, has plugged himself into his iPhone and is listening to Will Young. Marge, for the moment, is holding her tongue.

It's not until they see the first signs for the Medway services (which they still for some reason refer to as Farthing Corner) that anyone speaks.

"Can we stop at the services?" Bertie asks, yanking out an earbud. "Only, I'm starving."

Martin runs his tongue across his teeth and turns to look at Victoria for a response but she merely shrugs. He considers saying, *I would have preferred a slice of that lasagne to a floppy Farthing Corner sandwich,* but restrains himself.

"I think we had better," Marge says. "I could do with a wee."

Martin turns back to face the road. "Settled," he says, then, "Limp sandwiches all-round." Despite his best efforts, the words have slipped out.

"I'm sorry, OK?" Victoria says, sounding not very sorry at all.

"I wouldn't have any regrets if I were you," Marge says, finally deciding to chip-in. "If you hadn't argued before dinner, you would have argued during."

Victoria sighs and turns back to the side window.

"You know how they eat around there," Marge continues. "You know how much mess they make. And you know how it drives you insane."

"Yes, thanks, Mum."

"And after all that work you put into cleaning the kitchen as well. It was like she was messing it up on purpose almost."

Victoria nods silently. She imagines saying, *word,* one of Bertie's newer linguistic tics, picked up from all the American TV the kids watch these days.

"The last time I was there," Marge says, "that cat was all over the dinner table. We came in to eat and it was sitting on my plate ripping lumps out of the chicken."

Victoria imagines this and literally shudders.

"They didn't even mind," Marge continues, "and Max and Chloe have no more table manners than the bloody cat. Max is forever dipping his fingers in the serving bowls. Why he can't just serve himself..."

"Gran!" Bertie protests.

"I'm merely stating the truth. You behave far better than they do, Bertie. Am I right, Vicky, or am I right?"

But Bertie only hears the beginning of the phrase. He has plugged his earbud back in and turned the volume of the music up to a near-deafening maximum.

"You're totally right," Victoria replies.

"They eat like animals in that house," Marge says. "Animals!"

"They do."

"Do you remember calling her *Miss Piggy*," Marge asks, with laughter in her voice.

"That was you, not me," Victoria replies.

"On no. You definitely started that one."

"You still do call her that," Martin comments. "*And* you call Max and Chloe *the piglets*."

"Well, it's not un-fitting," Victoria says, "as any mealtime will demonstrate."

"They eat like pigs," Marge says. "You're right, Vicky. They really do."

Once Chloe and her friend Amy have arrived, Penny calls the family to table.

"Where did everyone go?" Chloe asks, eying the set table suspiciously.

"They had to leave early," Penny tells her.

"Why?"

"You'd have to ask *them* that," Penny says.

"It's because Mum called aunt Vicky a bitch," Max mumbles.

"What did you say?" Penny asks, shocked by her son's insolence.

"Well, you did."

"How dare you!" Penny says. "I never said anything of the sort. I don't talk to my sister like that. So, take that back."

Sander clears his throat and raises one finger. "Hey honey," he says, nervously. "You know I'm not that keen on contradicting you. But as you're effectively calling Max a liar, I do feel I have to point out that you *did* say that. We *all* heard you say that. You shouted it."

Chloe glances at Amy, restrains a smirk, and then, even though she personally *didn't* hear the famous phrase being spoken, she nods gravely to confirm it as truth.

Penny stares at Sander and opens her mouth in outrage. She licks her lips, takes a deep breath, and finally, staring at her plate, says, "Then I'm sorry Max. I'm sorry for contradicting you, and I'm sorry for saying it."

Max shrugs. "It's cool," he says. "But if I called Chloe a b–"

"Max!" Penny interrupts. "Don't push it, OK?"

"Your mother's right," Sander tells him. "The secret in life is to quit while you're ahead."

Max bites his lip, pulls a face and nods. "OK!" he says emphatically.

"So did they really just leave because you argued?" Chloe asks. "That's lame."

"Oh this was not any old argument," Max says, quoting a well known advertisement. "This was an M and S argument."

"Max!" Penny says sharply. But even Max can see that she's constraining a smile.

Chloe rolls her eyes at Amy, who giggles.

"My mum argues with my aunt too," Amy says.

"Right," Penny says. "Now, if we can just move on."

"Did anyone decide about Chr–" Max starts. But Sander is blinking slowly at him and shaking his head, so he drops the subject. "Hold the Christmas!" he says, raising one hand and grinning broadly.

The meal which was intended to be an extended, relaxed, semi-luxurious affair, gets reduced to the strict minimum and while Penny loads the remaining lasagne into a series of Tupperware containers and freezes it, Sander sets the kids up with a film in the lounge.

Finally, dragging Penny and one of the unopened bottles of Prosecco away from the messy kitchen, which he *says* he will clean up later, they head upstairs to their bedroom.

"God, she's even tidied up in here," Penny remarks.

"Maybe it was your Mum."

"No. This is definitely Vicky's work," Penny says, looking at the polished rows of perfume bottles on her dresser.

"You need to *relax*," Sander tells her. "Maybe you need a joint."

"I think you're right," Penny concedes. "I think I do."

When Sander has returned with his little wooden box and skinned up and lit the joint, he hands it to Penny and rolls onto his back beside her.

"She really is a bitch, you know," Penny says. "I don't just imagine it all. I don't make it all up."

Sander shrugs. "I didn't say you do," he says. "But other than having a stupid point of view on the Syrian crisis – which probably half of the population of this country would share – I'm not sure what she did to upset you, to be honest."

"It's not *what* she says," Penny says, speaking through smoke. "It's the way that she says it. It's like every single phrase has a little dig built in. That's the trouble. They come back and bite you once the conversation is over. You run the conversation back through your mind once she's left, and all the digs come back and nip you on the heels like a herd of rabid Chihuahuas."

"A herd of Chihuahuas?" Sander repeats, sniggering.

"A pack, then," Penny says. "Whatever. You know what I mean."

"I do," Sander says, still grinning as he takes the joint from Penny's hand.

"It's like the cleaning," Penny says. "I've got nothing against her spending her weekend cleaning my house if that's what rocks her boat. Really, *nothing*. But then she walks in and says, 'Ooh, this is all looking a bit out of control. Would you like me to help you get it *back* under control?'"

"Did she really say that?"

"Pretty much. Even Bertie had a go, the smug little fucker."

"Bertie?" Sander repeats, grimacing. He's pretty used to Penny slagging off her sister, but when she spreads the blame to her nephew as well it makes him feel distinctly uncomfortable.

"Yes! He came in at the end, purportedly to say 'goodbye'. But do you know what he said to me?"

"Nope."

"He asked if he could come and live here."

"Really?!"

Penny shakes her head exaggeratedly. "No," she says. "*Not* really. He was just being a snidey little dick. He looked at the messy kitchen and said – in this really goody-two-shoes little voice, right? *'Oh, aunty Penny, please could I come and live here, aunty Penny? It's sooo much nicer than home, aunty Penny'.*"

"Wow," Sander says. "And you're sure he wasn't serious?"

"Of course he wasn't serious."

"Well, you know," Sander says. "Don't blame the boy. It's not his fault."

"I know," Penny agrees. "You're right. But it was completely uncalled for. It was smug and condescending and totally unnecessary."

"It will just be stuff his parents say," Sander says. "You can't blame people's children."

"Yes," Penny says. "Yes, I'm sure you're right."

Sander rolls onto his side and slides one hand between Penny's thighs.

"And I'm not sure what makes you think I'm in the mood for *that*," Penny says.

Sander wriggles towards her and begins to nuzzle her neck. "Um?" he says. "Aren't you? In the mood for that?"

"Not really," Penny says.

But encouraged by the laughter in her voice, Sander continues. He kisses her cheek, then her neck. He pulls back her blouse and nibbles at her clavicle. "They say that it's a very good stress reliever," he says.

"Is that right?" Penny asks, reaching down to take Sander's chin in her hand so that she can turn his face towards her for a kiss. "Is *that* what they say?"

It's just after five and Penny and Sander have barely begun to clean up the kitchen when the landline rings.

"Can you just ignore that, please?" Penny tells Sander. He is already moving towards the handset and his capacity to be distracted from anything that resembles a chore drives Penny to distraction.

"Sure," Sander says, checking the display on the handset before returning it to the shelf. "It's only your Mum, anyway."

Penny sighs and wipes her hands on her jeans as she hesitates. "Oh, what the hell," she says, crossing the room. "Give it here."

"Hi Mum," she says, sounding pre-exasperated before the conversation has even begun. She's pretty sure her mother is going to tell her off about the argument again. In fact she's not even sure why she did choose to answer the phone. Some kind of Pavlovian reaction, no doubt. Some kind of umbilical whiplash.

"Hello," Marge says brightly. "It's just a quick call to let you know I got home OK."

"That took a while," Penny says, glancing at her watch.

"Well, we stopped off to get a bite to eat, didn't we. Everyone was starving."

Penny clears her throat. "Yes," she says. "That happens when you storm off just before dinner."

"Don't be like that," Marge says. "Of course, we realised in the car that we hadn't spoken about Christmas at all."

"Who realised that?"

"I'm sorry?"

"Who brought up Christmas?"

"Oh. I did."

"Right. OK."

"I suppose you don't want to think about it right now, do you?" Marge says.

"No. You're right. I don't."

"OK then."

"I'm actually thinking of cancelling Christmas altogether after that little performance."

"Oh, Penelope. You can't do that."

"If it's going to be anything like today..." Penny says, "I can. Just watch me. And please don't call me Penelope."

"Why? It's a perfectly good name."

"A perfectly good name which you never ever use."

"Only because you don't like it."

"You're right. I don't."

"Anyway, that would be a bit selfish, don't you think?"

"Selfish?"

"Yes. We *always* spend Christmas together."

"So maybe I'm thinking we should try something different this year," Penny says, addressing now both Sander, who is staring at her in surprise, and her mother.

"Oh, that's not an option, and well you know it. You know how difficult Christmas is for your sister – how difficult it is for all of us. Plus I'd have to choose, wouldn't I? I'd have to choose one of my daughters over the other. And that wouldn't be fair."

"Sure," Penny says. "Well, you'd have to be invited first, wouldn't you, Mum? We might want to spend it *completely* on our own. So that might simplify things for you."

"Oh, you cheeky girl," Marge says, forcing herself to treat the remark as a joke. "But I know what you mean. She can be difficult. In fact she was saying pretty much the same thing in the car."

"What same thing?"

"Oh, you know, about... I mean, you won't quote me on this, will you? She'd never forgive me. But she was saying that perhaps it would be better to organise things differently this year as well."

"Did she now?!"

"Yes. She can be quite critical when she gets going. As you know. I'm sure it's only because she's a perfectionist. I'm sure she doesn't mean anything by it."

"What did she say, Mum?"

"Oh nothing really. Martin wasn't happy though. He said it will be a while before he sets foot at yours again. But I expect he'll change his mind the next time there's a sunny bank holiday. I wouldn't worry."

"He said *what*?"

"You mustn't say anything," Marge says. "I promised not to tell you any of this."

"And Vicky. Did she agree with him?"

"Oh, she didn't say much. Other than the obvious."

"What's the obvious?"

"Oh, I can't tell you everything everyone said. She'd never forgive me."

"Mother. You know I never tell Vicky *anything* you tell me."

"Look, it was nothing really. She just said about the mess, you know. And the lack of hygiene, that's all. But you know what she's like about germs and things. And I'm sure she only said it because she was angry."

"God, she's got a nerve," Penny says, starting to feel truly angry herself. "I spent the entire bloody week decorating and cleaning for her, and…"

"In a way," Marge interrupts, "she was probably only joking. And I think she was only talking about Max and Chloe really."

"Max and Chloe?" Penny repeats. Beads of sweat are starting to sprout on her forehead. "What did she say about Max and Chloe?"

"Oh, not much. And, like I say, I'm sure it was just because she was upset. People say things they don't mean when they're upset. You know that."

"Mum. Tell me what she said."

"No, it wouldn't do you any good to know. Gossip never helps anyone. And Lord knows, I'm not the gossipy type."

"Mother," Penny says. "If you don't tell me exactly what she said right this minute, I swear I shall hang up the phone."

"I can't, I–"

"I *will* hang up. *And* you can spend Christmas in their stuffy little well-bleached flat eating M&S ready-meals."

"I promised I wouldn't say anything," Marge says. "You're putting me in a very difficult position."

"OK. I'm hanging up. Bye Mum."

"Oh, all right! But you won't say I told you? You promise?"

"No. I won't say you told me."

"*Well*," Marge says, sounding almost excited. "She said you eat like pigs, actually."

"I beg your pardon?"

"We were talking about table manners and the like. And she said you eat like pigs."

Sander, who has now put down his sponge, is crossing the room towards Penny. He's repeatedly mouthing the words, "What is it?" at his red-faced, perspiring wife.

"She actually said that?" Penny says, then for Sander's benefit, "She actually said we eat like pigs?"

"Now, try not to be too hard on her," Marge says. "Forgive and forget and all that."

"Forgive and forget?" Penny stammers. "Are you bloody kidding me?"

"And I think she only meant the kids," Marge says. "I don't think she really meant you."

"How *dare* she," Penny says. "How dare she insult my children. I mean, really... I...I... God! How, bloody, *dare* she!"

"Look, don't blow this out of proportion," Marge says.

"Out of proportion? Out of bloody proportion?!"

"I'm sure you'll get over this. You always do. You know what you girls are like."

"I... I have to go now, Mum," Penny says, her voice trembling as Sander reaches out to stroke her arm. "I... yes... I have to go. That's all. I have... um... a kitchen to clean. There you go. I have a kitchen to clean. No, it's not a kitchen, it's actually a bloody pigsty. So there you go. Bye."

Part Two

Two Christmases

It is the morning of Christmas Eve – without a doubt the most challenging day in Victoria's calendar.

It's after nine and Martin has just driven off to pick Marge up from her nearby flat in a sheltered housing facility. She's coming here for lunch before being driven down to Whitstable where she'll be spending Christmas with Penny's family.

Yes, it's just Victoria, Martin and Bertie for Christmas this time, and Victoria is feeling scared.

She glances down the hallway towards Bertie's bedroom. She knows he'll sleep for at least another hour.

She slides the blister pack into view from the top shelf and strokes it for a moment. She had promised herself that she would wait until at least twelve to pop her second pill, but she's realising that she's not going to make it. *Perhaps half now,* she thinks. *Perhaps half now and half later, and a sneaky forbidden cigarette. It is the worst day, after all.*

She crosses to the sink where she fills a glass of water and swallows the half-tablet before crouching down and pulling the hidden Marlboro packet from behind the cleaning products beneath the sink.

She lets herself out onto the roof terrace and slides the bay window closed behind her.

It's a cold, blustery day, but the sky is blueish and the sun is filtering through, albeit weakly. She walks to the far corner, where she knows she can't be seen, then crouches down and pulls a cigarette and lighter from the packet.

"Christmas," she mutters as she lights the cigarette. "Bloody Christmas."

The cigarette makes her head spin. She understands most of the things that she does but cigarettes are the exception. They don't taste nice. They don't make her feel better. And they're clearly not good for her, either. She drags so deeply on the cigarette that she hears it crackle.

Martin told her that Sander smokes marijuana and she wonders if it's anything like Valium. Perhaps she should have tried it when it was offered to her in the nineties. Perhaps she still should. According to Martin, Sander gets hold of pretty-much unlimited quantities of the stuff, and without having to go through all the rigmarole of consulting outrageously expensive Harley Street doctors either.

Indoors, everything is ready – red tablecloth, gold luxury crackers and the best silverware. The plastic tree is up and sparkling, and Bertie's gifts – unusually generous this year in an attempt at compensating for what he keeps calling their "broken Christmas" – are wrapped, piled up beneath the tree.

Four individual Christmas dinners are waiting in the refrigerator (she only has to heat them up) and the Champagne is nicely chilled.

Having Christmas dinner on Christmas Eve is Sander's fault, of course. It's how they do things in Denmark apparently, though Sander has always struck Victoria as about as Danish as fish and chips. But what with Christmas Eve being such a problematic day to negotiate, it was a shift in tradition they had all gratefully accepted. At least this way everyone is kept busy. At least this way they never find themselves alone as the hour hand sweeps onto the dreaded number three.

The cigarette having now burnt down to the butt, she stubs it out thoroughly on the underside of the windowsill and, sliding the packet into her pocket, crosses to the wall.

She looks out over the rooftops and thinks of Penny, then Marge and then, finally, Ed.

I was eight, she thinks. *Now I'm forty-eight.*

Forty eight! At least halfway through my entire life, and still dosed up to my tits on Valium just to get through the day.

She shakes her head and then thinks again, *Halfway through. Is this all there is? Can this really be all there is?*

The sound of a car catches her attention and she looks down to see Martin's BMW pulling up. Marge must have been waiting, ready for him. Victoria imagines her sitting in the lobby with her handbag on her knees, watching and waiting for another twenty-fourth of December to begin. She sighs deeply and heads indoors.

"Gosh it's blowy out there," Marge says when she enters the flat. She's fiddling with a stray wisp of hair, trying to push it back into place. She's clearly been to the hairdresser's.

"Your hair looks nice," Victoria tells her, even though she thinks her mother's hairstyle looks more and more like a crash helmet every time she sees her.

"It did before I went out in *that,*" Marge says, still pushing at the breakaway lock of hair.

"I'll get you some hairspray in a minute," Victoria tells her. "Don't worry."

"Thanks," Marge says, then turning to Martin who is standing in the doorway behind her, "Did you remember the presents?"

"I did," he says, raising her Sainsbury's bag and waving it as proof.

"Careful," Marge says. "There are breakables in there."

Marge unbuttons and hangs her coat, then follows Victoria to the large kitchen-dining room. "Gosh!" she says. "What's all this, then?"

Victoria looks at her with an air of surprise. "Um, Christmas dinner, maybe?" she says.

"But it's only the twenty-fourth, love."

"Yes. We always have Christmas dinner on Christmas Eve. You know that, Mum."

"Yes, on Christmas Eve *evening*," Marge says. "Not on blooming Christmas Eve morning."

"It's for later, for lunch time," Victoria says. "I thought it was better that way. Seeing as we won't be together this evening..."

Marge huffs. "I don't know how I'm supposed to eat two Christmas dinners," she says. "And I still think you should change your mind about this. You're being terribly stubborn."

Victoria laughs. The Valium is kicking in and she's starting to feel soft and floaty and vaguely amused. "I'm not being stubborn at all," she says. "We simply haven't been invited."

"I'm sure Penny wouldn't mind," Marge says.

"Are you?" Victoria replies, still managing to smile.

In search of support, Marge turns to Martin, behind her. "Surely *you* can't agree with all this silliness?" she says.

Martin shrugs. "I don't mind the change, to be honest," he says. "And pretty much anything's preferable to what happened the last time we went down."

Bertie, in pyjamas, has surfaced. His hair, which he has been growing, has fallen across one eye. The effect somehow reminds Marge of a pirate.

"Oh, please can we go?" he whines, leaning in to kiss his grandmother on the cheek.

"You see?" Marge says. "The boy sees sense."

"We've been through this a hundred times, Bertie," Victoria tells her son. "And the answer, this once, is no."

"Just let *me* go then," Bertie pleads. "I could go down with Gran. There's room in the car."

"That's true," Marge says (rather unhelpfully, Victoria thinks.) "He could."

"That's lovely, son," Martin says. "That's *really* flattering."

"It's not that–"

"I don't care what it is," Martin interrupts. "We're having Christmas here, all right? End of discussion."

"God!" Bertie says, now turning and heading back to his room in exasperation. But as he walks down the hallway he mutters, just loud enough for everyone to hear, "It's so boring here. I feel like my head's going to explode or something."

"I'll personally explode his head if he doesn't stop complaining," Martin tells his wife.

"The poor lad," Marge comments. "You can't blame him for not wanting to spend Christmas on his own."

"Only he's *not* on his own, is he, Marge?" Martin says. "He's with his beloved parents."

Victoria squeezes past her husband and calls to Bertie down the hallway. "Bertie, darling! If you want your presents

– and believe me, you really do – then you need to get up and get showered and get dressed in those clothes I put out."

"And put a bloody smile on that face!" Martin shouts.

"Don't worry," Victoria says, softly. "He'll be fine."

"So what are you cooking?" Marge asks Victoria once Martin has moved to the lounge. "This all looks very posh."

"Oh! I got these," Victoria says enthusiastically, opening the refrigerator door to reveal the four packaged meals.

"Oh, how funny!" Marge says. "Your sister said you'd be doing M&S ready meals. I wonder how she guessed."

"Did she, now?" Victoria says, both annoyed and bemused at the same time. "Well, you can tell Nigella bloody Lawson that she's wrong." She slams the refrigerator shut. "Those, Mother, are not from M&S at all. They're from *Harrods*, actually."

Victoria fills the day as best she can. She serves teas and coffees, then Champagne and snacks.

She press-gangs her son and husband into playing charades only to fail, through her veil of Valium, to guess a single one of their clues. But busy as they are, it is *not* the same as spending the day with her sister. She knew from the start that it couldn't be.

She had imagined how slowly these hours would pass, had understood that they would be even more painful than usual. But the reality is worse, even, than anything she had imagined, and she can almost hear the second hand as it creaks from one notch of the kitchen clock to the next.

Nothing, not the excitement of Bertie's new iPad, nor the surprise of emerald earrings, can do anything to speed it up. It's as if the air within the flat has been replaced with something viscous, replaced, perhaps, with that green slime that Bertie used to play with.

So, despite the meal, which is delicious, and the gifts, which are exaggerated, and despite everyone's efforts to make the best of a bad job (and even Bertie tries his best), the simple prospect of surviving the final hour to three o'clock becomes so utterly exhausting that she's actually relieved when Penny's friend Will appears, early, to whisk Marge off to Whitstable; when Bertie vanishes to his bedroom to set up his new iPad, and when Martin apologetically settles in front of the television to watch a football match he recorded.

Finally, she's able to give in to the path of least resistance. Finally, without witnesses, she can cave in to the inevitability of downing her remaining half a tab of Valium, and lying on her bed and watching, simply watching, as the hour labours its way towards, then through, then finally *past*, the dreaded void that is three o'clock.

It strikes her that it's actually easier this way, and she wonders if all the keeping busy of these past years hasn't been counterproductive after all. Perhaps what was always needed was not exhausting resistance, but passive, lazy, abandonment to pain, to guilt, to the shame of it all.

※ ※ ※

Penny is so busy preparing Christmas dinner that she almost escapes the dreaded three pm anniversary. But then a shiver runs down her spine, as if a gust of chilled wind has passed through the room, and she glances at the kitchen clock and sighs. It's one minute to three. Gotcha!

She pauses peeling spuds and respectfully waits for the minute hand to move on. She wonders if Victoria and her mother are OK and briefly considers phoning them to check. But they're together, she reminds herself. They'll be fine.

She tries to summon Ed's face in her mind's eye, but though she can picture the individual components – his smile, his goofy teeth, his nose, his blue eyes – putting them together seems almost impossible. It's not that her memories have faded as the years have passed, it's that they were never very good to start with. She had been too young to understand that brothers weren't necessarily around forever. No one had warned her they could disappear. So she failed, it now seems, to stare at Ed sufficiently. She failed to properly record the details of her brother's face, of his voice, of his essence.

The kitchen door opens and Sander's face peeps comically through the gap. "Are you OK?" he asks, and Penny could weep (if she let herself) for the simple fact of Sander's kindness, for the simple truth of being married to someone who loves her enough to remember the anniversary of something he never personally lived through.

Instead of weeping, she clears her throat. "Fine," she says. "A bit bored with peeling potatoes, but fine." She isn't really bored with peeling potatoes at all – it was simply the first thing that came to mind, the first conversational theme she could think of which wasn't to do with Ed.

"Here," Sander says, moving to the sink and bumping her hip with his own as he pushes her aside. "Let me do that."

"You're cute when you want to be," Penny says, pecking him on the cheek and trying to think what she should do now she's been liberated from spud duties.

"That sounds like a super-power," Sander replies, taking the peeler from her hand and picking up where she left off.

"I'm sorry?" Penny says. Her mind's still partly on the clock – the minute hand has just moved on a notch.

"Being cute whenever you want to be," Sander says. "It sounds like some brilliant super-power."

"Oh," Penny says. "Yes, I suppose it does." Sander, she realises, is already stoned; he's already on a different wavelength.

Penny is taking a break, sipping from a mug of too-hot tea and staring out at the whitecap waves when a pale blue Beetle chugs into view outside.

She glances at the time on the broadband box. It's just after four-thirty and they're way in advance of the agreed schedule. "What the hell are *they* doing here?" she says, watching Will – for it is indeed Will – as he climbs out, stretches his back, and, grinning broadly, waves up at her.

"Really?" Sander says, leaving his armchair to join her at the window. With a snigger, he adds, "Maybe they got bored at Vicky's."

Ben, Will's boyfriend-of-the-moment, appears from the passenger seat. He waves as well, and then both men begin the delicate process of extricating Marge from the back seat of the car.

"I'd better go and help them," Penny says. "Poor Mum." But by the time she reaches the car Marge has been freed.

"I've just been telling this friend of yours he needs a new car," she announces. "A car with proper doors at the back."

"Hi Mum. Hi Ben."

Ben waves his fingers at Penny over the top of the car. Something in his expression reveals that he has found the journey with Marge to be something of an ordeal. He's not as used to her as Will is, after all.

"Marge only wants to travel in Rolls Royces from now on," Will announces with a smile and a raised eyebrow. Then he kisses Penny on both cheeks and says, warmly, intimately, "Hello you."

"Hello *you*," Penny replies.

Marge turns to the car and shakes her head. "How old is this wreck of yours, anyway?"

"Erm, well, it's younger than you, for starters," Will says.

"Oh, you're a cheeky one," Marge tells him. "He's been cheeking me all the way down the motorway."

"I'm glad to hear it," Penny says.

"How are you, sweetie?" Will asks.

"Good," Penny replies, "What time did you set off?"

"Two thirty-ish. I was a bit early. You know how excited I get about Christmas. *And* seeing my bestie, of course."

"Of course," Penny says. Then realising that they will have left before three, she turns to Marge. "How was Vicky?" she asks. "Was she OK?"

"Fine," Marge says. "I mean, we left early, but she seemed fine. We had a lovely meal. From Harrods it was. And some very expensive gifts. Bertie got an iPad and they gave me a lovely cashmere sweater and..."

"You had dinner already?" Penny interrupts.

"Yes. Your sister's so thoughtful," Marge says. "They had dinner early just so we could be together. Isn't that nice?"

"Yes," Penny says, thinking, *Just to beat me to it, more like.*

"It was gorgeous. Rolled turkey and cranberry sauce, Yorkshire puddings and–"

"God, I hope you saved some space for this evening."

"This evening? You're not doing both meals again, are you?" Marge asks.

"Yes, Mum," Penny says. "Just like every year. Danish Christmas this evening, and normal Christmas tomorrow."

"Yess!" Will exclaims, making a winning gesture with one fist and turning to Ben. "I told you. The only house in England where you get two full Christmas dinners."

"Or in my case *three* full Christmas dinners," Marge says, mournfully. "What are you cooking anyway?"

"A roast," Penny says, taking her mother's arm and leading her towards the house. "Well, two roasts. With all the trimmings."

"Turkey again?" Marge asks.

"No. Salmon today and chicken tomorrow. The salmon thing is quite ambitious, actually. It's a whole one and I'm cooking it – or attempting to cook it – the Danish way. You cover it in rock salt. It keeps all the flavour in, apparently. Sander found me the recipe online."

"Oh, well, in that case, I'm sure I'll be fine," Marge says. "If it's just a bit of fish and a bit of chicken, I'm sure I'll manage."

Penny frowns and wonders how her mother has managed to make both of her Christmas dinners sound like understated failures before they're even cooked. "You know you said Harrods, Mum," she says. "Are we talking ready meals, here?"

"Yes," Marge says. "But not like any ready meal you've ever had. Some top chef – I've forgotten his name now – puts them together. Gorgeous, they were. Bloody gorgeous!"

When they enter the house, Chloe, Max and Sander have formed a welcome party at the bottom of the stairs. "Hi Gran," they say in unison. "Merry Christmas."

"It's not Christmas until tomorrow," Marge says, leaning in to kiss them, and for some reason pinching – painfully – Chloe's cheek between finger and thumb as she does so.

"Ouch!" Chloe shrieks, rubbing her cheek.

"It's Bill and Ben the flowerpot men," Max announces as Will and his boyfriend arrive.

"Don't call them that!" Penny snaps. "Sorry Ben. You'll have to forgive Max. He has absolutely no manners."

Will and Ben just grin. "Hello Little Weed," Will replies, which leaves Max looking confused.

"He's never even seen Bill and Ben," Penny tells them as they remove their coats and move to the lounge.

"I have, too!" Max says. "It's on YouTube."

"Oh yes, *everything's* on YouTube," Will agrees.

"That's quite good actually," Ben says, quietly. He has a soft, West Country accent. "I never thought of us as Bill and Ben before. I quite like it."

"What time's dinner, Mum?" Max asks.

"About six," Penny replies.

"Which means, in reality, about eight," Sander adds.

"So can I get a snack?" Max asks.

"Sure," Sander says. "You can help me get snacks for everyone. We've got a load of mini pizza things to heat up."

"And are we getting dressed up for dinner and stuff?" Max asks hopefully. They always have to dress up when Victoria is here for Christmas, and Max rather likes the excuse.

"I don't care," Penny says. "Dress however you want, dear."

"I'm not dressing up," Sander declares.

"No surprise there, Dad," Max says. "We're all just praying there's a new favourite jumper under that tree somewhere."

Sander glances down at his chest, then turns to Penny, who shrugs. "You might want to put something else on," she says. "It *is* Christmas."

"Well, we're dressing up, aren't we, Ben?" Will says, causing Ben to smile and blink in agreement. Will turns to Penny and wiggles his eyebrows. "I have a special Christmas jumper," he tells her.

Penny squints. "Ouch," she says. "Like a proper one? With Father Christmas on it or something?"

"Better than that," Will says. "You'll love it, Pen."

"Right. So, what I suggest," Penny says, "is that you stick your bags upstairs – you're in the top back bedroom which has been repainted and everything. And then you can get changed into your Christmas garb, or your lairy jumpers or whatever, and we can get some gin and tonics served. How does that sound?"

"Sounds good to me," Will says.

"I think I should phone Victoria," Marge says. "Just, you know, to check she's all right."

"You were just there, Mum," Penny says.

Will and Ben squeeze past them and bustle their bags from the room, then start to make their way upstairs.

"I just want to give her a quick call," Marge says.

"Fine," Penny replies. "But do *not* pass me the phone, OK? I can't be doing with it, not today." Penny has not spoken to Victoria since October.

Marge rolls her eyes. "You two!" she says. "What are you like?"

Penny shrugs. "Like two sisters who have chosen not to spend Christmas together, I imagine. Anyway, I need to get back to that kitchen."

But Marge grabs her arm to retain her and nods towards the door. "Where did that one pop up from?" she asks, confidentially.

"Ben?"

"Yes. I thought he was with… what was his name? The tall one."

"Frank," Penny says. "But they split up in, oh, I don't know… In March or something."

"Lord, he doesn't hang around, does he?"

"It's not like Frank died or anything, Mum," Penny murmurs. "He just ran off with some air steward. There's no official mourning period or anything. He doesn't have to wear a veil."

"All the same," Marge says. "I think I preferred Frank. He was so much more chatty."

"Oh, Mum! Just give them a break. Anyway, I think Ben seems lovely," Penny says. And it's true, she does think that. With his neat beard and brown eyes, with his long lashes and his short little legs, Ben reminds her of some friendly woodland elf.

"You just think that Will can do no wrong," Marge says.

"You're right," Penny confirms. "That's exactly what I think. Now, go and phone my sister, and then we can settle into having our own Christmas, here. All right?"

Ten minutes later, Sander has returned with drinks and Will (complete with reindeer jumper) and Ben (dressed in a rather dandy waistcoat and purple tie) have added their gifts to the pile beneath the tree. It is finally starting to feel like Christmas.

"I put some dodgy Christmas songs on my iPhone," Will says. "What do you think?"

"Definitely," Sander tells him. "Go for it. There's a speaker thingy in the corner. Chloe will show you."

Chloe groans and hauls herself to her feet with all of the energy of an eighty-year-old. "I'm sure Will knows how to use an iPhone dock, Dad," she whines, leading the way all the same.

Max reappears wearing his floral shirt, which he has visibly ironed himself, badly. He looks at Will's jumper and declares it, "Truly horrific."

"I know," Will replies, wide-eyed. "Fabulous, isn't it?"

And then Max notices Ben's outfit. "Wow!" he declares. "So you finally found a boyfriend with some dress sense, Will."

Ben grins broadly. "I'll take that as a compliment, shall I?" he says.

"Ben's a buyer for a clothes shop," Will explains. "He gets lots of freebies."

"Right," Max says. He feels suddenly self conscious. "Um. Is this all right, Ben?" he asks. "It's just that this is the only decent shirt I have. But I'm not sure if it's still fashionable or anything."

Ben laughs. "It's nice," he tells him. "Very cool. And still very much 'in.'"

Max blushes deeply but looks pleased with himself all the same.

"Compliments from the homos," Sander jokes. "You know you've got something right when that happens."

"Oh yes!" Will says, tweaking the pompom nose of his reindeer jumper. "We homos are *right* at the cutting edge of fashion!"

"*He is,*" Max says, nodding at Ben. "*Your* jumper is only vaguely better than Dad's."

"All right, all right," Sander concedes. "I'll change it. OK? I'll change the bloody jumper, and then everyone can just stop bitching."

Gin and tonics are served, quickly followed by refills, and soon everyone has migrated through to the kitchen, purportedly to help Penny.

"We'll be your kitchen slaves," Will tells her, but all any of them really achieve is to distract her from the task at hand.

So it's almost nine pm by the time they finally sit down to dinner, and so many snacks have been eaten, so many drinks have been drunk, that no one is even hungry anymore.

But the salmon, once broken from its rock-salt envelope, is succulent and delicious, the vegetables crispy and brown. With the exception of the hollandaise sauce, which is so lumpy that Penny has to pour it though a strainer, the meal is as good as she had hoped it would be. And, hungry or not, everyone digs in. Even Marge, for once, smiles, albeit lopsidedly, through the whole affair.

Solomon, the cat, summoned by the smell of salmon, jumps up onto the table. After much begging by Chloe, he's even allowed to remain. It's Christmas for cats, too, Chloe insists, as she feeds him scraps of salmon from her plate.

Marge isn't happy about it, but at least Penny draws a line when Chloe suggests that her guinea pig should join them too.

Chloe provokes some hilarity by announcing that she's going to become a vegetarian in the new year, and Penny has to remind her that she doesn't like vegetables. "Maybe I'll like them in the new year as well," Chloe declares.

"You could start now," Penny suggests, nodding at her plate. "You could start right now with those sprouts on your plate."

"Sprouts are rank," Chloe says. "Even Solomon won't touch them, look!"

"Apparently they taste different until adolescence," Will says. "I read a thing about it."

"OK, forget the sprouts, Chloe," Penny says. "How about you eat that parsnip?"

Chloe pulls a face.

"No," Penny says. "I thought not. Not *quite* ready to be a vegetarian, are you?"

"She likes chocolate," Max says. "That's veggie. Maybe she could live off Mars Bars. Then she could be a fat chav instead of just a chav."

"Oh, shut it you," Chloe tells him. "You think you're so funny."

The three course meal meanders slowly on, woven around random phone calls from various friends, and long, slightly drunken conversations about Will and Ben's lives in London. Regularly, someone vanishes to the lounge and returns with a gift to be opened as well, so it's almost midnight by the time they leave the dining room.

Marge makes her excuses and heads upstairs, and Sander puts music on and starts to dance with Penny. Both Chloe and Max express their disapproval of their parents' embarrassing behaviour, and yet neither of them leave the room.

"You two need to loosen up," Sander tells them. "Or you'll never have any fun."

"If you mean the dancing-to-the-Bee-Gees-like-a-nob kind of fun," Chloe says, "then you're right. It's never gonna happen, Dad."

But then Ben, who she secretly thinks is sexy, begins to dance too, and then Will joins in as well, so she starts, poutingly, to move her hips in time with the music.

"See, she's good," Ben shouts to Sander. "The girl's got rhythm."

And Chloe, still pouting, but now blushing as well, starts to dance properly, just to show Ben what she's capable of.

The next morning, Penny wakes up late. She has a hangover and the idea of cleaning up the kitchen and dining room only to make them dirty again leaves her feeling dispirited. It's almost eleven by the time she heads downstairs.

She finds her mother in the lounge watching television. "Morning Mum," she says.

Marge turns to look at her. "So you are here, after all," she says. "I was beginning to think you'd all run off on me. The house is so quiet."

"No," Penny says flatly. "Still here. Tea?"

"No thanks," Marge says. "I just had one."

Penny stares for a moment out at the beach. Everything, this morning – the sea, the sky, the pebbles – is grey. She feels distinctly grey herself, actually. Too much gin will do that, she thinks. She sighs and shuffles down the hallway towards the kitchen, pausing to peer in at the dining room en-route. Both rooms look horrific, and she fondly remembers coming downstairs to a spotless kitchen during Victoria's last visit. She should, perhaps, have been more appreciative.

She decides that Sander is going to have to help out, that's all. He's perfectly capable of being efficient when pushed. So, today, she'll just have to push.

She fills the kettle and then looks around at the disorder and wonders where to start. She crosses to the dishwasher and crouches down to begin emptying it. She wonders how many times, in a life, she'll have to fill and empty the damned thing.

"Hey, let me do that."

She turns to see Sander standing in the doorway. "You must be exhausted," he says.

"A bit hungover, that's all," Penny says, "but I *could* do with a hand today."

"We'll all chip in," Sander says. "It'll be fine. You'll see."

"If we can just get the kitchen sorted out before Will and Ben get up," she says.

"They are up. They're out, actually," Sander says. "They went for a walk, I think."

"A walk?" Penny says, feeling a brief pique of anger that they didn't, like Vicky, choose to scrub the kitchen instead.

But then the front door opens and Will's excitable voice rings out, somehow changing the entire atmosphere within the house. "Her boobs were so huge once she transitioned that it was a wonder of the modern world that she could still stand up," he's saying. He peers into the lounge, says, "Hi Marge! Merry Christmas!" and then joins them in the kitchen.

"So!" he announces. "Ben and I have been talking, and we're going to clear up and make breakfast for everyone so you get a break. How does that sound?"

"We were just going to…" Penny starts. But Will crosses the room to join her, and then steers her by the elbows from the room.

"Step *away* from the dishwasher," he jokes.

By the time the kitchen has been cleaned and breakfast has been served and cleared away; by the time the chicken has been stuffed and roasted, it's five pm.

Christmas, everyone is realising, is messier, later, and far less organised without the presence of the Cunningham family.

But it's also, surprisingly, more fun.

Without Victoria's moderating influence, they drink more than usual, they laugh at slightly ruder jokes, and function less as a well trained army, and more like a well-meaning hippie commune. It's less efficient, certainly, but it's actually a rather nice change.

The final gifts are opened at the dinner table just before six: a new jumper for Sander, new shirts from Will to Max, makeup for Chloe, and an M&S voucher from Marge to Penny.

"Well, that was lovely," Marge says, as they clear the things from the table. "Proof, if ever there was, that you don't need expensive iPads and emeralds to have a lovely time."

"No," Penny replies. "No, you don't."

She had been hoping, desperately, not for emeralds, but for a contribution to a new washing machine. She had even dropped numerous hints to her mother about it. Still, at least, she consoles herself, she can use the thirty-pound M&S voucher to buy food. What with Christmas and gifts, their January budget has been all but spent. She just needs to find the right moment to tell Sander.

• • •

It's the thirteenth of July. This means that tomorrow is the fourteenth – Victoria's birthday. She'll be forty-nine, but she feels more like a hundred. She's never felt lower.

She's had bad days before. Over the course of her life, she's probably had almost as many bad days as good days. But today, she just feels empty. She feels hopeless. It's the doctor's fault – the Harley Street guy, not her regular NHS GP.

She had been about to embark on her first course of hormone replacement therapy to relieve her early menopausal symptoms, which, lately, have reached an almost unbearable crescendo.

For on top of the dryness, which she had almost got used to, has come wetness, in the form of embarrassing, unpredictable leakage. And on top of the depression, which she's had so long it feels like part of her, and on top of the anxiety, which, with Valium, she manages just about to control, has come bouts of fogginess when her mind is quite unable to concentrate on anything at all. It's not a sensation that's easy to explain, but it's a bit like trying to think using someone else's eyeglasses. Her mood swings, too, have been terrible, and she's found herself shouting at Bertie, and then breaking out in a sweat, before crying at Martin.

So the solution they had come up with, after detailed discussion within her five-minute segments (Doctor Dailey is a serious man but with far too many patients) was to try HRT.

They'd been discussing it, building up to it, for a year now, and in January, she had finally decided that she was ready. Ready to admit she was menopausal. Ready to do something to stave it off, too.

But she had made the mistake of talking to Doctor Wilson-Coombe, her Harley Street guy, her second doctor who, unbeknown to Doctor Dailey, she sees in order to double her Valium prescription. She had never really considered Wilson-Coombe as a proper doctor, had aways seen him as more of a pusher really, an expensive dealer of Valium, if you will. So she had been surprised when he had such a strong opinion on HRT. He had sent her for some outrageously expensive genetic tests just because she had mentioned a great aunt who might have had cancer.

And then, just yesterday, he had dropped the bombshell. She is a carrier of a gene sequence which puts her at risk for cancer. Whether HRT would increase this risk was unsure, he said, but "well within the realms of possibility," whatever that was supposed to mean. It was certainly something to consider before starting HRT, he said. As was having an ovariectomy, a hysterectomy, and quite possibly a double mastectomy, as well.

Why don't you sew on a penis, while you're at it? she had thought, obtusely. Because what kind of woman would she be after that?

Something new to consider, she thinks again, running the doctor's words through her head. As if she was likely to ever think of anything else, ever again.

Beyond her fear of cancer, which has always been acute, but which is now overwhelming, is the fact that the one option open to her to relieve these dreadful symptoms is being wrestled from her grasp. Because if it does turn out that she can't have HRT – and she really does need to find a way to discuss this within her five minute window with Doctor Dailey – then what's left of her life?

Though their sex life had never been fabulous, it had had, at least, the merit of existing. But the wrong kind of dryness combined with the wrong kind of wetness does not sexy foreplay make, so now she's become *that* woman as well. She's become the woman who hasn't had sex with her husband in nearly a year.

Martin is avoiding her too, she can sense it. He's working three nights a week, yet he's not at the office (she's checked). So where is he?

She couldn't blame him really, could she? Every woman knows that, as far as men are concerned, needs must – a man will do what a man's gotta do. And yet, she'll leave him if she finds out for sure, she knows she will. She just has to decide whether she *wants* to find out for sure. Or not. She struggles to see how a divorce could make anything better.

So here she is, lying in bed, thinking about everything, thinking about nothing, but mainly thinking about Valium which might just stop her thinking about the rest.

She's taking too much of the stuff. Both of her doctors have told her so, even though neither of her doctors know about the other, even though neither of them know she has effectively doubled the dosage.

She's tried to cut down, really she has. It's just that when she does, everything else, the cleaning, the hand washing, the anxiety, it all gets worse.

She pulls her hands from beneath the covers and looks at them now. They're raw and pink from all the scrubbing, from the bleach, from the nailbrush.

"Are you OK?" Martin asks, and she physically jumps at the shock of his presence. That's another thing which keeps happening recently. She keeps drifting into herself, keeps disconnecting from the outside world, then being shocked when it suddenly forces its way into consciousness. Is it the Valium or the menopause, or her endemic anxiety that's the cause?

She turns to look at Martin. He's standing in front of the wardrobe, knotting his tie, smiling at her expectantly. He looks young, fit and healthy. He looks like the opposite of her, in fact. *He's going to leave me,* she thinks. *Of course he is.*

"Yes, I'm fine," she tells him, faking a smile. "I'm absolutely fine. And you?"

"Oh, you know," Martin says, glancing at his watch. "Running a bit late. That's all."

Once Martin has left for work, Victoria gets up. She pulls on her dressing gown and heads through to the kitchen. It's just before nine and she'll have to go and wake Bertie up soon. He has a late start today on account of the swimming pool being closed for repairs.

She prepares the coffee machine and switches it on, then sits at the kitchen table and listens to it cough, wheeze and splutter.

She thinks about Bertie next, for even Bertie is drifting away from her. He's still nowhere near as bad as Chloe, but he's spending more and more time in his room and less and less with his parents.

She does her best to remain chipper around him, but perhaps he's picking things up all the same. They say that children soak everything up like a sponge, don't they? They say that even your subconscious affects their development.

He had been good company for her when he was little, such good company in fact that she had felt guilty for monopolising him. But now he spends his time talking to girls on Facebook, and for much of the day, she finds that she's effectively living alone.

Somewhere along the line, not only did she forget to make new friends to replace the occasional, inevitable departures (people move away, they decide they don't like you, and sometimes they even die), but she also forgot *how* to make friends. She finds herself approaching fifty, and she has no idea whatsoever how women her age might even go about meeting new people. It's not like she's going to meet them at the school gates, after all. She's not going to bump in to new people at work, here in the kitchen, is she?

She's nearly fifty, and friendless, and jobless, in a failing marriage to a probably adulterous husband. She's mother to an increasingly alienated son, and sister to an apparently angry Penny. In fact the only person she still really talks to is her mother. It's not looking good.

It's not the first time she has felt this bleak, she reminds herself. The black dog of depression has visited her regularly as the years have gone by. But it had always seemed that there was something on the horizon to look forward to – there was some event marked in red in the calendar which would shake up the routine if she could just hang on in there. There would be Christmas at Penny's, or a coming summer holiday in Corfu, there would be books to read and pools to lie next to.

Even the holiday, this year, has gone tits up. For Martin, who must be having his very own midlife crisis, wants to camp. He wants to walk all day and sleep in a tent. He wants to prove just how young he is by sleeping in flea-infested Spanish hostels. And there's just no way she can participate in that madness. It would send her over the edge, that's her fear. It would push her off the cliff and the only place to land would be in the deep dark sea of clinical insanity.

The current plan, then, is for Martin and Bertie to go walking the Spanish hills together. It will do them good, Martin keeps saying. And it's indisputable that they need to do *something* to fix their relationship. Bertie hardly speaks to either of them these days, but he seems to hold Martin in special disregard.

In his bedroom, Bertie is not asleep. He's chatting to his friend Michelle on Facebook. In a strange kind of synchronicity that neither he nor his mother will ever be aware of, he too is worrying about the upcoming walking holiday.

M: So why isn't your mum going?

B: Mum? Camping? You've got to be joking!

M: Why?

B: Freaks out if there's a stain on a teaspoon.

M: True. I forgot.

B: There's no way.

M: Spain's cool. We went last summer. The sea was HOT.

B: You went to the Costa Not A Lot. V. Diff.

This is walking every day. Miles and miles and miles. Blister distances.

M: Yuck. Whachagonnado?

B: Dunno. I need an escape plan.

M: We'll come up with something.

B: I could tell them. That would put an end to it.

M: You wouldn't dare.

B: I might.

M: You wouldn't

B: I might.

M: They'll freak.

B: I know. But at least he won't want me on hols anymore will he?

M: True. But you wouldn't dare.

B: I might.

M: Repetition.

B: You too.

M: True. Gotta go anyway. Mum's calling.

B: Mine too. Love ya.

• • •

It's just gone eight and Victoria, freshly returned from her appointment with Dr Dailey, is Googling HRT on the iPad.

She finally plucked up the courage to tell him about her *other* doctor (though she didn't mention her principal reason for *having* another doctor). Still, she's glad she broached the subject, she's glad she was brave, or at least, braver than usual. Because Doctor Dailey, who seemed very sure of himself, claimed that Doctor Wilson-Coombe was a "little behind the times" as far as HRT was concerned. Specific clinical trials have shown, he claims, that HRT does not increase the risk of cancer beyond the level which her genetic disposition implies. And even that isn't as clear cut as Wilson-Coombe had implied. With regular checkups, she should be fine, he said.

Of course words like *should* only make you feel better until you have time to think about what they mean, but she is feeling at least a tiny bit less depressed about the whole thing.

But the whole Google business is frustrating her, and she wishes she could ask someone for help. Both Bertie and Martin find answers to their questions instantly, whereas she can never find a damned thing.

The front door to the flat opens, making her jump. She switches off the iPad, but then thinks better of it and switches it back on again, closes the HRT search window, and then switches it back off again. She doesn't want anyone stumbling upon *that*.

"Hello," she says, as Martin enters the room. He drops a large carrier bag beside the door and places his briefcase on the chair. "You're late again," she says.

Martin nods. "Rush job," he says. "Another Saudi needing British nationality yesterday."

"It sounds like they all want to be British these days."

"They do," Martin says. "The Middle East is a mess."

"I'm surprised we let them in. What with all the fuss about immigrants at the moment."

Martin shrugs. "We only let in the extremely rich ones who can afford apartments in One Mayfair and expensive immigration lawyers like myself. None of those horrible poor people."

"No..." Victoria says. She's not entirely sure if he's mocking her, or joking, or perhaps even being serious.

"So how are you?" Martin asks.

"Good," Victoria replies, crossing to Martin and kissing him on the cheek. She breathes in deeply in an attempt at detecting some clue as to where he really spends his evenings. And there *is* something there, isn't there? A sweetness to his breath. "Have you been eating something?" she asks.

"Ah, yes," Martin says. "Turkish delight. A gift from a client."

"Right," Victoria says, picturing belly dancers and veils. Was there something shifty in his expression as he replied to her, or is she being paranoid? She nods at the carrier bag. "What's in there?"

"Ah!" Martin says, brightly. "Camping stuff. An amazing two-man tent. It weighs less than two kilos. And two ultra-light sleeping bags. Do you want to see them?"

Victoria shakes her head, so Martin moves to the kitchen table and, as he loosens his tie with one hand, picks up a letter with the other. "Bertie's report card?" he asks as he shakes the sheet of paper open.

"Yes," Victoria replies. "Five As and two Bs."

"He's a clever lad," Martin says, then, "Hum. A+ in sport? That's my boy. Is he in his room?"

"Yes. And tell him dinner's ready, will you?"

Martin removes his jacket and walks along the hallway to Bertie's door, on which he knocks.

"Yes?"

"Can I come in?"

"I'm busy," Bertie says. "Um, homework."

"Come on," Martin says. "I only want to congratulate you."

There's a scuffling sound on the other side of the door and then it is unlocked and opened just enough for Bertie to peer out.

"You got secret visitors in there?" Martin asks, trying to peer in past his son's body.

"Nope," Bertie says, flatly. He grimaces, throws the door wide open, and gestures theatrically.

"I only wanted to congratulate you for the report," Martin says.

"Yeah. You said."

"Those are really good results."

Bertie nods. He looks bored.

"And an A+ in sports!" Martin says. "You're going to walk the legs off me on holiday."

Bertie vaguely restrains a yawn.

"I got a tent," Martin says. "Ultra light. It weighs two kilos. Less, actually. Do you want to see it?"

"Not now, Dad," Bertie says, then, "Are we done here?"

Martin sighs deeply. "I guess," he says. "But dinner's ready, so..."

"OK," Bertie says. "I'll be there." And then the door re-closes in Martin's face.

He stands, staring at the door for a moment as he tries to control his anger. Should he kick the door down and beat the boy? Perhaps. Then again, maybe he should just wait for the holiday to fix everything. He focuses on the plaque on the

115

door. It says "Albert". It is decorated with images of Thomas the Tank Engine. He swallows hard. He feels like he could cry. But then he licks his lips, stretches his jaw, and forces a smile. Keeping on smiling is his speciality, his one great skill in life.

"So how are you?" he asks, on re-entering the kitchen.

Victoria looks at him strangely, as if he has just said something incomprehensibly stupid.

"What?" he asks.

"We already did the whole *how are you thing*," she says, "that's all. I mean, we can do it again if you want..."

Martin clears his throat and nods sadly, then slumps into a chair at the kitchen table. "Wow," he says. "I just *love* living here."

Victoria, who isn't really listening, opens the oven door, slips on her oven gloves, and lifts the dish from the shelf. She places it in the middle of the kitchen table.

"Yum," Martin says. "Cauliflower cheese, my favourite."

"It's mushroom soufflé," Victoria corrects.

"Yum," Martin mugs, sotto voce. "Mushroom soufflé, my favourite."

Victoria stares at him blankly for a moment. She's still thinking about Turkish delight.

"What?" he asks.

"Nothing," she replies. "Did you call Bertie for dinner?"

Part Three

Two Secrets

With just over a week remaining until Victoria will have to drive Martin and Bertie to Gatwick airport, the pile of stuff they're intending to take now takes up one entire corner of the lounge. Victoria can't imagine how they are possibly going to carry it all, and she can't imagine, either, how she's going to get through their two week absence. It will be the first time she has slept alone in the flat since Bertie was born.

As if that wasn't challenge enough, Martin has had to fly off to Dubai for three nights for one of his immigration cases, leaving only herself and the increasingly isolationist Bertie in the house.

In her more optimistic moments, she imagines spending the coming two-week hiatus reading (also for the first time in years), sipping red wine, and listening to classical music. She visualises herself feeling centred and calm.

But she suspects that the truth will be rather different. Valium, chocolate, and rubbish TV are more likely candidates to fill the void. That and a binge of her new cyber-chondria – this obsessive Googling of cancer and HRT side effects with which she now fills her spare time.

Still, she's getting the bathroom retiled while everyone is away, so there will be lots to clean up after that. And the grouting, that horrible grey grouting, will finally be gone from her life. Even Marge agrees that the bathroom is looking dirty. Just thinking about it makes Victoria's hands itch.

She crosses to the kitchen sink and pulls the nailbrush and bleach from the cupboard. But there's no point trying to clean the bathroom grouting now. It will be gone in ten days.

Dirty, she thinks. God how she hates that word. *Dirty Deirdre*, she hears – a voice from the past. *A dirty Deirdre, that's all you are my girl.*

She pours the bleach onto the brush and starts to work at the fingernails of her left hand. That's where the bacteria hide, in the folds of skin and beneath the nails. The stiff brush is hurting her hands – they're already pink and sore – but the pain feels good. It feels real. It feels like she's alive.

She's supposed to make a fresh appointment to meet Doctor Dailey this week, but she's been putting it off. He wants to talk to her about reducing her Valium dosage (if he only knew) and has been commenting on the state of her hands as well. She had told him she had been using white spirit while decorating, which seemed to placate him, but she won't get away with it next time.

Perhaps she can deal with it all while everyone's away. Maybe she can bin all the Valium and bleach and lock herself in the flat like some heroin junky going cold-turkey. How hard can it be, after all? Surely all she has to do is prevent her own hand putting a tablet in her own mouth, stop her right hand scrubbing away at the left.

She pauses briefly. She even sets the nailbrush down. She stares out at the London rooftops, watches a bird soaring and then landing on a chimney stack. It's going to be a lovely, sunny day. Perhaps she should go out for a walk. She could go to the park.

When she looks back at her hands, they're already brushing again, her left hand now working on the right. By the time she has finished, the root of one of her fingernails is bleeding a little. It's just past eight o'clock, so she's allowed, thank God, to take her first Valium tab.

She crosses to the corner of the room and fumbles blindly on the top shelf until her fingers touch the edge of the blister pack. But to her surprise, it comes up empty. The little blue tablets have gone. Which is confusing because a) she's certain she had two left, and b) she never keeps an empty pack. She stretches and leans and pats every inch of the shelf but finds no second pack lurking out of sight. She grabs a chair from beneath the dining table, drags it across to the shelf and climbs up. The shelf is dusty. She needs to clean it. It is dusty, but empty.

She frowns and climbs down. She pulls her handbag from the hall closet and rifles around for the missing blister pack. She returns to the kitchen and empties the bag onto the table. She pads through to the bedroom where she opens the drawer of her bedside table, and sighs in relief at the sight of the Valium box. But to her shock, it too is empty. What should be a full, fresh box containing three blister packs, each containing ten tablets, is entirely empty as well.

Did God hear her thinking about the need to go cold turkey? It's a silly thought, but it's the first one that comes to mind. But if God's too busy to stop a war in Syria, how likely is he to intervene in the case of Victoria Cunningham's Valium? *Not God then,* she thinks. *Martin, perhaps?* Could Martin have decided that she needs to quit? Has he emptied the entire flat of Valium?

Feeling increasingly panicky, she checks the pockets of her various jackets in the closet, the drawer on Martin's side of the

119

bed, *beneath* the bed, in the bathroom cabinet, and beneath the kitchen sink where she hides her cigarettes. And then, still fingering the cigarette packet, and by now sweating profusely, she sits at the kitchen table to phone Martin.

He answers immediately. "Hey," he says, "You missing me already?"

"Hello," Victoria replies. "Um I... Look... there's no nice way to ask this, but, have you... Oh, I didn't wake you, did I?"

"Nope," Martin says. "It's late morning here. So what's up?"

"I can't find my Valium. It's all gone." She can hear her voice wobbling. She needs to get a grip on that.

"Okay..." Martin says, dubiously.

"I had two tabs left in one pack, and a full box in the bedside table, but they're all gone."

"I don't think I can buy Valium here, if that's what you mean," Martin says. "They're pretty strict about–"

"No, that's not why I'm calling," Victoria interrupts. "I just needed to check, you know... that *you* didn't... I mean... it's not you, is it? *You* haven't taken them?"

After an uncomfortable silence during which she can almost hear Martin fidgeting in his seat, he says, "Are you actually telling me that you think I took your Valium?"

"Not really, no."

"Well, I didn't."

"You didn't?"

"No. Of course not. Why would I steal your bloody Valium?" Martin asks, sounding angry.

"I didn't think you *stole it*," Victoria says.

"Well, what then?"

"I thought maybe you hid it."

"Why on earth would I hide your Valium?"

Even though Martin can't see her, Victoria shrugs. "I don't know," she says meekly. "Maybe you think I take too much."

"I think we both *know* that you take too much."

"Yes. Maybe."

"Definitely. But now's not the right time for that conversation. I'm at work. I'm with a client, dear."

"OK."

"So, you got confused. And you put it somewhere else, all right?"

"All right," Victoria breathes.

"Sorry, but I've gotta go. Talk later."

"Yes. Yes... I'm sorry. Really I am."

"It's fine. Goodbye."

Victoria remains at the kitchen table. She puts down her mobile and pushes it around the glass tabletop with one finger as she tries to think. Martin's outrage at being accused was totally convincing, plus he's a terrible liar, so that leaves only three remaining possibilities. Either she's going mad and has forgotten moving the Valium to a new hiding place, or someone broke in and stole it in the night, or...

She gasps. She clicks on her phone to check the time. It's twenty-past eight. Bertie should be up by now.

She stands sharply, knocking her chair over, then runs to his bedroom door. It's locked. She bangs on the door. There's no reply.

She raps on the door more loudly. There's still no reply. "Bertie?" she calls out, her heart starting to race. "Bertie? Bertie?! BERTIE?"

She's starting to cry, so she raises one hand to cover her mouth. She tries the doorknob again and pushes harder but it won't budge.

She knocks harder still, now hammering on the door, then pushes at the door with her hip. She pictures the lock on the other side – a simple sliding bolt. There's no way to open it from the outside. They should never have let Bertie fit it, of course, but it's too late now.

She runs to the kitchen and picks up her phone again. She calls Bertie's number, but he doesn't answer, so she renews the operation from outside his bedroom door and can hear it vibrating inside the room.

Pointlessly, she tries the door again, knocks again, calls out again. And then with difficulty – so hard are her hands trembling – she selects Martin's name from the list on the phone. But that's a stupid idea. Martin's in Dubai. He can't help her.

She closes her eyes and pinches the bridge of her nose, and tries, desperately, to think. She could call the police, the firemen, an ambulance, and get them to kick down the door perhaps? But they take ages. She needs something quicker than that.

She strides to the door of the flat, and then after a single second's hesitation due to the fact that she's in her dressing gown, she opens it and runs barefoot downstairs to the flat below.

Dawn, her Caribbean, thirty-something neighbour, opens the door immediately.

"Can you... Sorry! Hello. Um... Look... I need help..." Victoria splutters. "Is your husband in?"

Dawn nods nervously. "Justin!" she calls out. "Come quick."

A door opens and Justin appears. He's a massive presence, both tall and overweight. He's wearing boxer shorts only, and his ginger brush of hair is flattened from sleep. "Oh!" he says, seeing Victoria in the doorway.

"Victoria here needs your help," Dawn tells him over her shoulder without breaking eye contact. "I think it's urgent."

"Right!" Justin says. "I'll.. um... Hang on. Just let me get some clothes on."

"Be quick, please," Victoria says. Once he has vanished from view she continues, more loudly, "It's my son. He's locked in his room. I think... I think he might have done something stupid. Please be quick."

. . .

Victoria sits, her head in her hands. She listens to the heart monitor beeping, as regular as a metronome. She listens to – and breathes in time with – the wheezy rush of the ventilator.

Beside her, Bertie, who has been pumped out, fed with laxatives, activated charcoal and God knows what else, sleeps peacefully. He looks blissful, completely unaware of the angst he has put everyone through.

It had taken Justin a single kick to open the bedroom door and less than ten minutes to carry Bertie to the car and drive him to St John's Hospital. It was faster than an ambulance, he insisted, and Victoria, who has seen with her own eyes how slow ambulances can be, had agreed.

The doctors, initially frowning and urgent, quickly shifted to something that looked far more like "relaxed", that looked, at times, like "amused", even. Because Valium, it seems, is a terrible way to commit suicide. Or, one of the best ways, depending on how you look at it. It would take hundreds of tablets, the doctor had told her, to do any damage at all. In fact the only real risk was that Bertie's breathing might be affected.

Wheeze, goes the ventilator. Wheeze, click, whoosh.

And so the terror has abated now, leaving room for a whole bunch of other emotions. Confusion – why would Bertie do such a thing? Guilt – how could she not have known how unhappy he was? Anger with Bertie – for is he not a spoilt little brat with an iPad, an iPhone, two loving parents and a lockable private bedroom in Maida Vale? The shame – for what kind of mother sees two doctors in order to get extra Valium prescriptions? And what kind of mother leaves the stuff lying around the house? The doctor's questions made her feel like a junky who had left her smack lying around. And is that not, really, exactly what she is?

There's a sense of fear, too – fear of what Bertie will say when he comes around. Because perhaps there's something going on that she doesn't know about. Something at school, perhaps. Or even something at home. It happens in families. She's seen *that* with her own eyes, too. So she won't phone Martin just yet. She'll wait until her son has explained the inexplicable. She'll wait until she knows just what she's dealing with.

• • •

It's seven pm, and Victoria is in a taxi, travelling home.

Bertie is still out for the count, still snoring and grinning in his sleep in a way which makes her want to slap him hard. There will be no meetings with psychiatrists until tomorrow, there will be no revelations, no explanations, no cracks shooting across the thin ice of her life until then. No, everything's on hold until tomorrow. So she just has to somehow get through the next fourteen hours.

There will be no more Valium until tomorrow, either.

To her shame, she had asked Bertie's doctor for a prescription – in a round-about way, of course. "I was just wondering," she had told him, as convincing as an actor in one of those latin American sitcoms, "As he stole all my Diazepam... I was just wondering, well, is it safe, for me to stop? So suddenly, I mean?"

Doctor Bednarski had frowned at her. "After this..." he had said, gesturing at Bertie in the bed, "You want I give *more* Valium?"

"No," Victoria had replied, faking indignation. "I just wanted to check I'm not going to die or something if I suddenly stop!"

"Pfff," the doctor had said. It sounded like a special Polish noise.

But then as he studied Bertie's chart, and as Victoria blushed and sweated even more profusely than previously, his facial expression had softened. "How much have you been taking?" he asked without looking her in the eye.

"Um, ten milligrams. Four times a day. It's a lot. I know. I've been talking to my GP about reduc–"

"For how long have you have take this dosage?"

"A year maybe. Perhaps two."

"Pfff..." Doctor Bednarski had said again. But then he added, "I get a nurse to bring you some. Just until tomorrow. But you must see your doctor to taper this." He had wiggled his finger at her. "This is too much, OK?"

"Thank you," Victoria had said, then, "And I know. I'm... you know... I'm on it."

"Yes," the doctor replied. "Yes, I know you're on it."

But now, she has taken both tablets. So no, there will be no more Valium today.

As the taxi pulls up outside the house, she imagines facing Justin, facing Dawn. She wonders if they've told anyone else in the building.

"He's fine," she'll tell them. "He's sleeping. I'm so sorry to have troubled you."

And then she'll let herself into the empty flat, and she'll try not to think about what went wrong in this family, her family. She'll try to get through this night, try to get through it without Martin, without Bertie, without Penny, without Valium.

It's no worse than she deserves, after all.

* * *

"Come in, come in!" Doctor Cheeder says, beckoning through the open door.

Victoria is surprised. She has no idea why she assumed the psychiatrist would be a man, but she had totally assumed that. Perhaps it's simply because both her GP and her Harley Street Doctor (who she saw just an hour ago), as well as Bertie's doctor on the ward, are all men. Or perhaps she's just a bit more sexist than she realises. Wasn't there a riddle Bertie used to tell about a car accident and a surgeon, a riddle which tripped everyone up precisely because everyone imagined that the surgeon was automatically a man?

She enters Dr Cheeder's office, leaving the man with the nervous twitch and the girl with the bandaged wrist in the waiting area.

Doctor Cheeder – Doctor Trudy Cheeder, according to her name tag – leans over the desk and shakes Victoria's hand warmly. A shadow crosses her expression. "OCD?" she asks, nodding at Victoria's still outstretched hand.

Victoria frowns, so Dr Cheeder expounds, "Your hands. That's compulsive hand washing, isn't it?"

"Oh, um, no..." Victoria says, looking down at her shiny pink hand, then, "Actually, yes. I suppose it probably is something like that."

"Sorry," Dr Cheeder says. "It's an occupational hazard, spotting stuff like that... Please, sit down."

"Thanks," Victoria says, sitting and then struggling to know where to place her incriminating hands.

"Just before we move onto your son, are you seeing anyone for that?"

"For my hands?"

"Yes. We have a specialist here, Graham Masters. They get very good results with CBT – that's Cognitive Behavioural Therapy. It works wonders."

"Really," Victoria says, starting to blush.

"You can get your GP to refer you and I'm sure Graham can help you."

"Thanks," Victoria says. "I'll, um, think about it."

"So, onto Albert," the doctor says, glancing down at her notepad. "Because that's why we're here, isn't it?"

"Bertie, yes. He prefers Bertie. We all call him Bertie."

"Of course. So Bertie nicked all your Valium, eh?"

Victoria nods. "I should have locked it away. I feel terrible."

"I wouldn't worry about that too much," Dr Cheeder says. "If someone wants to attempt suicide then there's always a way. And most of them are far more likely to succeed than Valium."

"Yes," Victoria says. "I suppose. So *is* that what he was trying to do? To... you know..."

"Was he trying to kill himself?"

"Yes," Victoria says, suddenly fighting back tears.

"Sometimes an act, a violent act, or a desperate act, is the only way someone feels they can express themselves."

"Yes," Victoria says, pulling a tissue from her pocket and dabbing at her eyes. "Like a cry for help?" she adds. "That's what they always say, isn't it? A cry for help."

"In Albert's case, Bertie's, I mean, I'd say more a cry to be heard," Dr Cheeder says.

"I'm sorry," Victoria says, wiping away fresh tears. "I can't seem to stop crying today."

"I'd be surprised if you *didn't* cry," Dr Cheeder says, kindly.

"But I don't understand why he... why *this*. We're a good, close-knit family, you know?" Victoria says, her voice wobbling madly. "Bertie can tell us absolutely anything."

"It would seem he doesn't feel that he can."

"I'm sorry?"

"It would seem that Bertie *doesn't* feel he can tell you absolutely anything."

Victoria purses her lips and blows gently through them as she waits for this idea to sink in. "Has he told you something, then?" she asks.

"He has told me many things."

"But has he told you something's wrong? Something that he can't tell us?"

The doctor nods. "He has."

Victoria's first reaction is to feel insulted that her son has spoken openly to this woman he has never met before. "God! He told *you* what's wrong?"

"Yes, he did. And I'm really pleased that he did. It's a huge step forwards."

"So, is it school? Is he being bullied?"

"Not that I'm aware of."

"Is it—"

"Look," the doctor, interrupts. "It's not that there's anything wrong with Bertie... it's just that there are certain issues he doesn't feel he can express at home, right now. And I'm afraid my consultations with Bertie are in strictest confidence. They have to be. To gain his trust."

"Oh, really?"

"Yes," the doctor says, smiling. "Does that surprise you?"

"Well, he's a minor, still. I'm his mother."

"I'm aware of that, yes."

"But you're not going to tell me what's wrong with my own son?"

The doctor shakes her head gently. "It's for Bertie to tell you, when he's ready."

"And what if he's never ready?"

"That's entirely up to him."

"Gosh," Victoria says. "So what... I mean... How can I help him if I don't know why he did this?"

"You can just be there for him. You can love him. You can be understanding."

"But I don't understand."

"No."

"That's why, well... I really think you should tell me."

"Yes. I'm sure you do. But I'm not going to do that."

"OK..." Victoria says, doubtfully. "So, what now?"

"Well, you need to keep an eye on him, obviously. For a few days, at least. I consider him very low risk, but you should keep an eye on him. That won't be a problem, will it? You don't have too many other commitments at the moment?"

Victoria shakes her head. "Not really, no. And the overdose... he's fine? There aren't any side effects? Any, repercussions, I mean."

"None that we've detected. Everything seems fine."

"Thank God for that. I just wish I knew why."

"Well, as I said, Albert, Bertie, will tell you when he's ready. In the meantime, I'd avoid asking. Tell him that you're there for him, that you're ready to listen to anything he wants to tell you. Make sure he understands that there's nothing he could say which would damage your love for him. But then leave it at that. It can be very tempting, in cases like this, to try to wheedle it out of them, to try to pressurise them into telling you something."

"I can see that, yes."

"But you need to *not* do that. And make sure your husband understands that as well."

"OK. I'll tell him."

"If he seems unusually depressed, or agitated, or withdrawn, or upset, you can phone me." The doctor pushes her card across the desk and Victoria slides it to the edge and picks it up. She fiddles with the card as she tries to think what to say, what to ask, what to think. "And I've asked Bertie to come back and see me next week. The secretary will phone to make an appointment."

"So that's it?" Victoria says. "I just take him home and act like nothing happened?"

"Not at all," the doctor says. "You take him home, yes. But you impress upon him that he can talk to you, that you love him. Even if it doesn't appear that he wants to hear these things – he is an adolescent – or, suppose he doesn't appear to believe you, tell him anyway. It all sinks in, eventually. And try to keep the energy in the household as calm and encouraging as you can. If you need to argue with your husband, for instance, do that elsewhere."

"We never argue. Did Bertie say we argue?"

"No. But most couples do at some point."

"Yes, I suppose they do. But we don't."

"That's very unusual. In fact, if true, it's quite extraordinary."

"Well, it *is* true. We're not the arguing kind."

"OK. Fair enough. Anyway, you're probably feeling angry about what Bertie has done, too. But you need to vent that anger elsewhere for the moment. It's not what Bertie needs."

"Of course."

"I would suggest you see your GP and get him to refer you to an addiction counsellor and a therapist, too."

"An addiction counsellor? Is Bertie taking drugs?"

"No. That's for you. Yourself. To work out what you're going to do about your Diazepam habit. The doctor in A&E posted a note in Bertie's file about it and, well, forty milligrams a day – that's a high dosage. And Bertie mentioned it repeatedly, too, so don't, you know, assume that he's unaware."

Victoria whispers the word, "God," as a fresh bout of tears spring forth.

"You could see this as an opportunity. To heal together. As a family."

"Yes. I suppose."

"I would advise family therapy too. For all of you. Together, with your husband. It will help you communicate better. Again, your GP can organise that."

Victoria dabs at her tears again and then blows her nose. "Of course," she says. "I'll, um, talk to Doctor Dailey."

"And there's one final thing," the doctor says. "One thing Bertie specifically authorised me to discuss with you."

"Yes?"

"There is a holiday planned, I believe?"

"I'm not going. It's just Bertie and my husband. They're leaving next week. Oh, actually, Bertie won't be able to come and see you next week, because–"

"Sorry," the doctor says, interrupting, "But your son, it appears, doesn't want to go."

Victoria nods. "I know," she says. "I'm aware of that. But Martin, my husband, he thinks it's important. For their relationship. They haven't been getting on so well."

The doctor nods and blinks slowly. "I understand," she says, "But this once, I would strongly advise letting your son get his own way."

"Cancel the holiday, you mean?"

"He *really* doesn't want to go. And he doesn't feel anyone's been listening to him about that. So, yes. I think allowing him to tell you that he doesn't want to go is as good a place as any to start. You can use his follow-up appointment here as an excuse if your husband's resistant to that idea."

Victoria nods and chews her bottom lip. "Is it Martin?" she asks.

"I'm sorry?"

"Is Bertie... I don't know... Is he scared of being alone with Martin?"

The doctor frowns deeply and leans forwards. She licks her lips. "Is there some reason Bertie might be afraid of his father?"

"I don't know," Victoria says. "That's what I'm asking."

"But you have suspicions?"

"No."

"Is your husband ever violent towards Bertie?"

"No. Never."

"Does he threaten him with physical violence?"

"No. Never."

"Does he abuse Bertie in any other way?"

"No, of course not."

"Hum," the doctor says, now relaxing back in her chair. "And you're certain about all of that? Because if ever there was a time to air your suspicions, it would be now."

"I don't have any suspicions," Victoria says. "But you've just told me that my son doesn't want to go on holiday with his father. So something must be wrong."

"Right," the doctor says, now restraining a wry smile. "Well, I'm sure there are plenty of people who want to walk a hundred miles across a Spanish mountaintop in July. And there are probably just as many people who don't, yourself included, from what Bertie says."

"That's true. It's my idea of a nightmare."

"Well, it's Bertie's idea of a nightmare too," the doctor says, earnestly.

"Ah. Yes. I see."

"So, listen to your son. He's almost fifteen. He knows what he wants."

"Of course. Yes. Are we terrible parents, do you think?"

"No, I don't think that. And nor does Bertie."

"Good. But... I mean... is that all this was, then? A way to get out of the stupid holiday?"

"Something like this is rarely about just one thing," Dr Cheeder says. "But a part of it is certainly about Bertie's believing that he can't be heard. So listening to him on this issue is a great place to start, as I said."

"Of course," Victoria says. "I'll explain it all to Martin when he gets back. He's away with work at the moment. In Dubai. Do you think I should tell him? I haven't yet. Told him, that is."

"I think that's something you can discuss with your son," the doctor says. "Now, shall we go and see if he's ready to go home?"

"OK," Victoria says. "Yes. Let's do that."

. . .

When Martin steps out through the sliding doors at Heathrow airport, he glances straight at Victoria before turning and, following the crowd, dragging his suitcase away to the left. In his pinstripe suit and white open-necked shirt, he looks, somehow, generic, impersonal, not like her husband at all. It's only when she calls out his name, when he pauses, turns, focuses on her face and smiles, that he starts to look like the Martin she knows.

"Vicky!" he says, as he ducks under the barrier. "What the hell are you doing here? I almost walked right past you!"

"I thought I'd come and meet you," she says. "And don't worry, I saw you even if you didn't see me."

"It's just such a surprise," Martin says. "I mean, I have a shuttle booked and everything."

"Oh, I didn't think of that," Victoria replies. "Will they be waiting for you?"

"No, it's fine. I'll phone them," Martin says, pulling his phone from his pocket. "But why the change? What's this in aid of?"

"I just thought it would make a change. I thought we could get lunch together. There's supposed to be a Jamie Oliver place somewhere here, I think."

"That's Gatwick," Martin says. "And it's really nothing special. So no, let's get out of here and stop at a pub somewhere. I think I've had my fill of airports."

"OK," Victoria says, looking around. "Then, it's, um, *that* way. I'm in the car park over there."

As they start to walk, with Martin's case trundling behind them, Martin asks, "Nothing's wrong, is it?"

"No," Victoria lies. "But there is something I need to talk to you about. Over lunch. A few things actually."

Martin glances sideways at his wife. "Sounds ominous," he says. "You're not running off with the milkman again, are you?"

"We don't even have a milkman," Victoria replies in such a deadpan manner that Martin's not even sure if she has realised he cracked a joke.

They end up outside a pub called The Three Magpies in Hounslow, just minutes from the airport. "Are you sure this is what you want?" Victoria asks, looking up at the facade. She's surprised and little disappointed at Martin's choice.

"Yes," Martin says, pushing the door open and ushering her in. "A pint and a pie. After Dubai, it's *exactly* what I want."

The pub is almost empty – it is Tuesday lunchtime, after all – so they're able to order quickly and choose from almost any table in the place. Despite having many more comfortable options, Victoria chooses a cramped table in the corner for the simple reason that it's as far away as possible from the barmaid and the other clients.

"So, how was your trip?" Victoria asks as Martin puts the drinks on the table.

"Oh, you know, fine," he says, even though the words tedious, tense, and exhausting would more accurately describe his trip. It's simply that he has learnt over the years that expressing it doesn't make him, or the listener, feel any better. "And you?" he asks. "How was your mini break from hubby?"

"It was... um... interesting," Victoria says.

"Interesting?"

"I'll tell you," she says, "But if we can just wait until the food arrives."

"OK. But why?" Martin asks.

"I don't know," Victoria says. "I think I need something to do with my hands while I tell you everything."

"Okay..." Martin says, then, "Oh, come on. You're driving me crazy here."

And so Victoria attempts to tell Martin what has happened.

At first she struggles to frame the narrative, finds herself unable to decide what to tell Martin first and which words to use. But then she gives up and decides simply to tell it like a story, in chronological order. It makes things much easier.

"Do you remember when I called you?" she asks, starting again. "When I couldn't find my Valium?"

"Of course," Martin says.

"Well, after I hung up, I still couldn't find them. I looked everywhere."

"OK..."

"I searched the whole flat."

By the time she has finished, Martin is looking pale. In fact he's looking slightly green-tinged.

"So where is he now?"

"Bertie? He's at home, of course."

"On his own?"

"No, with Mum. I didn't want to leave him on his own, so I got Mum to come over."

"So you told her."

"Yes. I had to. I needed her to keep an eye on him."

"You should have told me," Martin says.

"I am telling you. But there was nothing you could do from over there. And there was no point you rushing home."

"No," Martin says. "I suppose not. And he won't go on holiday with me?"

"I'm afraid I really don't think he wants to. I mean, we haven't discussed it again. He won't talk about any of it, and the shrink – at the hospital – she said not to force him to talk. But seeing as that was the only thing he authorised her to tell us, I think we can be pretty sure."

They are interrupted by the waitress bringing their food. Pie and chips for Martin and a *Salade Niçoise* for Victoria.

"I'm not sure how I feel about that," Martin says, once she has left.

"About what?"

"About any of it. I mean, don't you think it's her responsibility to tell us what's wrong with our own son?"

"I did think that. But she explained that her main responsibility was to make *Bertie* feel better."

Martin sighs deeply. "I suppose," he says. "Though I can't see why those are incompatible. I'll just cancel, I guess."

"Maybe. I'm not sure what's best, really."

"You don't think I should go, surely? Not on my own?"

Victoria shrugs.

"Is it me?" Martin asks. "Or is it the trip? Because, I mean, I can cancel and organise something else. For all of us."

Victoria shakes her head. "I don't know," she says, forking some tuna to her lips. "But my feeling is that we should just drop the whole subject of holidays, really. Just never mention it again, whether you go or not. It has become... I don't know... emotionally charged, I suppose. Do you see what I mean?"

Martin nods, but is looking confused. "If it's me he hates, maybe I *should* go. Give you all a break from me. See if that does him some good."

"He doesn't *hate* you," Victoria says. "But he did say that you should still go."

"Did he indeed?" Martin says, laughing sourly, and pushing his plate away. "I think I lost my appetite," he explains.

"You need to eat something," Victoria says, pushing it back towards him.

"What words did he use?" Martin asks, lifting a chip disdainfully from the plate.

"When?"

"When he said that I should go anyway."

"Oh, well, he asked me if I thought you'd cancel. And then he said that you'd been looking forward to it for so long... that you should still go. I think he just doesn't want to feel guilty about mucking your holiday up."

"He *has* mucked my holiday up."

"I know," Victoria says, reaching across the table for Martin's wrist. "But maybe don't let him know that. The doctor, she said that we should keep things as emotionally low key as possible."

"Low key, huh? Well, don't worry. I'm not going to shout at him," Martin says. "But all the same... I'd like to know what the hell this is all about. I mean, what did *I* ever do to upset the boy?"

"I don't know," Victoria whispers. She looks up at Martin. She studies his face. "There isn't something I don't know about, is there?" she asks. "There hasn't been some incident I'm not aware of?"

"No!" Martin says. "Jesus! What kind of *incident*?"

"I don't know," Victoria says. "I'm just trying to understand here, that's all."

"Bloody-hell," Martin says. "So now you think *I've* been hiding something from you?"

"No. I don't. Like I say, I'm just trying to understand what's happening. And so far, none of it makes any sense to me."

"I'm going to ask him, straight off the bat," Martin says. "It's the only way."

"The shrink said specifically not to do that."

"Yeah, well. Maybe I don't care."

"I'm sorry sweetheart, but I think we *need* to care. She's an expert."

"An expert on what? On my son? On *our* son?"

"Of course not. But she's... well, she's an expert on repeat suicide attempts, I suppose."

"Right," Martin says. "So is that a possibility, then? That he'll try again? Is that what she said?"

"She said he's low risk. But she also said not to pressure him. She said to let him come to us."

"Hum."

"So, there's one more thing we need to talk about," Victoria says. "And I need you not to get angry."

Martin bows his head and silently fakes screaming into his hands before looking up at his wife. "Go on," he says.

"He, um... He wants to go to boarding school."

Martin leans towards Victoria. "What?" he asks in astonishment.

"Bertie. His, um, friend, Aaron, he's gone to one in Bedford. And Bertie asked if he can do the same."

"That's crazy," Martin says.

"I know."

"I mean, for one, he's doing brilliantly at St George's. You've seen his report cards. It's one of the best state schools in the country. And for two, he's fourteen. No one wants to change schools that close to their GCSEs. And three, he'd never get into Bedford anyway. They're not going to take him with two years to go. And four, if they did, it would cost a bloody fortune."

"I know all that."

"So what's this about? Is it the Catholic thing at St George's? Because..."

"No, it's not that. I asked him, and it's not that. He doesn't care about that."

"So what, then?" Martin asks.

"He... Look, Martin. This is going to be hard to hear. It was hard for me too, OK?"

"What? He hates us?"

"No, he doesn't hate us. But he doesn't want to live at home anymore, either."

Martin is changing colour now, shifting from pale green to red, like a traffic light shifting to STOP. "What?!" he spits. "WHAT?"

Victoria shrugs. "I don't know..." she says. "I honestly don't know. And I'm going to try to talk to the doctor again when he sees her next, but that's what he's saying. That's what he's asking us for."

Martin drops his head into his hands again, but this time he remains there long enough for Victoria to start to feel concerned. "Martin?" she says, reaching out to touch his arm through his shirt sleeve. "Martin?"

"I'm sorry," Martin says, finally lowering his hands to reveal glistening eyes. "I'm just... I mean... Jesus. Are we that bad as parents? Are we really?"

The following week is hellish because, despite the hospital psychiatrist's advice, Martin alternates, seemingly randomly, between attempting to be Bertie's best friend and trying gently, tenaciously to bully him into submission.

This good cop, bad cop routine understandably deepens Bertie's stony disdain for his father, as well as for his mother, who Bertie no doubt sees as his accomplice in all of this. Yet despite her understanding, she struggles to side with her son. It *is* deeply wounding to find oneself with a suicidal child who won't even trust you enough to tell you what's wrong. It's as if everything they ever did for the boy has been wiped out. They are, suddenly, not only strangers, but hostile strangers.

She sits at the dinner table and watches Bertie, who only a few months ago was full of beans, as he miserably pushes his food around the plate. And she remembers, as if his life was flashing before *her* eyes, every major milestone from the first time she held him to her breast, through his first day at school, to this moment of sadness, of failure, here at the family dinner table. "What's wrong, Bertie?" she asks him over and over in her mind. "Just tell me, for crying out loud. You can tell me anything." And sometimes the effort of not saying those words, of not shaking him until he speaks, of not locking him in his room without food until he simply lets her love him again, makes her weep – something she manages to do silently, in their bedroom, out of sight.

So, in a way, she's grateful, she's hopeful, even, when Martin dares to ask the forbidden question, even if she knows, with the logical part of her brain, that he shouldn't. And she watches Bertie every time; she holds her breath and waits to see if this time he will crack, if this time he will say something. Because there is truly nothing she wouldn't fix, nothing she wouldn't do, in order that this child, her son, her flesh, should get his smile back again.

But Bertie, in his misery, is seemingly more determined than any of them. He shuts himself in his room (though the lock is broken and won't be coming back). He slumps sullenly at the dinner table. He sits zombie-like in front of the television set or stares disdainfully at Martin as he tries to buddy him, or with sad hopelessness, when his father attempts to bully him instead. And his only answer to any question is "boarding school." He hates it here, he says. He needs to get away. And still he won't say why.

It's so sudden and so hurtful, and so inexplicable, that it drives Martin to the edge of insanity. Victoria has never seen her husband look so tired, so confused, so broken.

Victoria, for her part, was at the gates of lunacy before this happened, and now feels, if anything, a little less mad than before. Bertie's pain takes her out of herself, it would seem. It gives her something real to think about, something urgent to focus upon. It has reminded her of her one true purpose in life, and she stops thinking, for whole days at a time, about the menopause, about HRT, about cancer.

But remembering one's purpose is not to know how to achieve it, and she's failing – she knows she is. The low-key atmosphere the psychiatrist advised is anything but present and in fact, as the days go by, the family home comes to feel a little more like a pressure cooker every day. With Martin's mood swings becoming almost as difficult to manage as Bertie's misery, she begins to wish that Martin *would* go on holiday on his own.

She understands his resentment against the boy, of course. She feels his mounting fury as if it were her own. But the mixture of so many emotions, the seemingly mathematical product of three people's mood swings at this time of crisis, begins to feel overwhelming, and she starts to long for simplicity, instead. She starts to believe that, alone, with her son, she would perhaps stand a chance of finding out what is wrong. Alone, maybe, she can really fix this.

What's more, she can't help but notice that Bertie's alienation is more marked – far more so in fact – towards Martin than it is with anyone else. And she can't help but wonder, though she hates herself for it, exactly why that would be.

She has always had nightmares. They have polluted her sleeping hours so faithfully since childhood that they mostly feel like normal. That these have increased in intensity and regularity since Bertie's suicide attempt strikes her as little more than inevitable. But these last few days they have morphed into horrific scenes involving not only Bertie, but uncle Cecil as well. Could her subconscious be trying to tell her something?

When, on the fourth morning after Martin's return, she wakes from one nightmare involving Bertie and Cecil, only to doze off directly into another about Cecil and Martin, and when the simple fact of Martin laying one arm across her makes her scream as if her life were in danger, both in the dream and apparently outside of it, too, she knows she needs to act.

She has to find a way to convince Martin to go away, to leave them alone for a while. She needs time with her child to find out what is happening here, or, at the very least, to find out if she *can* find out what is happening here.

. . .

Martin feels ashamed, not of anything he has done, but of his feelings themselves.

Because, as Victoria drives away, and as he heads towards the airport entrance, his overwhelming feeling, *other* than shame, is a sense of relief.

He feels utterly, shockingly, almost ecstatically relieved to be escaping the family home.

There no longer seems to be a single aspect of his life at home to compensate for everything that is lacking. And this is not, he doesn't think, how married life was supposed to be.

His wife, once young and fun (if never actually fun*ny*) is turning, before his eyes, into a zombie. Her face, once smooth and beautiful, now looks permanently pinched. Her eyes, once so green he wanted to dive into them, look glazed, or vacant or occasionally both. And when she doesn't look glazed or vacant, she looks as if she is worried about some secret thing which can never be discussed.

He has no idea, he has realised only recently, what she actually does all day. The years of nappies and feeds are long gone, so other than shopping and bleaching worktops, both of which she does assiduously, he really can't work it out.

Even sex, once the thinly spread glue which held them together, has run dry.

Now his son, his beautiful baby boy, apparently hates him as well. Could there be any rejection more painful for a man than the rejection of his wife and his son?

He feels cheated, really – that's the thing. He feels as if he signed a contract for X only to find himself with Y. Or more specifically, he feels as if he signed a contract for X, Y and Z only to find himself with nothing whatsoever.

He works hard at his job, he really does. He works long, gruelling hours for hateful clients who have no respect for anything or anyone except money and those who have more of it than themselves. These rich Saudis, these billionaire Kuwaitis who want British nationality not because they respect anything British, not because they see value in an ancient civilisation, or a three-hundred-year-old democracy, or in a thousand years of English literature, but because British nationality is another thing they can buy, therefore why not buy it?

So he works long hard hours, yes. He has worked long hours for years and the truth of the matter is that if he didn't have a wife who likes Valium and shopping, and if he didn't have a son who hates him so much he prefers the horrors of boarding school to home, he would be rich enough to never work again. What's the *point* of them? he wonders, hating himself a little more for thinking it, but thinking it all the same. What's the point of Victoria? What's the point of Bertie? What do they contribute to the family, to the country, to anyone?

If it weren't for them, he could buy a little open-topped Jeep, he thinks, hitching his backpack up a little higher, and spend the rest of his life driving around Asia in shorts. It's so bloody unfair.

The doors of Gatwick airport slide open to greet him, and as he steps inside, he glances back to check that the BMW really is out of sight, that Victoria isn't even now swinging back to tell him she's changed her mind. But no, the car has vanished. He really has escaped.

So he feels relieved, yes. Utterly, shockingly, *shamefully* relieved.

Two weeks in Spain, alone. It's going to be incredible.

And perhaps, just perhaps, by the time he gets back, a little of the nonsense which has been swamping his life will have blown over.

As Victoria drives home, she runs a tiny movie over and over in her mind's eye. It's nothing more than her last few seconds with Martin, that moment when he waved goodbye, when he blew her a kiss and turned away.

He had looked sad, of course, but it had been a lazy, fake kind of sad which had almost made her laugh. And as he turned and hitched his backpack higher, there had been a youthful ease to his movement which she had understood and recognised. That's the trouble with living with someone – it becomes impossible to dissimulate. After twenty years, you can read each other like a book.

He'll leave her when he gets back – that's the next thought that comes to mind and a lump forms in her throat, and her eyes mist as she imagines the scene. "Being in Spain gave me time to reflect," he'll say, "and I think we'd both be better off if we went our separate ways."

"This hasn't been working for either of us," he'll say, and how could she argue with that?

She had dreamt of so much for them, once upon a time. She had actually believed that their life together would be fun, would be an adventure. But fun and adventure turned out to be challenging for her, though she doesn't know why that's the case. So they have settled into this life which is not a life, which, as time goes on becomes less and less like a life and more like facsimile of a life – a work of fiction or a piece of theatre, and not even a very good one at that.

She thinks, for no apparent reason, of a video that Max had shown them all a few Christmases ago. It had been an advert, on YouTube, and Max had liked the music.

The video, a three minute advert, or an infomercial as the Americans would call it, had been for a brand of motorcycle, or perhaps for camping equipment, she can't quite remember which. It had shown a group of friends on motorbikes riding through pine forests, the sun slanting through the trees. It had shown them camping by streams and the film had seemed realistic – these were not particularly young, or particularly beautiful people – and in fact the woman in the film, who looked a lot like herself, had even seemed distinctly worse for wear as she washed her face in the stream in the cold morning light.

"Isn't that cool?" Max had said once it was over, "I love that song."

And they had all agreed that, yes, it was cool. "It's very pretty," she had commented. "I wonder where they filmed that?"

But that little film had troubled her for weeks. It had even invaded her nightmares a few times, yet she hadn't been able to work out why; she hadn't been able to decode what it was about that film that unsettled her so profoundly. Because she had never liked camping and had certainly never dreamt of going anywhere on the back of a motorbike. She is, if anything, terrified of the things.

But today, suddenly, unexpectedly, she understands. She doesn't know why that film has popped back into her mind but today she gets it.

She pictures Martin with his backpack, hiking enthusiastically away, and she understands that the film upset her because it was about dreams – not dreams of comfort, or dreams of wealth, or dreams of safety; not dreams of cars or furniture or luxury, not dreams in fact, of any of the things they have spent their lives pursuing. No, what the film had shown was a dream of... of... *being there*, perhaps – of simply being *present*. Dreams of riding through a forest and shivering, dreams of seeing your breath in the early morning air, dreams of waking up to too-cold feet and washing your face in an icy river, of being *alive* quite simply.

It's been so long since she felt alive, that's the thing.

She should have gone with Martin, she thinks, briefly. They all should have gone together. Only she couldn't go with Martin. She isn't the hiking, camping, stream-washing kind of woman, is she? She doesn't even have the capacity to be that person momentarily, even if Martin, apparently, does.

So yes, she thinks, he will leave them. He will come home and say, "I've had time to think and I've realised what's been missing. I've realised I haven't been happy, I haven't been living. I haven't been alive. So, I'm leaving you."

And who could blame him for that?

It's just after eleven when Victoria gets home. Marge, who has stayed the night, is bashing the vacuum cleaner into the skirting boards and doesn't notice her arrival.

"Mum?" she calls out from the doorway to the kitchen. "MUM!"

Marge jumps visibly and turns to face her. "Lord, you nearly gave me a heart attack," she says as she struggles to balance on one foot in order to kick the off switch on the Dyson with the other.

"Why are you hoovering, Mum?" Victoria asks, once the machine has whined to a halt.

"Oh, I spilt a little sugar," Marge replies, "that's all."

"Right," Victoria says as she shrugs her way out of her jacket. "Well, I wouldn't worry too much. They're coming round later today to rip those worktops off."

"They're coming *today*?"

Victoria nods. "I'll be so glad to see the back of them. We'll have brand new ones by Saturday. And then the new washing machine and dishwasher are coming on Monday. It's going to look lovely by the time Martin gets home."

"That'll be nice," Marge says. "But what's wrong with this dishwasher?"

Victoria shrugs. "They're looking a bit tatty," she says. "I thought it would be nice. Plus, the new worktops are grey, so the new ones will match. I thought Penny might like the washing machine, to be honest. I think hers has been playing up. It is a good one, after all. Maybe you could ask her for me?"

"Maybe you could ask her yourself," Marge says. "But, to be honest, she'd probably just be insulted. You know what a chip she has on her shoulder about inheriting your castoffs."

Victoria nods. "Yes, you're probably right. She's so prickly these days." She notices some grains of sugar lurking beneath the kitchen table and can't help herself. She takes the handle of the Dyson from her mother and kicks it back into life.

Once the floor is clean and the vacuum cleaner has been stowed, she fills the kettle. Marge, now sitting at the kitchen table flicking through *Elle* magazine, asks her if Martin got off OK.

"I don't know," Victoria says. "I just left him at the drop-off point. He was in a hurry. We were running late. But I assume so. Any sign of Bertie?"

Marge shakes her head. "No, he's still sleeping," she says. "Chloe's the same. She sleeps all the time. I wouldn't worry."

"Hard not to worry," Victoria says, "the way things are."

"I did peep in on him. He's OK," Marge reassures her.

"Good," Victoria replies, pouring ground coffee into the glass pot of the French press. "I'll wake him up in a bit. He has his hospital appointment this afternoon. Coffee?"

Marge nods. "That would be nice. Is this appointment with the… the… um… doctor?" she asks. She refuses for some reason to say the word 'psychiatrist.'

"Yep," Victoria replies, "with the shrink."

"Are you going to talk to her about this boarding school nonsense?"

"I'm certainly going to try."

"I suppose you do need to at least know if *they* think it's a good idea," Marge says, "though it all sounds like madness to me."

"I was thinking about it on the way home, actually," Victoria says. "I mean, if that's what he really wants, well… I'm tired of fighting everyone about everything. I was thinking about Penny, too. I need to phone her. This whole... thing... has gone on too long."

Marge smiles serenely and nods. "That's a good idea," she says. "Forgive and forget."

"I don't know about forgetting," Victoria says. "But we can't not talk to each other forever. It just gets silly after a point."

Marge nods. She chews her bottom lip, a gesture that Victoria knows from experience means that she's considering saying something delicate.

"What is it?" she asks, leaning back on the worktop and tipping her head sideways.

"It's just that... well... if you are going to phone her, there's something you perhaps need to know."

Victoria's brow creases. "Yes?"

"I wasn't going to tell you, but if you're going to phone her... well, *she* might tell *you*. And I don't want you getting angry – not when you haven't spoken for ages."

"Go on."

"The thing is, I spoke to her the other day, on the phone, about Bertie."

Victoria screws up her features and shakes her head. "Oh, Mum!" she laments. "You didn't tell her? I specifically told you–"

"Not about... you know... the hospital," Marge interrupts. "I didn't tell her that. I know you don't want her to know about that."

"So what, then?"

"I just said about Bertie wanting to go to boarding school."

Victoria closes her eyes and pinches the bridge of her nose. "Oh," she groans. "I can just imagine how that went. I can just imagine how smug she was about our own son wanting to leave us."

"Not at all," Marge says. "But the thing is, she knew already."

"She knew what?"

"That he wanted to leave home."

Victoria straightens her body, suddenly alert. "She what?"

"Penny knew that Bertie wanted to leave home," Marge says again.

"But how? Did he tell Max?"

"No," Marge says, confidentially. "And that's the thing."

"What is?"

"Well," Marge says, leaning forwards and glancing down the hallway towards Bertie's bedroom. "Apparently, Bertie asked Penny if he could go and live there."

"I'm sorry?"

"Bertie asked them if he could go and live with them. In their house. In Whitstable."

"He *what*?"

"It was when we were down. In October."

Victoria opens her mouth to speak but then closes it again and shakes her head. She rubs one finger lightly across her lips as she struggles to take in this new information. "God, so now I *have* to phone her."

"Yes," Marge says, then, "Sorry, why?"

"Well, if Bertie said he wanted to leave all the way back in October, then maybe he told her the reason. God, I can't believe that she didn't tell me, though."

"He didn't tell her why, I'm afraid," Marge says. "I asked. But you're right. It's very remiss of her not to have told you."

"She really should have," Victoria says, feeling both tearful and angry at the same time. "And this happened back in October, you say?"

Marge nods.

"So she's had *nine months* to tell me."

"In all fairness to your sister, I don't think you've spoken to her once since then."

"But all the same," Victoria says. "This is important."

"I know," Marge says. "And she should have told you. You're right."

Victoria shakes her head. "God, I used to think we were close," she says, laughing sourly. "But this…"

"You *are* close," Marge says, "so, don't say that."

"If she had just let me know, we could have sat Bertie down and spoken to him," Victoria says, now slipping into outrage. "None of this need ever have happened."

"I know," Marge says.

"That's… just…" Victoria splutters.

"Unforgivable?" Marge offers.

"You're right," Victoria says. "It's unforgivable. It totally is."

As Victoria drives, she runs through various possible scenarios for a telephone conversation with her sister. But whether she phones her to shout, or she phones her to cry, in her mind they all end badly. Her ultimate realisation is that she simply can't talk to Penny without a) being the first to climb-down (and after today's revelations, she's really not in a mood to do that) and b) telling her about the overdose, which would make it no longer a simple mishap but something that Bertie (and they) have to live with evermore, and c) explaining where the Valium came from (when Penny warned her to get off it years ago) and d) and, this is perhaps the most

153

dangerous, without giving Penny the possibility of telling her exactly where her parenting has gone wrong. Because with Penny seeing herself as such a successful parent, *and* such a successful psychologist, that could really grate on her. That could push them past the point of no return.

Once they have dropped Marge off, Bertie moves to the front seat.

Victoria has never been particularly good at discussing things, but it has always seemed slightly easier, or at least a little less difficult, to do so in the car. It's perhaps the lack of eye contact, or the security provided by locked doors; it could be because movement makes escape impossible, or the fact that the driver is too occupied to make any sudden gestures, but whatever the reason, it has always struck her as the least worst place to broach a difficult subject. She takes a series of deep breaths and prepares herself.

"How are you feeling?" she asks after a moment, and she's happy with her voice which sounded casual yet optimistic. "Does it make you nervous going to see Doctor Cheeder?"

Bertie, beside her, shrugs. "Not really," he says.

"Is she easy to talk to?"

"Uh-huh," Bertie says. "Fairly."

"Is she... easier to talk to than me, for example?"

Bertie simply shrugs again in response, but there's the vaguest hint of a snort through his nostrils, a snort which says, *I know what you're doing, and I'm not falling for it.*

"I want to ask you something," Victoria says, "and you don't have to answer, OK?"

Bertie turns away now. He stares out of the side window.

"Is that OK?" Victoria asks, then, "Hello? Planet Earth to Bertie. Are you receiving me?"

"I just thought I was getting a break from all that with Dad away," Bertie murmurs.

Victoria manages to sigh entirely silently. She runs her tongue across her teeth before continuing. "Are you glad he's away?" she asks.

"I was," Bertie says, still without turning.

"What does that mean?"

"I *was* glad until you took over his role as chief inquisitor."

"That's not fair," Victoria says, softly. "I don't think you're being very fair to me."

They drive on in silence for a few minutes before Bertie finally replies, "Sorry, you're right. I'm not being fair to anyone at the moment."

Tears immediately spring forth, and Victoria is glad that Bertie is still looking away. It's the first real thing her son has said to her in weeks.

"That's OK," she says, her cracked voice betraying her. "We're all in a strange place at the moment."

"I know," Bertie says. "It's my fault."

"It's not," Victoria says, reaching out to touch his leg and then restraining herself. This is going so well, after all. Better not to take risks.

She negotiates a roundabout before asking, "So, can I ask you my question?"

Bertie sighs. "If you have to," he says.

"Did you ask Penny if you could live with them?"

"Oh, Jesus!" Bertie says, now turning disgustedly to face her. "You've been talking about me behind my back?"

"Not at all," Victoria says, calmly. "She said something to Mum about it, that's all. She said you'd asked to stay there or something. I just wondered if it was true."

"Gran's such a shit-stirrer," Bertie says as he turns away anew. "And she just laughed at me anyway," he adds, too softly for Victoria to be completely sure of his words.

"I'm sorry?" she prompts.

"Nothing," Bertie says.

"But you did ask her?"

"Yeah," Bertie says. "Sort of."

"And did you say that she *laughed*?"

Bertie half-shrugs.

The sign to the hospital has come into view and Victoria suddenly wishes she had chosen a longer route. "Are you sure you don't want to tell me why?" she says as she indicates and pulls into the hospital complex. "Are you *sure* you don't want to just tell me why Penny's place, or even boarding school, is preferable to here? It would make everything so much–"

"Yeah," Bertie interrupts. "I'm sure."

Victoria sits and waits. She alternates between staring at the closed door behind which her son is no doubt telling his deepest secrets to a complete stranger, looking down the long, shiny corridor, and checking her phone which obstinately refuses to access the internet now she finally, for once, wants it to.

After ten unbearably slow minutes, she stands and makes her way back to reception and then on up to the hospital restaurant where she buys a cup of coffee which she sips as she stares, instead, out at the lawn.

Despite the hopping blackbird and the weeding gardener, the hour continues to pass slowly and by the time she returns downstairs she's feeling nervous and highly strung, but she has resisted, at least, the desire to pop another Valium. Not only is she aware that she needs to be alert for this meeting with Bertie's doctor, but she's scared, too, that the doctor will somehow be able to tell. *"You're stoned off your face on Valium, aren't you, Mrs Cunningham?"* she can imagine her saying.

At exactly one minute to twelve, the door opens and Bertie steps out, closing it quickly behind him as if to keep the secrets locked in. "Hi, Mum," he says flatly.

"All done?" Victoria asks as she stands.

"Uh-huh."

"I just need a quick word with her, myself," Victoria says, touching her son reassuringly on the arm with one hand and reaching for the door-handle with the other. "I won't be a minute. Just wait there."

"I'm not sure you can..." Bertie starts, but Victoria is already inside, already pushing the door closed behind her.

Doctor Cheeder looks up from her notes and frowns deeply. "I'm sorry," she says. "But can I help you?"

"Yes, I'm, um, Bertie's mother," Victoria reminds her, taking a seat even though she can already tell that she's not going to be invited to do so.

"Yes, I know who you are," the doctor says. "But unless I'm mistaken, we don't have an appointment."

"I know, but I need to talk to you," Victoria says.

"That's as maybe, but you'll need to make an appointment. I have my twelve o'clock waiting outside."

"There's no-one there yet," Victoria says. "And I only need five minutes. Please?"

Doctor Cheeder licks her lips and sighs. She covers her notes with an orange file and nods. "OK. Five minutes. But I can't tell you anything Bertie has said to me in confidence. You know that, right?"

"Yes," Victoria says. "It's just that there's this boarding school thing. I assume he has told you he wants to go to boarding school?"

Doctor Cheeder smiles blandly. "I'm afraid I can't possibly comment."

"OK, so let's assume he *has* told you," Victoria says – she has prepared herself for this. "Let's pretend that you know that he wants to go to boarding school, all right? So my question is, theoretically of course, supposing *you* had a child who was going through a difficult time, who you were worried about, who you felt you needed to keep an eye on... Would *you* consider that sending him away to a boarding school was a good idea? Even if that's what he wanted? Because I'm really not sure what to think, here. And I really don't want to take the wrong decision."

Doctor Cheeder crosses her fingers and clears her throat. "It's extremely important that Bertie doesn't think I have betrayed his confidence," she says. "His trust is the most important thing there is right now, believe me."

"I understand that. But surely we can talk theoretically?"

"Yes, well... theoretically, then, as you say, if I *did* have a son in the situation you describe, I might think, having treated a few boarders in my time, that he possibly has an inaccurate idea of what life at boarding school is like. So I might try to negotiate with him in order to find some *other* way for him to obtain the space and distance he currently craves."

"OK," Victoria says. "I think I see."

"Personally, I have a brother, so perhaps I'd ask him to help. I might ask him if my theoretical son could come and stay for a while. Do you see what I'm saying?"

"Yes," Victoria says. "Yes, I *do*... But I only have one sister, and we're not even on speaking terms."

"In order to discuss your relationship issues with your sister, you really would need to make your own appointment. But those are *your* issues, not Bertie's. If you catch my drift."

"I do," Victoria says. "I catch it perfectly."

"We all need some space sometimes," the doctor continues. "As a parent of a child who is in the process of becoming an adult, our job, sometimes, is just to recognise that. And to facilitate, perhaps, a non-permanent, non-damaging way for our child to separate from us, just as much as they need – without having to throw the baby out with the bathwater, so to speak."

"So the boarding school is a bad idea," Victoria says. "That's what I thought."

"I've said all I'm going to say right now," Doctor Cheeder says. "And I'm afraid I really do need to write up Bertie's notes and get on to my next patient."

Victoria glances longingly at the sheets of paper peeping out from under the orange folder as she sighs and stands. "Right," she says. "Thank you. Thank you so much."

"One final thing," the doctor says, glancing at the door.

"Yes?"

"As far as Bertie is concerned, we didn't speak about him. Not even theoretically. We spoke only about you, OK? I can't impress on you sufficiently how important it is that he doesn't doubt the confidentiality of our meetings."

"Of course. Thanks again."

"You're welcome, Mrs Cunningham. Um, if there's a pale teenage girl sitting out there, tell her I'll be just five minutes, would you?"

"Of course," Victoria says. "Yes, of course I'll tell her. Sorry to have held you up."

"It's fine," Doctor Cheeder says. "As you say, these decisions are difficult but important."

Outside, in the car, Bertie fastens his seatbelt, then asks, "Why did you need to talk to my doctor?"

"I'm sorry?" Victoria says, as she manoeuvres out of the parking space. "Oh, that's not really your business. It was private really. But it wasn't about you, if that's what you mean."

"Yeah, right," Bertie says.

"It really *wasn't*," Victoria tells her son. "It was about my Valium, if you must know. I've been taking it for too long and I was asking her about reducing."

"Oh, OK," Bertie replies, his tone softening. "What did she say?"

"I'm afraid that really is private," Victoria says. "But I'm going to deal with it, OK? So don't worry. How was your session?"

"All right, I suppose."

"Did you ask her what she thought about boarding school?"

"Nope," Bertie says.

"Maybe you should have," Victoria says. "She might be able to help you decide."

"I have decided," Bertie says.

They drive in silence for a moment, then he adds, "Will we ever see the Anderssons again?"

"Penny and Sander?" Victoria replies. "Of course we will."

"Right," Bertie says. "When?"

"I'll talk to your dad when he gets back from his holiday. We'll see what we can arrange, OK? Maybe you can go down for a weekend or something without us."

"Really?"

"Uh-huh," Victoria says, even though she can't think how she could possibly organise such a thing without speaking to her sister. "Would you like that?"

"Yeah. That would be cool."

• • •

It is Monday morning, and Penny has a long, difficult, and almost certainly exhausting week ahead of her. As she sips her morning coffee, she leafs through the pile of unpaid bills and tries to decide which one to pay first. She is hesitating between paying the most overdue ones, such as the broadband bill, or the most essential ones, like electricity.

Their money issues have really been getting to her recently, and have, for the first time ever, caused her bouts of actual insomnia.

She's been lying awake obsessing about potential remedies. They could sell the house, for instance. They could then pay off all their debts, buy a nice four bedroom house inland somewhere, and still have a couple of years' salary to stash in case of future disasters.

But she knows how deep Sander's attachment to the house is. She loves the place too, of course, but Sander's relationship with the place is on a whole different level. It's a symbol of his manhood, really, of his ability (past) to provide for his family.

They could take in a lodger – that's the other idea she has been chewing over. And if she could get Sander to admit that he's never actually going to paint anything ever again, they

161

could even take in two. But she's loath to introduce such random elements into the midst of her otherwise successful family life. It's impossible to know what effect a new person in the house might have on them all. And didn't Will's aunt get burgled by her own lodger, after all?

And so she shuffles through the bills and hesitates between broadband and water, between rates and electricity, and feels a little sick.

She glances at the clock. It's eight fifteen, so she'll have to leave soon.

Her job has been getting her down recently. She has an ever increasing caseload of kids who have lost their parents, and asylum seekers stuck in hopeless bedsits, and bereaved parents who need to be taught how to grieve, and there's virtually no hope, under the current government, that anyone will ever be recruited to second her.

The result is that she's spreading herself ever thinner, doing her job less and less well. She's going to meet new clients having read their case notes at night when she was half asleep, or in some cases going to meet them having not found the time to read them at all, and she hates herself for it, hates herself for bluffing her way through interviews about the most traumatic events people will ever have to live through.

Sander, this morning, is sulking too. She had asked him, over coffee, to reduce his considerable drug budget, just until they get things back on an even keel.

He has been spending – she finally worked it out – almost two-hundred pounds a month on grass, a figure which Sander flatly denied.

"I spend no more on dope than you spend on wine," he had claimed, which, seeing as Penny knows exactly how much she spends on wine (twenty nine pounds ninety eight pence on two boxes of white, Australian chardonnay from Lidl) is completely untrue.

When Penny had told him this, Sander had simply uttered the word, "Jesus" and left the room. So nothing is resolved. And she will have to attempt the conversation all over again.

She swigs down the last of her coffee and grabs her car keys and coat from the hallway – it's raining outside. But then she remembers the washing machine. She just has time to hang the stuff on the radiators before she leaves.

Downstairs in the basement, the machine is silent despite not having finished its cycle. She can see, quite clearly, that the drum is still full of water. "Not again," she groans, reaching down to pull off a shoe.

She whacks the machine on the side next to the timer, exactly as Sander has shown her, and for a second it looks as if she has succeeded – the machine lurches into action, the pump begins to whir and water begins to sluice. But then there's a faint popping noise, and the room, with the exception of a faint hum, is suddenly silent again.

"Not now," Penny tells the machine as she turns the knob to "spin" and whacks it again. She tries the "drain" position, too, but nothing happens. The machine is resolutely on strike.

She unplugs and plugs it in again, bashes the on/off button with her fist. Nothing. "Shit!" she mutters, checking her watch and pulling her shoe back on before heading upstairs.

When she pushes the studio door open, Sander looks startled. He looks guilty, in fact. Clouds of sweet smelling smoke hang in the air.

"The machine's stopped again," Penny tells him. "Can you fix it, please?"

"The washing machine?"

"Yes."

"Hit it with a shoe," Sander replies, speaking in smoke signals.

"I did. It won't budge."

"Hit it harder?" he offers, doubtfully.

"I did. Believe me."

"Maybe switch it–"

"Off and on? Done that too. I've tried everything, and I'm late. So can you please just deal with it, Sander?"

Sander shrugs. "Sure," he says. "I'll try. But you know at some point..."

"Yes, I know, I know. We need a new one."

* * *

By the end of the day, when Penny gets home, she is both physically and emotionally exhausted.

The house is quiet. The kids are in their rooms and Sander is (unusually) absent. The radiators, worryingly, are not covered in drying clothes.

She returns to the basement only to find the washing machine still full of water. Across the top of it, Sander has written, in red chunky marker, "I am utterly, definitively, dead."

"That's helpful," Penny mumbles, attempting, yet again, to kick, twist or jolt the machine back into life and becoming increasingly angry as the machine refuses to budge.

"Right, that's it," she says, now furious.

She climbs the stairs to the lounge and pulls her ancient laptop from behind the sofa. She plugs it in and switches it on, and with an increasing sense of despair, she stares at the screen as Windows attempts to start up, then after ten minutes, feeling almost tearful, she gives up, closes it and stuffs it back behind the couch.

She climbs the stairs to Max's bedroom and knocks, then enters.

Max, who is listening to music via headphones, visibly jumps. "Ugh!" he exclaims, yanking out an earbud and sitting. "Mum!"

"Can I use your computer?" she asks. "I need to do something online."

Max has an ageing MacBook, one of his uncle's cast offs. It's the only computer in the house that consistently works. "What's wrong with yours?" he asks, scrambling to reach the computer before she does.

"It won't start," she says. "It just says *Windows Loading* all the time, and then nothing ever happens."

"I told you, it's got a load of viruses on it," Max says. "You need to get a Mac."

"Well, I can't afford a Mac," she retorts. "In the meantime, can I use yours? I need to order a new washing machine. The old one has finally given up the ghost."

"Um, OK," Max says, sitting at his desk and rapidly closing incriminating windows. "Where from?"

"Currys," Penny says.

"There you go," Max says, vacating the chair once the website is loading. "But can we afford a washing machine?" he asks, then, "And does Dad know?"

"Can we afford it? No. Do we have a choice? Not really. Does Dad know? I suggest you go and find out," Penny says sharply.

As Max backs out of the bedroom, Penny watches Currys' homepage as it loads, and right in the middle of the page is an

165

advert for a summer special, a nine kilogram Hotpoint SmartWash with a thirty minute quick cycle.

She studies the photo, notes the half price deal, and suddenly feels ecstatic. "Thirty minutes!" she says, quietly. "That'll do nicely."

She quickly clicks through to the order confirmation screen where she types in her address details. The machine can be delivered tomorrow afternoon, the screen informs her. They'll take away the old monster free of charge. *Isn't modern life wonderful?* she thinks as she types in her debit card details.

The cursor hovering over "Confirm Order", she hesitates for less than a second before, with a smile and a sigh of anticipation, she clicks on the button. She does her best to resist the shopping urge, but a new washing machine really will change her life.

As the little onscreen wheel spins, she tries to remember exactly how close to their overdraft limit they had been. Surely there's enough leeway for a two-hundred pound washing machine, isn't there?

When her debit card is declined, she repeats the operation with the Barclaycard. Yes, the interest rate is crazy, and yes, she had promised herself never to use it again, but this is, after all, an emergency. She's a working mother and she needs a bloody washing machine; she needs, specifically, a slate grey, nine kilo Hotpoint SmartWash with a thirty minute quick cycle. The cost is only about the same as Sander's monthly drug spend, after all.

She clicks the confirm button again. The little wheel spins for slightly longer than the last time which she takes to be a good sign. She chews her fingernail. She fiddles with the credit card, flipping it over and over as she waits.

And then, unexpectedly, as the words *Your transaction was declined* appear for the second and final time, she bursts into tears.

She covers her eyes with one hand and shudders and sobs. "I'm so tired of this," she splutters. "I'm just so tired of it all."

By the time Sander gets home half an hour later, Penny has both pulled herself together and repaired the damage to her makeup.

"Where were you?" she asks, looking up from the frying pan, in which she is browning onions for bolognese sauce.

"I went out for a walk," Sander says. "I went to look at that second-hand place to see if they had any cheap washing machines."

"At this time?" Penny says, glancing at the clock. It's almost seven in the evening.

"Yeah," Sander says. "I didn't realise how late it was. They were closed."

"Right," Penny says, partially mollified that Sander has at least tried to do something. "We really do need to find a solution, and soon."

"I tried to fix it, but it's really dead this time. It is about a hundred years old."

"I know," Penny says. "I went to order one online. There's a half price deal on a Hotpoint one at Currys. But the card was refused."

Sander frowns. "Really? The debit card or the Barclaycard?"

"Both."

"Ouch."

x

167

"Yes, ouch…" Penny says flatly. "Look, we've used up our overdraft limit *and* the credit card is over the thousand pound mark."

"Jesus," Sander says.

"So, we're in a pickle."

Sander nods. "I… I don't know what to say, really. I'm sorry."

"Unfortunately, 'sorry' doesn't fix this one," Penny tells him. "We need to do something. We're at the end of the road here, Sander."

"Sure," he replies. "But what?"

"You *could* stop smoking."

"Oh, Jesus, that again?"

"Yes," Penny says, switching off the hob and turning to face her husband. "Yes, that again. A washing machine costs almost precisely what you spend on dope each month."

"I do *not* spend two hundred quid on dope."

"But you do. You're just in complete denial about it."

"Do you really want to have this whole conversation all over again?"

"How can I *not* have this conversation again?" Penny asks. "We're overdrawn at the bank. We're up to the limit on the card. The electricity, broadband, water and rates all need paying. And the only thing I can possibly think of that we could spend less on is your stupid dope habit."

"It just so happens…" Sander says.

"I'm sorry?"

"It just so happens that the only thing you can think of is the only thing I actually spend any money on."

"No, Sander," Penny says, now raising her voice. "It doesn't *just so happen*. We've cut back on everything else already. We don't go on holiday. We don't buy nice clothes. We don't eat out. We buy our food from bloody Lidl. We don't spend a single extra penny on anything."

"OK, OK, I'll stop," Sander says. "Happy now?" He then turns and storms from the kitchen, slamming the door behind him.

But even as he climbs the stairs to his studio, he knows that it's not true.

He won't stop smoking because he *can't* stop smoking. And he's not, in truth, in denial about it at all. He has noted and fully accepted his complete inability to stop smoking. He uses the word 'addict' within the confines of his own head to describe himself. And he has even worked out some of the reasons why he can't stop smoking.

The fact, for instance, that when he does try to stop, time stretches horribly. His days become vast, desolate wastelands to be got through, where the only thought that manifests is that he should work, he should paint – only he can't think *what* to paint. Yes, stoned or straight, he's out of ideas. With or without dope, he's no longer an artist. With or without it, he's just an ever fainter memory of an artist. It's just that it's a lot more painful without dope than with it.

Once the bolognese sauce is ready, Penny returns to the basement. By removing the filter she manages to drain the washing machine into a basin without spilling too much on the floor. She then piles the sudsy washing in the sink and pummels it beneath running water until it's clean, until her fists hurt, and until her rage finally dissipates.

* * *

It's nine-thirty on Saturday morning, and while her coloureds tumble over each other in the drum of one of Whitstable launderette's industrial machines, Penny walks to the nearby seafront.

It's a beautiful July day, one of those days when you can sense, in the air, the heat that is to come – one of those days when the world feels almost like energy itself, bottled up. Perhaps she'll go for a swim this afternoon if she's feeling brave.

When she reaches the shore, she sits on a wall and looks out at the pebble beach on which holidaymakers are already setting up windbreaks, and at the deep grey strip of sea beyond.

She pulls her phone from her pocket and after a moment's hesitation, dials the number. She's been meaning to phone her mother for days, and she's hoping that the confirmed death of their washing machine might inspire a little charitable donation. It's a bit ridiculous at forty-five to find oneself soliciting handouts from one's mother, but when there are no other options...

"Hello," she says, as soon as Marge answers. "It's Penny."

"Penny?" her mother says. It's her usual way of expressing reproach.

"Yes, your youngest daughter," Penny says, playing along. "Remember me?"

"Just about," Marge says.

"Come on," Penny laughs. "It wasn't that long ago."

"No," Marge says. "If you say so. So what's new down at the seaside?"

"Nothing much. It's a lovely day here. It actually feels like summer for once."

"Lucky you," Marge says. "It's all grey here. Are you outside? Only, I can hear seagulls."

"I am!" Penny says. "I'm on the seafront. I'm waiting for my washing to wash. I had to take it to the laundromat. Our machine has finally given up the ghost."

"It's been giving up the ghost for years," Marge says.

"You're right. It has. Only this time it has totally given up. Even Sander can't resuscitate it. What we really need is a new one. They're only two hundred pounds, but we can't even afford that at the moment."

"You're lucky you have a launderette nearby, then," Marge says, doggedly refusing to take the bait. "I used to have to hand-wash all of your clothes when you were little."

"Well, I've done a few hand-washes too. But what we really need is a new machine."

"That's such a shame," Marge says. "I just realised. Your sister threw hers out only yesterday."

"That red Smeg one?"

"Yes. They're having new worktops and cupboards fitted, and the red ones didn't match."

"But it was almost new."

"Oh, it was a few years old, I think. But perfectly good. But you know what they're like. They've more money than they know what to do with, those two."

"But Mum..."

"Still, I suppose we should be happy for their success and all that, shouldn't we? Jealousy's a terrible thing when you think about it."

"But has she *actually* thrown it out? Or is she just about to?"

"Oh, it's *gone*, darling. They did the worktops last week and the new machines came on Friday."

"Machines? She changed the dishwasher too?"

"Yes, I told you. She wanted grey ones. To match the new cupboards."

"But Mum. I mean, we really *need* her old machine. Are you sure it's too late?"

"Oh, definitely," Marge says. "But what a shame. If only she'd thought of you first. Still, she always was a selfish child. Even when she was little, she never wanted to give you her toys, even when she didn't want them anymore. Do you remember?"

"I do."

"Of course, if you were actually speaking to her at the moment, then you could have told her yourself."

"Yes, well. That works both ways, doesn't it?" Penny says.

"She's getting the bathroom retiled this week too. She wants it all done before Martin gets back from Spain."

"Right," Penny says miserably. The red Smeg washing machine is still revolving in her mind's eye. "So how's that going? How is Martin's Spanish adventure?"

"Fine, I think," Marge tells her. "Vicky hasn't mentioned it much, to be honest. I think they might have had an argument or something. Or perhaps she's just too busy with the workmen and everything. And Bertie."

"Is he all right, then?" Penny asks sounding disinterested.

"I think I heard Vicky saying she was going to ask you if he can come and stay, actually."

"I'm sorry?"

"Yes, he's been... well.... a bit funny, lately."

"Funny?"

"I told you about the boarding school thing."

"Well, no one could blame the boy for wanting to get away," Penny says. "Vicky's hardly low maintenance. I'm surprised he didn't go with Martin, though, to Spain."

"Yes," Marge says. "Yes, we were all surprised at that. He's been a bit under the weather, I think. That's why Vicky thought a seaside break might do him good. A change of scenery and that."

"Poor Bertie. He probably needs a change of *family*."

"Well, quite. So you'd agree then?"

"To Bertie coming to visit?"

"Yes. I'm sure Max would be pleased. They seem to get on well, those two," Marge says.

"Yes they do. But she'd have to ask me first, wouldn't she?"

"I could perhaps let her know you don't mind," Marge says. "That might ease things a little."

"No," Penny says, still thinking about red washing machines. "No, if Vicky wants something, then let her call me and ask me herself."

. . .

Victoria is in the process of putting the final finishing touches to the bathroom as she waits for Martin to get home.

Both the bathroom and the kitchen are looking gorgeous, and she has almost finished erasing the last tell-tale signs of all the renovation work – the smears of grouting across the corners of the tiles, the smudges of paint around the edges of the new worktop and the fine sawdust that seems to keep re-depositing itself in every corner.

But the initial buzz of the restyled kitchen and bathroom is already wearing off. She's back to worrying about Martin, now.

She has spoken to him on the phone a couple of times in the last two weeks, and he has sounded normal enough. But she's convinced that it's only when she looks into his eyes that she'll know for sure if he's going to leave her or not.

She has just succeeded in forcing Bertie to come into the kitchen for lunch when the front door opens and a red-faced, skinny, younger looking version of Martin pops his head around the door. Which is frustrating, because, with Bertie present, he clearly isn't going to give anything away.

"Hello!" he says brightly, removing his backpack and propping it up against the wall.

Victoria rinses her hands beneath the tap and walks down the hallway to join him. "Hello," she replies, drying her hands on a tea-towel. She feels unexpectedly shy in his presence, as if, not knowing whether he's loving her or leaving her, she doesn't know quite how to interact with him.

He smiles at her and leans in for a kiss, so she pecks him on the lips and tries desperately to decode the depths of his regard.

"Hi, Dad," Bertie says. "Was it fun?"

Martin nods. "It was amazing," he says, and Victoria's heart flutters a little. "But I'm shattered now."

"You should have let me come and pick you up," Victoria says. "I did offer."

Martin laughs and leads the way through to the kitchen, removing his now-grubby hiking jacket as he does so. "Oh, it wasn't the half an hour on the Gatwick Express that tired me," he says. "It was walking two-hundred kilometres in the baking sun."

"Did you really walk two hundred kilometres?" Bertie asks, then, "How many miles is that?"

"About a hundred and forty, I think," Martin says. "Give or take. About the same distance as down to Penny's place and back. Farther, actually."

He carries the kettle to the kitchen tap to fill it, but Victoria prises it from his grasp. "Sit down," she says. "I'll do that."

"Thanks," Martin replies, pulling out a chair from beneath the kitchen table. "I'm gasping for a decent cup of tea."

Victoria fills the kettle and switches it on before turning back to face the room. Bertie, who is opposite, looks uncomfortable too, she can see. Perhaps he can sense the possibility of Martin's departure, as well.

It reminds her of something she once read about Shrödinger's cat, which, as far as she can recall, was neither dead nor alive until someone opened the box to check.

Right here, in this kitchen, her marriage seems neither dead nor alive until Martin opens the box that reveals what's going on in his head, what's happening in his heart.

"The kitchen looks nice," he says.

"It looks just like before, only a different colour," Bertie quips.

"Don't keep saying that!" Victoria tells her son, forcing herself to feign laughter as she speaks.

Martin looks around and considers the changes before declaring, "No, no, it definitely looks nicer."

"It took them all week," Bertie says. "We had to eat noodles and pizzas. It was like we were camping too."

"Huh," Matin says. "I would have given anything for a pizza some nights. The food in the hostels wasn't all it might have been."

"But you enjoyed yourself?" Victoria asks, still looking for clues. "Despite the food?"

"It was amazing," Martin says. "It was really... Look, I know you'll both laugh at this, but it was really quite... quite *spiritual*, I suppose. I really felt like I found myself up there."

This doesn't make Victoria want to laugh at all. In fact she suddenly finds herself blinking back tears.

"Right," Bertie says. "Wow."

She adds milk to Martin's tea and plonks the mug down in front of him, and as he looks up at her a shadow crosses his features – concern perhaps, or confusion; sadness maybe. And she suddenly knows she was right. He's going to leave her.

"The, um, landscape was amazing," Martin says. "I'll show you the photos after lunch if you want."

"Great," Bertie says, unconvincingly. But at least he's making an effort, just as Victoria asked him to.

She would make an effort herself, only she feels as if she's been ushered onstage in the midst of an unknown theatre piece and she has absolutely no idea what role she is supposed to be playing.

"I made a pie," she says, grabbing at the first, easiest role that springs to mind. "And a salad. If that's all right for you?"

"Great," Martin says, clapping his hands together, and looking, for all the world, like an actor playing 'Dad'.

Between Bertie's presence and a host of emails and errands that Martin needs to catch up on, it's not until they're in bed that night that they're finally able to talk.

Feeling quite literally terrified – trembling, in fact – Victoria climbs into bed next to Martin. Realising that he's almost asleep already, she bounces around just enough to wake him up, then asks, "Are you too tired to talk?"

"No," Martin replies sleepily. "I mean, I'm *tired,* but I can talk. You have no idea how nice it is to sleep in a proper, comfortable bed."

"But you had a nice time all the same? You're glad you went."

"Yes," Martin says. "Like I said, it was great."

Victoria sighs. She won't get any sleep tonight unless she asks the question, but then she won't get any sleep tonight once she gets the answer, either. She rolls onto her back and looks up at the dark ceiling, at the tiny speck of orange light leaking through the curtains from the streetlamp outside, and she tries to decide.

"Are *you* OK?" Martin asks. "You seem strange."

Victoria laughs sourly. "Thanks," she says, then, "I'm fine."

"You're not," Martin says. "I'm not sure what you are, but fine isn't it."

"OK, I'm not then."

"What's wrong?"

Victoria shrugs and Martin, beside her, feels the mattress move just enough to know that she has shrugged. "Is it the kitchen?" he asks. "Are you disappointed?"

"No. Of course not."

"Is it Bertie, then? He seemed a bit better to me, but..."

"No, it's not Bertie, either."

"So, what then?"

"I don't know," Victoria lies. "I think... well I think, I think..."

"Yes?"

"I think I'm scared, actually," she says, her voice starting to crack despite her best efforts.

"Scared?" Martin repeats. "Of what?"

"I'm not sure," Victoria says, her voice trembling strangely.

Martin rolls onto his side. "See, I knew something was wrong," he says. "Tell me."

"It's this whole Spain thing," Victoria replies. "I mean, I know you had a good time. And I know you didn't miss me at all. But..."

"Of course I missed you."

"But now I'm scared that you've realised you can have a better life without me. Without any of this rubbish." The tears are starting to roll down her cheeks now and she's glad that it's too dark for Martin to see them.

"But..." Martin says.

"I know I've been useless," Victoria interrupts. "I know I *am* useless. But I didn't mean to be. It just happened. I didn't expect things to turn out like this. I didn't want them to be like this."

She jumps at the sensation of Martin's fingers touching her chin in the dark. "Shhh," he says, softly. "I did miss you. Of course I did."

"You didn't say it. Not once."

"It's just..." Martin says.

"Go on, say it. I need you to say it, I think."

"It was a strange trip," Martin says quietly. "I realised a lot of things. I don't think I've had much time to think lately, what with work, and Bertie, and all the rest, and I realised things, about myself, about us. We've... we've fallen asleep really. We're getting old, we're somehow just getting old together when we should be living. We should be having adventures, and fun, and enjoying life. I mean, we're going to die. But we're not having fun, are we? We're just getting old together."

"You see," Victoria says. "That's what I was afraid of."

"But I'll tell you what I also realised," Martin says, softly. "I realised that I can't really enjoy myself if you're not there. I liked all the walking, I really did. And I saw some amazing things. I mean, you saw the photos, right? But I hated every bloody minute of it. Every thing I saw, I wanted to show *you*. Every time I felt happy, I suddenly felt sad again because you weren't there to share it with me."

"Really?" Victoria breathes as she swipes at the tears with the back of her hand.

"I didn't want to tell you because... because I felt embarrassed, I suppose. I didn't want to admit it. But I was bloody miserable without you, Vicky. And I spent the entire time missing you. I spent the whole bloody holiday wishing that I had never gone at all."

● ● ●

It is Monday afternoon, but to Penny, it feels more like a Thursday. Having suffered from insomnia for two nights in a row, she doesn't feel as if she has had a weekend at all.

Saturday night's insomnia had been caused by their financial woes. She had lain awake until four am creating virtual balance sheets in her mind, trying to find some magical solution whereby they could fix things without moving house. By Sunday night, she was feeling feverish, something she attributed initially to over-exhaustion. But as she had lain there sweating she had decided that she was probably coming down with a dose of summer flu, and then, terrifyingly, she had begun to wonder if these weren't the hot flushes everyone talks about. And so, she had begun to worry about the menopause instead.

She blinks hard and tries to pull herself together. Sosamma Cherian is entering the consulting room and Penny's worries pale into insignificance when compared with Sosamma's. Being fully present for her client is the absolute least she can do.

Sosamma, who, according to her case notes, is a thirty-eight-year-old Syrian refugee living in yet another one-room bedsit with her husband, eighteen-year-old daughter and eleven-year-old surviving son, is a pretty yet fragile looking woman. She's wearing a purple headscarf and has the largest, bluest eyes that Penny has ever seen.

"Hello," Penny tells her, speaking slowly. "Please take a seat. If you could close the door..."

Sosamma blinks shyly at her, pushes the door to, and sits down, perching elegantly on the edge of the seat.

"Before we start, Sosamma – can I call you Sosamma? Or would you prefer Mrs Cherian?"

"Sosamma's OK," she says, with a nod and another eyelashey blink.

"Great, well, I'm Penny. Penny Andersson." Another nod. "So, before we start, can you just confirm for me how comfortable you are in English? I know you haven't been here very long."

Sosamma licks her lips and stares at her feet as she replies, "It's OK. My father learnt me. And a little at university, too."

"That's great," Penny says. "What did you study at university?"

"Chemistry," Sosamma says. "I s... specialise – is that right? Yes? I specialise in organic chemistry."

"Gosh," Penny says. "I was terrible at chemistry."

"That's OK," Sosamma says with a faint smile. "You don't work as chemist."

"Well, your English is excellent, which makes this much easier for me. So thank you for that."

"You're welcome," Sosamma says, blinking and nodding again.

"How good is your understanding of what I do?" Penny asks. She has wasted whole half hours in the past with women who thought she was a GP warming up for a medical consultation.

"You are helping with the things that happen to me, yes?" Sosamma says. "Psychological things. With my bad dreams?"

"Yes. Well, I'll try. I'm a trauma counsellor. And from what I've read here, you've had more trauma in the last six months than most people go through in a lifetime."

"Trauma?" Sosamma repeats uncertainly. "I'm not so sure of this word."

"Difficult experiences," Penny explains. "Upsetting, distressing things that happen."

"Yes," Sosamma says. "OK."

"You're having nightmares, you say? Bad dreams?"

Sosamma nods.

"Can you tell me what they're of? What happens? Do you remember when you wake up?"

She nods again. "Yes. My son. He dies. In my arms. Every night."

"I see," Penny says, gently. "That must be very upsetting. And is this person in the dream recognisable as your son?"

Sosamma shakes her head. "No. He looks different. But I know. In my dream – I know. It's my son."

"Is this Chandy, or..." Penny glances at the file, "or, Kuriakose? I'm sorry. These names aren't familiar to me, so they're hard to remember. And to pronounce."

"It's Zachary in English, I think," Sosamma says. "You can say Zachary if it's easy."

"No, I need to learn," Penny says. "So, in the dream, is it Kuriakose, or Chandy?"

"It's Chandy," Sosamma says. "The dead one."

"I see."

"It's in the church. Where he died. Everything the same."

"So it's actually a memory of what happened to you, not an invented dream?"

"Yes. It's like memory."

"Would you like to tell me what happened? Or is that too painful for you?"

"Not," Sosamma says. "Not tell, I think."

"That's perfectly fine," Penny says.

"But maybe you can answer this question," Sosamma says. "Is it good to talk about or not to talk about? My husband, he says I am..." She mutters something in Arabic. "Deny? This is the word?"

"He says you're in denial?"

"Yes. I think. He says I should talk about. So maybe you can tell me this. To talk or not to talk. For the dreams to go away. Which is better?"

Penny clears her throat and leans forward. "As a general rule, talking about it, when you're ready, will probably help. With something like... what happened to Chandy, when we lose someone close, especially a child, there is a lot of pain. And when you tell the story, you feel that pain quite strongly, yes?"

Sosamma nods and brushes a stray tear from her cheek.

"But the pain will get less with time. That will seem impossible now, but it's true. It will become easier."

"It will go away?" Sosamma asks. Then pointing to her chest she says, "It hurts. Like real pain. Here."

"Yes. Well, it probably won't go away completely. No. But it will get easier to think about it. It will become a part of you. And telling the story, that's part of that process."

Sosamma nods and pulls a tissue from her sleeve, then dabs at a tear in the corner of her eye. "So you think that Avrachan is right? That I must talk?"

"No. Not necessarily," Penny says. "Things like this, they can sometimes feel too hard to bear. They can feel impossible. Sometimes *not* talking about it feels like the only way to survive. So sometimes denial is the only reasonable place to be, the only place you feel safe."

"Yes," Sosamma says. "Yes, I think this is true for me. But I think, too, I must do something. For the dreams. It's every night. I'm so tired. I'm so scared. I try not to sleep."

"Perhaps what's needed is for you to let yourself talk about what happened just a little bit. From time to time. You could try telling me a little piece of the story, just as much as you can bear. Maybe that would let a little bit of the pain out?"

"I'm scared," Sosamma says.

"What are you scared of?"

"I'm scared if I cry... for Chandy. I'm scared I never stop crying."

"It's a very common fear," Penny says. "Many people worry about this. But it's not true, in fact. You cried just now. But you stopped."

"Yes."

"And that's a process. A client once said that it was like a bottle full of pain, if you can imagine that. And each time you let yourself remember, each time you let yourself feel the pain, each time you cry, you empty the bottle a little bit. So it becomes easier to carry. Do you understand?"

"I think. Like a bottle of tears, yes?"

"Yes," Penny says, thinking that it's rather a beautiful image. "If you like. But you can protect yourself, as well. You can do it slowly. At your own pace. When *you're* ready. Not when anyone else thinks you should."

"Pace?" Sosamma says. "I don't think I know *pace*."

"It means speed. You have to do it at your own speed. Not too fast and not too slow."

"I see," Sosamma says, now blinking back fresh tears and looking at the ceiling. "So can we try?"

"I'm sorry. Try what?" Penny asks.

"Can I try to tell you?"

"If you want to," Penny says. "But only if you want to. There's no obligation at all. It's for you to decide."

"I like you," Sosamma says, forcing a tiny smile through her rolling tears. "So maybe we can try."

Penny swallows with difficulty, and pushes the box of tissues across the desk towards Sosamma. "OK," she says. "At your own pace. Your own speed. Just stop whenever you want to."

"OK," Sosamma says, taking a deep breath. "We were in the church. We're Christian. You know this, yes?"

Penny nods.

"The... the rebels, I suppose you call them. They were all around the town. Like a circle. And the Americans, they are dropping bombs, yes? Our building is damage. So we hide in the church. They have a..." she gestures with her hand.

"A basement? A room below ground floor?"

"Yes. We hide in the basement. All of us. Avrachan, Kuriakose, Eliamma, and little Chandy. There are others, too. Friends, neighbours. A priest. The children are crying. Some people are hurt. Avrachan is bleeding from a bomb before..." She waves over her shoulder. "We are very scared."

"It must have been terrifying."

Sosamma covers her eyes with one hand and nods as if the visual memory is just too much to bear, as if covering her eyes might somehow make it stop. "Then they come," she says. "The rebels come in the church. They don't care. These are bad men. Not ISIS, but the same. And they come with machine guns. The children, they are screaming. The women are crying. Some men, too. Some people, they run, and the rebels, they, they..."

"It's OK," Penny says. "Take your time, Sosamma."

"They shoot them down," she weeps. "All the ones who run, they shoot them down. Man, woman, child, they don't care. My Chandy, he ran. I was holding him but he got away. And he ran."

Once Sosamma has left, Penny sits and stares at the empty chair opposite.

She has a forty-five minute lunch break before her next appointment, and she had intended to nip to the nearby supermarket to pick something up for tea tonight, only she can't seem to find the energy to leave her chair.

She's surprised at this at first, but after a moment's reflection, she realises that this is more than tiredness. This is her body telling her to pause, to reflect, to give itself time to

185

process whatever has just happened. Because something *has* happened. And so she sits and stares at the empty chair and waits.

Perhaps she needs to let herself feel Sosamma's pain, she decides. She's an expert, has *become* an expert, at *not* feeling other people's distress. She has learned – in order to continue doing her job without having a breakdown – to concentrate on process, not emotion. She has made herself an expert on techniques for guiding people through and beyond their pain, for teaching them, if you will, how to deal with it, rather than dealing with it herself.

But today, for some reason, seems different. Today she needs to let herself feel it, she thinks, perhaps just to prove to herself that she still can.

She starts by picturing, in her mind's eye, the scene. She imagines beautiful, fragile Sosamma, sweaty and scared in the basement of a church. She imagines her gripping the sleeve of eight-year-old Chandy, pictures him breaking away, Sosamma begging him to return, or perhaps too scared to even speak; seeing him shot down, seeing others who have run to their own children falling too. She can almost sense the tension in her own body, the tension of being caught between impossible choices: to run to one's son and die with him, or to stay with the other children when their need is just as great.

And then, finally, she lets herself imagine Sosamma's dream: Chandy, dying in her arms, his blood, and his life, slowly seeping away.

By the time she has finished, only seven minutes have passed, but Sosamma's case notes are wet with Penny's tears. The ink has not run (she writes with a ballpoint pen) but the paper is buckled and transparent where her tears have landed.

She thinks of Sosamma's conceptual bottle of tears – such a delicate image for the pain we all hold.

Our first reaction to death or loss is so often to avoid thinking about them, to block whatever is causing the pain by thinking about other things, by taking, in many cases, drugs, whether legal or illegal, by doing almost any thing which will stop that pain. But *not* thinking about it can drive a person insane.

She thinks, now, of her own life traumas. She compares them with Sosamma's loss of her son, her house, her country... There's no comparison really, but every person's biggest trauma is still that person's biggest trauma. There is no relativity within the realm of one's own subconscious. So Penny wonders if she perhaps doesn't let herself think sufficiently about the things which have happened to her.

She "dealt" with them, of course, during her own therapy, before she even became a therapist in her own right. But as she has just told Sosamma, these things never go away. They only become easier to bear. And she wonders if she hasn't been too busy helping everyone else, too overwhelmed by the heft and scale of their problems, to think about her own.

She visualises again, the bottle of pain, Sosamma's bottle of tears. Because she still has her own bottle she carries around – of course she does.

She takes a deep breath and pulls the box of tissues back to her own side of the desk. She glances briefly at the closed door and calculates the risk of a colleague coming in. And then she lets herself remember.

* * *

The second uncle Cecil had left (he had closed the front door behind him so quietly it was as if he was scared of waking someone) Ed and Vicky had begun to run riot.

Their excitement about Christmas was bubbling over and, once they had verified that Cecil had not taken his gifts with him, they had started to run around the house, releasing pent-up energy. It was as if Cecil had been the cork holding all the fun in and the second he was gone they became happier and freer and lighter. Penny could feel it too, and whatever had gone on before was now clearly over. Christmas could finally begin.

The three of them had run around the house and then out into the small back garden. It was a sunny day, a windy day, and Penny can remember the sensation of her cold knees peeping out beneath her skirt, of the thick blue jumper she was wearing.

Vicky had pushed her on the rusty old swing, and then Ed had taken over, pushing her higher and higher until the feet of the metal frame lifted and the rope went slack – until Penny got scared.

But, unarguably, it was too cold outside, so when Marge had rapped on the lounge window and called them indoors, they had executed her orders immediately.

Marge had been dozing, Penny recalls, and when she woke up she had been strange – both angry and sad at the same time. She had seemed, somehow, like a wind-up toy at the end of its spring. Indoors, Ed and Vicky, their energy inversely proportional to Marge's, had chased each other around until she came out to shout at them. She was watching a film, she said, and she couldn't hear herself think.

So they had all moved upstairs, first to Ed's room at the top of the house, then to the landing where they began to slide down the bannisters. But when Penny tried to join them, Ed had said she was too little. It was almost certainly true, Penny now realises. She had been unable to even hook her leg over the shiny mahogany bannisters without help from Ed or Vicky. But she had been upset, all the same, to be excluded from the fun and games.

And so, she had gone down to tell Marge. Sliding down the bannisters, as fun as it undoubtedly was, was strictly prohibited, so she had opened the door to the lounge and sidled to her mother's side with the intention of dobbing them in.

Her mother was asleep again, and snoring loudly, a bottle of sherry and an empty glass at her side. On the television screen was a film. Penny can't remember which film it was but it had been someone her mother adored, perhaps Errol Flynn or Mario Lanza. Yet despite the film, and the sherry – things which generally made her amenable – she had seemed, once woken, severe and irritated, or perhaps disappointed and upset. Whatever was wrong with her, it made Penny uneasy and hesitant about executing her plan to stop Ed and Vicky's fun upstairs.

"Shhh!" Marge had slurred, when Penny tried to speak to her. "I'm watching this."

At that moment, the clock had struck three. God! She had forgotten the grandfather clock, but she remembers it now, she remembers the exact sound of the chime. It had struck three and Marge had leant forward in her chair the better to concentrate on her film. Deciding to try again, Penny had reached for the sleeve of her cardigan and had tugged on it. "But Mum," she had started to say.

And that's when it had happened.

There had been a thud – a horrible, sickly body-blow which had reverberated through the floorboards.

Both Marge and her daughter had frozen, perhaps for only a second, or perhaps for much longer. They had turned to look at the closed lounge door and they had frozen, mother and daughter in a shared moment of not-yet-actualised terror. And then Vicky had broken the absolute silence of the house with a scream.

Marge then ran to the hall. She began to wail in a way that Penny found terrifying. "No," she kept screaming, over and over. "No. No. No."

Penny had stayed put. She had stood there in the lounge, with Errol Flynn on-screen (yes, she's sure now that it was Flynn), and the horrible wailing coming from the hallway, and she had done absolutely nothing. She had been too scared to move.

After another indeterminate amount of time, Marge had called for her help. "Penny!" she had said, her voice so deformed by tears as to be almost unrecognisable. "Go get Cecil. Run to the station and make him come back. Penny! Go as fast as you can."

Penny had stood, her hand on the china doorknob. It had tiny pink flowers painted on it. She was too scared to step out into the hallway, too scared to see whatever was out there, too scared to discover what had happened. "Penny!" Marge had shouted again. "Now! Or you, Vicky! Jesus! Will one of you, please, go?"

Eventually, though she doesn't remember it, she must have slipped through that door. But there's a gap here, a big black hole bang in the middle of her memories. She must have seen

Ed's body at the base of the stairs. She must, almost certainly, have stepped over him to get to the front door. But she cannot remember it. She never has been able to. Is it possible that she didn't look? Is it possible she covered her eyes?

Victoria had been standing at the top of the stairs, this she remembers.

Penny now covers her eyes with both hands and tries, yet again, to remember. But though she can see the pattern of the hall floor mosaic, though she can imagine, perfectly, the newel post, that bulbous final bannister which Ed's head must have struck, there's a vacuum right there in the middle of her memories.

Next: outside in the chilled December air, Penny is running to the train station. They lived about half a mile away, but though she was crying, and though her little lungs were smarting from the freezing temperatures, she had run all the way.

She had reached the station in time to see Cecil standing on platform three in his three piece suit and his big grey overcoat, his brown leather suitcase at the side of his shiny brogues. But she did *not* run to his side. She did not call out.

She would have needed, in theory at least, a platform ticket to reach him, and for the longest time she told herself that this – the lack of a platform ticket, the lack of money for a platform ticket, even – was the reason she had remained out of sight in the shadowy interior of the station building. But she worked out years ago that this was not the truth. She still has no idea quite *why* she did not do as she was told, and even now, even at forty-five, other than remembering a sick feeling, a nightmare sensation of having jelly-legs which refused to advance, she can't come up with a plausible explanation. But she could have stopped uncle Cecil leaving. And she didn't. Of this much she is sure.

Eventually a train arrived, blocking her view of Cecil, and when it vanished, he too, had gone.

She remembers walking home slowly. Perhaps she was in shock, but, whatever the reason, she was definitely in no hurry to return.

She remembers, she thinks, banging a stick against some railings. She remembers sitting on a doorstop and running away when the front door suddenly opened. She remembers crying at one point, and a kind man asking her what was wrong.

By the time she got home, Mister Michaels from number nineteen was, incongruously, she thought, mopping their hall floor and Mrs Michaels was standing at her gate in an overcoat.

"There you are!" she had exclaimed, speaking though a handkerchief. "We've been worried sick. Come inside. Everyone's at ours."

By "everyone", Penny had thought she meant *everyone*. As in, her mother, her sister, and her brother. She remembers feeling elated, feeling momentarily overjoyed. She had misunderstood the situation, that was all. She remembers her confusion when she ran into the Michaels' lounge to find only Victoria, wide-eyed and silent, and her mother bent over on the sofa, still weeping.

"Where's Ed?" she had asked, looking around the room and then up towards the Michaels' own, identical staircase.

Victoria had blinked and shaken her head, and Penny hadn't been sure if she was telling her not to ask this question, or if the head-shake was somehow an answer in itself.

"Where is he?" she had asked again.

"He..." Mrs Michaels had begun to say.

But Marge had interrupted her. "He's at the hospital," she had croaked. "The ambulance took him, and he's at the hospital."

Victoria, she noticed, was still shaking her head.

• • •

It is ten am on Saturday, and Penny, still in bed, is reading the *Guardian* on her smartphone. It's the first weekend of August and the sun is streaming in through the salt-stained windows, warming her shoulders. From outside, through a cracked window, she can hear waves, seagulls, and some shrieking swimmers. It's a gorgeous combination.

As she clicks on the culture section of the *Guardian* website, Sander's phone begins to buzz on the bedside table.

"Sander?" she calls out. "Sander! Pho-oh-ne..." But Sander, next door in the en-suite, does not reply, so she rolls to her side and reaches for his phone.

WILL the screen says, which is strange, because Will is her friend, not Sander's. In fact she's not sure she can ever remember Will having phoned Sander. What's more, she has been waiting for Will's call, herself. He is due to pick Marge up and bring her down for the weekend, and he almost always calls before they set off from London.

She swipes at the screen and raises the phone to her ear. "Hey, Will," she says. "You got the wrong number. This is Sander's phone." On the other end of the line she hears what sounds like the faintest of groans, and then a click before the line goes dead.

"That's weird," she tells Sander, who, still naked, is reentering the room. "That was Will, but on your phone not mine. And as soon as I answered, he hung up."

Sander smiles and as he rounds the bed says, "Maybe he wanted to talk to me." Then, jiggling his privates, he adds, "Maybe he wants a bit of this. Maybe Will and me have secret things going."

"*Really?*" Penny laughs as he climbs back into bed. She places the phone in Sander's outstretched hand and then pokes him in the ribs. "You're welcome to each other," she says. "Be my guest. Call your boyfriend and see what he wants."

Sander snorts and taps at the screen before raising the phone to his ear. "Hey Will," he says. "My wife says you want to talk to me, and only me. Which I kind of understand. She does get boring sometimes."

Penny rolls onto her side and watches her husband's expression as the smile slips away to be replaced with confusion, and then a deep, wrinkled frown. "Um, yeah. Of course," Sander says, his voice transformed as he slides from the bed. "Hang on." He stands and heads back towards the bathroom. "Just, um, wait a minute," he tells Penny. "There's some kind of problem."

Penny watches as the bathroom door closes, then pulls a face. She sits up and plumps the pillows behind her as she tries to imagine what possible kind of problem would involve speaking to Sander rather than herself. A problem with Will's old car, perhaps? But if that's the case, Will really has phoned the wrong number. Sander wouldn't even know where the engine is.

For the first minute, Penny stares at the closed bathroom door as she waits for Sander to return. She then turns her attention back to her telephone and attempts to continue reading the newspaper article on the screen. But she quickly gives up – she can't concentrate – and stands, instead, and pulls on her dressing gown.

"Sander?" she whines, knocking on the bathroom door. "What's going on?"

"Just a minute," he calls back. After this she hears him say, quietly, "Yes. God! Yes, of course."

When he finally does open the door again, he finds Penny sitting on the edge of the bed, waiting for him. "Well?" she asks.

Sander looks at her strangely. He chews his bottom lip.

"What is it?" she asks again.

"It's Marge," Sander says. "She's..." He clears his throat. "Look, there's no easy way to do this, hon." He exhales sharply before continuing, "She's dead, I'm afraid, Penny. Your mother's dead."

Penny blinks at him exaggeratedly and smiles crookedly. "I'm sorry?" she says.

"Will and Ben," Sander explains. "They just turned up at Marge's place. And..." he shrugs, unable to make himself say the words a second time.

"If you're joking," Penny says, "then it's in very bad taste, Sander. Because that's not funny *at all.*"

"I'm not joking," Sander replies, now moving to her side and sitting. He slides one arm around her shoulders and takes her hand in his. "I wish I was."

"Really?" Penny says. "Maybe *Will's* joking. He can be a real arsehole sometimes."

Sander shakes his head soulfully. "It's not a joke, Penny."

Penny raises one hand to cover her mouth. "But how?" she murmurs, as tears start to well up, clouding her vision. "I spoke to her yesterday and she was fine."

"In her sleep, they said. They found her at breakfast."

Penny shakes her head at Sander. "But that doesn't make sense," she whispers. "They serve breakfast at silly o'clock over there. Mum's always complaining about it. If they'd found her at six or seven or whatever, they would have phoned, surely? There must be some mistake."

"That's the other thing," Sander says. "They did. They phoned Vicky, apparently. They told her hours ago."

• • •

Victoria squeezes the button on her car key and opens the hatchback of the BMW. "Here you go," she says. "Put that bag in there."

"Are you sure this is a good idea, Mum?" Bertie asks.

"Why wouldn't it be a good idea?"

"It's just that Dad said he'd be home by lunchtime," Bertie points out. "Maybe we should wait and all go together."

"No, he had his adventure in Spain," Victoria says. "It's our turn, now."

She walks around the car to the driver's side and climbs in. "Well, come on!" she shouts. Bertie is still peering at her warily through the open hatchback.

"Weird," Bertie mumbles. "Truly weird." He slams the hatch and rounds the car, then climbs into the passenger seat. "Why won't you tell me where we're going?" he asks, as he fastens his seatbelt.

"I told you, it's a surprise," Victoria says, smiling blandly at him.

Bertie shakes his head. There's something wrong with his mother this morning, but he can't put his finger on what it is. Beyond her sudden, inexplicable desire for adventure, her eyes have a crazed glassy stare about them. Her face seems expressionless, her makeup thicker, and her skin looks somehow smoother, younger, robotic almost. Even her movements, usually nervous and jerky, like a scared little rodent, are smooth and placid this morning. It's all most unsettling.

Victoria starts the engine and then claps her hands. "Right!" she says.

"Do *you* know where we're going?" Bertie asks, noticing his mother's hesitation.

"Hum," Victoria says. "Well, I know *where* we're going. I'm just not that sure how." She reaches for the GPS and starts to jab at the screen. "But I'm sure this little box knows the way. You can be my map reader, if you want."

"You don't need a map reader with a GPS," Bertie says. "That's the whole point."

"Why not?"

"The GPS *is* a map reader, Mum."

"You can still look at the screen and tell me what's coming up, can't you? I hate having to look at it while I'm driving."

Bertie sighs and shakes his head. "Whatever," he says, despairingly.

He watches as Victoria configures the GPS, but as she clips it to the screen, it momentarily displays the destination. "Blackpool?" Bertie says. "Why are we going to Blackpool, Mum?"

"Damn," Victoria says. "You weren't supposed to see that."

"That's miles and miles and miles away. That's, like, up north or something, isn't it?"

"It's not *that* far."

"Mum," Bertie says. "You're scaring me."

"Scaring you?" Victoria repeats, reaching down and engaging *Drive*. "Don't be so silly. Don't you want to go on a mini-adventure with your old mum?"

"Yeah... No... Not really. Why Blackpool?"

"I have my reasons, trust me," Victoria says, glancing in the wing mirror and pulling out into traffic. "Can you look at that thing and tell me if I'm going the right way? I'm never sure which direction to take at the beginning. I always end up having to turn around."

"If you mean to go to Blackpool then you're going the right way, yeah," Bertie says, wriggling to pull his phone from his pocket.

Victoria glances at him and frowns. "What are you doing?" she asks, suspiciously.

"Just phoning Dad," Bertie says.

In a smooth, precise gesture, Victoria snatches the phone from his grasp and slides it into her door-pocket. "No, you're not," she tells him, flatly.

"Now you're *really* scaring me."

"Oh, please do stop being so whingy."

"I'm not. You're being weird, Mum. You're like some kidnapper in a film or something."

"What rubbish!"

"Jesus, it says four hours and eighteen minutes."

"I'm sorry?"

"The GPS. It says it's gonna take four hours and eighteen minutes to get to Blackpool."

"Gosh, that *is* a long way, then."

"What time will we even get home?" Bertie asks.

"Oh, I don't think we'll be coming home today," Victoria says. "If it's four hours and eighteen minutes, it's a bit far for that, don't you think? I expect we'll have to stay in a hotel and make a weekend of it. It'll be fun."

"Mum," Bertie says, sounding genuinely upset. "Listen to me. I don't want to go to Blackpool."

Victoria glances over at her son and rolls her eyes. "You've become such a bore, Bertie. I mean, I'm sure that's my fault. Nature or nurture, I suppose it still comes down to me. But you really have. Where's your sense of adventure?"

"I don't have one," Bertie says. "And nor do you, usually."

"Which exit here?" Victoria asks as they arrive at a busy roundabout.

"Third exit," Bertie says miserably. "A5. You know, you *could* just switch the sound on – on the GPS."

"I don't know how to," Victoria says. "So maybe you can do that for me."

"Mum, please," Bertie says, sounding almost tearful. "This is mad. Are you leaving Dad? Is that it?"

Victoria laughs. "Of course I'm not. Don't be so daft."

"What, then?"

"Oh, for God's sake," Victoria says. "All right. I wanted it to be a surprise, but all right. Do you know where the biggest, fastest roller-coaster is?"

"What?"

"In the country. Which town has the biggest fastest roller-coaster?"

Bertie shrugs. "Alton Towers, maybe?" he says. "But that's not in Blackpool, Mum."

"No, it's not in Alton Towers, sweetheart. It's called The Big One. And it's in Blackpool Pleasure Beach. Which, as the name suggests, is in…"

"Blackpool?"

"Very good."

"Oh," Bertie says. "And that's where we're going? Blackpool Pleasure Beach?"

"Yes," Victoria says. "That's where we're going. If you can just stop whinging and start map reading."

"Oh," Bertie says again, sounding less upset but still a little dubious. "OK."

"It goes at a hundred and something kilometres an hour," Victoria tells him. "Imagine that."

"Cool," Bertie says. "So, are you going to come on it, too?"

"You never know. I might."

"Wow."

"So, you see…?" Victoria says, now moving into the fast lane and accelerating.

"I mean, that's still a bit mad, Mum. To just suddenly decide to go to Blackpool. Just for a funfair thing."

"I know," Victoria says. "But like you said, it's cool too, right?"

"Yeah," Bertie concedes. "Yeah, it is kinda cool. But it's mainly still just mad."

* * *

As Sander drives her up the M2 motorway, Penny cries. Occasionally, unpredictably, the tears stop, and she attempts to phone her sister, then her nephew, yet again. But neither of them are answering their phones. It's most upsetting.

Martin, who she *has* spoken to, has promised to phone her back the second he finds out where his wife and son have vanished to. But that doesn't stop Penny calling him twice during the journey, just in case.

By the time they reach the halfway point, she feels all cried out and just sits, numbly, watching the countryside spin past. Occasionally she glances at her phone again to check, but the only text is from Will letting her know that he and Ben have arrived in Whitstable, and that the kids (who, still sleeping when they left, have not yet been told of their grandmother's death) are both fine. Which is at least one thing she doesn't have to worry about.

On arrival at Vivian Court, they are led into the manager's office and offered cups of horrible, bitter coffee.

"I *can* do this for you," Sander tells Penny for the third time. "You don't need to be here."

"She's my mother," Penny breathes. "Well, she was."

"OK," Sander says, reaching for Penny's hand.

"Don't do that," Penny says, snatching her hand away. "Don't be nice to me or I'll cry. And I need not to cry. At least until we're out of this horrible place."

"OK," Sander says. "You old monster."

"Do I look terrible?" Penny asks, fumbling in her bag for her compact. She removed her makeup in the car, but is suddenly unsure whether makeup-less red eyes are any better than panda-eyes.

"You look fine," Sander says. "That was just me not-being-nice as requested."

Mr White, the facility manager, a suited young man who looks more like an accountant than anything else, arrives with a second tray of coffees. "Oh, you already have coffee," he says. "Oh well." He slides the tray onto his desk next to the first,

201

identical one, and then takes a seat. "You *are* Mrs Thompson's daughter?" he asks.

Penny nods. "Yes," she says.

"I thought I remembered you," he says, even though they have never met before. "But I do have to check. It can be terrible in this job if you get people mixed up."

He explains that Marge's body, or Penny's "mother" as he still refers to her, has been transferred to the local hospital. "You'll have to go and... you know... visit her," he says vaguely.

"Visit her?" Penny repeats, suddenly grasping at a foolish hope that there's been some kind of mix up and sitting up straight in her chair.

"Yes, you'll have to, you know... identify the body, I'm afraid. It's procedure," he says. "I'm so sorry."

"Of course," Penny says, slumping back down, devastated anew. *You stupid man,* she thinks.

He asks if they would like to visit Marge's flat, an offer which Penny declines. "I'm not ready for that, I don't think," she says, her voice wobbling.

"And her things?" Sander asks. "Do we need to do anything about those today?"

Mr White shakes his head. "This is her key," he says, sliding an envelope across the desk towards them. "No one will go in there until you return this to us. It's her private space still."

Penny looks at Sander enquiringly. She can't even think what she might need to ask here.

"Um, how long do we have?" Sander asks. "To sort out her things?"

"As long as you want," Mr White tells them. "But the lease continues until you hand back this key. And as long as the lease continues then rent will accrue. Mrs Cunningham has been paying that, I believe."

"No, Mum paid it with her housing benefit," Penny corrects him.

"That didn't really cover it, I'm afraid," the man says. "So Mrs Cunningham has been paying the shortfall. And as her housing benefit will have ceased, of course, the whole amount will accrue. That's why most families try to get things sorted out within a few weeks."

Outside in the sunshine, Penny sits on a bench and weeps anew, while Sander tries yet again to phone Victoria.

"It's just not fair," Penny splutters as they start walking towards the car. "I shouldn't have to do this on my own."

"No," Sander says, sliding one arm around her shoulders. "You're right. You shouldn't. Still, *I'm* here."

"Yes," Penny says, managing the tiniest of smiles through her tears. "Thank God."

Once they reach the car, Sander asks, "So what now? Home? We don't have to go to the hospital today. We can come back tomorrow and do it with Vicky if you prefer."

Penny shakes her head. "No," she says. "Let's get it over with. Do you know how to get there?"

Sander taps at his smartphone screen. "Just looking now," he says, then, "Oh, that's easy. It's down the road."

It takes them just ten minutes to drive to St Mary's, and another ten to find the mortuary. The mortuary thing comes as a fresh shock to Penny. She has no idea why, but she had imagined seeing Marge in a hospital bed. Silly really, but shocking all the same.

A male nurse leads them to a vast, chilly room, and just like in *Dexter*, it contains a wall of metal drawers. He slides out number three-seventeen and pulls back the white sheet, and, as if playing a well studied role, Penny goes weak at the knees and collapses into Sander's arms.

As the death has been referred to the coroner, the nurse tells them, the body may not be released immediately, potentially not for two or three weeks.

Penny nods and thanks the young man, but takes in none of what he says. The whole scene feels surreal.

"I'm just realising," she tells Sander, as they step back out into the incongruous sunshine. "I have no idea how to do any of this."

"What's that?" Sander asks.

Penny shrugs. "Funerals. Wills. Any of it."

"We'll sort it out together," Sander says. "Don't worry."

"All the same," Penny says. "I'm sure there's loads of things we have to do."

"Sure," Sander says. "But you heard the man. We have a couple of weeks to do it all."

"Is that what he said?" Penny says. "I don't think I was listening."

"That's what he said," Sander confirms. "They're keeping the body for up to three weeks. So we have plenty of time to sort things out."

"I wonder why?"

"Why the delay?"

"Yes."

"Well, he said it's been referred to the coroner. So I suppose it's so they can... you know..." Sander pulls a face.

"So they can do a postmortem. Is that it?"

Sander nods.

"Yes, of course," Penny says. "I hate that idea."

"It may not come to that."

"I should know all of this. I talk about all this stuff every day. It's just... well..."

"It's different when it's your own family?"

"It really is," Penny says. She unexpectedly gasps, covering her mouth with one hand.

"What is it?" Sander asks, moving to her side.

Penny shakes her head slowly. A fresh batch of tears roll down her cheeks.

"What?" Sander asks again.

"I just realised," Penny says. "I've no parents left."

"Oh, babe."

"I... I don't know why. It just hit me," Penny says. "I hadn't thought about it."

They have reached the car, so Sander asks, "So what now? Home? Lunch maybe? Vicky's place?"

"I don't know," Penny says. "Maybe you can just hold me for a bit until we decide?"

"Of course," Sander says, opening his arms wide and embracing her. "And then food, I think. Despite it all, I'm starving."

• • •

As Victoria drives, Bertie alternates between feeling excited about riding The Big One and worrying about the incomprehensible change to their daily routine.

He'd feel a lot happier if his mother would at least give him his telephone back, if he could talk, even briefly, with his father. But she won't even let him use it to Google *The Big One*.

They stop, only once, at the Hilton Park service station. "So where do you want to eat?" Victoria asks.

"Burger King?" Bertie replies, testing whether his mother's character-shift extends as far as letting him eat junk food.

"Yes," Victoria says, confirming his worst fears. "Let's do that. I haven't had a burger for years. It'll be fun."

By the time they reach Blackpool seafront, it is two pm.

Victoria drives straight up to the first hotel she sees – the Hilton. "This will do," she declares.

"Can I have my phone back now?" Bertie asks, as they climb out of the car.

"No, you can't," his mother replies. "It will do you good to spend a few hours without being glued to a screen."

"But what if I want to take photos?"

"I'll take them on mine. And I swear that if you ask me one more time, I'll leave you in the hotel and go to the funfair on my own."

Bertie briefly considers the strategic advantages of being left alone at the hotel. He could use the hotel phone to call his father, after all. But it would be a shame to come to Blackpool and *not* go on The Big One. He can imagine his friends asking him about it and having to explain that he chose to stay in his room so he could phone his daddy. He feels ashamed just at the thought of it. It's not as if his mother's craziness is actually life threatening or anything.

"OK," he says. "Whatever. I only wanted to tell Dad where we are. He'll be worried."

"Oh, well, if that's all you're worried about," Victoria says, "then don't. I left him a note. He'll be fine. So relax."

Victoria chooses a family room because it has bunk beds. "You always wanted bunk beds," she tells Bertie. "Do you remember?"

"That was when I was five or something," he says. "And it was only because Max and Chloe had them."

But the room is bright and modern and the sea view is stunning, and despite his protestations otherwise, Bertie *is* vaguely excited about the idea of sleeping in the top bunk in a tower block.

"Do you want to have a shower and change or anything?" Victoria asks him as she stares out at the seascape.

"I'm fine," Bertie says. "Anyway, I didn't *bring* any clothes."

"No," Victoria replies, dreamily. "No, of course you didn't. We didn't know we were staying over, did we?"

Bertie climbs onto the top bunk and dangles his legs over the edge. From up here, the view from the window is quite vertiginous. He jumps down again and joins Victoria, still staring from the window.

"Are you all right, Mum?" he asks.

Victoria swivels her head to face him. "I'm sorry?" she says. "I was miles away."

"Are you all right?" Bertie asks again.

"Honestly?"

Bertie nods. "Honestly."

Victoria shrugs. "I don't know, honestly," she says. "But this is all fine, really, isn't it? So if I were you, I'd just roll with it. Make the most of it while it lasts."

Bertie nods. "OK," he says. "OK, I'll try."

They take a tram from the hotel to the funfair. Running straight along the seafront as it does, it's a gorgeous ride.

"I love the sea," Victoria says. "I always wanted to live by the sea."

"Like aunty Penny?"

"Yes. Well, we grew up by the seaside. You know that, right?"

"Yeah, in Margate," Bertie says. "I suppose Dad needs to be in London for his job, though."

"Yes," Victoria says. "Yes, I suppose he does."

"Did you really leave him a note? Does he really know where we are?"

"Yes, I told you I did."

"OK," Bertie says. But he knows that she is lying. She has never been able to lie convincingly about anything.

"Look," Victoria says, pointing. In front of the tram, to the left, the vast structure of the roller coaster is rising up before them.

"Wow," Bertie says. "Awesome."

"It's certainly big."

"Are you really going on it with me?"

Victoria pulls a face. "Maybe," she says. "Maybe not."

It's a sunny, August weekend, so they have to queue for fifteen minutes to buy day passes, yet once inside, the park is surprisingly calm.

"It fills up later, about four," a man tells them when Victoria comments on this.

Bertie heads straight for The Big One, which also has the longest queue. He's so excited about the ride that by the time they reach the gates, he has completely forgotten the unorthodox nature of their day-trip. "So, are you coming,

Mum?" he asks, just as a train thunders down the first hill, and the occupants all scream.

Victoria grimaces. "Would you mind terribly if I sit this one out?" she says. "I think I'd like to warm up on something a bit gentler. I haven't been on anything like this for years."

"No worries," Bertie tells her. "We can do it again, later. Together."

Victoria kisses him on the cheek and steps out of the queue. "Be brave," she says. "You can tell me all about it. I'll take photos."

She weaves her way behind the barriers, and then walks to a bench where she sits. She waves to Bertie as his train trundles away. He looks radiant and she remembers him at five years old, looking exactly like this, one Christmas morning.

Once he is out of sight, she pulls her phone from her bag and switches it on. She has seventeen voicemails and twenty three text messages, but she doesn't consult any of them. Instead, she sends a short, simple text message to Martin.

"Don't worry," she types. "I'm with Bertie, and we're fine. I just needed to get away for twenty-four hours. I'll see you tomorrow."

Bertie, in the carriage, now clankingly ascending to the summit, attempts to borrow his neighbour's smartphone so that he too can text his father.

But the girl, a fifteen-year-old with bleached blond hair isn't having it. "Bog off," she tells him. "You'll just drop it or sommat."

"But I need to send my dad a text," Bertie protests. "It's urgent."

"Sorry," the girl says, then, "God, I'm shittin' a brick 'ere."

And when Bertie looks down at his tiny mother on the bench below, he forgets about texting Martin instantly. "Me too," he says. "Me too."

Bertie rides the Big One four times that afternoon, as well as managing to ride on almost every other ride in the park.

Surprisingly, of all the attractions, the one which scares him the most is the theoretically tame *Wild Mouse*. It's not the speed or the height of the ride which makes it the most fear-inducing in the end, but its rickety, ancient nature. It feels as if the car could jerk off the track at any minute.

"Now, you see," Victoria says, as she clambers out of the car, shaking, "that's quite enough excitement for me."

"It was pretty scary, Mum," Bertie admits. "You should try The Big One. Really, you should. It feels way safer than that thing."

"No," Victoria says, definitively. "No, I don't think so."

It is half-past six when they return to the hotel.

"I just need to lie down for half an hour, and then we can go out and find somewhere for dinner," Victoria says. She discreetly popped a Valium after the Wild Mouse, and is feeling suddenly sleepy.

"Fish and chips?" Bertie suggests.

"If you want."

"Can I have my phone, then?" Bertie asks, as they pass into the lobby. "Just so I've got something to do while you sleep."

"No," Victoria says. "You can watch television if you're–" She freezes. Because there, in the lobby, is Martin. He has his legs crossed, and he's reading a newspaper.

Bertie follows her gaze and then shouts, "Dad!" and runs to join him with unusual enthusiasm.

"Hello!" Martin says, standing and ruffling Bertie's hair.

"So Mum really did leave you a note," Bertie says. "I didn't believe her."

"A note?" Martin repeats, then, "Oh, yes. Of course."

"Hello," Victoria says, stopping a few meters from her husband and crossing her arms. "This is a surprise."

"I thought I'd join you," Martin says. "You made it sound so much fun in your *note*. It seemed too good to miss."

"Here," Victoria says, uncrossing her arms and fumbling in her handbag for the room key. "Take this and we'll see you up there."

"OK, but..."

"Just do it, Bertie."

"But can I have..."

"Bertie!" she says, raising her voice.

"OK, OK," Bertie says. "God, I only wanted to phone Dad, anyway."

"Here, come and sit down," Martin says, once Bertie has left them alone. He returns to the sofa and pats the space beside him. But Victoria takes the armchair to his left, instead.

"So what's going on, hon?" Martin asks.

"I don't know," Victoria says. "How did you find us?"

"Bertie's phone," Martin tells her.

Victoria frowns and shakes her head. "His phone?"

"It has a function. It's called *Find My iPhone*. It's in case you lose it. It shows you where it is on a map."

"But it's in the car outside."

"I know. I saw it was next to this place and I phoned them. And they confirmed that you were here. So here I am."

"Really?"

"Really. Modern technology, huh?"

"And you... what... rented a car?"

"Train," Martin says. "It's quicker. Only three hours."

"I see."

"Did you not *want* to be found?"

"Apparently not," Victoria says. "Seeing as I *didn't* leave you a note."

"May I ask why?" Martin asks.

Victoria shrugs.

"Is this to do with... I mean... I take it you know. I take it you've listened to at least some of your messages."

"Yes," Victoria says. "Yes, they phoned this morning. Just after you left for work. Vivian Court. They phoned me first thing."

"And how are you feeling?"

"I don't know," Victoria says. "How are *you* feeling?"

"Mainly worried about you."

"Worried?"

"Yes, you don't seem yourself to me."

"Don't I?"

"No, you don't."

"OK then," Victoria says. "Who do I seem like?"

"Running off to Blackpool is not the most obvious choice of action when..."

"When my mother dies?"

"Exactly."

"OK," Victoria says.

"OK?"

"Look, Martin. Here's an idea," Victoria says, sounding exasperated. "Why don't you tell me how I'm supposed to react, and then I can just try to fulfil everybody's expectations, OK? Because I'm at a bit of a loss, here."

"It's not about expectations," Martin says. "It's about..."

"Yes?"

"It's... Well, I think you're having some kind of breakdown to be honest, honey."

Victoria sighs and looks down at her hands. She fiddles with a cuticle for a moment, then says, "Maybe I am. It's possible. I mean, how would I know?"

"Honey..." Martin says. "Listen..."

"And then again," Victoria continues. "Maybe I'm not. Maybe I just don't care."

"You don't *care*?"

"Yes. Maybe I just don't care. Maybe I actually feel relieved. And maybe I just needed a little space to try and work out why that might be. Still, that's not happening now, is it?"

* * *

Penny hangs up the phone and pulls it to her chest. She closes her eyes and sighs deeply.

"You OK?" Sander asks, on entering the kitchen.

Penny reopens them and sighs again. "Yes. They've been found. Everyone's OK. And the kids?"

"Sad... upset... you know."

"Normal upset, or ... ?"

Sander nods. "Chloe's crying a bit. Max is more... more like angry, really."

"Good," Penny says. "They need to let it out, one way or another."

"So, they've been found, where? Was that Victoria on the phone?"

Penny shakes her head and glances at the handset before putting it down. "Oh, no," she says. "No, that was Martin. You're not going to believe this."

"Why?"

"He found them in Blackpool."

"Blackpool?"

"Uh huh."

"Up by Liverpool?"

"It's closer to Manchester. And Preston, I think. But yeah."

"What the fuck are they doing in Blackpool?"

Penny stares into the middle distance and shakes her head slowly. She's trying to imagine the scene – she's trying to make it make sense. "She took Bertie to the funfair, apparently."

"I'm sorry?"

"You have to stop making me say everything twice, sweetheart. I'm too tired for it. She took him to the funfair. In Blackpool."

"So, she didn't even know?"

Penny snorts sadly. "Oh, yes, she knew, all right. She got the message first thing this morning. And then she put Bertie in the car and drove him to Blackpool."

"But that's..."

"Crazy?"

"Well, yeah."

"You're right. It is. Martin thinks she's in shock. And it sounds like a pretty good diagnosis to me. Still, at least they're OK, I suppose."

"And they're still there? In Blackpool?"

Penny nods gently. "Martin's staying with them – she booked them into the Hilton apparently – and then he's driving them back tomorrow. He's going to tell Bertie about..."

She clears her throat before continuing. "He's going to tell Bertie about Mum after dinner. And then I suggested he take her to see someone tomorrow."

"Who? Oh, a shrink? Does Victoria *have* a shrink?"

"I don't think so," Penny says. "But I think she needs one."

"I think she does, too," Sander says, now joining Penny and resting one hand lightly on her arm. "She's taking it really badly, then?"

Penny shrugs. "I don't know," she says. "It's a funny one, isn't it? I mean, Martin says she's absolutely fine. A bit too glazed and a bit too happy, but otherwise fine. So I suppose we have to deduce that she's not fine at all. Because being fine isn't really a normal reaction, is it?"

"Maybe she's in denial," Sander says. "You're always going on about people being in denial."

"Yes, it will be something like that, I expect."

"Are you worried about her?"

Penny pouts and shakes her head. "No," she says, her voice cracking a little. "No, I think I'm too upset about Mum to care about Vicky right now. I don't think I have any space left. You know, in my heart."

"Did you actually speak to her?"

Penny shakes her head. "She didn't want to speak to me. And Martin says there's no point anyway. She's too out of it to be any use. But there's plenty of time, isn't there?"

At that moment, the back door opens and Will and Ben appear. "Hey," Will says. "You OK?"

"Just about," Penny offers, smiling vaguely.

"Posh got found," Sander tells them. "Up in Blackpool."

"Blackpool?!" Will exclaims.

And so Penny tells the whole story again.

When she has finished, Ben says, "So, we've been talking, Will and I, and I think we should go. I don't think you want us here right now. Not at a time like this."

"Don't be silly," Penny says. "It's nice that you're here. And anyway, it's too late."

"It isn't. We can leave now and still be home by ten," Ben says, glancing at his watch.

"No, please stay. I'd like you to stay."

"See," Will says, addressing Ben. Then to Penny, he continues, "In that case, I thought we'd go and get some dinner. The options are what? Fish and chips?"

"Fish and chips from the place you know," Sander replies. "Um, Chinese. There are a couple of places that do Chinese. There's an Indian on Oxford Street. Or pizza from the High Street."

"They're all too expensive," Penny says. "I've got plenty of stuff in the freezer."

"This is our treat," Will says, looking back at Ben. "Isn't it?"

"Absolutely," Ben says.

"I'm not hungry anyway," Penny tells them. "So..."

"But which option are you the least not hungry for?" Will asks. "Chinese? You like Chinese, don't you? You love a bit of MSG."

Penny shrugs. "I'm really not hungry," she says. "Ask the kids. See what they want."

"The kids will say pizza," Sander informs them.

"But what about you?"

"Chinese or Indian," Sander says. "But the kids will say pizza. They always say pizza."

"We can manage both, can't we?" Will asks Ben. "Chinese and pizza?"

"Definitely," Ben says.

"Then, I could perhaps manage a mushroom chop suey," Penny says, doubtfully. "If you're definitely going there anyway."

Once Will and Ben have left, Sander takes Penny's hand and leads her to his studio where he pulls his dope box from the shelf.

Penny crosses to the window and stares out at the sea, lit orange by the setting sun.

She remembers being little and asking her mother why the sky turned pink at sunset. "Because it's pretty," Marge had told her. "They made it pink because it's pretty." And she had imagined a team of painters, like the men who were at that time painting the seafront railings, having a meeting to decide the best colour.

When Sander taps her on the shoulder, she jumps, then turns to face him. Seeing the tears in her eyes, he wraps his arms around her.

"It was just too soon," Penny tells him. "I wasn't ready."

"I know," Sander replies. "I know, babe. Here. Have a smoke."

"Thanks," Penny says, "but not today."

"Really? I thought..."

Penny shakes her head. "It hurts, but, you know, that's normal. I *want* to feel this. It's... it's a process."

"OK," Sander says, adding guiltily, "You know, this is my first. I haven't smoked all day."

"God, that's true," Penny says. "I didn't notice."

"I try so hard," Sander says, his voice expressing irony. "But nobody ever notices."

"Well, I have kind of had other things to think about, today, Sander," Penny says, brushing a lone tear from her cheek.

* * *

One week to the day after Marge's death, the coroner releases the body. She died, it has been established, from a massive hemorrhagic stroke.

Having googled the subject extensively, Penny suspects that this could logically have resulted from the multiple blood thinners Marge was prescribed after her previous stroke. Were she American, she would probably attempt to sue someone. But she knows that the anti-coagulants were a logical choice after Marge's blood clot, and she has no desire to make life more difficult for any of the lovely NHS staff who treated her, so she mentions her findings to no-one. Money and blame won't bring her mum back anyway.

She thinks about all of this and tries to imagine a suitable funeral as she drives up the M2 in the pouring rain. She worries, too, how her meeting with Victoria will go. It will be the first time she has seen her since their mother died, the first time they have even spoken, in fact, since their argument the previous October. She imagines them hugging and weeping together. She imagines Marge's death being the thing that brings them back together. But she suspects she's guilty of wishful thinking, especially as Martin has warned her that she is still "pretty strange."

By the time she arrives in Maida Vale, the rain has stopped, but the sky is still dark, the streets are wet, and, for August, it's shockingly cold.

She leaves the car in a car park (it's a stunning eight pounds for two hours) and then heads to her sister's flat.

Victoria buzzes her in immediately, which is at least something. She had fully imagined a scenario whereby she would have to go on to the funeral parlour on her own because her sister had absconded to Blackpool again. Or some other "fun" destination.

When she reaches the top floor, the door is ajar, so she lets herself in.

"I'm in the loo," Victoria calls out. "I won't be a moment."

Penny hangs her raincoat on the coat-stand and walks through to the airy kitchen. She moves to the window and looks out over the rooftops.

"Sorry about that," Victoria says, and Penny turns to face her.

"It's fine," Penny replies. "I was just looking at your view. It looks quite stormy over there. It's all purple – quite pretty actually."

"It's not much compared with your view," Victoria replies. "Cup of tea?"

Penny nods and takes a seat at the kitchen table. So they aren't going to embrace, she realises. Or at least, not yet.

"So how have you been?" Victoria asks as she fills the kettle.

Penny frowns. "Since October? Or since Mum died?"

"Either. Both."

"OK, I suppose," Penny says. "I'm coping. Just about. You?"

"I'm fine," Victoria says. "You know, the usual."

"Nice kitchen," Penny comments, "I like it."

"Thanks," Victoria replies, stepping back to reappraise it herself.

Penny opens her mouth to say something about the new washing machine but then closes it again. They have more important things to talk about today, but she can't work out how to get there. It's as if Victoria has built a business-as-usual wall she can't break through.

After a moment's reflection, she stands and crosses to Victoria's side, intentionally invading her personal space. She reaches out and touches Victoria's arm. "So how have you *really* been?" she asks.

Victoria looks at her confusedly. "I've *really* been fine," she says, using the excuse of fetching teabags to break away.

"Vicky," Penny says. "You *can't* be. Not really."

"Um?" Victoria replies, then, "What can't I be?"

"Fine."

"Because Marge died?"

Penny chews at a fingernail. She can't remember Victoria ever calling their mother Marge. She has always been "Mum." She's struggling not to slip into professional counselling mode. She wanted to keep this honest and intimate and personal and shared. But it's hard. Because Victoria truly is still *pretty strange*. "Oh, come on," she says. "This is me you're talking to. She was your... she was *our* only remaining parent."

"I know," Victoria says. "Everyone keeps telling me that I can't feel OK about that, but I do. I started seeing someone. Did you know that? Of course you know that. Martin tells everyone everything."

"No, I didn't know," Penny lies. "Who are you seeing?"

"A psychiatrist. He's ancient. Nice, but ancient. Anyway, he spent the first two sessions telling me I was in shock. And then yesterday he agreed that I might not be after all."

"Were you somehow expecting it?" Penny asks. "Is that it?"

"Her death?"

"Yes."

"Well, we all knew she'd die eventually, didn't we?" Victoria says as she dunks the teabags. "We all knew she wasn't going to go on forever."

"That's true," Penny says. "But all the same."

Victoria shrugs and places the two mugs in the middle of the table, then returns to the refrigerator for milk. "So the funeral," she says. "That's what you're here for, isn't it?"

"Yes... well, no," Penny says. "I'm here to see you, mainly."

"OK. Well, here I am," Victoria says. She says it in such a neutral manner that Penny really doesn't know how to take it.

"But yes," Penny says, "we *do* need to talk about the funeral. In fact we need to go there. In an hour. I thought cremation. I mean, I don't feel like I need somewhere to visit her, do you? And burial is crazy expensive."

Victoria shakes her head.

"And an open casket thing would be difficult of course."

"Because?"

"Because of the postmortem."

Victoria pulls a face.

"I know... So, cremation?"

"Sure."

"And the service. C of E, or...?"

"I don't think Mum believed in God."

"No, but..."

"I mean, she never mentioned God. Well, except when she was swearing."

"It's just that otherwise," Penny says, "the service might be a bit... you know... empty."

Victoria shrugs. "Just do it how you want," she says.

Penny's eyes are beginning to water, now. This is just too hard to bear alone, and she does feel as if she's truly bearing it alone. She pinches the bridge of her nose for a moment before continuing. "There's no will. So everything just gets divided up between us."

"Fine," Victoria says. "She didn't have anything anyway."

"She has a savings account," Penny says. "Had. It's got ninety thousand in it. From the sale of the house, I suppose."

"Ninety thousand?" Victoria exclaims. "God, the cow!"

"Vicky," Penny whines. "Please."

"You know she had us paying for everything, right? Because she was supposedly broke?"

"I didn't know that actually. I mean, they told me, at Vivian Court, last week. But I didn't know until then."

"We paid half her rent, we paid her rates, her TV licence... we paid everything."

"Perhaps she wanted to save it for us?" Penny offers, doubtfully.

"Well, it's a funny way of doing it," Victoria says.

"Yes. I suppose it is," Penny agrees, sipping at her tea. "Look," she adds. "Can you help me out a bit, here?"

Victoria looks surprised. "Help you? What with?"

"I don't know," Penny says. "Our mum's dead. A little bit of emotion wouldn't go amiss."

"Emotion?" Victoria says.

"Yes. Emotion! Oh, come on, Sis, I know you're upset. *You* know you're upset. What's all this... I don't know... this... *pretending?* Why are you pretending to be fine?"

"Do you want me to fake something? Is that it? I can cry if you want."

"Vicky," Penny pleads. "I don't understand."

"It's because you're not listening. As usual."

"That's not fair, but... OK. I'm listening," Penny says. "So tell me."

"It's not what you want to hear, believe me."

"OK. But tell me anyway."

"I've worked through all of this with Doctor Muller."

"Doctor Muller?"

"Yes, he's Austrian. Like Freud."

"Okay..."

"I've been through all of this, and I'm pretty certain I'm being honest with myself. I know nobody believes me, but I am."

"Right. So?"

"And I just don't care. That she's dead, I mean. I've looked deep inside myself, and I just can't identify anything that feels like giving a damn. Does that make me a monster? Maybe. But it's true."

"But you were so close," Penny protests, her eyes starting to tear.

"Maybe we weren't," Victoria says. "Maybe that was me pretending."

"Really?" Penny says. "Was it? Did you feel like you were pretending? When you had her over for dinner twice a week? When you took her shopping? When you filled her fridge with food? When you nursed her after the stroke? When you spent a whole week looking for that bloody turquoise cardigan she wanted?"

"I don't know," Victoria admits. "I honestly don't know. But I think I was just on... just on a sort of autopilot, really."

Penny pinches her nose and breathes into the palm of her hand. She peers at her sister opposite and tries to understand. "You see," she finally says, caressing her brow. "That just doesn't make any sense to me. Not personally *or* professionally. I'm listening. I really am. And I'm trying to understand. But it just doesn't make any sense to me."

"What's new?" Victoria says.

"What's that supposed to mean?"

"Perhaps I *am* the cold, selfish person you accused me of being the last time I visited you."

"Oh, Vicky!" Penny protests. "Are you still holding on to *that*?"

"Why wouldn't I be? My only sister calling me a selfish bitch... it's not that easily forgotten."

"We both said things we didn't mean that day," Penny says, softly. "You know that. It was just a silly, childish argument."

Victoria sips her tea and shakes her head gently. "Was it?" she says. "Was it really?"

"Of course it was. But, look... I'm sorry, OK? If that helps, I'm sorry. I don't think you're a selfish bitch at all. They were just... just random words. I say things I don't mean when I'm angry. We all do."

"Hum, well, thanks for the apology, anyway."

"But that's no reason to... I mean... today we need to talk about Mum. And I just don't believe that you don't have *any* emotional reaction to it. Even you must see that that's... unlikely. Don't you?"

Victoria licks her lips, then turns away to look out of the window. It's starting to spot with rain again. Penny waits for her to continue, then, after almost a minute, she touches her on the arm. When Victoria turns back, her eyes are watering.

Finally, Penny thinks. "You see," she says. "You just don't want to let yourself feel anything. But it's not healthy to keep it all bottled up, trust me. I had this Syrian woman in my office the other day and she described it – rather beautifully, I thought – as a bottle of–"

"It's not what you think," Victoria interrupts. She's clearly not interested in Penny's analogy. "That's the thing."

Penny cocks her head and reaches out for her sister's wrist but she pulls it away. "What isn't?"

Victoria sniffs and dabs at the corner of one eye with her finger. "This," she says.

"Of course it is. And that's fine. I'm just glad to see that you're alive in there."

"Alive?"

"Yes. And capable of some emotion. You've been so controlled about this. So cold."

Victoria laughs sourly. "You don't want to hear this, Penny," she says. "So just leave, will you? Can you do that for me? Can you just leave before I say something I might regret?"

"But there's nothing you could say that I wouldn't want to hear," Penny tells her. "You're my sister, and I love you. And no, I won't leave. I can't leave anyway, because we have to go to the funeral parlour together."

"I'm not coming," Victoria says. "So just do it how you want. I don't care."

"But I told them you'd come. I came by car so I could drive us both there. We have an appointment. To choose the coffin and the flowers and everything."

"I don't mean today," Victoria says. "I mean, I'm not coming today *either*, obviously. But no, I meant the funeral. So it doesn't matter. Just do it how you want."

Penny frowns deeply. "I don't understand," she says.

"Which bit?" Victoria replies, sharply.

"You're saying you're not coming to the funeral *at all*?"

"That's right."

"Oh, this is madness," Penny says. "I'm not sure what's going on with you, but this is absolute madness."

"Oh, please leave," Victoria says, sounding exasperated.

"What?"

"Please. Leave. My. House," she repeats, pointing at the door. "I want to be alone now."

"No," Penny says. "I won't leave. I'm not going anywhere until you tell me what the hell is going on."

"Please, Penny."

"No. No, I won't."

Victoria sighs and looks outside again. "OK, you've asked for this," she says, turning back, looking suddenly pink and angry. "You want to know what's going on? You want me to get emotional. You really want to know what's going on in this head of mine, do you?"

"Yes," Penny insists. "Yes, I do."

"Good. OK. Well, I'm glad she's dead."

Tears spring instantly to Penny's eyes, clouding her vision. Her chest feels tight as if her heart is about to burst. "But Victoria..." she pleads.

"I am. I'm *glad* she's dead. I feel liberated," Victoria says, tears running down her own cheeks now. "That's how I feel. I *hated* her. I didn't realise it because I couldn't let myself realise it. Because it was... I don't know, like a tautology, or something. Hating your mother. That's impossible, right? But I did. I hated her. And I'm glad she's dead. And the first thing I thought when they called me, the first emotion I felt when Vivian Court phoned, was joy. It's not what I expected, but it is what happened. I thought, *I'm free. Finally, I'm free. She's dead. And thank God for that.*"

Penny is crying freely now. It makes it difficult to speak. She rummages in her handbag for a tissue, but can't find one. A brief scan of the kitchen has not revealed any kitchen roll to hand either. "But that doesn't... I mean... why?" she splutters.

"Not listening again," Victoria says. "You see?"

"But I *am* listening. It just doesn't make sense."

"Because I *hated* her. I couldn't let myself admit it when she was alive, but I couldn't stand the woman. I've hated her since I was *eight*."

"But that's just not true. You're rewriting history," Penny whimpers. "I don't know why you're doing this... well, I do actually – you're just scared of what you'll feel if you let yourself realise. She's gone, Victoria. Our mother. She's gone."

Victoria snorts. She crosses to a wall cabinet and returns with a roll of kitchen paper from which she rips a sheet before plonking it in the middle of the table. "Here," she says, then, "I knew that there was no point. I knew you'd be like this."

"But you were closer to her than I was," Penny insists. "You saw her all the time. You paid for everything, like you said. You looked after her. You worried about her."

"Yes, I did," Victoria says, sounding angry again. "You went swanning off to the seaside and left me to do it all. So I did it. But now it's your turn, OK?"

"My turn?"

"Yes. So please. We'll pay for... whatever. If that's what you need. We'll pay. But just leave me out of the whole thing, OK? Just do it however you want and let me know when it's over."

"You're really not coming?" Penny whimpers, a fresh batch of tears rising up.

"Sorry, Sis," Victoria says. "But no. I'm not."

"But why?" Penny asks, shaking her head dolefully. "I still don't get it."

"Because no one wants to hear what I have to say about her," Victoria says quietly. "And you can trust me on that one."

On the way to the funeral parlour, Penny is forced to pull over. She can't see the GPS for her tears, let alone the traffic beyond the windscreen.

She bumps the car up the kerb and cries freely for a minute. It's only when the tears have subsided that she realises she's on a red route. She also happens to have stopped right in front of a video camera. The fine will no doubt follow shortly. "Brilliant," she sniffs. "Bloody brilliant."

It is late afternoon when she gets home and Sander is cooking. "Hello," she says. "Something smells nice."

Sander wipes his hands upon his apron. It has a bra and panties printed on it and he looks utterly ridiculous. "Curry," he says. "Chickpea curry. I was going to make prawn curry, but we're out of prawns."

"They were a bit expensive," Penny says. "Anyway, your chickpea curry is lovely. Plus it's been ages since we had that."

"I know," Sander says, returning to stirring the frying vegetables. "That's why. So how was it? Horrible?"

"The funeral parlour was OK, I suppose. It looked like the one in... what was that series called?"

"Six Feet Under?"

"That's the one. It looked exactly like that. I was so spaced out by the time I got there... I just randomly said yes and no to things, really. It's all madly expensive. But they can get paid straight from Mum's bank account, so at least we don't have to worry about that."

Penny hesitates for a few seconds before continuing. She does this every time she catches herself referring to her mother's this, or her mother's that. It sounds like a grammatical error. It sounds as if she hasn't accepted her death or something. And yet it's not her mother's *old* bank account, either, is it? Her *old* mother's bank account, perhaps? She shivers.

"Barclays – her bank – I went there too, they said they'll make an exception to pay funeral expenses. I had to go to the register offices to register the death as well. The woman there was totally incompetent. It was like a bloody Monty Python sketch. It took her forever. I've never seen anyone type so slowly."

"You say 'I,'" Sander says, frowning at his frying pan. "Where was Posh during all of this?"

"Oh, she didn't come," Penny says, lightly.

"What, to the register place?"

"To any of it. She's not coming to the funeral either. Or so she claims."

"She isn't? Why?"

Penny shakes her head and sinks into one of the dining room chairs. "Pour me a glass of wine – a big fuck-off glass of wine – and I'll tell you all about it."

When she has emptied the glass of its contents and recounted her story, Sander shakes his head despondently. "Wow," he says, simply. "Just, wow."

"I suppose we do have to have a funeral, do we?" Penny asks. "I didn't really stop to wonder if it was even necessary. I mean, it's not like anyone's going to be there."

"We'll be there," Sander says. "And Martin and Bertie, I would think."

"If she lets them."

"Oh, I don't think Martin ever needed Victoria to let him do anything," Sander says. "Then again... And I called around like you asked. Three people are coming from that place where she lived."

"Vivian Court?"

"Yeah. And her neighbour from Margate. Mrs Michaels?"

"Aww, Mrs Michaels," Penny says, cutely. "Bless. She made the world's best fairy cakes. They used to have those little silver balls on them. The ones that break your teeth."

"Well, she's coming if her son can drive her. She's a bit old to travel up on her own, apparently."

"I'll bet. She was old when I was little, so... Was it Peter? The son's name?"

"She didn't say," Sander says. "Oh, and Cecil. I think I found your uncle Cecil."

"Really?" Penny says, sitting up straight. "Are you sure?"

"I think so. There's a Cecil Stone on Facebook who looks about the right age. He lives in Orpington. Does that sound about right?"

"I'd need to see a photo. But it might be. He lived on the outskirts of London. That's all I remember, really."

"I wrote to him. On Facebook. To ask if it's him," Sander says. "So, we'll see."

"He's a bit old to be on Facebook, isn't he?" Penny says.

"Maybe he's a silver surfer," Sander says as he opens a tin of chickpeas and tips them into the pan.

"Even if it *is* him, he might not come," Penny says. "I mean, they definitely fell out about something."

"Maybe we'll find out why."

"Maybe," Penny agrees. "You know, Vicky said a strange thing. She was in full flow and–"

"Full flow?"

"Yes. She went off on a bit of a rant. She wouldn't say anything for ages, and then she suddenly lost it and got all shouty on me. And she said, in the middle of all that other stuff, that she has hated Mum since she was eight."

"Which is when Ed died, right?"

"Exactly."

"Any ideas?" Sander asks.

Penny shrugs and shakes her head. "I didn't think to ask," she says. "It didn't really register until afterwards when I was in the car." Sander has reached for the potato masher and is crushing some of the chickpeas in the pan. "Sorry, why do you do that?" Penny asks him. "Why do you squash them like that?"

"It makes it taste better," Sander says. "It gives it a better texture."

"Fair enough."

"Are you going to ask her?"

"Ask Victoria what happened when she was eight?"

"Yes."

Penny sighs. "Not right now," she says. "I don't think I have the energy for another dose of my sister. It was pretty full-on."

"I can imagine."

Penny's phone vibrates in her pocket, so she wriggles in her seat and pulls it out. "Is Chloe at Matilda's? Only she wants a lift home."

"Yes," Sander replies. "Do you want me to go?"

Penny nods. "I'm shattered," she says.

"Tell her I'll be there in half an hour," Sander says. "As soon as I've finished this, I'll go."

"You haven't been smoking?"

"Not yet," Sander replies. "Good, aren't I?"

"Very. I'm impressed."

"Me too," Sander says, then, "I suppose Cecil might know. If it is him."

"I'm sorry?"

"What happened to upset Posh. I mean, I'm assuming these things are all related."

"I'm guessing they must be," Penny says.

"That was some Christmas, huh?"

"Oh yeah," Penny confirms. "That was some Christmas. I was remembering in the car, actually. Mum *was* kind of strange with Vicky after Ed died."

"Strange?"

"Yes. She was upset, obviously. She was devastated, really. But she was... well, she was nasty to her, really. To Vicky. Ed was sort of her favourite. Actually, he was *totally* her favourite – there was never any doubt about that. But when he died, it was as if Vicky got passed over. It all somehow came to me. I think I became the favourite, after that. I never stopped to think why before."

"Hum," Sander says. "Well, that would explain a lot."

"About?"

"About your relationship with your sister. I mean, if she grew up feeling jealous of you. Because you got all the attention."

"Perhaps," Penny says. "I'm not sure, really. I was way too young to remember much. But I do remember Mum being sort of *off* with Vicky. So maybe something else did happen."

• • •

Mrs Michaels had produced a plate of her famed fairy cakes that day. It seems incongruous, thinking about it now, to have offered around a plate of pretty fairy cakes at a moment like that, but Mrs Michaels always seemed to have a freshly cooked batch of cakes to hand, and the day Ed fell was no exception. Thinking back on it now, Penny realises that they had probably been baked as a Christmas treat.

Anyway, Penny had sat eating hers, picking the silver balls from the icing and one by one crunching them between her teeth while Marge (who refused the offer of a cake) sat and cried, and Vicky, still white as a sheet, stared silently at hers.

Eventually – for it seemed like forever, time passed slowly that day – Mr Michaels came back. "There," he said, softly. "All spic and span." And that had been enough to set Marge off again. She had wept for another half an hour.

"We should go," she had said when she had calmed down enough to speak. "Thanks. Thanks for everything."

"Are you sure?" Mrs Michaels said, wringing her hands. "You can stay as long as you need. You can stay the night if you want."

"No," Marge insisted. "No, the girls will sleep better in their own beds. And it's like getting back on a 'orse, isn't it? If we don't go back now..." And so they returned to their own house which suddenly smelt of bleach.

Leaving Vicky staring strangely up the staircase, Penny stepped back into the lounge where the tree reminded her that it was still Christmas. Some of the gifts were Ed's and she remembers wondering whether they would get to open them for him, or whether they would have to wait for his return to see the contents.

The doctor had arrived just then, and had taken Marge to the dining room, where he spoke so softly that they couldn't hear what he said. There was a lot of whispering in the weeks to come, there were many secret conversations. The doctor had given Marge an injection to calm her down, but it had made her incredibly sleepy instead.

"Look after your sister," she had instructed Vicky, sharply. "I'm off for a cat-nap." But it would be no cat-nap. She would sleep solidly until the next day.

Once her mother was gone, Penny had crossed the room to the tree where she sat cross legged. As she squeezed the packages one by one, she expected Vicky to tell her off, but she had just watched silently, her expression glazed.

When she had finished squeezing all of the smaller packages, she lifted the largest box of all. "Is this Ed's train thing?" she asked.

Vicky nodded in reply.

"Will we open it for him?" Penny asked. "Or take it to the hospital?"

Vicky frowned then.

"I think we should take it there."

"He's gone, Sis," Vicky whispered.

"I know," Penny replied. "But when they've stitched him, he might need it or something."

Andy, the little ginger boy at playgroup had fallen from the climbing frame just two months before. He too had been wheeled off on a stretcher. But other than a few angry stitch marks across his forehead, he was fine now.

"He's dead, Penny," Vicky explained. "He's gone to heaven."

Penny frowned then as she attempted to concentrate on thinking about this new concept. She stared at the pretty holly packaging on Ed's gift, and tried to work out what Vicky was telling her. "Isn't he coming back *ever*?" she asked, tears starting to form.

Vicky shook her head very slowly.

"Is it my fault?" Penny asked. "Is it because I didn't get Cecil?"

Again Vicky shook her head. "No," she said, quietly. "No, Cecil would have made everything worse."

• • •

Penny had wondered then, as she wonders now, just what her sister meant by that. For how could anyone's presence have made anything worse that day?

She was too young to understand what was happening. She was too young to fully understand what death meant. But Victoria understood.

Despite her elder sister's reassurance, Penny continued to feel responsible, or at the very least, *partly* responsible for Ed's death. For who could say for sure that the presence of a calmer, more cool-headed adult than her mother mightn't have saved Ed's life as he lay there, as his lifeblood pooled away from him onto the tiled hall floor?

In fact, Penny realises, she *still* feels guilty about not having done as she was told.

Nowadays, being an adult, she can, of course, reason with herself. The logical part of her brain can inform the emotional part that there is nothing Cecil could have done.

But so many mysteries remain.

Penny is forced to take a week off work. Her boss is very sweet about this, but Penny feels horribly guilty all the same. In a job like hers, you simply can't take time off without knowing that you're letting down the most vulnerable of people. But there are so many things to be done when someone dies that there's really no other option. And as Victoria is demonstrating her expertise in the art of passive resistance – she does not answer her phone and only responds to voicemail or text messages once it's too late – it all falls to Penny. So she travels up and down to London on the train, collecting copies of death certificates here and delivering them via the Underground to bank managers, solicitors, and undertakers there.

It's madness really that society expects a newly bereaved person to jump through so many hoops. Perhaps, Penny thinks, the whole process has been designed to take one's mind off the loss. Or perhaps it's been designed, rather, to hammer home that loss – it can seem so hard sometimes to truly integrate the fact that someone has died.

Penny is supposed to be an expert on bereavement, of course. It was a part, a large part, of her training. But never having gone through the process herself – or at least, never when she was old enough to understand it – she's discovering aspects that she never thought about before. She's discovering, for example, that the human brain expects permanence. The cup is where you put it. The car is where you parked it (if it hasn't been towed away). The wine is still in the refrigerator where you left it. It's only people, the most complex, important, influential, life-changing elements of our lives, who are there and then are shockingly not-there. And it's surprisingly hard to get one's brain around that.

So she wakes up every morning, and, just for a second, she doesn't know that Marge is dead. She forgets and, momentarily, she wants to phone her. She pulls a recipe book from the shelf and sees the recipe that her mother likes so much and thinks that she'll make it the next time she comes down. Time and time again she has to remind herself that she's dead, that's she's gone, vanished, that she'll never be seen again.

There's a new awareness of the absolute nature of oblivion, too, an understanding, a sensation, almost, that we're all heading that way. These are concepts that we all, as adults, understand. We know that we shall die. But Penny has never understood it physically before. She has never been aware of the speed and trajectory of her life towards it, she has never felt before, on a cellular level, the inevitability of that gaping, waiting void. *Your parents are dead*, the universe seems to be telling her. *Now you're next.*

Is Victoria feeling it too? With her avoiding nine out of ten phone calls, it's impossible to know.

The day before the funeral, Victoria answers Penny's call immediately. Penny takes this as a good omen, a sign that her sister has finally relented.

"Hello darling!" Penny says warmly. "How are you feeling?"

"Fine," Victoria says, her new stock answer. To hear her speak, she has never felt better. "I just got back from my session with Muller."

"How did that go?"

"Fine. You know I can't talk about that."

"OK then. I... I just wanted to talk about tomorrow," Penny says nervously.

"Tomorrow," Victoria repeats flatly.

"Yes, tomorrow. We're all coming up for the funeral, as you know. It's at eleven."

"Yes. I know. I just got Martin's suit from the cleaners for him. It's not his nicest suit, but it's black."

"So...?"

"Do you want to come here first or something?" Victoria offers.

Penny exhales sharply and her eyes tear. Tears and sighs seem to be never far away these days. "Oh, I'm so glad!" she says. "I was so scared about having to send her off without my big sister by my side."

"I'm not *coming*," Victoria says. "I didn't say I was *coming*! I just said you could come here before, if you want. That way Martin and Bertie can drive over with you."

Penny is momentarily speechless. It happens rarely, essentially when her emotions are performing a crunchy gear-change from joy, for example, to anger.

"Hello?" Victoria says.

"I... I'm speechless," Penny tells her.

"Huh. I've been saying exactly the same thing all week, so I don't know why."

"I don't know what's got into you," Penny says. "I just can't see how that's possible – letting your son go to his grandmother's funeral on his own? That's just... well, it's outrageous really."

"He won't be on his own, will he? He'll be with his father."

"God, Mum said you were selfish, and she was right," Penny says, wincing even as she says it. It's not a nice thing to say, and it's not going to take this conversation anywhere she wants it to go. But it's too late now. It's said.

"Selfish?" Victoria repeats. "Selfish?!"

"Yes. Selfish. You're showing no regard for me, or for your son, or for your husband, or, for that matter, for your dead mother. It's all just *you, you, you,* isn't it? Mum was right. I should have listened."

Victoria snorts. "She said this when? Oh, was it when I was filling her fridge? I'll bet that's it. Or maybe when I was paying her rent? Was it, perhaps, when I visited every bloody sheltered housing place in London? Was it then? Or was it when she spent every weekend watching Noel bloody Edmonds on our television? And where were you, then, Penny? Huh? Where were *you*? And you dare to call *me* selfish? Well, fuck you, Penny. Fuck you!" The line goes dead.

"OK, we *won't* drop by," Penny says, her voice taut with emotion.

She looks up to see Sander standing in the doorway. "That didn't go well, I take it?" he says.

Penny shakes her head. "No," she says. "Not really."

Later that day, Penny phones Martin to try to enlist his support getting his wife to the funeral.

"I'm doing everything I can, Penny," he says. "Believe me. It's like I said before. I really think she's having some kind of breakdown. But she'll snap out of it eventually. At least, I'm assuming she will."

"Only by the time she does, she will have missed her mother's funeral," Penny tells him.

"That's true," Martin says.

"There are no re-runs of this one, Martin."

"Also true," he says. "But what do you want me to do?"

"I just think it's a bit convenient," Penny says, another batch of words which have slipped out in spite of her best intentions.

"What do you mean by that?" Martin asks, sounding suddenly prickly.

"Oh, never mind," Penny says. "There's no point anyway."

"Goodbye, Penny," Martin says. "I'll see you tomorrow. At eleven."

Brilliant, Penny thinks. *Now I have his back up as well.*

．．．

The next morning, Penny is awake before sunrise. She sits in the lounge nursing a mug of coffee and listens to the creaking house as it sleeps, and to the waves as they crash and wheeze against the pebbles outside, until slowly the horizon brightens, first a deep, sumptuous blue, then purple, then red, and then orange. It's going to be a beautiful day – a beach day, Penny thinks, not a funeral day.

Sander comes downstairs at seven. He rests one hand on Penny's shoulder and looks outside as well. "You OK?" he asks.

"Uh huh," Penny says, turning to look up at him. "Gosh, you look nice." He's wearing a white shirt and black trousers. The full outfit cost her less than fifteen pounds at Primark, but you really couldn't tell.

"Thanks," Sander says. "But it feels like school uniform. I seem to have disguised myself as Max."

"Well, it's nice to see you in a shirt for once," Penny says.

"It's gonna be nice, then," Sander comments, nodding at the blue sky beyond the window. "Good job I didn't waste money on that jacket after all."

Chloe, unusually, wakes up of her own accord. At eight, she appears in pyjamas, looking as tired as Penny feels. "I couldn't sleep," she says. "I kept thinking about Gran."

"Me too," Penny tells her daughter as she strokes her hair from her eyes.

"What time are we leaving?"

"In an hour. So make sure you're ready, OK?"

"OK. But do I really have to wear that dress? Only I thought..."

"You do," Penny tells her. "We both do. It's just one day so..."

Chloe rolls her eyes, but she knows better than to argue today. "Can I do my nails, then?"

"You can," Penny says. "But not black, and not purple, OK?"

Chloe pulls a face. "It's a funeral, Mum," she says. "Everything's *supposed* to be black."

"You're almost right," Penny tells her. "Everything except makeup."

"Gran wouldn't have minded," Chloe says. "She told me she liked the emo look."

"That," Penny says, actually managing to laugh, "I very much doubt."

The drive to London is sombre.

Sander and Max, in matching school uniform, are stoney faced, while Penny is permanently on the edge of tears. Only Chloe, stuck in childish resentment about having to wear a black Primark dress, seems unfazed. But Penny knows that won't last.

When they get to Hendon Crematorium, they cross paths with the departing relatives from the previous service, some of whom are red-eyed while others are still weeping. The two parties nod at each other respectfully.

"Who are all those people?" Chloe asks. She thinks, for a moment, that these are secret friends of her gran.

"The previous batch," Max explains. "One lot comes in as the last lot go out. It's like a production line."

"That's weird," Chloe says, "when you think about it."

"You're right," Penny says. "It is weird."

Inside the crematorium, the coffin is already in place as requested. Penny couldn't be sure there would be enough people to carry a coffin, and hadn't wanted to pay for pall-bearers they didn't know. Plus, all that coffin carrying business has always struck her as a little absurd, a bit Laurel and Hardy somehow – little more than an opportunity for horrific, slapstick disaster. And she can see that she was right about the numbers. Despite Sander's best efforts, only five people are present: an old lady and an overweight man, an elderly chap with a walking stick who Penny thinks she recognises from Vivian Court, and another aged couple already seated at the front.

On seeing Penny, the overweight man stands and helps the woman to her feet.

"Hello," she says, when Penny reaches them. "I'm Flo. From next door. Do you remember me?"

"Of course I do," Penny says. "You're Mrs Michaels who baked all the cakes."

"And which one are you?" Mrs Michaels asks.

"I'm Penny. The youngest."

"Ah, good," Mrs Michaels says. "Don't tell your sister, but you were always my favourite."

"Hi Penny," the man says, and Penny suddenly realises that this is Peter. Peter who was seventeen years old the last time she saw him. Peter with the blond mop and the blue eyes – Peter who Victoria had a childhood crush on. It barely seems possible that he can have become this overweight, red cheeked man. But then Penny thinks about the fact that Peter must be approaching retirement now, and then terrifyingly visualises herself through Peter's eyes. *Yes,* she thinks, *he's not the only person to have changed.*

"Is Vicky...?" Peter asks. He blushes an even darker shade of red, and Penny somehow picks up that he's afraid he has put his foot in it – he's afraid that Victoria has followed Ed's premature trajectory to the other side.

"She's fine," Penny says. "But she probably can't make it today."

"Oh?" Peter says.

"Oh!" his mother exclaims. "That *is* a shame."

"Yes, I was hoping to see her," Peter says.

"Well..." Penny replies, casting around for a quick change of subject. "Um, this is Chloe, my youngest." She gestures to Chloe, who is lurking behind her, to step forward. But Chloe shyly raises one hand and waves instead. "And this is Max, my son. And Sander, my husband."

As they all shake hands, Penny explains, "This is Mrs Michaels. She lived next door when I was little. She used to supply us with cakes. And this is her son." Internally she frowns at the fact she has mentioned cake and the overweight Peter in almost the same sentence. She wonders if he noticed.

"Your mother fell asleep in my daffodils once," Mrs Michaels tells Chloe. "She broke all the stems."

"I was about five," Penny says. "So no memory of that whatsoever. Personally, I think it's a myth."

"Victoria will remember," Mrs Michaels says. "You just ask her."

"So, Victoria's not coming?" Peter asks again. "What a shame. I was hoping to see her."

"Yes," Penny says. "Yes, so was I."

"Is there a wake thingy after?" Peter asks.

"Just a drink," Penny explains. "In a pub. Chequers. It's just down the road. You're welcome to come if you'd like to."

"Thanks. That would be nice, wouldn't it, Mum?"

Mrs Michaels nods. "If I'm not too tired by then. I tend to wear out quite quickly these days, dear."

Moving forwards, Penny crouches down next to the elderly man with the walking stick. "Hello," she says. "You're from Vivian Court, aren't you?"

"I'm sorry dear?" the man says, tapping on his hearing aid, then, "Oh, yes, Vivian Court. That's right. Are you the other daughter?"

"Yes, that's me."

"We saw the other one more. Veronica, is it?"

"Victoria? My sister?"

"Yes, that's right. She came a lot. Lovely girl."

"Right," Penny says. "Well, thanks so much for coming."

"And Veronica? Is she here?" the man asks, looking around the room.

"Not yet," Penny says. "But I'm sure she'll be here soon." She has decided that it's perhaps easier just to lie.

"Where do we sit, Mum?" Max asks. He's tugging gently on Penny's sleeve.

"Front row," she says.

"What, next to them?"

"Yes," Penny tells him.

"Who are they?"

"I don't know dear," Penny says. But then the man in the end seat turns to look at her and she recognises him.

"God, isn't that Marge's brother?" she hears Mrs Michaels say.

"Cecil!" Penny exclaims, straightening and moving to his side. "You made it!"

As Max, Chloe and Sander take their seats, Penny crouches down next to Cecil. "There was me wondering who those cheeky people were in the front row," she tells him. "And it's you!"

"Sorry, are we...? Would you like us to move?"

"Of course not!" Penny says. "You're family. I just hadn't seen your face. I wasn't sure I'd even recognise you to be honest, but you've hardly changed at all."

"I wouldn't say that," Cecil says. "This is my wife, Janine. Janine, Penny. Penny's my niece."

Penny shakes Janine's hand. "Pleased to meet you," she says.

"Likewise," Janine says, though she doesn't look pleased at all. In fact the expression on her pinched face looks a lot like profound disapproval. But Penny can tell by the deep wrinkles around her mouth that Janine is a woman who has been pursing her lips for many years now, so she decides not to take it personally.

"So, how's my little Penny?" Cecil asks. "How long has it been?"

"Forty years, give or take. And I'm OK, considering the circumstances."

"Yes, of course," Cecil says. "It's all very sad."

"That's my husband, Sander," Penny says, pointing along the row. "And my children, Max and Chloe."

"Lovely," Cecil says, fiddling with his threadbare tie. Penny notices, now, the tatty nature of his collar, his worn brogues

245

and his shiny trousers. Cecil, it would seem, lost a bit of his sheen at some point. "And your sister?" he asks.

"I don't know, actually," Penny says. She glances around the room and sees Martin and Bertie lingering in the entranceway. "Ah, that's her husband arriving now. Sorry, you'll have to excuse me."

She returns to the entrance and embraces Martin and Bertie. Bertie, she can see, has been crying. "Thanks so much for coming," Penny tells them. "It means a lot."

"Mum's outside too," Bertie tells her. "She's smoking a cigarette."

Penny pulls a face. "She's here?"

"Yes."

"And she's smoking?"

Martin nods. "It's a whole new thing," he says drily. "She's only on ten a day at the moment, but she's working at it. She's progressing every day."

As Penny brushes the sleeve of Bertie's blazer with one hand and steps outside, Martin murmurs, "Go easy on her, eh?"

"Of course," Penny casts back over her shoulder. "Of course I will."

Outside, there is no sign of Victoria, so Penny walks across the courtyard and around to the graveyard at the side, where she finds Victoria seated on a bench, her back to her.

"Hey, give us a ciggy," she says, as she approaches the bench, and Victoria visibly jumps and turns back to face her.

"Oh hello," she says, speaking in puffs of smoke.

"Hello."

"Do you have time?" Victoria asks. "I was just about to stub this out."

"Let them wait," Penny says, smoothing her skirt and taking a seat next to her sister. "They can't start without us, can they?"

Victoria pulls a Marlboro packet from her handbag, opens the lid, and offers it to Penny.

"So, you came," Penny says, as she pulls one from the packet.

"I'm not speaking, though," Victoria says.

"Nor am I. There's an officiate. He's going to do the Lord's Prayer or something and that's about it. Max wanted to speak, but he changed his mind this morning. And I can't..." she sighs. "I just can't face it."

"Right," Victoria says, reaching out to light Penny's cigarette. Anyway, when did you ever smoke cigarettes?"

"Only at times of great stress," Penny says. "And you?"

"Only at times of great stress," Victoria retorts.

Penny has barely taken her first dizzy-making puff when Max appears. "They're starting," he says, breathlessly. "Dad says you have to come quick."

Back inside the chapel, the officiant is already standing at the lectern so the sisters scamper to their seats, feeling, beneath his angry glare, like naughty schoolchildren late for class.

"Well, thank you all for coming," he tells the essentially empty room the second they have sat down. "We are here today to pay our last respects to Marjorie Thompson, who most of you knew simply as Marge..."

Victoria nudges Penny at this point and nods towards the end of the row. "That's not... is it?" she says. "It can't be. Can it?"

Penny nods. "Sander found him," she whispers. "Now, shh!"

The service groans by with all the grace of an unwanted works' dinner.

It's a pretty lacklustre affair, Penny admits to herself, and for the first five minutes she feels swamped not by grief, but by guilt. She should have spent more time planning what this stranger would say about her mother; she should have forced Victoria to share a few stories he could tell; she should, perhaps, have asked Cecil about her mother's childhood. She should have had the nerve, above all, to speak herself. Because this, what is happening now, the Lord's prayer, a dreadful poem and a litany of platitudes, has little to do with the life of spunky, feisty, single-mother Marge. Marge who did everything for them. Marge who managed all that Penny manages and more.

But Penny has been swamped, that's the thing. She has had so many, many things to deal with and so little help from anyone else to do them. Surely no one could blame her, could they? Surely Marge, if she is watching, understands?

So this is it, she thinks. A shabby, impersonal sendoff in an almost empty chapel. *I'm sorry, Mum, I let you down.* Even the flowers look tired.

Unexpectedly (for this was not agreed) the officiant starts to recite a poem by Mary Elizabeth Frye. It's a simple, pretty poem, but it somehow saves the day.

Do not stand at my grave and weep / I am not there, I do not sleep

It's clearly not what the author intended, but weep is exactly what Penny now does. It feels as if the poem is reaching deep into her innards and yanking out fistfuls of pain – the pain of this all-consuming loss.

I am a thousand winds that blow / I am the diamond glints on snow

Salty tears stream down Penny's face and she unashamedly lets them flow.

To her right, swamped by her mother's distress, Chloe can no longer blank out what has happened either. Because, no, Chloe didn't agree with her gran about her emo makeup or anything much else. And no, theirs was not a touchy-feely relationship. And no, Marge's gifts were rarely generous or thoughtful or even wanted. She was a tight-fisted, stern old gran, in fact. But, despite it all, Chloe suddenly realises, they loved each other. And now that she's gone she *does* miss her. And she'll miss her forever, now, because Gran is never coming back. *Never. Forever.* These are not concepts Chloe has ever thought much about before. *Gone forever!* She leans against her mother's heaving shoulder and lets herself cry, too, for the suddenly understood irreversibility of death.

I am the sunlight on ripened grain / I am the gentle Autumn rain

Max and Sander join in too, bravely attempting to blink back their own tears, while Bertie, sandwiched between his mother and Max, holds out a moment longer. It's only when Max slides one arm around his cousin's shoulders that Bertie begins to cry as well.

When you awaken in the morning's hush / I am the swift uplifting rush

Only Victoria remains dry-eyed. In truth, she's struggling to even follow the proceedings. She's lost in a bubble of Valium and a sea of resurfacing memories, lost in the shame of what she said to her mother forty years ago, as well.

For how is she going to be able to look Cecil in the eye after what she did? How can she possibly stand and chat to him in a pub after all the things she said?

Of quiet birds in circled flight / I am the soft stars that shine at night

Unless, of course, what she said was true. But how could she possibly know? How can she trust her memories when it was so long ago? Because it was *so* long ago. She had been seven years old... or perhaps eight. You see? She's not even sure about that anymore.

So, no, she *can't* trust her memories. She can't differentiate any longer between what happened that day and what she's told herself since.

Bertie once told her that his friend Aaron had killed Smurf, the family cat. So Victoria had gone round there to have it out with Aaron's family, to warn them about their psychopath of a son, only when she got there, Smurf had been sitting proudly on the bonnet of the car cleaning his paws. Everyone knows that kids make stuff up. They can even convince themselves that their lies are true, given enough time.

Bertie, poor Bertie, is crying now, sobbing freely into his hands, and Victoria thinks that she too should really be crying. She consciously reconfigures her features into a more convincing expression of grief. She doesn't want to add lack of emotion at her mother's funeral to her already extensive repertoire of shame.

If that *were* to be the case, if she *had* made it all up, then of course, Marge would have been right to treat her the way she did. Even *without* knowing the full extent of Victoria's crimes, she would have been justifiably furious with her daughter just for having driven Cecil away. And if Marge was right and

Victoria was wrong, then she should be feeling sadder today. She got off lightly, perhaps, after all.

She leans forwards and glances along the row at Penny who, through tears, notices this and looks up at her sister as the officiant reads the last verse of the poem.

Do not stand at my grave and cry / I am not there, I did not die.

Something tickles Victoria's cheek and it's only when she reaches to scratch it that she understands that she too is crying. *Oh, Mum*, she thinks, simply. *Oh! Mum!*

She brushes away the tears with her index finger and then closes her eyes as she attempts to listen to the officiant's words as he reads the final blessing, but again she drifts off into memories not of Marge, whose life they are supposed to be celebrating, but of Ed, and of Cecil, and of a shameful little girl called Victoria she once knew. A little girl who did terrible, terrible things. A little girl who caused nothing but suffering and mayhem to everyone who knew her.

"May Christ the Good Shepherd enfold you with love, fill you with peace, and lead you in hope..." the officiant reads.

It's only when a crescendo of sobs from Penny's direction drags her from her trance, that Victoria opens her eyes and discovers that the coffin has miraculously vanished.

Everyone is standing. The service, it seems, is over.

Outside, Penny dabs at her eyes and thanks people for coming. Will and Ben are now present too, beautifully dressed in dark, modern suits.

"Hi Will," Penny says, hugging her friend. "I was crying so much, I didn't even see you."

"We arrived late," Will explains. "There was a... an incident, let's say, on the Bakerloo line. So we snuck in halfway through. I'm ever so sorry, Pen."

"It doesn't matter," Penny says, sniffing. "It was all a bit Heath Robinson anyway, to be honest."

"I thought it was nice," Ben says, sweetly. "I liked your choice of poems, too."

"Thanks," Penny says, brushing his cheek with the back of her fingers. "You're cute. A liar, but cute."

On the other side of the courtyard, Cecil is waving his car keys agitatedly at his wife, so, worrying that they are leaving, Penny crosses to join them. As she reaches them, Cecil says, a little sharply, it seems to Penny, "Just do it! I'll be right there."

Janine opens her pursed little mouth to respond, but then seeing Penny arriving, she simply closes it again and takes the keys from Cecil's outstretched hand. She turns and leaves, clip-clopping across the courtyard in her heels.

"Is everything OK?" Penny asks.

"Sure," Cecil says. "You know how it is."

"Not really," Penny replies. "But you are coming, aren't you? To the pub, I mean. I need to talk to you a bit about all the things that happened."

"*What* about what happened?" Cecil asks. And there's an incongruity between his sharp tone of voice and the gentle way Penny asked him to stay that puts Penny's nerves on edge. He sounds as if he's responding to a threat of interrogation rather than a softly delivered plea for intimacy.

"Me too," Victoria says, with meaning, and Penny turns to see that her sister has joined them.

"I… well, I could…" Cecil stammers.

"You are coming, aren't you?" Victoria asks. "You're not going to just vanish again, surely?"

"It's… it's just that Janine's with me," Cecil says. "So, you know…"

"Doesn't she want to come?" Penny asks.

"Oh no, it's not that. I mean, she doesn't, you know… *know*."

"What doesn't she know?" Penny asks.

"About any of that," Cecil says. "About why we fell out and stuff. And I… I mean, I'm sure you'd agree, there's no point bringing all that up now, is there?"

Penny frowns deeply and glances at her sister in case her expression might provide some clue as to what is going on here. But Victoria's face, though glassy and strange, explains nothing. "There's no point *what*?" she asks, turning back to Cecil.

"There's no point *telling her*," Victoria offers. A realisation is sweeping over her, a truth, a feeling, communicating as if through the air, from Cecil's sweating pores to some primeval sensory organ within her. A realisation that maybe, just maybe, she was right.

"I can… can trust you, then?" Cecil stammers. "If we come, I mean… not to…"

"Not to tell your wife?" Victoria says.

"Yes. It's just that, well, what happened. With Marge. That was punishment enough," Cecil says. "Don't you think?"

Penny opens her mouth to express the fact that she has no idea what Cecil and her sister are talking about, but Victoria raises a finger to silence her. She doesn't want her sister's big boots stamping their way through this one. "Was it?" she asks gently. "Was it enough, do you think?"

"I lost my sister. I never saw her again," Cecil says. "You know that. *And* you two. My lovely gals. I didn't get to see you growing up or nothing."

"No," Victoria says. "That's true."

"And it's not like anything..." Cecil continues, apparently encouraged. "I mean, it's not like anything ever... Well, it's just... you need to know that it was just that one time. And it wasn't only *my* fault. He was different to other people. He really was. We had, I don't know, a special bond, I suppose you'd call it. I mean, it was wrong, of course. But he wanted it to happen too. And it never happened again, I promise you that. You need to know that. You have to believe me. I mean, we have kids, we've got three of them. And they'd tell you. They think the world of me. They love their old dad. And he did too, you see? That was why... You do understand, don't you?"

Penny feels lost. She feels almost surreally lost in fact. She was already feeling overwrought with emotion from the funeral before this strange encounter happened. It's as if she's lacking the spare capacity to work out what's happening here. She feels as if she has stepped into the cinema halfway through the film. But something definitely *is* happening here. The colour has completely drained from Victoria's face, and Cecil's has gone a deep shade of pink. Despite the gentle breeze, they are both sweating profusely. Yes, something is definitely happening here – something deep and dark and perhaps even dangerous.

Victoria, on the other hand, feels un-lost for the first time in forty years. It's as if someone has turned a light on and she can suddenly see where she is. Because she was right, wasn't she? She really did see what she thought she saw. She didn't make it up, so she isn't a liar, and she isn't mad, either. What she told her mother was the truth, then. She can tell from the fear in Cecil's eyes that it was the truth. And in that case, her mother's allegiances at the time were hopelessly, hatefully, tragically wrong. Unexpectedly, she feels wise and strong and vindicated. But above all, she feels incredibly, *incredibly* angry.

"So, come for a drink? I mean, of course," Cecil is saying, still rambling in a bizarre fashion. "I just needed to be sure... I mean, you wouldn't have asked me here to the funeral, would you, otherwise? Not if you didn't want things to be... better. But as long as we're all agreed that we've... well, we've moved on, haven't we? It was ages ago all that. Forgive and forget and all that, eh? What do you think? Because I'd love another chance. To get to know you. My lovely gals. And your lovely families. Right?"

He looks pleadingly at Victoria, who remains as still as a statue, then, more hopefully at Penny. "Right?" he says again.

"I'm sorry," Penny starts, "but I have absolutely..."

"OK," Victoria says sharply, cutting her short again.

"OK? Oh, thank-you," Cecil says, raising his hands as if in prayer. "I've been... well, quite nervous about this, really. That's why, it's been... you know... forty years. I mean... *forty years!* But you can see, now, can't you? You can see what happened, it was a very unusual thing. A one-off thing. And you do, you understand, don't you?"

"Yes, I understand," Victoria says, her voice completely devoid of intonation.

"And Marge, I'm sure you realise, she wouldn't have wanted it all being dragged up again. Not at her funeral. Not now."

"No," Victoria says. "No, you're absolutely right. Mum wouldn't have wanted anyone to talk about any of it ever again."

At these words, Cecil visibly relaxes. But Penny, who knows her sister so much better than Cecil, who can decode the tiniest subtleties of her sister's voice, the smallest shifts in her body language, instead tenses up.

"So, do you want to know what I think?" Victoria asks, her voice now sugary sweet with mock compassion.

To Penny's dismay, Cecil falls for it hook, line and sinker. "Yes?" he asks, nodding enthusiastically.

"You really want to know?" Victoria asks again, and Penny sees the first shadow of doubt cross Cecil's brow, even as he nods again.

"This," Victoria says. "*This* is what *I* think."

As she begins to work her mouth strangely, Penny thinks she understands what is about to happen. *But no,* she tells herself. *She can't. She can't possibly do that. Not at Mum's funeral. She just can't.*

But then she *does* do that. And it's exactly what Penny feared.

Victoria pulls in her cheeks and then spits, generously, at point blank range, directly into their uncle's eye.

"You're a disgusting, dirty bastard," Victoria says, as Cecil covers his face with his hands. "That's what *I* think."

Time stretches, and a few seconds seem to last for minutes. Cecil wipes his eye with the back of one hand and glares hatefully at Victoria while Penny looks from one to the other and then back again, her mouth agape. Around them, people are turning to look, their conversations are fizzling out; some are covering their mouths in shock.

And then the moment is over, and Cecil is striding away, the hard soles of his shoes pounding the courtyard as he leaves.

Penny watches him go and then turns to ask her sister what just happened, but she too has vanished.

She looks around and, deducing that Victoria can only have returned inside, she starts to follow her, but is retained momentarily by Martin who has had to run in order to intercept her. "What was that?" he asks, grabbing at her arm.

"I don't know, Martin," she says.

"But she did just...?"

"She spat in his eye. Yes."

"I should go to her," Martin says.

"No," Penny tells him forcefully. "No, it has to be me. Trust me."

She finds Victoria in the corner of the chapel. Her cheeks are wet with tears and she's fumbling madly in her handbag. As Penny reaches her, she pulls her cigarettes from the bag.

"You can't smoke here," Penny tells her, grabbing the shaking hand holding the lighter.

"I don't care," Victoria says.

"Here," Penny instructs. "Out here." She gently pulls her towards a fire exit where she pushes the bar to release the door. As they step over the threshold, Victoria lights the cigarette.

"What just happened there?" Penny asks her sister.

Victoria leans against the wall of the building and drags deeply on the cigarette. "He proved me right," she says, incomprehensibly.

"I don't understand. About what?"

"I hate him," Victoria breathes.

"Yes, I got *that*," Penny says. "But why?"

"He... Oh God, I can't tell *you*, Penny. You're so much better off not knowing. You've been so *lucky* not knowing. But he's a bad person. He's a terrible person. You shouldn't have invited him. Did you? Did you actually *invite* that... that man?"

"Yes. Yes, I did," Penny says. "But if you won't tell me anything... I mean, why wouldn't I? He's Mum's brother, for God's sake. Other than us, he's her only relative. Here, give me one of those, would you?" Penny nods towards Victoria's handbag, which she opens and offers so that Penny can reach inside. "You know," Penny continues, once her own cigarette is lit, "I think I need to know what's going on. I think it's time."

"Not today," Victoria says, dabbing at her eyes. "Not at her funeral."

"That just happened at her funeral," Penny says. "So tell me, will you?"

"I can't, Penny. Really, I can't. But stay away from that... stay away from him. And keep him away from your kids. I thought he was dead. I *hoped* he was dead."

"Did he...? He didn't... *abuse* someone, did he?" Penny says. "Because that's what it sounded like."

Victoria nods almost imperceptibly.

"It wasn't... Oh God," Penny says, closing her eyes and feeling sick. "It wasn't Ed, was it?"

. . .

It was the morning of Christmas eve and Vicky had woken up early. She was too excited about Christmas to stay in bed.

Fun times were few and far between in the Thompson household. Since their father had died, just two years after Penny was born, things had been pretty awful, really.

Marge had taken a job at the local Tesco supermarket but there still wasn't enough money for coal, or sometimes even for electricity.

The girls would come home to a cold, draughty house and an empty refrigerator. They would sit together in the kitchen (the least-cold room thanks to the afternoon sun) and wait for Marge to return with something for dinner, usually whatever she found in the bargain basket of her workplace. The bargain basket made for some unusual dinner combinations.

But Christmas was different. Christmas was the exception.

Uncle Cecil always came to stay at Christmas and with him he brought money for coal and food, and gifts for them all. He worked as a salesman and things were going well for him. He wore elegant suits and smoked cigarettes from a gold cigarette tin with a clasp that Vicky liked to play with.

Marge, so glum since Dad died, changed when Cecil arrived, too. She dressed prettily and wore makeup and perfume. Even her accent changed slightly when Cecil was around.

Vicky was the first person downstairs. The clock on the mantlepiece said six-thirty, which meant that Marge wouldn't be up for at least an hour. She liked her "lie-ins" on her days off, and would punish anyone who interrupted them.

Vicky sat next to the Christmas tree and memorising the gifts so that she could put them all back in the exact same spot, she gently lifted them one by one until she came to hers. It was a biggish package, just about the right size and weight for a cassette player, the thing she had asked for, the thing she had dreamed of.

She lifted the package to her ear as if she might hear the music within, and imagined herself dancing around to The Three Degrees, or ABBA, or the Bay City Rollers.

Then, thinking she heard movement above, she carefully replaced the packages.

Checking one last time that the pile looked undisturbed, she returned to the hallway and looked up the stairs. But the house remained silent.

In the kitchen, she opened the usually empty refrigerator and stared at the contents.

There were bottles of Babycham, and Cecil's Pale Ale. There were Ski fruit yoghurts and sliced ham and cheese and a half-made trifle. One of the bottles of milk had been opened, so she raised it to her lips and sipped at the cream floating on the top.

Back in the hallway, she hesitated about what to do next. But then she remembered her book – *The Lion, The Witch and The Wardrobe.* She was excited to read what would happen next. She began to climb the stairs.

When she reached the landing she heard movement coming from Ed's room on the top floor. He had been bragging, the previous evening, about having squeezed the packages. He knew, he said, what was in them. Only she did now, as well. She would tell him. He would be impressed at her nerve.

As she opened his door, strange noises met her ears, and she wondered if Ed was doing his exercises. He had decided recently to be a professional footballer, and had started doing sit-ups and press-ups. Footballers have to be incredibly fit, he had told her.

But when she peeped around the door, she found not Ed doing press-ups, but Cecil. At first she didn't understand what she was seeing. Why would Cecil be doing exercises in Ed's room? But then she realised that Ed was *beneath* Cecil. Cecil was doing his press-ups *on* Ed.

Ed looked up at her just then. He had tears in his eyes. He didn't look happy.

She jerked back out of the door as if she had accidentally burned her hand in a flame. And then she had gone to her room and cried about whatever it was she had seen. Because she really wasn't sure what that was.

* * *

The sisters have slumped to the ground. They are sitting, side by side, their backs against the wall.

"I feel sick," Penny says, once Victoria has finished.

"Welcome to the club," Victoria says. "I've been feeling sick for forty years."

"So, did you tell Mum?" Penny asks.

"Please don't make me go through the rest of it," Victoria replies. "I just can't, Penny. I can't."

"OK," Penny says. "But just tell me that you told Mum. And that's why she sent Cecil away?"

"I told her."

"Did she report it to anyone? Or did she just banish him?"

"Penny," Victoria says. "That's enough."

Penny sighs deeply and slides one arm around her sister's shoulders. "OK," she says again. "Have you even told any of this to a professional?"

Victoria silently shakes her head.

"I think you need to."

"Of course you think that."

"Because I'm a psychotherapist?"

Victoria shrugs.

"Maybe that's true," Penny says. "But I still think that you should talk to someone. I think you need to work through it all. Did you talk to your Austrian guy about this?"

"Doctor Muller?"

"Yes."

"No. I can't. I can't talk to anyone about this."

"I understand that," Penny says. "It's a huge childhood trauma. But maybe you could, now. I mean, you've just told me."

"I suppose," Victoria says, vaguely.

"There isn't more, is there?" Penny asks, suddenly frowning.

Victoria looks away.

"Cecil... he didn't... ?"

"Me?" Victoria asks, turning back. "No! Of course not! I wouldn't have let him near me. I would have cut his dick off."

"Kids sometimes don't feel they have the choice," Penny says. "I'm sure Ed didn't."

"Well, he didn't," Victoria says. "And that's it. That's the whole story. Honestly."

"Good," Penny says. "Well, thank God for that." But even as she is saying it, she is realising that she doesn't really believe what her sister is saying.

• • •

The ambiance in Chequers is workaday. The place is busy, filled with men in suits eating burgers and secretaries picking at salads, and the mourners have to elbow their way through the lunchtime drinkers to order at the bar. With only seven of them present from the funeral, their little meeting feels more like a work's lunch than a wake. But neither Penny, nor Victoria, is in any state to care.

Victoria is feeling as angry as she has ever felt, and is alternating between hoping Cecil will come so that she can punch him (her spitting gesture, she now feels, was insufficient) and praying that she'll never see him again.

As for Penny, her sister's revelations are washing over her in foul, nauseating waves. Images of Cecil and Ed keep swamping her mind, and there's nothing she can do to stop them. It feels like she's bobbing around in a sea of sewage, trying desperately to keep her mouth above the waterline in order to breathe.

She's unexpectedly angry with the people around her as well. "Stop laughing!" she wants to shout. "My mother is dead. My brother, whose life was cut obscenely short, was sexually abused! In God's name, stop laughing, will you?" It's just too much to think about, too much to take in, especially today, which was supposed to be about remembrance, which was supposed to be about celebration of Marge's life, after all. It's as if her mother's funeral has been sullied by these revelations, and, as she said to Martin, there's only one chance to get this day right – there are no replays. Will her mother's funeral be associated forever more with a paedophile uncle and an abused brother?

She's angry with herself for inviting Cecil and angry, too, that she repeatedly asked Victoria to explain it all to her. She's even angry with Victoria for replying, for telling her, and not knowing what to do with any of this anger, it's spilling over making her hate everyone around them as well. And Cecil! Above all, Cecil! For how could he possibly imagine anyone would ever *forgive and forget* something like that? Has the man no sense of remorse? Has he no shame?

She's standing in a small group with Sander, Martin and the old chap from the sheltered housing complex whose name she has forgotten, and she notices now that Sander is staring at her strangely. He has, she deduces, been speaking to her.

"Um?" she asks, sipping at her gin and tonic.

"I said, are you sure you're all right?" Sander asks.

"Yes, I'm fabulous, darling," she says, sourly.

"You don't seem fabulous."

"No? It's a funeral, Sander. What do you expect?"

Sander pulls a face and glances at Martin beside him, who sighs and asks, "Any idea where my wife and son went?"

Penny shrugs. "No," she says. "No I don't, Martin. Blackpool, perhaps?"

Martin now pulls a face as well and, using the search for Victoria and Bertie as an excuse, vanishes into the crowd.

Sander seizes Penny's free arm and telling the old guy, "Excuse me one second," he pulls her to one side. "OK, tell me what's going on, Pen," he says, "because you're being really strange now."

"Am I?" Penny says.

"Yes. You're bitching at everyone."

"I'm sorry," Penny says. "It's just... this is hard."

"But something's wrong, isn't it?" Sander asks. "Something else? Why won't you tell me what happened with Posh?"

"Another day," Penny says. "I told you in the car, I'll tell you another day! Are you even listening to me, Sander?" she asks, rapping her knuckles on his forehead.

"Ugh..." Sander groans.

"Well, you keep just asking me the same thing, over and over. Why won't you just listen to me?"

"Excuse me for trying to help," Sander says, releasing her arm and turning back to the old chap.

Penny gasps in exasperation, and, spilling a man's pint as she does so, she barges her way through the crowd to the door and steps out into the sunlight. All the tables in the beer garden are taken. It's unsurprising really, it's a beautiful day.

On the other side of the road, beyond the railings, she can see identical empty benches and tables belonging to Middlesex University, so, still holding her gin and tonic, she walks to the end of the road, passes through the university gates, and, ignoring the stares of the students, crosses the green and takes a seat. She's aware that these benches have not been provided for overflow from Chequers, but she needs to be alone and, today, seating etiquette is just not something she has any capacity to care about. In fact, if someone were to challenge her, she'd probably enjoy it. She feels like she might be in *need* of a good, lively brawl. But she's disappointed – her anger must be radiating from her skin. Everyone stays clear of the glaring woman with the gin and tonic.

The solitude plus the drink and a tweeting magpie in the tree above her combine to calm Penny's nerves, and by the time her glass is empty, she is feeling more centred and, above all, guilty about playing truant from her mother's funeral. She downs the final drips of gin and tonic from her glass, crunches the remains of an ice cube, and heads back.

On reaching the pub, she spots Bertie at the rear of the car park sitting on a wall drinking a Coke, so she crosses the beer garden to join him. "Hello," she says softly, on arrival. "Are you OK over here by your lonesome?"

Bertie shrugs.

"Funerals are hard," Penny says. "We go through all kinds of different emotions. And that's all fine."

"Right," Bertie says, looking away.

"Have you seen Max and Chloe?" Penny asks, glancing around.

"Nope."

"Do you want me to leave you alone?" Penny asks. "Is that it?"

By way of reply, Bertie shrugs and nods at the same time.

"OK," Penny says reaching out to stroke her nephew's shoulder but then abandoning the gesture when he flinches from her touch. "I understand that," she adds. "I had to have a bit of time-out myself just now."

When she steps back indoors, she sees the crowd is thinning out a little. On the far side of the pub, Martin and Sander are talking, presumably about the football on the Sky Sports screen in the corner. Max and Chloe are present, half-heartedly playing pinball, and Penny thinks that she'll give Bertie ten more minutes and then she'll send Max out to fetch him. She crosses to the bar where Victoria is chatting to Old Guy and as they come into earshot, she hears him say, "She was lovely, though. A heart of gold, your mother had."

Victoria groans. "It's not like you even really knew her, is it?"

Penny swoops in and leads her sister away. Over her shoulder she tells her mother's admirer, "I'm so sorry – emotions are all over the shop today." She feels vaguely reassured by her sister's outburst. At least she's not the only person suffering from randomly directed anger today.

"What?" Victoria asks as she's led away. "What did I do now?"

"You can't say that, that's all."

"Why not? It's true. He *didn't* know her. You know he told me he only arrived there six weeks ago, right?"

"I know but..."

"It's just so hypocritical. Whenever someone dies, no one's allowed to say what they really think. I can't stand it."

"He's the only guy here who wasn't family," Penny says. "Well, except Will and Ben. But Will is sort of family too. Actually, where are they? I haven't seen them here at all. They said they were coming."

"I don't know," Victoria says.

"Anyway, all he was saying was that she was lovely. And it's true. And she *did* have a heart of gold. So just... I don't know... give everyone a break. Just for today. OK?"

Victoria gives a little shake of her head but seems to be calmer already. "Let's go outside," she says. "I need to smoke."

"Here, this way," Penny tells her, leading her towards the main entrance. "Bertie's out back, and I think he needs to be on his own for a bit."

Out on the street, Victoria leans against the wall and lights a cigarette. "So, is he OK? Bertie?"

Penny nods. "In an angry kind of way. Everyone seems angry today, to be honest."

"I'm not surprised," Victoria says. "He has plenty to be angry about."

"You didn't tell him, did you?" Penny asks. "Not about Cecil?"

Victoria wrinkles her brow and shakes her head. "Of course not," she says. "I thought you meant he seemed angry with *you*."

"No," Penny says.

Victoria snorts and drags deeply on her cigarette.

"You smoke too much," Penny comments. "You seem to have gone from zero to twenty-a-day in about a month."

"I know," Victoria says. "I have a death wish, I think. But I'll stop. Soon."

Penny wrinkles her nose as she replays bits of the conversation in her head. "Bertie's *not* angry with me, is he?" she finally asks.

Victoria gives her a "look". It's the same look she used when Penny was little and had said something stupid.

"What? He *is*? Why?"

Victoria gasps. "Oh, come on, Pen," she says. "You didn't expect him to just forget, did you?"

Penny frowns. "I don't understand. Forget *what*?"

"October. Last year."

"You mean us? Our argument?"

"No! I mean him asking you for help and you telling him to bugger off."

"I don't understand," Penny says again. "Bertie has never asked me for help."

"He told you he was unhappy," Victoria says. "He trusted you and you let him down. And God knows, he didn't trust anyone else."

"I still don't know what you're talking about."

"Mum *told* me," Victoria says.

"What? What did she tell you?"

"You know full well."

"Jesus, Victoria," Penny says. "I love you. I do. But you're really not making any sense today. I suppose that's to be expected, but…"

She's interrupted by Victoria's sour laughter. "You can't get away with this, you know," Victoria says. "You can't just pretend that it never happened. Especially not with Bertie. I mean, he was there."

"Pretend *what* never happened? I have absolutely no idea what you're talking about."

"So, Bertie *didn't* ask you if he could come and stay?" Victoria says. "Both he and Mum lied about that?"

"Oh, that!" Penny says. "Yes, that's true. He asked. But he was only joking. At least, I thought he was joking. He was, wasn't he?"

"He tells you he's unhappy. He tells you he wants to leave home. He asks if he can live with you, for God's sake. How is that a *joke*?"

"But he didn't, Vicky," Penny protests. "He didn't tell me anything. *Was* he unhappy? *Is* he unhappy?"

"He tried to *kill* himself, Penny," Victoria says.

"He *what*?"

"He asked you for help and you laughed in his face and did fuck-all. You didn't even tell *me*. He could have *died*. And all you had to do... at the very minimum, was let me know. We could have done something. We could have intervened. Hell, I'm angry about it."

For the third time that day, Penny senses the blood draining from her face. "But I don't know anything about that. When was this?"

"When was what?"

"When did Bertie try to kill himself?"

"At the beginning of last month. He took a load of Valium."

"God, that's dreadful. Thank God he's OK. But that isn't what happened," Penny protests. "I promise you. Is that what he told you?"

"He said you laughed in his face, yes."

"Oh, Bertie," Penny says, now close to tears. She turns to her right as if she might see Bertie around the corner, sitting on his wall. "Oh, Bertie. I had no idea."

"Mum said he told you everything," Victoria says.

"Well, he didn't. He just asked if he could live with us and I thought it was a joke. I would never... you know... I just wouldn't. I'd do anything for Bertie. You have to believe me."

"I do," Victoria says. "That's the worst thing."

Penny shakes her head enquiringly.

"It was Mum. Again," Victoria explains. "I'm just playing it all back..." She points at her head and makes a circular motion. "And it was Mum. She said he'd told you everything and you had sent him packing. I was furious. Mission accomplished."

"But why?" Penny says. "Why would she say that?"

Victoria shrugs. "As I said when you asked me to speak at the service, you're not going to like this," she says. "Especially not today. But Mum wasn't..."

"She wasn't what?"

"I don't know," Victoria says. "It's like... Do you remember that poem thing Margaret Thatcher famously read out when she got into power? *Where there is discord / may we bring harmony...*"

Penny nods. "It's a prayer by Francis of Assisi, I think. No one knew Thatch' was being ironic at the time."

"No, well, Mum was kind of the opposite."

"The opposite of Thatcher?"

"No, the opposite of the verse. Mum was kind of *where there is harmony / may I bring discord.*"

"Oh don't," Penny protests. "Please?"

Victoria shrugs. "I said you wouldn't want to hear it," she says. "I didn't want to realise it myself for years. But it's the truth, Sis. She spent most of our lives playing us off against each other. She was, as Bertie would say, one crazy stirring bitch."

Penny opens her mouth in horror. "Bertie didn't say that, did he?"

"Oh, no. Not about Mum," Victoria says. "No, keep your hair on. Bertie, like everyone else, is lost in the dream."

"Lost in the dream?"

Victoria nods. "Yeah, he thinks she was a saint, too. But she wasn't. She really wasn't."

It's two thirty and, essentially because Penny has drunk four gin-and-tonics, Sander is driving them home.

A bank of cloud from the west is slowly obscuring the sun as they drive, and the forecast, Max informs them, is for rain.

"Why didn't that Cecil bloke come to the pub?" Chloe asks.

"That *Cecil bloke* is your mother's uncle," Sander tells her.

"Yeah. I know. But why didn't he come?"

Penny twists in her seat in an attempt at looking back at her daughter. "I don't know," she lies. "I expect he had to be somewhere else."

"Bertie said aunty Vicky spat at him," Max says.

"What a silly thing to say," Penny replies.

Sander, who saw what happened but doesn't yet know why, turns to look at his wife accusingly. "I'll tell everyone everything tomorrow," she says quietly. "Just not now, OK?"

271

"So what about Bill 'n Ben?" Chloe asks. "I thought they was coming too."

"They *were* coming," Penny corrects, "not *was*. And I have no idea what happened there. Actually, I might call Will now and check they're OK."

As she fishes her mobile phone from her handbag, she murmurs, "I do hope she wasn't watching."

"Who?" Sander asks as he negotiates a roundabout.

"Mum. I mean, it was hardly sendoff of the year, was it?"

"It was fine, hon," Sander says. "It was her funeral. No one expected you to party like it was nineteen-ninety-nine."

"Why nineteen...? Oh... Prince," Penny mutters, still fiddling with the phone and then raising it to her ear. "Yes, well," she says. "All the same. It was all a bit naff. I was half expecting Victoria to say something, but... Hi Will, it's me. Just wondering what happened to you. I hope you're OK."

"Voicemail?" Sander asks, as she returns the phone to her lap.

"Yes. Oh, but hang on, I have a text message from him." Penny jabs at the screen a few times and comments, "Weird."

"What does he say?"

"Sorry Penny, but something personal came up," Penny reads in a monotone voice. "So, so sorry. But there was really nothing I could do. Forgive me. Love you. See you soon."

"Something personal?" Sander repeats. "You think they argued?"

"In the half-mile between the cemetery and the pub?"

Sander shrugs. "Maybe," he says. "We've argued in less."

"Who knows," Penny sighs, casting the phone into her handbag, and turning to look out of the side window. "Why are we going this way? We didn't come this way on the way up, did we?"

Sander shakes his head. "It's quicker. I checked Google maps. It's almost half an hour quicker."

"But this is the Dartford Crossing, right? We have to pay."

"Oh, shit, yes," Sander says. "Do you want me to find a different route? I could turn south and go through the centre."

"Then we'd have to pay the bloody congestion charge," Penny says, retrieving her phone from her bag again. "No, carry on. I'll pay it now. I have the app."

"It's ridiculous you can't pay at a booth thing anymore," Sander comments.

"You're right. It is utterly ridiculous. I have no idea how the oldies manage it all. And with the congestion charge as well, it's getting impossible to drive anywhere without a smartphone and a credit card these days."

Sander glances in the rearview mirror and, seeing that the kids both have their earbuds in, tests to see if they're listening. "Kids?" he says quietly. "Are you receiving me? Anyone want pizza tonight?" When there's no reply, he adds, glancing at Penny, "They're all plugged in."

"So?" Penny asks.

"So, I don't want to be shouted at again, but I'd really appreciate it if..."

"Please, Sander," Penny pleads. "Tomorrow. I said I'd tell you tomorrow. And I will. But not now. I don't have the energy to go into it all now. I really don't."

"Fine," Sander says.

"Go into what?" Chloe asks, from the back seat.

Penny sends Sander a knowing look. "Nothing," she says. "Listen to your music, darling."

Part Four

Let the Light Shine

It is Saturday morning, and despite an exhausting week at work trying to catch up on the backlog, Penny is driving back to London. It is almost the end of August, and if her mother's flat isn't emptied by the end of the month, a full month's rent will fall due. Victoria, who has been paying the bills while they wait for probate, has said that she doesn't see any point in paying for an empty flat. She has promised to be there today. She has promised to help.

Though Penny is scared of the emotions which are bound to surface as she goes through her mother's things, she's looking forward to getting it over and done with too. Because once this is done, the only remaining task will be the scattering of the ashes. And there's no hurry for that, after all. Lots of people wait years before they do that.

As she drives, she listens to Woman's Hour on the radio. They're discussing the menopause with refreshing honesty and Penny wonders if the various symptoms they're describing as being associated with being perimenopausal mightn't explain the fact that she's completely lost her sex-drive lately. In fact, even when they have "done it" recently, it hasn't been easy, or particularly agreeable, either. She decides to ask Victoria if *she* has had any symptoms yet. Well, she'll ask her, she decides, if an appropriate moment comes up. Because given the fragile nature of their relationship lately, that's not exactly a given.

Though she reaches Vivian Court fifteen minutes after schedule, Victoria has not yet arrived, so she phones her and leaves a voicemail message before heading to her mother's flat. She inserts the key in the lock and lets the door swing open.

To her surprise, absolutely nothing appears to have been done since her mother died – in fact, it looks as if no one has set foot in the room since then. The curtains are drawn, leaving the room in green-tinged semi-darkness. The surfaces are coated in a fine layer of dust and there's even a half-drunk cup of tea on the table, now covered with a thin crust of mould.

She stands in the doorway and surveys the scene. She tries not to cry.

"Hello there!"

Penny turns to face the woman behind her, a pretty, Asian-looking member of staff.

"Hello," Penny says. "I've come to clean her stuff out."

The woman nods gently. "I'm sorry for your loss," she says. "Are you OK? These things are hard."

"They are," Penny agrees.

"For what it's worth, Marge was in fine spirits the night before," the woman says. "I don't suppose that helps, but..."

This woman knew her mother! This woman remembers her name! Penny swallows with difficulty and fights back tears. "You spoke to her?" she croaks.

The woman nods. "I was in the canteen. I'm Dina, by the way. Yes, she said she was going away or something. The seaside, I think. She was looking forward to it."

Penny dabs at the corner of her eye and sniffs — her nose is suddenly running. "That's us," she says. "We live in Whitstable, down in Kent. She was coming to see us. Only..." Her voice peters out.

"Whitstable's nice," Dina says. "I went there once. Anyway, she was on fine form. And like I say, she was looking forward to it – lots."

"Thanks," Penny says. "That does help, actually."

"If there's anything I can do..." Dina offers. "If you need help with anything heavy, or you want boxes or anything."

"Thanks," Penny says again. "My sister's coming, so I should be fine. Though a couple of empty boxes might be useful. I spent all week collecting them but then left them back home."

"I'll get you some right away," Dina says.

Penny lingers in the corridor until she returns with three nested boxes, then takes a deep breath, and steps into the room, closing the door behind her.

She sighs deeply and puts the boxes down. She crosses to the window and peers out between the curtains. She feels somehow as if she is both herself and her mother as she looks out at the view. She wonders if some essence of her mother isn't still present, still floating around in the ether, looking out with her, or perhaps even lurking inside her, looking *through* her eyes, using them as her own.

"Mum? Are you here?" she whispers.

When no answer comes, she sighs jerkily and pulls back the curtains flooding the room with light, then looks back out again. She can see her car down there, she realises. But the feeling is gone. She's alone again.

She turns back to face the room. She walks slowly around the small flat, dragging her fingertips across the dusty surfaces.

They say that most house dust is dead skin, don't they? She lifts her fingertips to her nostrils and sniffs at them, then, perhaps because she saw the gesture in a film, she crosses to her mother's closet and sniffs at the clothes instead. But surprisingly, only the vaguest scent of *Timeless*, her mother's favourite perfume, remains. She pulls the strongest smelling garment, her mother's much loved cardigan, into her arms, then, glancing behind to check her position, she sinks onto the bed. "Mum," she says, simply, as she caresses it.

Eventually, after a few minutes, she gently folds the cardigan and puts it to one side. She looks around the room and wonders where to start.

The closet, she decides, is as good a place as any, but as she fingers the clothes, she realises that though she only wants to keep two items – the cardigan and a hat – she can't begin to get rid of anything else until Victoria tells her which items (if any) *she* would like to keep. So without her sister's presence, the whole process is impossible, really.

She phones Victoria again and leaves another message, then phones Martin and does the same all over again.

She lifts, one by one, her mother's dowdy skirts and dresses from the rack and lays them on the bed. None of these items of clothing "speak" to her – none of them shriek, "Keep me!"

In fact, her main sensation on going through the closet is sadness, not only sadness that her mother is gone, but sadness that she didn't have nicer clothes. Sadness that her life, ultimately, was nothing more and nothing less than a very ordinary life. She deserved more, Penny thinks. She deserved excitement and adventure and at least an occasional dash of good luck. We *all* deserve more than Mum got, she thinks.

She pulls a box from the shelf and puts it on the bed, then kneels before it and removes the lid. It contains her mother's accessories: some cheap jewellery, a string of fake pearls, some gaudy gold earrings, a headscarf; an old, empty purse that she remembers from way back... She doesn't know why, but she slips the fake pearls into her pocket.

She returns to the closet for a second identical but much heavier box. She sits on the bed and removes the lid. The box contains photos, hundreds of them. Here is Victoria in a baby dress sitting on her mother's knee; here an empty pram with a teddy bear in it; next, a proudly taken photo of a homemade birthday cake, a view of Margate seafront, the two sisters on the beach building sandcastles... Here, now, is Ed in the sticky process of eating candy-floss.

"I can't," she breathes, through tears, returning the photos to the box and putting the lid back on. "I can't do this on my own."

She stands, dries her eyes on a tissue from her mother's box of Kleenex, and then pulls on her coat. "And there's no reason why I *should* do this on my own," she adds, as she swipes her keys from the counter. "Bloody hell, Vicky. Where are you?"

When Penny gets to her sister's place it is Bertie who opens the door. He's still in his dressing gown.

"Hi, Bertie," Penny says. "Is your mum in?"

Bertie shakes his head.

"Oh," Penny says. "Do you know where she is? She promised to help me with something today and she's not answering her phone."

Another shake of the head, then, "Mum's not brilliant with promises at the moment. Or phones."

"No," Penny agrees. "No, she isn't, is she? Is your dad around?"

"Work," Bertie says. "But he should be home soon."

"Right. Well, can I come in and wait, then? Would you mind?"

Bertie shrugs and steps aside.

Once the front door is closed, Penny removes her coat and hangs it on the stand. Bertie is already heading for his bedroom, so Penny trots in an attempt at getting there before his door swings shut. But she's too late and has to knock to get him to open it again.

"Look, I know I'm not your favourite person at the moment," Penny says, tentatively, "but do you think I could have a word with you?"

"Sure," Bertie replies, albeit unenthusiastically. He backs into his bedroom and plops himself on the edge of his unmade bed.

"Were you sleeping?" Penny asks.

"Facebook," Bertie says, nodding in the direction of his laptop.

"Right. Well, I wanted to talk to you the other day, actually. At the funeral. But your mum said it was better to wait."

"She told me."

"She told you what?"

"That it was all a misunderstanding and everything."

"Yes. It really *was*," Penny says. "If I'd realised you were... you were having a hard time, I would have definitely said yes. I just thought you were joking. It was right in the middle of my argument with your mum and I just thought you were taking the Mickey to be honest."

Bertie nods. "OK," he says.

"Can I sit down?" Penny asks, nodding at the chair next to Bertie's desk.

"If you want."

"So, your mum told me you had a really bad summer," Penny says, moving clothes from the chair to the desk and sitting down.

"Yeah. Kind of."

"Can you tell me what's been happening? Only if you want to, of course, but..."

"Nah," Bertie says. "You're all right."

"Oh." Penny hadn't been expecting that. "Well, can you at least tell me if things are still bad?"

Bertie shrugs.

"So, you don't feel the need to come and stay with us anymore?"

Another shrug. But then, just as Penny is beginning to despair, an opening comes. "They wouldn't let me anyway," Bertie says.

"Who wouldn't?"

"Mum and Dad."

"But you'd like to? If you could? Would you like me to talk to them? Would you like me to see what I can arrange?"

Bertie shrugs yet again but also nods. "I guess," he says. "Maybe Will could come and pick me up. Like he used to come and get Gran?"

"That's possible. I could ask him."

"I just need to get out of here," Bertie says. "I hate it here."

"Why is that, Bertie?" Penny asks. "Why don't you tell me?"

Bertie pushes his bottom lip out. "They're always asking me questions. All the time. I can't stand it. It's like a police interrogation or something."

Penny clears her throat. "Right," she says. "Message received."

"Sorry," Bertie says. "It's just..." He shakes his head.

"No, I know *exactly* what you mean, actually," Penny tells him. "Sometimes you just want to keep things to yourself, don't you? Sometimes you just want some time to think about things without everyone asking you to explain yourself before you even know what you think about it all."

"That's exactly it," Bertie says.

"So, leave it with me. And I'll see what I can do, OK?"

"You'll ask Mum and Dad? Really?"

"Yes. I'm not promising miracles, but I'll ask if you can come for weekends from time to time. That should be doable."

"And you'll ask Will if he can come and get me?"

"Yes. I mean, even if Will isn't coming down, you're still big enough to jump on a train, aren't you?"

"Sure," Bertie says.

At that moment, the front door to the apartment opens. "Ah, someone's home," Penny says.

"That's Dad."

"How do you know?" Penny asks.

Bertie shrugs. "He drops his keys in the bowl when he comes in. Mum leaves hers all over the place. And then we all have to help her look for them otherwise she cries."

Penny steps out of Bertie's bedroom to find Martin in the hallway; he's shrugging out of his overcoat while simultaneously fiddling with his iPhone. "Oh! Hello Penny!" he says. "I was just reading your text messages."

"Sorry," Penny says. "I didn't realise you were at work. I was just trying to find my sister, really."

"She's gone AWOL again, has she?" Martin asks, hanging his coat on the rack.

"Yes, she was supposed to help me with Mum's flat, but she didn't turn up."

"Huh," Martin says, now loosening his tie and undoing his top button. "How's that going? Cup of tea?"

"Sure," Penny says, following him through to the kitchen. "And it's not really going at all. I tried to start going through her stuff, but I couldn't face it on my own."

"I can imagine," Martin says. "Actually, I'm hungry. I'm going to make myself a sandwich. Do you want one?"

"A sandwich would be good," Penny says. "Would you like me to do it, though? You don't want to be getting butter over your suit."

Martin shakes his head. "It's fine," he says. "Take a seat. And then if Vicky isn't back by the time we've eaten, I'll come and give you a hand with the flat. How does that sound?"

"Oh, um, that sounds lovely," Penny says. "But totally beyond the call of duty."

"It'll be easier for me," Martin says. "I mean, I loved the old dear, but she wasn't my mother."

"No."

"Bertie? BERTIE!!" Martin shouts.

Bertie pops his head around the door and shouts back, "What?"

"I'm making sandwiches. Do you want one?"

"No thanks," he shouts back.

"I don't know why I bother," Martin mutters.

"Adolescence?"

"Something like that," he says, pulling bread from the bread-bin, then cheese and butter from the refrigerator.

"That is a lovely suit," Penny comments. Martin's sheer, teal suit is catching the light as he moves around, shimmering almost.

"This?" Martin says. "It's pretty ancient actually. But Vicky won't let me get rid of it. She got the trousers adjusted a while back. Middle-aged spread." He taps his stomach through his shirt.

"Oh, you're looking pretty good for..."

"For my age?" Martin laughs.

Penny smiles. "We all put on a bit of weight. It's called being human. But most guys approaching fifty look terrible. I have a single girlfriend, Terri, and you should see the guys she meets online. You're still pretty fit and sporty, aren't you?"

"I do my best," Martin says. "You and Vicky are doing OK, too. You're both good looking women."

"Thanks," Penny says. "But Victoria has her weight far better controlled than I do."

"Ah, that'll be her cast-iron willpower," Martin says.

Penny wishes briefly that he had contradicted her instead. "Yeah," she replies, vaguely.

She sits at the kitchen table and watches Martin as he assembles the sandwiches. It's actually quite strange to find herself alone with him. She's spent shockingly little time alone with Martin since her sister married him twenty years ago. It's simply not something that ever seems to happen and in fact, she has never really had the time to work out what she thinks about him. He's a good looking man, that's for sure. He's a smooth, snappy dresser, too. But beyond that, she's never quite been able to decide whether he's shockingly congenial or merely superficial and boring. Whichever it is, he's certainly easy on the eye.

"So, how's life at the seaside?" Martin asks.

"Oh, you know," Penny says. "Same same."

"Work OK?"

"Work's horrific. But that's entirely normal."

"Ha! I know what you mean there," Martin says.

"We're just waiting for probate to come through, really," Penny admits. "We have this whole backlog of things that need buying, or fixing, or replacing... The kids need new... new *everything*, really. Sander wants to buy some canvases or something. And a load of weed no doubt."

"Is he painting again?"

Penny shrugs. "Not really, no. But he reckons he has an idea. Though I've heard that one before."

"The money's got to come through soon, hasn't it?" Martin asks as he pours boiling water into mugs. "It can't be that complicated."

"I certainly hope so."

"We could lend you some," Martin offers. "In the meantime, I mean. If that helps."

Penny wrinkles her nose. "Thanks," she says. "But I'll give it another week and see if it comes through. If not, I might well take you up on that."

As Martin puts the two plates on the table, his phone on the countertop buzzes, so as he pours milk into the mugs of tea, he studies the screen.

"Your sister," he says. "She says she's gone to see a specialist. She's sorry but it was the only appointment available."

Penny blows out through pursed lips.

"She's let you down a lot lately, huh?" Martin says. "I'm sorry about that."

Penny gestures vaguely with her hands. "I just..." She sighs. "I don't know what's got into her, really. She seems so

285

different. So unpredictable. Is she like this with you as well, or is it just me?"

"She's pretty strange," Martin says. "I think she's going through some kind of change. And we're all kind of waiting to see if it's for the better, in a way. Or not for the better."

"When you say change. Do you mean *The change?*"

Martin pulls a face. "The menopause?" he says. "No, I think she's a bit young for that, don't you? No, she's just a bit all over the place. And of course your mum dying hasn't helped."

Penny thinks that her sister isn't *too young for that* at all, but that she should probably leave that clearly undiscussed subject undiscussed. "So, what kind of specialist is she seeing on a Saturday morning, anyway? Or is it personal?"

Martin shrugs. "Probably someone who will give her even more Valium," he says. "Or perhaps someone who will help her get off the stuff. Hopefully the latter."

"I *thought* she was taking something," Penny says. "I caught her popping pills a couple of times. And she sometimes seemed... I don't know... kind of vague?"

"Oh, she's so stoned sometimes, you can't even have a conversation with her," Martin says as he hangs his jacket on the chair-back and takes a seat next to Penny. With his close physical proximity, the moment seems even stranger. "But I think it's one of the things she's genuinely trying to deal with at the moment. Has she never spoken to you about it?"

Penny bites into her sandwich and shakes her head. "She never talks to me about anything," she says. "Well, nothing important, anyway."

"No, me neither," Martin says as reaches for his own sandwich. "Anyway, bon appétit!"

"Bon appétit," Penny replies, through a mouthful of cheese and bread.

Martin remains relaxed and amenable throughout lunch. He seems pretty "happy in his skin" as the French would say, but then Martin's skin has always been almost irritatingly flawless. It must be a fairly easy skin to be happy in, Penny thinks.

When, in their separate cars, they arrive at Vivian Court, Martin switches to "stunningly efficient" mode. It's a side of him that Penny has never seen before. It must be, she reckons, how he is at work. No wonder he has done so well.

As she watches Martin ruthlessly clear the food cupboards and refrigerator directly into bin bags, Penny realises that it's truly easier for someone who isn't emotionally involved to help out.

As he repeats the operation with Marge's clothes, Penny watches numbly. She truly doesn't want to keep any of these items and yet she's certain that she would find herself totally unable to bin them without Martin's logical, emotionally-neutral help.

When they reach the box of photos, Martin says, "The easiest thing is just to seal them up and put them in your loft – or ours – for later. There's absolutely no reason to look at them today. In fact, I would think that's just about the worst thing you can do."

"You're totally right, of course," Penny admits. "It was looking at those that threw me off my stride this morning."

"And I'd suggest you do the same for all her knick-knacks," Martin says, picking up a china bell from a shelf and ringing it. "Stick them in boxes and tape them up. You'll enjoy going through them one day, but I don't think today is that day."

Penny swallows with difficulty, takes the horrible bell – a horrible bell that graced her childhood home from birth until the moment she left – and starts to wrap it in newspaper. "God, I am so glad you're here," she says.

Martin smiles blankly and winks at her. "It's my pleasure," he says. "It should have been Vicky really, but to be honest, I think you're better off with me. She would have been useless at this."

"Like me."

"You're not useless," Martin says. "But it's your mum's stuff, isn't it. It's bound to be hard. If you want to pay me back you can help me out when my two finally pop their clogs. *If* that ever happens."

"It's a deal," Penny says. "Actually, how are they? You never mention them. They're in Edinburgh, aren't they?"

"Just outside. And they're, you know... senile, grumpy, totally disinterested in anything except their aches and pains."

"They're old," Penny says, summing up.

"Yep," Martin says. "Coming soon to us all."

Marge's apartment having been rented fully-furnished, her possessions don't amount to much. They fill two large bin bags with rubbish and three with clothes. Her sheets and towels, they give to the warden. "People often need them," he says. "You'd be surprised."

Everything else, the junk jewellery, the bells, her collection of utterly pointless decorative thimbles, her pictures and paperweights and books and playing cards, fit into the three boxes Dina provided, and these they seal up with tape and load into the back of Penny's car. There are no surprises. There are no secret love letters, no unmentioned wills leaving everything to an unknown lover or child, no police statements about Cecil.

"It's not a lot, really, is it?" Penny says, staring, her hands on her hips, at the contents of the open hatchback.

"Well, you got rid of most of the junk when she moved in here," Martin says.

"That's true. There was masses of it. All rubbish, but masses of it. A whole houseful. But all the same, look," Penny says. "Is that really it?"

"I suppose it's not the stuff that counts, is it?" Martin says, gently. "I suppose it's the memories."

Penny sighs and nods. "You're right," she says. "Thanks Martin. You're a good man, aren't you?"

Martin wrinkles his brow. "Now why do you sound so surprised about that?" he laughs. "What has my wife been telling you?"

Penny frowns. "I didn't sound surprised," she says. But she realises that she probably *did*, because, in a way, she *is* surprised. She and Sander have, she realises, kind of boxed Martin in to a role that they alone defined for him: the high-earning, Tory-voting lawyer. And like all of us, he is far more complex than that. "Oh, I wanted to ask you something," she says, dragging her eyes away from the bin bags and boxes. "I spoke to Bertie earlier, and I know it's late notice and everything, but, well, Monday's a bank holiday. I was wondering if he could come back with me and spend the weekend with Max and Chloe. They haven't seen anything of each other for ages."

"Maybe," Martin says, leaning against the bonnet of the car. "But he's being very difficult at the moment. I have to warn you."

"He'll be fine with us, I'm sure he will."

"I'm not sure what Victoria's told you," Martin says. "About everything that's gone on this summer?"

Penny nods quickly. "She told me," she says. "About boarding school and the Valium and all that stuff. We'll keep an eye on him. You don't need to worry."

"Oh, I wasn't worried about that," Martin says. "It's just, I think he might drive you insane. He hates everything and everyone at the moment. Especially me actually. God knows what I've done."

"Well, he was OK with me," Penny says. "I mean, he's an adolescent boy... he just shrugs when I talk to him, really. But that's normal. I still think he'd like to come. Maybe it would do him good to get away. It would give you a break too. Things have been quite intense recently as far as I understand."

"They have," Martin says, with meaning. "Well, I'll ask Vicky. He can't come with you now because he has a friend's birthday party to go to tonight. But we could perhaps stick him on a train tomorrow morning. As I say, I'll need to get his mum's approval. Plus I'm off all week, so she might have planned something."

"Of course," Penny says. "My friend Will said he might come down tomorrow, so if he does, he could maybe bring Bertie with him. He could stay a few days. It would be nice."

Martin nods. "Sounds OK to me," he says. "But like I say..."

"Just let me know what she says," Penny tells him. "Either way, it's fine."

"You're not coming back now, then?" Martin asks, checking his watch. "I would think she'll be home soon."

"No, I'll just head back, I think. I have to take the keys back to the warden and pay for the cleaning and stuff. And I have to drop these clothes off at Oxfam or somewhere..." she glances nervously at the bin bags in the car. "And then home, I reckon. It's not like Vicky seems keen to see me at the moment or anything, so..."

Martin nods. "Try not to take that too personally," he says. "Like I said before, she's in a strange place right now."

"It's fine," Penny says, brushing a visualisation of the angst her relationship with her sister generates to one side with her hand. "Actually, it's not fine at all," she continues. "I'm furious with her about not helping with the funeral, and I'm even more furious about her not turning up today. But you being here has atoned for her sins, so I'm going to try to get over myself. But it really is best if I don't come back now. I think I'd kill her."

"Right," Martin says. "Um, I was thinking... why don't you dump those bags in my car and *I'll* take them to Oxfam. I can just see you driving around with those in the back for years."

Penny laughs. "You are so right about that," she says. "How did you know?"

Martin shrugs. "Intuition?" he says. "Go take the keys back and do what you have to do. I'll shift these bags to mine."

As Penny drives home with the sun in her eyes, she starts to feel lighter, actually physically lighter, as if a non-metaphorical weight has been lifted from her shoulders. She hadn't realised how much she had been dreading dealing with this. She hadn't understood how much the frozen stasis of her mother's apartment had been weighing on her.

An old Bill Withers song comes on the radio, a song she likes, and as she drives back towards their seaside haven, she first taps her fingers, and then, after a moment, even joins in a little. "Lovely day, lovely day, lovely day..." she sings. It's the first time she has felt sane in weeks.

She starts, too, to allow happy memories of her mother to surface. She remembers the time Marge tried to teach her to knit. It had been supposed to be a money saving gesture. It was meant to calm her pregnant nerves, too. But she had given up after less than ten rows. She had handed the mess back to her mother to sort out. She remembers Marge helping her paint Chloe's room, too. She thinks back to a day on the pier when her mother's hat had blown into the sea. She had had too much to drink that lunchtime and had danced a little as they walked home. Yes, despite Victoria's current downer on her, there had been good times too. There had been happiness. There had been love.

As she leaves the M2, the music is interrupted by a phone call from Sander. She has never quite got used to the hands-free phone thingy, and is always a little surprised when she manages to make it work. "Hello?" she says, tentatively pressing buttons on the steering wheel.

Sander's voice springs from the speakers. He tells her that he's in Canterbury at an art supplies shop. He asks her, then begs her, to join him there.

"Can't it wait till the money comes through?" Penny asks him, restraining herself from pointing out that seeing as he hasn't painted anything of note for fifteen years, another few days won't hurt.

"But it *has* arrived," Sander tells her excitedly. "I checked this morning, and there's over forty grand in the account. Please, babe? I'm on a roll, but I need these big canvases."

By the time Penny reaches Cowling and Wilcox, Sander has finished shopping. He's standing on the pavement with three vast canvases leaning against his side and a huge bag of materials at his feet.

"Thanks so much for this, babe," he says as they load them into the rear of the car. "I was going to struggle home with these on the train, but this is so much easier."

He asks Penny about her day, but she doesn't tell him much. She doesn't want to think about it any more, plus the hours spent with Martin feel strangely like some kind of infidelity. She's not sure why that is, but she asks Sander about his big idea instead.

"You know the old masters, like um, Millet and Eastman Johnson, people like that?" he says, almost breathless with excitement. "You know the way they used to paint the tradesmens? The families harvesting the corn, and the threshers, and the washer women and what have you?"

"Tradesmen is plural," Penny reminds him. "It contains the word 'men' which is the plural of man. So it doesn't need an 'S'. It's just that you asked me to point out when you do that S thing..."

"Sure, right..." Sander says, sounding annoyed that she has interrupted his flow. "But do you know what I mean?"

"Those harvest paintings?" Penny says vaguely. "I think so."

"Well, I'm going to do something like that," Sander tells her. "Only with the jobs people do today. Traditional, masterly oil paintings, but of checkout girls and UPS guys and pole dancers. It's gonna be awesome."

"I can see you coming from here," Penny says. "I can see the pole dancing research being quite time consuming. And expensive."

"Ha," Sander laughs. "I'll probably just work from photos for that one. But do you see the idea? Do you see how gorgeous it's going to be? The colours of all those packages

293

behind the checkout girl? The neon lights in the strip club. But really thick chunky paint – probably do it all with a pallet knife. And big – big enough so you can stand back and ignore the texture."

The images that manifest in Penny's mind aren't really gorgeous at all. In fact, the idea strikes her as quite horrific. But she hasn't seen Sander this excited for years. He seems younger and sharper and, yes, sexier even. And so she keeps her doubts to herself. "That sounds fabulous, dear," she says.

Her main fear recently as far as Sander is concerned has been that the second the money arrived he would rush out and buy a lorryload of weed. Because since he cut down, he's been so much more *present* in their lives, so much funnier and more useful around the house. So a sudden urge to spend money on materials is quite a relief. "You're not going to start smoking again, are you?" Penny asks, her fears slipping out. "Not like before?"

"I never stopped," Sander says, frowning now, suddenly knocked off his optimistic top of the hill. "Where did that come from?"

"I don't know," Penny says. "I guess I'm just thinking that it would be a shame if instead of creating these wonderful paintings you're telling me about you just started smoking joints and staring into the middle distance again."

"Oh," Sander says, then, "Just tell it like it is, honey. Don't beat around the bushes or anything."

"I think it's good. That we can talk honestly. Don't you?"

"I suppose," Sander says.

"I just like you more when you smoke less," Penny explains. "And I think it's done you good to cut down. I think that might even be why you're so excited today."

Sander sighs deeply, so Penny glances briefly across at him before returning her gaze to the road ahead. "What?" she asks. "What did I say?"

Sander shrugs. "I just hate it when you're right about stuff," he says.

. . .

The following morning, Will arrives just before ten. Bertie, having got home late from his party, is still sleeping, while Martin is already out playing squash.

"Hi Will," Victoria says. "He's still in bed, I'm afraid. But I'll wake him up right now."

"Ah, sorry," Will says. "We're early. It's kind of our speciality these days. Ben gets so excited whenever we go anywhere. He's like a little dog. He even does that whimpering thing."

Victoria laughs. "B-E-R-T-I-E-E-E!" she shouts. "Will's here. He's left the dog in the car."

"Actually I had better go and tell him to park," Will says. "He's just kerbed it outside for the moment."

By the time Will returns, Bertie is in the shower and Victoria has made a French press of coffee. "We couldn't find a space anywhere," Will tells her. "But Ben's fine in the car. He's reading something on his Kindle. Some novel about aliens or something."

"Oh, no!" Victoria says. "That's not fair. There's a car park around the corner. Do you want me to…"

"He's fine," Will interrupts. "Really. He's totally fine."

"Well, Bertie won't be long, anyway. He's pretty fast in the mornings. Even faster when it's to escape the horror of home."

As Victoria presses the plunger on the coffee pot, Will crosses to the window and looks out over the roofs. "This is a great apartment," he says. "Nice balcony-terrace-thingy too."

"Yes, it's OK," Victoria agrees. "It was expensive when we bought it, but it's worth silly amounts of money nowadays. But we like it. For London..."

"You'd rather live somewhere else? I mean, if you could. If Martin's job wasn't here?"

"I'm not sure," Victoria says. "I have a whole love-hate thing going on with London. I'd be tempted by the seaside, maybe. Or the countryside. Or somewhere hot – a Greek island, maybe. But I kind of like the bustle and grime as well."

"I know what you mean," Will says. "I think it's the anonymity I like. That you can dress however you want, that you can *be* whoever you want. I grew up in a village near Shrewsbury, and everyone knew everyone's business there. But here, no one gives a damn. D'you know what I mean?"

"I do," Victoria says, handing Will a mug of coffee. "Sugar?"

Will shakes his head.

"Yes, no matter how mad you are in London, at least you're never the maddest, right?"

Will smiles lopsidedly. "I suppose," he says.

"Here, come outside. I want to smoke."

They move to the small roof terrace and Victoria slides the door closed behind her. She lights a cigarette, offers Will one (he refuses) and sits down. Will leans against the wall and continues to look out at the view. "It's going to be hot, I think," he says. "We might even get a swim. A hot bank holiday weekend – it's a whole new concept!"

"Yes," Victoria says, her mind clearly elsewhere. "So, what happened to you the other day? I can't say I blame you, but you did a very efficient disappearing act after the funeral."

"Oh," Will says. "Yes. I was a bit embarrassed about that. Penny wasn't too upset, was she?"

"I don't know," Victoria says. "But I don't think so. She had other things on her mind, really. We all did."

"Right."

"So, what happened?"

Will shrugs. "I can't really go into it. But suffice to say Ben overheard a bit of your argument with your uncle. And it brought up... I don't know... a few *issues* for him, I suppose you could say."

"Oh," Victoria says, frowning. "You don't mean... I mean, Ben wasn't... Nothing like that happened to Ben, did it?"

Will shakes his head. "Sorry. I really can't go into it. It's all *very* private stuff. But we would have come if we could. Ben was just too upset."

"Oh, poor Ben," Victoria says.

"Yes," Will agrees. "Poor Ben. What with his schooling and his family, it's amazing he's still sane, really."

"Resilience," Victoria says.

"Indeed."

Victoria drags heavily on her cigarette then taps the ash over the edge of the balcony. "Look, Will, I need to ask you a favour, actually," she says.

"Okay..." Will says, sounding doubtful.

"It's... well... it's delicate."

Will nods. "Go on?"

"I feel like it's a bit of a nerve, really, me asking you. I mean, you're Penny's friend, aren't you? Not mine."

"It's fine," Will says. "Anyway, I like to think I'm friends with both of you."

"Thanks," Victoria says, even though they both know that it's not really true. "The thing is, it's... well, it's Bertie."

"He's been having a hard time, right?" Will offers, trying to make whatever Victoria has to say a little easier. "Penny told me a bit about it all."

"Yes."

"Is there something I can do to help?"

Victoria sighs. "I'm not sure, but there's this mystery, right? And it's making everything incredibly difficult."

"A mystery?" Will repeats.

"Yes, about what's actually wrong with him. He told the shrink, apparently, but he still won't tell *us* anything. It's incredibly frustrating."

"Can't you ask the shrink?" Will says. "I mean, Bertie's still a minor, right?"

"Yes, you'd think so, wouldn't you?" Victoria says. "But no. It's been going on for months and she won't tell us anything either. It's like living in a big dark cave without a torch."

"So you want me to try and find out?"

"I don't know," Victoria says. "I mean, he probably won't talk to you either. Why would he? But if you could try... maybe during the drive down, or while you're at Penny's... if the opportunity should present itself. I mean, don't force it or anything, but..."

"Have you any kind of inkling?" Will asks. "Any leads?"

"Not really, no. But I'm scared it's something here, I suppose."

"Something here?"

"Something at school, perhaps. I mean, he wants to go to boarding school, and we've been trying to organise that but there aren't any places available. Or something at home, maybe? Something we're doing that we aren't aware of. Or something one of us is doing that the other one isn't aware of, even. I don't know."

"Wow, things are really difficult, huh?" Will says.

"He never wants to spend time with us, these days. He won't even eat at the table unless we force him to. He doesn't want to live here, he says. And he won't go *anywhere* with Martin. I'm... I don't know. I'm scared something's going on and I'm somehow... failing him, I suppose," Victoria says, raising her cigarette to her mouth and trying to stay the trembling of her hand.

Will scratches his head and crosses the terrace to take a seat next to Victoria. "What kind of thing do you think might be going on?" he asks, seriously.

"I don't know," Victoria says. And it's true. It's suddenly true that she doesn't know. Her mind is mercifully blank. Because she simply can't let herself think that thought.

But if it *was* something serious, if it was something *like that*, then she'd believe him. That's for certain. She'd do everything in her power to protect him, to save him, to avenge him, even. Because not being believed, not being saved, well, she's been there. And that's horrific. That's beyond words.

"What kind of thing, Victoria?" Will asks again, sounding deeply concerned.

"I don't know, Will. I honestly don't. But..."

The door to the kitchen slides open and Bertie pops his head out, interrupting them. "I'm ready, Will," he says, his happy voice jarring against the angst of the moment and contrasting peculiarly with Victoria's depiction of him. "Super quick, huh?"

"Um, ultra-quick!" Will says, forcing a smile even as he glances worriedly at Victoria. "You... um... you should give Ben lessons, he takes hours. *And* he uses all the hot water."

Will gulps down his coffee and, as he stands, rests one hand on Victoria's shoulder. "Leave it with me. I'll see what I can do," he says, giving it a squeeze.

Victoria sends Will off with a travel-cup of coffee for "poor Ben."

"I won that in a stupid school raffle," Bertie tells Will as they step out onto the street.

"The cup?" Will asks.

"Yeah," Bertie says. "Best prize ever, huh?"

"Well, Ben will thank you for it, at least."

Will waits until the stressful navigation of inner London is over before attempting to talk to Bertie. "So how's life?" he asks, as they join the A2.

"Fine, you know... OK," Bertie says.

"You seem full of beans today, at any rate."

"D'you think we'll be able to swim? D'you think it'll be warm enough?" Bertie asks. "I haven't been swimming for ages. Well, except with school."

"Hopefully," Will says.

"Absolutely not," Ben laughs, glancing in the rearview mirror.

"Ben won't swim unless the sea is actually boiling," Will jokes. "He needs to see those bubbles rising to the surface otherwise he won't even dip a toe in."

"Hey, I swam in Greece," Ben protests.

"I rest my case," Will laughs. "So how *is* school? I heard you want to change or something."

"It's OK," Bertie says. "Does Max still have that helicopter thing?"

"The drone?"

"Yeah."

"Not sure," Will says.

"He crashed it, I think," Ben offers. "But it still works. It just steers funny."

"Cool," Bertie says.

"So, why do you want to change school, Bertie?" Will asks, wincing at his own attempts at sounding casual. "I thought you were a grade A student or something."

"Has Mum asked you to interrogate me?" Bertie asks.

"I'm sorry?" Will says. "Um, no. Of course not. Why would she do that?"

Bertie shrugs. "It's just there's lots of questions suddenly."

"Sorry," Will says, feigning umbrage. "But around here we call that *conversation*."

They drive for ten minutes in silence before Bertie says, "It's just that I wanted to go to boarding school, that's all."

"Boarding school?!" Ben asks, genuinely shocked. "Why in God's name would anyone *want* to go to *boarding school*?"

"Um, Ben went to boarding school," Will explains. "Didn't have the best time."

"And the understatement of the year award goes to Will," Ben says theatrically.

Bertie now slackens off his seatbelt and leans forward. Ben clearly has grabbed his attention. "Where did you go, Ben?" he asks.

"Winchester College."

"Oh, we looked at that one, but Dad said it was too expensive."

"Lucky you."

"No good then?"

"Oh, it's nice enough," Ben says. "If you like being beaten up every day. It's good if you're into finding dog-poo in your bed, as well. That's kind of a Winchester speciality."

"Eww," Bertie says.

"Ben got bullied a lot," Will explains.

"Constantly, in fact," Ben adds, lightly.

"Why?" Bertie asks.

"Why did they bully me?" Ben says. "I guess you'd have to ask them."

"You can probably guess why," Will tells Bertie, "if you try."

Bertie frowns deeply and slumps back in his seat.

"Are you getting bullied?" Will asks. "Is that why you want to leave?"

Bertie doesn't answer, so Will twists in his seat in order to look back at him, an effort Bertie rewards with a sullen shake of the head.

"So why then?" Will asks.

Bertie shrugs.

"Too many questions," Ben says. "Leave the lad alone."

"Yes. Of course. Sorry," Will says.

They drive in silence for a another minute, then Ben switches on the radio. But the second he does so, Bertie speaks again, forcing him to turn the sound down. "Ben?" he asks.

"Bertie?"

"Was it because... you know... Was it because you're gay?"

"Top marks to the boy in the back row!" Ben says, then, after another pause, "Of course everyone didn't hate the place.

In fact, if you're a homophobic bully then there's probably no better place to be."

"That's horrible," Bertie says.

"Yes," Ben agrees. "It was."

"I saw a film," Bertie says. "And it wasn't like that at all."

"Yeah?"

"Yeah. With Rupert Everett in it. An old film."

Ben and Will exchange knowing glances. "*Another Country*?" Will suggests. "About Eton?"

"It was filmed in Oxford, I think," Ben says.

"Yeah, but it was supposed to be Eton."

"Maybe," Bertie says, then, "Yes, I think so."

Will bites his bottom lip before speaking. "So, when did you see that, Bertie?" he asks nonchalantly.

"Ages ago."

"At the cinema?" Ben asks.

"Nah, it's ancient," Bertie says. "My friend Aaron downloaded it, I think. He downloads loads of films."

"Right," Will says, then, "And you watched it together?"

When Bertie fails again to reply, Will stretches and peers back at him. Bertie, he discovers, is staring straight ahead. His face looks swollen with as-yet unshed tears.

"Are you all right, mate?" Will asks, earnestly.

Bertie's face starts to distort.

"Hey, Ben," Will says, turning back. "Can you pull over somewhere?"

"Why?" Ben asks, struggling to see Bertie's face in the mirror.

"Hey, Bertie," Will says, shifting even further around in his seat. "Whatever it is, it's OK, all right?"

Tears are rolling down Bertie's cheeks now. "You won't tell anyone, will you?" he asks.

"Jesus, mate," Will says. "Of course not!"

A few miles later, Ben manages to pull off the A2. "There you go," Will says, pointing to a homemade sign on the roundabout.

"Nell's Cafe?" Ben asks, incredulously. "Are you sure? Are you sure you want to have *this* conversation in Nell's Cafe with all the long distance lorry drivers sitting in?"

"OK, forget it," Will says. "Just stop over there." He points to a gravelly strip of hard shoulder at the roadside.

But as soon as the vehicle has stopped, Bertie jumps out and begins to run off down the road. "Jesus!" Will exclaims. "Wait here. I've got this."

"Hold on," Ben says, grabbing Will's arm as he opens the door. "Is he gay or something?"

"I don't know," Will says. "But I've a feeling we're about to find out. Bertie? BERTIE!"

Will catches up with Bertie at a T-junction, where, unsure where to go next, Bertie has stalled. He is sitting on a concrete bollard on a tatty grassy verge as juggernauts rush by.

"Hey," Will says. "Don't run off on me like that. Jesus, imagine what your folks would say if I had go back and tell them I lost you near Nell's Cafe!"

Bertie sniffs. "Good riddance, maybe?"

"Now that I very much doubt," Wills says, bending over and struggling to catch his breath. "So, what's up matey?"

Bertie shrugs. "Nothing," he says.

"Well, this doesn't *look* much like nothing, does it?" Will says. "You seem pretty upset about something. Now, I have my own ideas why that might be, but it would be far better if you just told me."

"Told you what?"

"I don't know," Will says. "Anything you want."

Bertie shrugs again.

"OK, let's try this," Will says, through a sigh. He sits briefly on another bollard but, deciding that it's too far away, he stands again and crouches down beside Bertie. "Did you want to go to boarding school because you thought it would be... I don't know... easier, perhaps, to be who you want to be?"

Bertie sniffs and shrugs again.

"Did you think it would be like *Another Country*? Is that it?"

"It's just a film," Bertie says. "I know that."

"A film you watched with your friend Aaron?"

Bertie nods.

"And you liked it? The film?"

Bertie nods again, a little sheepishly this time.

"So why don't you tell me *why* you liked it?" Will says, trying a different tack.

Bertie wipes his eyes on his sleeve and looks up through his lashes at Will. "You won't tell him, will you?" he says.

"Who?"

"Dad."

"Oh, no! I won't tell anyone anything you don't want me to tell them. And that's a promise, OK?"

Bertie nods.

"So..."

"So, why did I like the film?"

Will nods encouragingly. "If you want, yes."

Bertie chews the inside of his mouth and sniffs repeatedly before replying, "Well, Rupert Everett is kind of hot in it, isn't he?"

Will snorts. Laughter bursts out of him in a swell of relief. Tears manifest in his own eyes, too. He scratches one ear then caresses his beard as he tries to decide how to respond. "He is," he finally says. "Rupert Everett is kind of hot. Though I preferred the other one, to be honest. The blond one who plays his lover. James something, wasn't it?"

Bertie nods. "That's what Aaron said. But I preferred Everett."

"Fair enough," Will says. "Each to his own. I'm still not sure it's a film that would make me want to go to boarding school, though. I mean, I haven't seen it for ages, but one of them commits suicide, doesn't he?"

Bertie nods. "Yeah," he says. "Well, I tried that too."

"Oh, shit, Bertie," Will says. "Things aren't like that anymore. It's not nineteen thirty or anything. You don't have to feel bad about who you are, whoever you think is hot."

Bertie shrugs. "You say that, but..." he says, then, "You know, I wanted to tell you for ages. But I was scared you'd tell Dad."

"Oh, you don't have to worry about that," Will says. "We homos are like a secret society. We never tell anyone anything."

"Right," Bertie says.

"So, just to be clear, here," Wills says, scared, suddenly, that he's jumping the gun. "Are you saying... I mean, you are saying, aren't you, that you think you might be gay, yeah?"

"Might be?" Bertie says, pulling a face.

"Yes."

"Do you think that you *might* be gay, Will?" Bertie asks, his tone of voice sarcastic.

"OK. Point taken," Will says, raising the palm of one hand. "So why are you so worried about your dad, anyway?"

"He'd disown me if he knew," Bertie says. "You don't know him."

Will frowns. "Hum," he says. "I don't know him *well*, it's true. But he's always been pleasant enough to me. And to Ben. Plus I think you'll find that parents disowning their kids is another thing that only really happens in films these days."

"He told me to man up," Bertie says. "He said everyone would think I was a fag otherwise."

Will pulls a face. "A *fag*?" he says. "Are you sure he said that?"

"A fag or a poof," Bertie says. "I can't remember, but he made me do more sports. So people wouldn't pick on me. I had to do judo and football and stupid rugby. He was worried they'd think I was gay otherwise... So you see?"

"Right," Will says, looking troubled. "Well, this is our secret then. I won't tell a soul. Now, lovely as it is here breathing in all these diesel fumes, how would you feel about going back to the car and then driving somewhere a bit nicer where we can carry on this conversation? Um?"

Bertie nods. "OK," he says. "Are you going to tell Ben?"

Will laughs as he straightens up. "Um, I think Ben worked it out already." Bertie looks concerned about this so Will adds, "Not because of you or anything. It's just the film. Not a lot of teenage heterosexual lads hunt down copies of *Another Country*, you know what I mean?"

"Bit of a give-away, then?" Bertie says.

"Yeah," Will says, putting one arm around his shoulder and giving him a squeeze. "Yeah, just a bit."

As they start to walk back towards the car, Bertie says, "You *won't* tell anyone else, though, will you?"

"No!" Will says. "I told you. I promised even. And Ben will promise too if you want. Don't worry."

"It's just that you're friends with Penny and everything. And she might tell Mum. And Mum would tell Dad..."

"I won't tell anyone. Not even Penny. But I'll bet you anything you like that your dad would be fine about it," Will says.

"I bet you he wouldn't."

"Everyone thinks that," Will says. "But they're hardly ever right. I was terrified when I told my dad, but he just said, 'Yeah, I know'."

"Really?"

"Really."

"How did he guess, do you think?"

Will shrugs. "I don't know really. I mean, I did have a bit of a thing for Barbie dolls. So that might have been a giveaway."

Bertie pulls a face. "Really?" he says. "Or are you winding me up?"

"Sadly not," Will laughs. "I used to borrow them from girls at school. Mum was fine, too, when I told her. I mean, she cried a bit. She was worried that I was going to be unhappy or lonely or something. But she soon got over it. And she *loves* Ben."

As they approach the car, Ben, who is leaning on the bonnet, gives them a thin lipped smile and a little upwards nod of the head. "All better now?" he says.

Will nods. "We're just talking about telling parents. Yours were OK too, weren't they?"

"I only ever told my Mum," Ben says. "She was convinced Dad would lose the plot, so we kept it a secret. But I reckon he would have been OK, really. I kind of regret not telling him. But it's too late now."

"Is he...?"

"Dead, yeah," Ben says. "My theory is to choose your moment carefully. You have to wait till something bigger or more urgent is going on so that it doesn't seem like such a big deal. Funerals are good, I reckon. Or flooded kitchens, exploding ovens... shit like that."

Bertie frowns. "I don't understand," he says.

"I told Mum when our car broke down in the middle of a crossroads," Ben explains. "She said, 'What? Why are you telling me this now? Help me push this bloody car.'"

"Oh, right," Bertie says. "I get it. So do you think I should have told them at Gran's funeral, maybe?"

"No," Will says. "Like I say, I think they'll be fine whenever you tell them. In the meantime," he adds, addressing Ben, "Bertie wants us to promise we won't tell a soul."

"Of course we won't!" Ben says. Jingling the car keys, he adds, "So, where to now?"

Will turns to Bertie. "That cafe over there, so we can talk in comfort? Or another nicer cafe... or a pub or something farther down? Or straight to Penny's? You choose."

"Penny's is fine," Bertie says. "We can talk in the car anyway, can't we?"

"Sure," Will replies. "Let's do that."

Once they are on the move, Will pulls his phone from his pocket and, below Bertie's line of vision, composes a text message.

Bertie, however, spots what he's doing. "Who's that to?" he asks.

"Just Penny," Will says. "Just saying we're running a bit later than planned."

But it's a lie. The text, addressed in fact to Victoria, reads, "Mystery solved. I can't tell you (I promised), but I'll work on Bertie... Relax and enjoy your weekend. And maybe don't mention it to Martin just yet. xxx"

• • •

Penny unfolds the ancient deckchair and drags it across their scrubby lawn until it is in the sun. She then returns to the kitchen and pours herself a jumbo glass of Prosecco. Now the money has come through, she is having a long awaited break from Lidl's boxed Chardonnay.

It's a stunning August Sunday, and Bertie, Chloe and Max are picnicking on the beach while Will, Ben and Sander have gone to the pub. It's the first time she has been both calm and alone in over a month and she's intending to make the most of it.

She returns to the deckchair (Solomon has curled up underneath it) and takes a hefty swig of wine – it's cool and delicious and fruity – and then after fidgeting briefly to get comfortable, she drops one hand to stroke the cat, closes her eyes and turns her face to the sun.

The heat on her eyelids, the red light filtering through, the purring of the cat, the distant screams of families playing on the beach at the front of the house... it's all lovely. She sighs with contentment.

She listens to the gulls screeching, to the distant swell of waves upon the beach. She thinks about her mother and feels the loss all over again, but in a softer, gentler kind of way. She thinks of Bertie, who seemed strangely, almost hysterically happy on arrival, and wonders if she will ever find out why he has been so unhappy at home. She thinks of Sander who claimed he was spending the entire weekend painting, but who has now gone to the pub instead. And then, as she starts to drift, she pictures Chloe swimming, and then Chloe painting a portrait of Bertie. She dreams of Bertie painting a portrait of the cat, and then the cat painting a seagull, and then the cat and Max jumping in a canoe and paddling off over the horizon.

She's dragged from her dream by the chime of the doorbell. She groans, tries to sit up, but then decides to ignore it and reaches for her wine instead. But the wine is now warm. She wonders how long she has been asleep.

When the doorbell chimes a second and then third time, she sighs and manages to lever herself from the deckchair.

She opens the front door to find Victoria standing on the doormat. "Oh!" Penny exclaims. "Gosh. It's you."

"Ha!" Victoria says, already squeezing past her. "I was worried no one was in."

Penny frowns and watches her as she advances towards the kitchen. She looks at Victoria's bag, pulls a face, and then turns and closes the front door again.

"Um, lovely surprise and everything," Penny says when she reaches the kitchen. "But why are you here?"

"Huh," Victoria says. "That's a nice welcome for your big sister, isn't it?"

Penny shakes her head sharply from side to side and blinks repeatedly. She's still struggling to wake up. "Seriously, Vicky. Why *are* you here?"

Victoria puts down her bag and turns to face her sister. "It's just something I needed to do, OK?" she says, mysteriously. "So are you going to make me a cuppa or not?"

Penny shakes her head. "Make yourself a cuppa," she says. "I'm on Prosecco."

Victoria shrugs. "That'll do," she says, reaching for a glass. "Yes, that'll do nicely."

Penny watches as Victoria opens the refrigerator, pours her own drink and then heads out to the back garden. "What a lovely day," she calls back.

Penny wrinkles her nose, mutters, "It was," and then pours a fresh glass for herself. The bottle is already almost empty. When she gets outside, her sister has stolen her seat, so she sets the glass aside and, feeling resentful, puts up a second deckchair. "Everyone's out," she says. "I was asleep in the sun, to be honest."

"Right," Victoria says. "Where are they all?"

"The kids are on the beach. I'm surprised you didn't see them, actually. And the men have, as tradition dictates, gone to the pub."

Victoria nods and sips at her wine. "This is nice," she says. "It makes a change from that horrible stuff in a box you usually have."

"Right," Penny says. "Well, that horrible stuff in a box is all we could afford. I'm sorry it offended you."

Victoria turns a frown on Penny. "Am I getting bad vibes here? Am I correctly sensing that I'm not welcome? Are you upset with me in some way, sister?"

Penny laughs. "What, you mean other than being upset about the fact that you broke your promise by not coming to Vivian Court?"

"Ah," Victoria says.

"Yes, ah," Penny mockingly repeats. "Plus the fact that Bertie is supposedly here so that you can all have a break from each other. I'm not sure how that works now."

"So you're still angry about Mum's flat?"

"It was yesterday, *sister*," Penny says. "So yes, I'm *still* angry about it."

"Martin helped you though, right?"

"Yes. Martin was lovely. But it was supposed to be you. You promised."

"I know..." Victoria says. She sighs deeply. "Look, I'm sorry. I am. Really. I needed to see this doctor. It was important, if that helps. And she could only see me yesterday, so..."

"You *promised* me. Promises aren't things you can just..."

"I'm sorry," Victoria interrupts, sounding less sorry already. "But I have things going on you don't know about. I have things I have to deal with. And sometimes they need to just take priority. But I'll make it up to you. OK?"

Penny blows through pursed lips. "Do you have any idea how hard that was for me? Going through her things like that? On my own?"

"With Martin."

"No. On my own. I got there and you hadn't turned up. And it was too hard, it was *so hard*, so I came around and you weren't even home. You just don't get it, do you?"

"Of course I do."

"Oh, whatever," Penny spits. "So what's wrong with you, anyway? What was so urgent that it just couldn't wait." *This better be good*, she thinks.

"I had to see a gynaecologist."

"Oh? Because?"

"I've been having troubles. With my pelvic floor," Victoria says, sounding aggressive. "And with my vag, if you must know."

"Ooh. That sounds bad."

"Yes. And it's not even the half of it."

"Is this... this isn't menopause stuff, is it?"

Victoria nods. "Yes, of course it is."

"I've been having hot flushes, I think," Penny says.

Victoria laughs. "If that's all it was! You have no idea what's coming, little sister."

"So, what? You're actually going through the menopause now?"

"I've been perimenopausal for two years. It's horrific."

"Tell me," Penny says. "Tell me what to expect."

"You don't want to know."

"I do. I think it's starting. I've gone a bit... you know... dry. Is that part of it?"

Victoria nods. "Plus cramps and night sweats and waking up at four am. My sex drive vanished pretty early on. I can't sleep – oh, I said that one already, didn't I? My tits hurt. I pee myself when I cough. Um..."

"Oooh," Penny says. "God, Vicky."

"I know."

"So what did the doctor say?"

"Well, I had already seen two. My GP said I should take HRT. But not for more than five years. My other GP said it was dangerous..."

"You have two GPs?"

"Yes. It's a long story."

"And he said it was dangerous why? Because of the cancer risk?"

"Exactly. He said I needed to *man up* and *knuckle down* and various stupid bits of advice like that. I'm telling you, *never* go and see a man about the menopause."

"And this new one is a woman?"

Victoria nods. "She's a world class specialist, actually. She's written papers on it and stuff. That's why I needed to see her. I wanted a definitive opinion. Plus she's old, of course. She's sixty-five or something... So she knows what we're dealing with here. Unlike Doctor Dickhead."

"OK, and?"

"You mean, what did she say?"

"Yes."

"Oh, it turns out the HRT cancer link is all a bit tenuous actually. Well, it isn't exactly tenuous, but the increased risk of breast cancer is offset by reductions in other risks, like colon cancer and what have you. It seriously reduces the risk of me throwing myself off a cliff, too, so that's got to be good."

"So you're going with HRT?"

"I already did. I started a few months back. I'm starting to feel tons better, but I was sick with worry about it. So yesterday was good. She really put my mind at rest."

Penny tuts. "Oh, poor you," she says. "You never mentioned any of this to me before."

"You never *asked* me about any of this before."

"Well, no..."

"But Mum must have told you, right?"

Penny shakes her head. "Nope. Not a word. I didn't even know... you know, that it was happening, yet."

"No? Mum being discreet? That's a new one. Anyway, the long and short of it is, never consult a man about women's problems – they have no idea."

"And you can take the HRT for five years, you say?"

Victoria shakes her head. "Uh-uh," she says. "I could potentially take it *forever* as long as the checkups are OK. Fabulous, isn't it? No menopause for me, sister."

"OK."

"And I'm feeling tons better. I'm telling you, if you're starting to have problems, just go get that HRT."

Penny nods. "Wow," she says. "You're like an HRT salesperson or something."

"I am. I feel quite evangelical about it, actually."

"And you really trust this doctor?"

"Totally. I mean, look... I've seen three people and had three completely different opinions. So at some point you have to choose whichever truth suits you, right? But she has the best credentials on the subject of anyone I could find. There's a seven month waiting list just to see her, only she had a cancellation five minutes before I phoned. That was why I had to go yesterday."

"OK. I hear you," Penny says. She downs the last of her drink. "More wine?" she asks.

Victoria nods. "Oh yes," she says. "More wine!"

When Penny returns, Victoria surprises her by looking up and asking, "Do you think we'll ever be friends again, Pen?"

Penny hands Victoria her drink. "Maybe," she says. "Is that why you're here, then? To patch things up?"

Victoria shrugs. "Partly," she says. "I mean, I really want that to happen. But I'm mainly here because of Bertie, to be honest."

Penny slides back into her deckchair. "Now that, you see, I *don't* get. I thought the whole point of Bertie coming was to give him, and you, some space. Martin even asked me if I could try to find out what he's so upset about, seeing as he won't talk to either of you."

Victoria looks shocked. "Martin asked *you* to find out?"

Penny nods.

"Oh. Gosh."

"Why would that be a surprise?" Penny asks. "He's bound to be as worried about Bertie as you are."

Victoria nods vaguely. "I guess," she says. "It's just, well, I was worried that Martin was part of the problem, I suppose."

"How so?"

Victoria shakes her head. "I don't know. But anyway, Will knows now, apparently. So hopefully he'll let us all in on the secret."

"Will?"

Victoria nods and sips some more wine. "He texted me," she says. "On the way down. Apparently Bertie opened up to him in the car. So we're just inches away from knowing what all this is about. Finally!"

"Ah!" Penny exclaims. "So *that's* why you're here. To interrogate Will? It's not about *us* at all."

"Oh, don't be like that," Victoria says.

"Don't be like what?"

"I don't know. Always looking for a reason to hate me. I'm happy to be here. We're talking again."

"We are," Penny says, flatly.

"We haven't spoken properly for ages."

"And that's *my* fault?"

"Of course not," Victoria says. "But I'm here now, so that's got to be good, hasn't it?"

"I suppose," Penny says, struggling to sound less doubtful than she feels.

The sisters continue to drink. When the first bottle of wine has been emptied, Penny pulls a fresh one from the fridge along with a tub of anchovy-stuffed olives.

The sun moves slowly across the patch of sky and the wispy clouds seemingly burn off, making the day even brighter, even hotter.

Penny repeatedly tells Victoria how angry she is about everything she has had to deal with, and Victoria repeatedly apologises. And yet neither of them sound particularly convincing, not Victoria in her sorrow, nor Penny in her anger. Because though they have managed to avoid the realisation for the last ten months, they are still sisters: there is a profound non-logical, non linguistic connection between them, a unity borne of DNA and blood and shared history. And deep down, Penny has always known, even as she pretended otherwise, that her sister would not have left her to deal with these things alone unless there was simply no other way. We all do the best we can, Penny knows this. No one sets out to disappoint or fail others, especially not their family members. And she now lets herself realise that this applies to Victoria as well. She lets herself understand that Victoria simply didn't have what it took to help her at that moment. And the more she lets her sister talk, the more she lets her explain what she's been going through, the easier that becomes to understand.

By three pm Victoria is slurring her words.

"So where's Martin, anyway?" Penny asks her.

"Ah," Victoria says. "Poor Martin. I left him a note. I'm afraid I've been treating him even worse than you lately."

"Really?" Penny says. "I find that hard to imagine."

"Yes," Victoria says, raising her glass and almost missing her lips. "I've been pretty mean to Martin."

"But why?"

Victoria shrugs. "Well, the whole *meno* thing hasn't been very sexy."

"No. No, I get that," Penny agrees. "Our sex life has taken a hit recently as well."

"Of course, that's all easing off now my oestrogen levels are back up. But all the same."

"All the same, what?"

Victoria shakes her head vaguely. "I don't know," she says. "It's this Bertie business, I suppose. I need it to resolve. It's been affecting me. It has been affecting everything, really."

"Because you think Martin's part of the problem?"

"I really don't know," Victoria says. "But that's what's so scary, isn't it? People never know."

"People never know what?"

Victoria shrugs and sighs. "Terrible things go on in some families, don't they? And everyone's always, kind of, *'Oh, I had no idea that aunty Flo was a satanist. I had no idea she'd been crucifying virgins in the cellar.'*" She runs her tongue across her teeth. She's having a little trouble getting it to curl around words like *crucifying*.

"You don't think Martin is... I mean, you surely don't think he has..." Penny stammers.

"No, I don't," Victoria says. "But my son wants to leave home. He took a bloody overdose rather than going on holiday with his father. So something's wrong, right? And I'm just desperately trying not to be... well, not to be like *her*, I suppose."

"Like who?" Penny asks.

They are interrupted by Will and Ben whose faces have appeared above the garden wall. "Hello ladies!" Will says. "Now, this is a surprise!"

"Hi Will," Victoria says. "Hi Ben."

"Can we come and join the party?" Will asks.

"Sure," Penny says, struggling to lever herself from the deckchair, then crossing the garden to unbolt the gate. "What happened to my husband?" she asks, peering down the alley.

"Oh, we sold him to some Thai prawn fishermen," Will says. "Ten years in slavery, but you get unlimited king prawns. Good deal, huh?"

"He's on the beach," Ben explains. "With the kids. We just came back for our swimming costumes, really."

"Damn!" Victoria says. "I knew I'd forgotten something. I didn't bring my cossie."

"I'll lend you one, I'll go get it now," Penny says, vanishing into the darkness of the house.

"So, Will," Victoria says, patting the deckchair beside her. "Tell me all."

Will smiles at her lopsidedly but remains standing. "I can't," he says. "I promised. And you shouldn't be here."

"Oh, don't be like that," Victoria says. "Come and sit down and tell me everything."

"You're pissed, aren't you?" Will laughs.

"So are you," Ben comments. "Actually, so am *I*."

"Yeah, but not as pissed as her. Look at her! She can hardly sit straight."

Victoria pulls a face. She tries to look sober and outraged but just ends up looking even more intoxicated. "So, come on," she says again. "Spill the beans."

"It's nothing serious," Will says. "That's all you need to know. I mean, Bertie thinks it's serious, obviously. But it isn't. And I can't tell you, so don't ask me to. I can try to persuade Bertie to tell you, and I'm working on that. But I won't break my promise to him. And you really shouldn't have come."

He looks up to see that Penny has returned. She's standing in the shadow of the doorway to the kitchen with a towel and an orange swimming costume in one hand. As she steps out into the sunshine, Will sees that she has a strange expression on her face, a look of amused illumination.

"I just worked it out," Penny says. "God, it's so obvious."

Will shakes his head solemnly, trying to interrupt her flow. But Penny isn't looking at Will. She's looking at Victoria instead, who is stretching and straining in her deck chair as she attempts to look back at her. "What?" Victoria asks. "What did you work out?"

"Well, he's gay, isn't he? That'll be why he told Will. Bertie's gay, that's all! God, I can't believe we didn't spot it before!"

"But..." Victoria says, straining to the side in an attempt at seeing Penny's face more clearly. And then suddenly, after the briefest of creaks and a short, sharp *crack*, she's lying on the floor, the collapsed deckchair beneath her.

Everyone bursts out laughing and when Will manages to say, "... so surprised, she fell out of her chair..." even Victoria manages a smile.

Ben holds out one hand and pulls her to her feet, and when Penny has managed to stop laughing Victoria says, "So, are you serious? About Bertie?"

Penny raises her palms. "Hey, don't ask me," she says. "Ask him."

Victoria turns to Will.

"This isn't fair," Will says earnestly. "It's not fair on Bertie, and it's not fair on me."

"But is it true?" Victoria asks. "For Christ's sake, just tell me."

"You're going to have to pretend not to know," Will says. "That's gonna be really important."

"Fine!" Victoria says. "I'll pretend anything you want. But is that really it? Is that really what's been going on?" She rubs her hip where it hit the frame of the deckchair when she fell. She's going, she thinks, to have a bruise.

Will nods reluctantly.

Victoria raises one hand to cover her mouth but then moves it up to her eyes and begins to cry.

Will, opposite, looks devastated by her reaction. He opens his mouth to speak but then closes it again when no words come out. Ben moves to his side and slides one arm around his waist. "Come," he says softly, trying to pull Will away from a scene which is clearly causing him pain.

"No," Will says, shrugging his arm off. "Wait!"

"I can't believe it," Victoria sobs.

"Jesus!" Will exclaims. "It's not *that* bad."

Penny moves to her sister's side and strokes her shoulder tentatively. She pulls an unhappy face at Will and then says, "Will's right, Vicky. It's really not the worst thing in the world."

"Oh, I know," Victoria splutters, finally lowering her hand to reveal her glistening eyes. "I'm just so relieved!"

"Relieved?" Will asks, his expression shifting from dismay to amusement.

"Yes!" Victoria says. "I mean, if that's all that's wrong? If the whole time, it's just been about that. God! Why didn't he just say? I need to call Martin."

"No you don't," Will says.

"I really do."

"Please," Will says. "Just hold off. Let's see if we can get Bertie to tell you first, OK?"

It takes Victoria fifteen minutes to regain her composure and another five to reapply her makeup. The four adults then pull on their swimming costumes and head to the beach.

"Don't forget," Will says, as they cross the road.

"Be surprised, yes, you said," Victoria replies, then, "How about I take you all out for a meal tonight? A sort of secret celebration that the mystery has been solved?"

"We're having pizza on the beach," Penny tells her. "It's all organised, I'm afraid."

"All right," Victoria says. "But I'll pay, OK?"

"There's really no need," Penny says.

"You can pay for mine," Will offers, cheekily.

The beach is crowded, and they struggle to find Sander and the kids for the simple reason that they are all swimming. But eventually Penny recognises three of their towels, so they lay their own beside them and head down to the water's edge. "They're over there," Penny says, pointing to a buoy in the distance around which four figures are floating.

Ben gets no farther than his ankles before saying, "Jesus! It's freezing."

"Of course it is," Will says, wading in.

"I'll, um, stay back here to guard our stuff, I think," Ben says, even though, other than towels, they haven't brought any stuff.

"Of course you will," Will laughs.

Victoria, who is now knee-deep, changes her mind as well. "I think I'll stay with you, Ben," she says. "I need to talk to someone about this whole Bertie thing, and you're as good as anyone."

"Why thank you, Ma'am," Ben says, his tone of voice caustic.

"So, what do I tell him?" Will calls back.

"Bertie?" Victoria asks.

"Yes. Why are you here? Officially, I mean."

Victoria shrugs. "I was jealous," she says. "Yes, tell him I was jealous of his weekend at the seaside. Tell him I decided to come and join you all. That'll do it."

"OK," Will says, "we'll go with that for now."

• • •

The next morning, Penny comes downstairs to find Victoria loading the dishwasher.

"Ooh, hello," she says. "The cleaning fairy has returned."

"Um?" Victoria replies distractedly, now closing the dishwasher and crouching down in front of the cupboard below the sink. "Do you really not have any bleach? Not even the bit I left behind last time?"

"Um, that was last October," Penny says.

"I know. I just thought that seeing as you don't use the stuff..."

Penny fills the kettle and switches it on. "Tea?" she asks.

"Sure," Victoria says, studying the various labels on Penny's ecological cleaning products.

"You know, I love that you're cleaning my kitchen," Penny says, leaning back against the counter-top and watching her sister, "but what's it all about? I mean, it's not like Mum's here to impress anymore, is it?"

"Um?" Victoria says as she straightens with a spray bottle of Green Clean. "What's it got to do with Mum?"

Penny shrugs. "Oh, you loved it when she used to tell you how clean your place was compared with mine."

"She never told me that."

"Well, she told *me* often enough."

Victoria holds the bottle up. "Is this any good?" she asks.

Penny crosses the room and takes the spray from her grasp. "It has slightly more cleaning power than tap water," she says.

"Oh."

"On the other hand, it won't destroy the planet, kill all the fish in the sea, or give you cancer."

"Right," Victoria says doubtfully.

"But seriously, Vicky, what *is* it all about? Why don't you just stop cleaning for twenty-four hours and have a break?"

"Well, I can't stop, can I?" Victoria says. "I would have thought that was obvious."

"You can't?"

"No. It's an OCD thing. Surely you realised that by now?"

Penny looks puzzled. She pushes her bottom lip out. "Actually, I hadn't. I just thought you were trying to show me up."

Victoria shakes her head. "Sorry sister," she says, "but strange as it may seem, not everything is about you."

"Which you have to admit," Penny says, "is a bit rich coming from you."

"Are we really doing this then?" Victoria says.

"Doing what?"

"The whole argument thing," Victoria says. "Again? Really?"

Penny reaches out and touches Victoria's elbow. "No," she says. "No, we're not. I'm sorry. I'm just grouchy because I haven't had my tea yet."

When the two mugs of tea are ready, the sisters make their way to the lounge. Outside, the day is silent and still. Around them the house sleeps.

"So is the cleaning really an OCD thing?" Penny asks after a few sips of tea. "Have you had a diagnosis?"

Victoria nods. "I have an appointment in March to see someone about it."

"In March? Why March?"

"Because it's the NHS," Victoria says. "And because there are a million immigrants in the queue before me, I imagine."

"It's more likely to be because this wonderful government isn't spending all the taxes those immigrants are paying on the NHS," Penny suggests, "but anyway... Why don't you go private? You've never cared about paying to jump the queue before."

"What's that supposed to mean? Oh, because I see a private GP in Harley Street?"

Penny shrugs. "Well, you do, don't you?"

"Only to get Valium," Victoria says. "If you must know, I'm addicted. I'm trying to wean myself off it, but for the moment, yes, I'm addicted. And the Harley Street guy is far more dealer than doctor."

Penny tuts compassionately at her sister. "Addicted? Are you really?"

"Yep."

"That's a tough one. Look, I'm sorry. I don't know why I'm being like this."

"It's an old habit," Victoria says. "Mum set it up when we were kids. I've thought about it a lot since she died. She created a whole *system* of resentment. A perfect *let's be mean to Victoria* syndrome."

"I don't think that's true at all," Penny says.

"No, well, you wouldn't."

"So how's it going? With the Valium, I mean?" Penny asks, after a pause for thought.

Victoria taps her wedding ring against her mug of tea. She shrugs.

"How much are you taking?"

"I'm down to thirty milligrams now. But I was on forty. I'm doing my best. And the HRT makes it a bit easier."

"That's all related, I suppose," Penny says.

"It seems so. I started getting these anxiety attacks at four am. And my GP gave me Valium, which got me back to sleep, for a while. When he wouldn't give me any more, I found another doctor who would."

"I get that sometimes," Penny says. "The four am thing. But I take Valerian root instead. It's natural."

Victoria laughs. "My neuroses are well beyond the reach of a bit of Valerian root, I'm afraid," she says.

"And the cleaning things? What's that about, then?"

"It's linked to the Valium, really," Victoria explains. "When I stop – between doses, I mean – it's all I can think about, really: How long till I can take the next dose? When I'm busy, cleaning and stuff like that, it helps, sometimes. The time goes faster."

"I see," Penny says, sounding more professional than she would like.

"My life's a bit empty," Victoria says softly, her eyes glistening a little. "That's the thing."

"Oh, don't say that," Penny says. "You have Martin. You have Bertie."

"You know, I really ought to call Martin and put him out of his misery. It's just that Will thinks I should wait until Bertie has told me himself."

"I think Will's right. Bertie made him promise not to tell anyone, and it really should be up to Bertie when he tells his father."

"I suppose it can wait another twenty-four hours. But I just hope Will convinces him to tell us *both* so we can put an end to all of this."

"He will, don't worry. But you see, your life *isn't* empty. You have Bertie and Martin to worry about."

"Bertie's getting older. He doesn't need much from me nowadays. And Martin..."

"Yes?"

"I don't know. I think he might... I mean, you couldn't really blame him, because I haven't been very... you know... sexual. But I think he might be fulfilling his needs elsewhere to be honest."

Penny looks shocked. "God, Vicky!" she says.

"Actually, I don't know at all. But he's been coming home later and later, so..."

"I don't believe that," Penny says. "Martin's lovely. And he loves you. He wouldn't. He just wouldn't."

328

Victoria shrugs. "Well, you would say that."

"Why do you keep saying that?"

"Because... I don't know," Victoria says. "I mean, it's all right for you, with your job and your house by the sea..." she glances around the room now as if to demonstrate the sheer luxury in which Penny is living. Penny follows her gaze and sees only the chipped paint on the fireplace and the threadbare couch that Solomon has spent the last nine years sharpening his claws on. "It's OK for you," Victoria continues, "with your touchy-feely arty husband and your career and your mini-me daughter."

"Huh!" Penny says.

"Huh?"

"Well, you finally said it," Penny says.

"Said what?"

"That you're jealous. I mean, I always knew you were jealous, but you never said it directly before."

"Of course I'm jealous. Just take any aspect of your life and compare it with mine, Penny."

"Any aspect?"

"Yes."

"What, like the fact that I work sixty hours a week but don't get paid overtime? Like the fact that we've been so broke I've been taking the washing to the bloody laundry for months because the machine's broken and we can't afford a new one? Like the fact that – just like you in fact – Sander is addicted to dope, which costs even more than Valium. Like the fact that my husband hasn't earned a penny since the beginning of the century?"

"Yes, but..." Victoria says.

"I have to do everything here," Penny interrupts. "I have to *do* everything and *pay* for everything. You have no idea."

"But you do love Sander?"

"Yes, I love him," Penny says. "But I'm so *tired*. I'm *so damned tired,* Vicky." Penny sighs deeply then continues, "I'd give anything, you know, for a week of your life. A week of zoning out on Valium in front of the telly, and wiping the odd worktop with bleach."

"That's so unfair," Victoria says. "I do not spend my weeks *zoning out in front of the television.*" She prays that Penny won't challenge her on what she *actually* does, all the same. Because she's really not sure what she would say.

But thankfully, Penny's thoughts take a different track. "You're right," she says. "I'm sorry. But you know every time Mum got home from yours, she'd phone me to tell me what a lovely time she'd had. She'd tell me how clean and organised it was. How relaxed you were."

"Relaxed?" Victoria says. "I used to take a double dose of Valium when Mum came. Sometimes I popped a few Tramadol too."

"Tramadol?"

"Yeah. GP number one prescribed them for menstrual cramping. They didn't help much, but combined with Valium and a glass of wine, they give quite a nice buzz. I've got a couple left if you want to try."

"No, you're all right," Penny says. "Anyway, Mum made it all sound quite idyllic at yours. And you have to admit, you've had it easier than me."

"Easier?"

"Well, yes. Martin earns a good wage. You've never had to work. You buy anything you want..."

"See, you've always done this," Victoria says.

"Done what?"

"I don't know. Pretended everything was easy for me. Pretended I have some kind of charmed life. You've always had a chip on your shoulder about things. That's what Mum always said about you, actually – that you had a chip on your shoulder. But that... that *resentment* stops good things from happening to you, Penny. There are loads of times I wanted to help you out, but I couldn't."

"Because of the chip on my shoulder?" Penny says, glancing at her shoulder and brushing it mockingly. Despite her best efforts, she's starting to feel quite angry again.

"Yes! At the funeral, for instance, I wanted to lend you some money, but I didn't dare. Because we all know how you would have reacted to that. It's like the washing machine business. I wanted to give you my Smegs. I even asked Martin if he'd agree to drive them down to you. But Mum said it would offend you. She said you'd always had a chip on your shoulder about my cast-offs. And she's right."

"That's so untrue," Penny protests.

"No, it isn't."

"I *asked* Mum about your washing machine. And do you know what she said?"

"No, I don't. But I think you're about to enlighten me."

"She said you were selfish. That's what she said. She said that even when you were little you wouldn't lend me your toys. She reminded me how even when you didn't want them anymore, I still couldn't have them. And she was right. You *were* like that. You *are* like that. And so knowing full well that we needed a new machine you sent it off to the tip."

"That's so unfair!"

"Only it isn't!"

"It is unfair," Victoria says. "I'm telling you, I wanted to give them to you. But Mum warned me not to."

"I'm sorry, but I simply don't believe you," Penny says.

"Well, that's up to you, I suppose."

"I mean, why *would* she say that? What could she possibly gain by lying? I asked *her* to help me out so that we could buy a new one, but she didn't have the money. And then..."

"Yeah," Victoria interrupts. "Like, she only had eighty thousand in her bank account, after all."

"Ninety thousand. And? Your point is?"

"Well, she said she didn't have the money to help you with a washing machine. Why would she say *that*?"

At that moment, Sander pops his head around the door. "Morning ladies," he says.

Both Penny and Victoria turn to greet him, but one look at their expressions has Sander beating a hasty retreat. "Oh," he says, stepping backwards and closing the lounge door.

"What's wrong with him?" Victoria asks.

"I have no idea," Penny says. "So, what's with this agenda to paint Mum as the root of all evil? What's that about?"

"I'm sorry?" Victoria says.

"Is it because painting her as some kind of monster makes losing her a bit easier?"

"Oh, do stop trying to analyse me, would you? I mean, I know it's your job and everything, but..."

"I'm not."

"Yes, you are. And you'd do better to analyse yourself and consider for one second that you might be wrong about something – that your world view might not be one hundred percent accurate like you always think it is."

Penny rubs one hand across her face then chews a fingernail. She tries to remain calm. Accusations of her lapsing into "shrink" mode always stop her dead in her tracks. Because it is, she knows, a genuine risk. "OK," she says, finally, "So, why don't you tell me?"

"Tell you what?"

"Tell me *your* world view. Tell me what it is I'm so wrong about. I'm listening. Really."

Victoria shrugs. "Well, you have this myth, don't you? Of the all-smiling, singing, dancing, loving mother. But Mum wasn't the person you thought she was."

"OK," Penny says, dubiously. "So, who was she? Tell me the Victoria version."

Victoria sighs and shakes her head slowly. She half stands and puts her empty mug on the coffee table and then returns to her seat and starts to wring her hands together.

"She was complex," she says.

"Complex?"

"Like everyone, I suppose. But she was a mixture of good and bad. It's just that you got most of the good."

"And you got most of the bad?" Penny says, her tone vaguely mocking.

"Yes," Victoria says emphatically. "Yes, I did. Mum hated me a bit."

"She did not *hate* you."

"She did. She made my life hell. I know you choose not to remember any of this, and I understand why that's easier for you, but she did. She used to mock just about anything I said. She would always go with your preference over mine. She was ten times stricter with me about everything than she was with you. She used to call me Dirty Deirdre. Do you even remember that?"

"I do," Penny says. "But she called me Piggy Penny."

Victoria snorts. "She did. But if you think back carefully – and honestly – you'll remember that she didn't say it in the same way. Piggy Penny was like a term of endearment almost."

"It was. That's exactly what it was."

"But Dirty Deirdre wasn't."

Penny twists her mouth as she struggles to remember. And yes, *hadn't* there been a certain curl to her mother's lip when she addressed Victoria? "You know what I never understood," Penny says, "is when Ed died – I mean, Mum worshipped Ed, right?"

Victoria nods vaguely.

"So, when Ed died, why did she skip over you? Why did *I* suddenly become the wonder child?"

"So you admit it?"

"I suppose, yes..." Penny says. "I mean, I don't agree that she hated you. But I suppose I did become the favourite. And I could never understand how she could do that. I mean, I could never choose between Max and Chloe. When you have children, you love them all equally, right?"

"Except that Max *is* your favourite," Victoria says. "And Chloe is Sander's."

"He is not."

"Well, I've always seen it that way," Victoria says. "But I just assumed it was the natural mother/son thing. The father/daughter thing, too. But maybe I got it wrong."

"Then maybe I need to watch that," Penny says thoughtfully. "But it still doesn't explain Mum. I mean, she ended up with two daughters. So why choose one over the other?"

"She was angry," Victoria says, with a shrug. "She was angry with me about Cecil – because he left. And she never forgave me for it."

"Because you told her what was going on?" Penny asks.

"Yes. Because I told her what was going on."

"But that would be horrible. I mean, talk about blaming the messenger."

"It *was* horrible. I mean, in her defence, she really *did* think it was all my fault."

"How could it be *your* fault?"

"Well, she didn't believe me, did she? So it became my fault. For making things up. And we all know how hard things became once Cecil vanished. I mean, you remember how broke we were, right?"

"It was horrible," Penny says. "Do you remember those bargain basket meals she used to come up with?"

Victoria nods. "Mashed potato for dinner and smashed up ginger nuts for tea?"

"A well balanced diet, if ever there was one," Penny says. "But when you say that she didn't believe you…"

"Yes?"

"Well, that doesn't really make any sense, does it? Because she sent Cecil away. I mean, if she hadn't believed you, she wouldn't have sent him away."

"Ah," Victoria says. "Well, you see, that, unfortunately, isn't quite what happened."

"It isn't?"

"No."

* * *

When she got back to her bedroom, Vicky had cried for a little while. But then, as childhood resilience prevailed, she had pushed what she had seen from her mind and started to play with her dolls instead. Barbara, her biggest, oldest, one-armed doll, had matted blond hair, and so she had emptied her toy box until she found the brush. She then sat cross legged on her bed. "Don't cry," she told the doll. "I know it hurts but it'll be over in a bit."

Five minutes later, her bedroom door had creaked open and Cecil's plump face – still flushed from exertion – appeared.

Vicky felt slightly scared of him for a moment, though, if asked, she could not have explained quite why. But then Cecil has asked her if she was OK in a friendly kind of way and had eased his way into the room. To her relief, he was fully dressed, in his three piece suit, his watch chain glinting where it crossed the straining buttons of his waistcoat.

"Are you OK?" he asked again, and Vicky had nodded solemnly.

Cecil still had one hand hidden behind his back, and when he brought it into view she saw that he was holding a shiny, foil-wrapped Father Christmas.

"I thought you might like some secret chocolate," Cecil said, closing the bedroom door behind him.

Vicky watched him warily as he advanced towards her brandishing the chocolate Father Christmas. She was both excited and scared about the offer of chocolate. Christmas chocolate before Christmas was strictly forbidden. They all knew that.

"So, do you want some?" Cecil asked, taking a seat beside her on the small bed.

Vicky bit her lip and nodded. "Yes please," she said.

"Good. I thought you might," Cecil said, his voice soft and kind. "But you mustn't let your mum know. It has to be our special secret."

Still holding the Father Christmas in his right hand, he slipped his left arm around her shoulders and gave them a squeeze. "This is nice, isn't it?" he said.

Vicky nodded nervously.

"But your mum would be upset if she found out our little secret," Cecil continued. "And you don't want to upset your mum, do you? Especially not on Christmas Eve."

Vicky, still tracking the chocolate from the corner of her eye, shook her head. "I can hide it in my toy box," she said, pointing.

Cecil looked confused. "Hide what?" he asked.

"The secret chocolate."

"Oh, yes," Cecil said. "Of course. Though I thought you might want to hide it inside your tummy, actually." He then reached across and tickled Vicky's tummy which made her laugh, but which also made her feel a bit sick too, as if, perhaps, she was imagining how she would feel if she ate all the chocolate.

"So, if I give you this, can you keep the other secret as well?" Cecil asked.

"What other secret?"

"The secret game I was playing with Ed. You mustn't tell your mum about it. After all, we don't want to get Ed into trouble, do we?"

Vicky frowned and shook her head even though she was unconvinced. With Ed being such a clear favourite in the household, *and* being the eldest, *and* being a boy, there were many occasions in her day when getting Ed into trouble was strategically important just to even things up a little.

"And your mum would be *so* upset," Cecil went on, "that she might cancel Christmas altogether, and we don't want that, do we? It would be a terrible shame if I had to take all those presents back to the shop."

Vicky nodded. "OK," she said. She knew she was being manipulated, but it seemed to her that, what with the chocolate and the Christmas gifts, it was probably worth it.

Finally, the Father Christmas passed from Cecil's right hand to his left, and then into her own small hands where it looked so much bigger. "You're a good girl," Cecil said, stroking her head. "I used to think Ed was my favourite, but now I think it's you."

Vicky forced an uncomfortable smile and dug one fingernail into the head of the Father Christmas.

"Do you want to do the *Ning Nang Nong?*" Cecil asked, patting his knee.

Vicky shook her head. She quite liked the *Ning Nang Nong,* but she would prefer it if Cecil left her to play with her dolls and eat chocolate, she reckoned.

"OK, then," Cecil said, ruffling her hair again. "I'll see you later. And remember, not a word."

Once the chocolate was eaten and the foil had been balled up and hidden at the bottom of the toy box, she made her way downstairs.

Her mother was busy mopping the hall floor. "If you go through now, you can't come back until it's dry," she warned her, her cigarette bobbing up and down as she spoke.

"Can I make tea?" Vicky asked. Her authorisation to use the dangerous kettle was recent, and she was proud of her new tea-making job.

"All right," Marge said, "but be careful, don't burn yourself, and don't take the teabag out too early. Not like last time, OK? I don't want a cup of gnat's pee."

In the kitchen, Vicky dragged a Formica chair to the sink, then climbed up to fill the kettle. She then returned to the sideboard and plugged it in, leaning her elbows on the edge of the counter and staring at the distorted room reflected in the polished sides of the kettle as it boiled.

She had just finished pouring water into the teapot when Marge joined her.

"You all right there, dumpling?" she asked, stubbing her cigarette out in the ashtray.

"Of course," Vicky said, proudly. "I'm very good at making tea."

But as Marge turned to look at her, a shadow crossed her features. "What...?" she said, crossing the kitchen and crouching down before her. She grasped the back of Vicky's head with one hand and dabbed at the edge of her lips with the forefinger of the other. And only then, only when Marge raised her finger to first her nose, then her lips, did Vicky realise that she had been rumbled.

"Chocolate!" Marge exclaimed, looking both puzzled and annoyed. "Now where did you get chocolate from, young lady?"

Vicky shook her head. "I didn't," she said.

Marge grabbed her wrist then. She dragged her through to the lounge and lifted her up so that she could see herself in the mirror above the mantlepiece. "Look!" she said. "Now, tell me what this is if it isn't chocolate?"

"I..." Vicky said. But she couldn't think of a way out, because the chocolatey evidence was there for all to see. It was all around her mouth.

"You eat like a pig," Marge said. "I don't know how you thought you was gonna get away with that." She lowered her brutally to the floor. "You've been stealing, haven't you? Where did you take that from?"

"I didn't," Vicky said.

"A thief," Marge said. "That's what you are. A chocolate thief! And the day before Christmas, too!"

"But I didn't," Vicky protested, starting to cry.

"Then tell me where it came from," Marge said, shaking her arm so violently that she feared that, like her doll's, it would come off.

"It's Cecil's," Vicky sobbed.

"You've been stealing from your uncle? But that's even worse," Marge shouted. "Do you have any idea how much he does for us? Look at that tree. Look at the presents underneath it. Cecil did all of that. Christmas wouldn't be nothing without Cecil."

"I didn't steal it," Vicky said, her tears now mixing with anger at the injustice of her mother's accusations. "He gave it to me."

"Oh, lies as well, now, is it?" Marge said. "Well, you know what happens to little girls who lie and steal, don't you? Father Christmas doesn't bring them anything. In fact, they don't get Christmas at all!"

"But he did give it to me, he did!"

"Maybe we'll ask him about that, then, shall we?"

"He did. He gave it to me and said not to tell you."

Marge paused to catch her breath. A rare doubt had infiltrated her usual certainty about everything. She crouched down to look Vicky in the eye. If Cecil had been undermining her rule then she wasn't going to be happy about it. "He said you shouldn't tell me?"

"Yes. It's a secret."

"Why would he do that? Why would he tell you to lie to me?"

"Because of the other thing."

"What other thing?"

"I can't say!" Vicky said, bashing her fist against her side dramatically. "It's a secret!"

"Oh, that's enough," Marge said. "I'll let Cecil punish you. And there'll be no Christmas presents for you, young lady. And no Christmas dinner, neither."

"The press-ups," Vicky said, through sobs. "They're doing press-ups. Secret press-ups in Ed's room."

Marge grabbed her daughters hips and shook her. "What press-ups? What are you on about?"

"With Ed. They took their clothes off and Cecil did press-ups. And he made me promise not to tell you and he gave me chocolate. But it's a special secret. I'm not allowed to tell you!"

At that moment, Cecil's voice boomed out from the landing above. "Who has been stealing chocolate from my suitcase?"

Vicky thought, obtusely, of her sister's favourite book, Goldilocks and the Three Bears. *Who has been sitting in my seat?*

"Huh," Marge said, now straightening up and putting her hands on her hips. "The truth comes out! I knew you was lying."

"Someone's been stealing chocolate from my suitcase," Cecil said again as he appeared in the doorway.

"Yes, it's this one," Marge said. "And that's not the half of it. She's been making up lies, too. She's been making up stories that would make a whore blush."

"But you *gave* it to me!" Vicky spluttered. "You gave it to me to keep the secret."

Ed appeared at that point, his face peeping out from behind Cecil. He looked pale and waxy and afraid. "What's going on?" he asked, his voice unconvincing like a bad actor in a cheap drama.

"Tell them!" Vicky pleaded. "Tell Mum about your secret game with Cecil. She doesn't believe me. He took his clothes off," she said pointing. "They both did. Tell her, Ed."

Ed had swallowed hard before replying. "She's mad," he said. "I don't know what she's on about, Mum."

. . .

"She slapped my face twice," Victoria tells Penny. "Once for lying and once for stealing."

"God!" Penny says. "That's dreadful."

"And then she sent me to my room."

"I remember that. I tried to come in and you wouldn't let me."

"That's right. And then a bit later, you came to tell me that he was leaving."

"So she *did* send him away?"

"No," Victoria says. "No, I don't think so. I think he was just too ashamed to stick around."

"He would have been scared, I would think. He would have been scared in case Ed told the truth."

"I suppose so."

"God, if I *had* gone and got him that day, if I had brought him back from the station, he would have known he was safe, wouldn't he? He would have known that Ed *couldn't* tell the truth anymore."

"I know," Victoria says. "That's why I was so glad when you didn't bring him back. I was scared of him."

"And because he *didn't* know that Ed was dead, he never came back."

"Yeah, that's how I read it, anyway."

They are interrupted by a banging noise carrying through the walls.

"What's that?" Victoria asks, looking concerned.

"It's just the washing machine," Penny says. "Sander got a second-hand one from the *Friday Ad* for twenty quid. But it's dreadful. It's going to explode one day."

"Would you let me buy you one?" Victoria asks, earnestly. "I'd like to do that for you."

"Ha!" Penny laughs. "Thanks, but I've ordered one. A brand new eleven kilo one with a built in dryer. It's coming on Tuesday. But thanks for the offer. Better late than never."

At that moment, Sander raps on the door and peeps in. "Is the coast clear?" he asks, "Only I wanted to watch last night's match."

"It's fine," Penny says. "Can we use your studio, though? We're having a bit of a heart to heart, here."

"Of course," Sander says, throwing the door wide open. "Be my guests."

"Or we could go for a walk?" Victoria suggests. "It looks lovely out there."

"You're right," Penny says. "Let's do that."

As the women pull on their shoes and prepare to leave, they cross paths with Will and Ben coming downstairs. "Coffee and toast?" Will offers.

"No, we're going out for a walk," Penny says. "Maybe later."

"Fair enough," Will says. "Have fun."

"Fun," Victoria repeats, as they step outside. "I'm not even sure what that means anymore."

The women head to the beach and turn left, away from the town centre.

"You know," Penny says, "it's amazing to me that you've never told me any of this before. It must have been incredibly hard to keep all of that bottled up."

"It was," Victoria says. "But it seemed better that way. I mean, when it happened you were too young to understand it all. So was I really, but anyway... And then later on, I thought that you were lucky not knowing. There didn't seem to be any point wrecking your childhood retrospectively, if you see what I mean. Plus I felt so ashamed of it all."

"But you have to let this kind of thing out. For your mental health, I mean."

"I know. And I've started to, now, haven't I? I've told Doctor Muller."

"And you've told me, too."

"Yes, I suppose." Victoria says. She scrambles up onto a wooden, barnacle encrusted groyne, and then pulls Penny up after her. She wraps her arms around herself and looks out to sea.

"Are you cold?" Penny asks. "Do you want to go back for a jumper?"

"No, I'm fine," Victoria says. "Gosh, it must be lovely getting up to this every morning. And that smell of seaweed and iodine or whatever it is. I love it."

"To be honest," Penny says, "I'm too busy most mornings to notice."

"I suppose," Victoria says. "I suppose we all get used to it wherever we are."

Penny, who has been running the conversation back through her head, now says, "Anyway, ashamed of what? You said you were too ashamed. But what did *you* have to be ashamed of?"

"Oh, I don't know," Victoria says, glancing away, somewhat shiftily it seems to Penny.

"Unless there's more?" Penny says. "I keep thinking there's more. Every time you tell me something, it feels like half the story."

"I think it's best if we leave it at that," Victoria says, blandly.

"So there *is* more. Did he abuse you? He did, didn't he?"

"No! No, of course not. Though I imagine that if he had stayed around he might have tried."

"Did he abuse *me*?" Penny asks.

"No," Victoria says, looking shocked. "Did he?"

"No, I don't think so," Penny says. "But you never know with things like that. People blank things out for years. I've had clients who have suddenly realised at sixty that they were abused."

"OK, no, then. I don't think he abused you."

"So, what then? Did Mum do something really awful to you after he left?"

"Mum did a million awful things to me after he left."

"But that's not it."

"There is no *it*, Penny."

"Only there is."

"There isn't."

"If you say so," Penny says.

• • •

Back at the house, Sander's match replay has been interrupted by the doorbell and a burst of staccato knocks on the front door. He hits the pause button on the remote control and rises from his seat.

"I was just going to get that," Will tells him when he reaches the hallway.

"It's fine," Sander replies as the doorbell rings again.

Sander opens the door to find a red-faced Martin on the doorstep. "Is she here?" he asks urgently. "Is my wife here?"

"Um, hi Martin," Sander says.

"Sorry, hi Sander."

"And yes. I mean, no. It's like... she's here, but she's not here."

"What?" Martin asks.

"Well, she's here," Sander says, wincing at his own inability to explain. "But she's gone for a walk with Penny."

"Oh," Martin says.

"Are you all right, mate?" Sander asks.

"No," Martin says. "I'm not all right. This is the third time in a month she's buggered off without telling me where she's going. And it's the third time I've inexplicably found myself car-less. And I'm sick of it. I'm sick to death of all of it."

"You, um, you'd better come in," Sander says, turning to throw a concerned glance at Will. But Will has discreetly closed the kitchen door to give them some privacy.

Sander attempts to settle Martin in the lounge but Martin will not be settled. He paces up and down the room constantly checking the street outside as he does so.

"I'll make teas," Sander offers. "Don't move."

"I don't want tea," Martin says. "I want my wife and son back so that we can actually spend some bloody time together."

"Yeah," Sander says. "Yeah, you'll get your wife. Don't worry. She'll be back soon. But in the meantime, I'll make teas."

By the time Sander returns with the mugs of tea, Martin has sat down, albeit on the edge of his seat, and in the only armchair with a view of the street.

"Here," Sander says, proffering the mug.

"Thanks."

"So, you're pissed off," Sander says, perching on the edge of another armchair.

"No. I'm... Yes, OK, I'm pissed off," Martin admits. "It's just been getting worse and worse."

"What has?" Sander asks. "What's been getting worse?"

"Everything," Martin says, his voice strained and brittle. "I took the whole week off so we could do something as a family. And so we could sort out Bertie's bloody schooling – because Christ alone knows what that boy wants. And I get home to an empty house. Again! *And* no bloody car. I mean, what am I supposed to do with that, Sander? Sit at home and wait? Sit at home and hope my wife and son will deign to spend a bit of time with me? I mean, what's that about, eh?"

Sander shrugs and shakes his head. "I don't know," he says. "I'm sorry."

"And why here?" Martin asks, looking around. "Can you tell me what's so fucking brilliant about here?" He grimaces and adds, "Sorry, I didn't mean anything."

"I don't know," Sander says again. "The beach, maybe?" he adds, tentatively.

"The beach?" Martin repeats.

"Yeah, people like beaches on bank holiday weekends, don't they? I'm just trying... Look, I don't know. I'm just guessing here."

"But the idea of us all going to the beach together? I mean, that's just too awful to contemplate, right?" Martin says. "The idea of an actual family holiday where we have some fun *together*, that's a total impossibility. Because my son can't stand me and given the choice, my wife would prefer to be just about anywhere else than wherever I happen to be. I mean, when did I get to be the bad guy, huh?" Martin's rant ends in a crescendo that reaches as far as the kitchen. "When did that happen, Sander?!" he shouts. "What did I ever do?"

A minute later, Bertie, awoken by his father's voice, appears in the kitchen.

"Why's Dad here?" he asks Will quietly.

"I don't know," Will says.

"Did you tell him?"

"No," Will says. "I didn't."

"He sounds upset," Bertie says. "He sounds, like, *crazy* upset."

"I think he *is*," Will agrees. "I think he's upset about your Mum coming down here without telling him, mainly."

"Can I say something?" Ben, who is seated at the kitchen table, interjects.

Will frowns and turns to face him. "Of course you can. Why would you even ask that?"

"Right. So the thing is," Ben says, winking at Will and then turning to Bertie. "You know that conversation we had about choosing your moment."

"To tell Mum and Dad?" Bertie asks, nervously.

"Yeah. Well, this is it," Ben says. "Your Dad's upset, but not with you. If you tell him now..."

"I'm not telling him *now*," Bertie says.

"I think you should. I think this is your moment."

"No way," Bertie says.

"What do you think, Will?" Ben asks.

Will chews the inside of his mouth for a moment before replying. "Ben could be right," he finally says. "I mean, if anything goes wrong..."

"Which it won't," Ben interjects.

"No," Will says. "But if it did, then we're both here for you, aren't we? And he might just be relieved. It might even calm him down a bit. If he understood, I mean, why you're here, with us."

"I think it will too," Ben says.

"It won't!" Bertie protests.

At that moment, the kitchen door opens to reveal Martin, looking no longer angry, but upset instead – his eyes are watery. "Bertie!" he says, then with the briefest of glances, "Will. Ben."

"Hi Dad," Bertie says. "What are *you* doing here?"

Martin opens his mouth to speak, then closes it again and sighs jerkily instead. "I... I don't know," he finally says.

"We'll, um, leave you to it, eh?" Will offers, making to leave.

But Bertie sends him a pleading glance. "No!" he says, urgently. "Please, Will, no!"

Martin glances between the two men's faces as he tries to understand, then takes three steps forwards and crouches down in front of his son. He takes Bertie's elbows in his hands and says, as if the realisation is only now dawning on him, "You're *scared* of me? Is that it, Bertie? Are you *scared* of me?"

Bertie rocks his head from side to side in a troubled manner. "No... I... I don't know."

"Why?" Martin asks, now straining against a second bout of unexpected tears. "What did I ever do to you, Bertie?"

Bertie shrugs.

"Did I ever hit you, Bertie? Did I ever once hurt you?"

Bertie, whose eyes are now tearing as well, shakes his head.

"Was I unfair to you? Was I mean to you?"

"No Dad," Bertie says, his voice cracking.

"Then why?" Martin asks. "What happened here? Never mind why am *I* here, why are *you* here, Bertie? Why aren't you at home? Why aren't we all off having a holiday somewhere? Why don't you... I don't know... You don't even seem to want to be my son anymore. Why is that?"

Bertie glances at Will again, who is chewing his bottom lip, then at Ben whose eyes are glistening as well. "It's time, Bertie," Ben says gently.

Bertie nods almost imperceptibly, then turns back to face his father.

Will steps forward and crouches down by Bertie's side. He blinks kindly at Martin (who frowns uncomprehendingly) then puts one arm around Bertie's shoulders.

Sander, who has appeared in the doorway, asks, "Shall I close this door and give you some space?"

Will shakes his head at him. "Go on, Bertie," he says. "I'm here. We're all here for you. Tell him. Get it over with."

"Tell me what?" Martin asks.

"No..." Bertie protests.

"Go on," Will says. "Do it. We're here. Ben and I are here for you."

"What?" Martin asks. "What is it? What's wrong, son?"

"I'm..." Bertie says, his voice wobbling. He scans the faces around him for reassurance one last time, then in a rush, he spits the words out. "I'm gay, Dad."

Martin releases Bertie's elbows now and sinks back onto his heels. "You what?" he says, flatly.

"I'm gay, Dad," Bertie says again as tears start to flow. "I'm sorry."

Martin's brow furrows. "You're *gay*?" he says.

Bertie nods shamefully.

"You... you mean, you don't like girls? You like other boys?"

Bertie screws his face up and nods again as tears run down his cheeks. "I'm sorry, Dad," he says again. "But I can't help it. I'm like Will and Ben."

Martin, now crying silently as well, shakes his head. "But why?" he pleads.

"I don't know," Bertie sobs.

"No one knows *why*," Will murmurs.

"Uh?" Martin says, now shooting Will a glance that implies he just said something really irritating.

"Well, they don't," Will tells him.

"I don't mean why is he *gay*," Martin says, incredulously. "I mean why are you telling me this, son? Why are you apologising to me? I don't get it."

Bertie dares to look up at his father.

"Well?" Martin asks.

"Because I know it's not what you want," Bertie splutters.

"What *I* want?"

"Yes," Bertie says, nodding miserably and sniffing. "You want me to be good at sports and all that. You want me to be one of the lads. You want me to be a footballer or something, so you can be proud. But I'm not like that."

"Oh, Jesus!" Martin exclaims, now opening his arms. "Come here, will you?"

Bertie glances at Will and then looks nervously back at his father. "Come here!" Martin says again, now moving forwards and wrapping his son in his arms. "Jesus! I don't care *what* you are, son," he tells him as he pulls him tight. He sounds outraged that anyone could have ever imagined otherwise. "I don't care what you do or who you are or who you fancy. I don't care about any of it. You can be a footballer or a dancer or a bloody Brazilian drag queen as far as I'm concerned. You're my son. You're my boy, Bertie. You're my beautiful baby boy! And I love you. No matter what. Don't you get that?"

• • •

On reaching the end of the footpath at West Beach, Penny points inland and says, "There are tea-rooms over there. Do you want to go and get a drink?"

"Not really," Victoria says. "You?"

"No, I'm fine." And so the sisters cross the beach and continue their way along the water's edge, walking on the narrow strip of sand between the pebbles and the sea.

"What are those for?" Victoria asks, pointing at one of the wooden breakwaters.

"The groynes? To stop the beach being washed away, I think."

"Of course they are," Victoria says, picking up a pebble and throwing it as far as she can. "I kind of knew that anyway. Do you remember Ed's stone-throwing competitions?"

"Not really," Penny says. "Should I?"

"It was kind of a speciality of his," Victoria says, "setting up competitions that he could win. He used to make you bet sweets and stuff and you were too little to realise that you'd always lose. It was quite mean, really."

"I don't remember," Penny says. "In fact, if the truth be told, I hardly remember Ed at all. I remember some of his toys, which is weird. I remember his steam engine, for instance. It had a funny smell."

"Methylated spirit," Victoria says. "It ran on methylated spirit. And you're right, it did smell funny."

"But that's weird, isn't it? Remembering that but not Ed? I mean, I can hardly make out his face, but I remember every detail of that steam engine. It was green and red and it had a big brass wheel that went round."

"Memory's a funny thing," Victoria says.

"It is," Penny agrees. "Especially when there's trauma involved. So what was he like?"

"Ed?" Victoria says, glancing back at their footprints in the sand. The trace of their passage is already fading. "Ed was OK, I suppose."

Penny frowns. That was not the response she had been expecting. "He was *OK*?" she repeats, mockingly.

Victoria shrugs.

"Did we get on?"

"You and Ed?"

"Yes. You just said he was mean to me."

"Oh, no, that wasn't anything serious. He just liked betting things with you and stealing your sweets. But half the time he gave them back when you cried. He was OK towards you, I suppose."

"He was OK towards *me*?"

"Yes."

"So I wasn't nice to Ed? Is that what you're saying?"

"You used to get him into trouble quite a lot," Victoria says. "We both did. But that was normal really. He was quite irritating because he was so clearly everyone's favourite. Mum treated him like he was her husband half the time. She used to ask him his opinion on stuff as if he was an adult. Which was pretty weird, a bit dysfunctional, if you look back on it now."

"And what about you two?" Penny asks. "I mean, you were closer in age. Did you two get on?"

"He was OK," Victoria says again.

"Did you love him?" Penny asks. "Did you miss him horribly when he died? Because I think I was too young to get it really."

Victoria looks away along the beach. "There are hardly any people over there," she says. "Let's go there."

"Did you love him?" Penny asks again. She's used to people avoiding the most pertinent questions when in therapy.

"I... look, do we have to talk about Ed?" Victoria says.

"No, we don't," Penny says after consideration. "But I'd appreciate it if we could. I've waited a long time to dare to talk about Ed. In fact it would seem I had to wait until my mother died. So now we finally have broached the subject, yes, I'd be grateful if you could tell me a bit about him for the simple reason that I don't remember much."

"It's best avoided," Victoria says. "As a subject, I mean. That's my honest opinion." And then she starts to head diagonally off across the beach. Despite the pebbles, which are hard going, she manages quite a pace. Penny is forced to trot to keep up with her.

"Hey," she says, when she finally manages to catch her sister's arm. "Wait!"

Victoria attempts to break away, so Penny grabs her belt, and it's only then, only as Victoria looks angrily back at her, that Penny realises she is crying. "Oh," Penny says. "Sorry. I didn't mean to upset you. Victoria?"

"It's nothing," Victoria says, swiping at her tears with the back of her hand.

"Only it's not nothing, is it?" Penny says.

"No," Victoria admits. "But please, let's not go there."

"Sit down," Penny says gently. "Just sit down and tell me."

Victoria shakes her head. "I can't."

"Please."

"Can't you just drop this?" Victoria says, sounding exasperated and angry and tearful at the same time.

"No," Penny says. "No, I'm sorry, but it's time. Sit down and talk to me!"

Something inside Victoria gives way. It's as if the physical strength she has been using to keep this secret all these years has suddenly deserted her. Unable to stand, she crouches, then sits on the pebbles, and Penny, who immediately joins her, throws one arm around her waist.

"Come on," Penny says. "How bad can it be?"

Victoria snorts sadly. "You have no idea," she says menacingly.

"So tell me."

"Oh, God. I'll tell you if you really want," Victoria says. "I'm too tired to care anymore. I'm tired from carrying it all, too. I'm tired of hiding it all the time. But I really need to know that you've heard me. Because I'm telling you, as your sister, as your friend, that you're better off not knowing."

"OK," Penny says. "I've heard you. And I don't care. So tell me."

"Give me a hug first, please," Victoria says.

"Now?" Penny asks, looking surprised. Her sister has never been the huggy type.

Victoria nods. "Yes," she says. "Because I don't think you'll want to give me one afterwards."

Penny briskly hugs her sister, then, when they separate, she asks, "And why would that be?"

"You'll see," Victoria says.

A man passes with a labrador on a lead. Both he and the dog look enquiringly at Victoria – it's as if the air around her is purple with angst. She crosses her arms and hides her face in them until they are past.

"He's gone," Penny says, eventually.

"So, Ed," Victoria says, lifting her head. "You asked me what he was like."

Penny nods and rubs her sister's back gently. "Yes," she says.

"Well, he was..." Victoria takes a deep breath. "Look, I don't want you to think that I'm saying any of this was his fault, OK? Because it wasn't. I've thought about this a lot, and I'm sure Ed was just doing the best he could to make sense of what happened to him, all right?"

"All right."

"OK," Victoria says, looking out to sea then taking another forced, mechanical breath. "So, you asked me if I loved him. The truth is that I was scared of him."

"You were *scared* of him?" Penny repeats, withdrawing, despite her best intentions, her hand from Victoria's shoulder.

"Yes. Scared. Terrified."

"But why?"

"Because he was damaged goods. That's what we'd say these days – damaged goods."

"Because of what Cecil did to him, you mean?"

"Yes. Because of what Cecil did to him. It had been going on for a while, that's the thing. The abuse. For months, definitely. For years, maybe."

"Years?" Penny says. "But he was only eleven. How could it have been going on for years?"

"I don't know. And I don't know what form it took *before* then. I mean, he might not have always... you know... done what I caught them doing that day. But he was always in Ed's room when he came to stay, you remember that, right?"

"Yes. Ed had a spare bed in his room, so..."

"So, when I caught them that day – on Christmas Eve – it was like something I knew already. Do you know what I mean? When something's more like a realisation than a shock?"

"I suppose I do, yes."

Victoria picks up two small pebbles now and begins to turn them over in the palm of her hand with her thumb. "It changed him, that's the thing. It wasn't his fault, but it changed him from a nice, ordinary boy, into something else. It wasn't his fault. But it wasn't right, either." Victoria covers her mouth with a trembling hand and looks away for a moment. "I feel sick," she mumbles.

"Me too," Penny says. "But go on. You're doing really well."

"It started one weekend in summer," Victoria says, looking down at her feet. "Actually, it was probably the same weekend as now. August bank holiday or something. He always came down on bank holidays. And it was after he left that it started."

"What started? Cecil abusing Ed?"

Victoria shakes her head. "No, that predated this, like I said. No, this was different."

"Right," Penny says, struggling to follow, then, "What was?"

Victoria blows through her lips. "Jesus, this is hard," she mutters. "So, Ed came into my room. He asked me if I wanted to play a game, all right? He told me to close my eyes and hold out my hand. And I didn't suspect anything. I mean, I was seven, right?"

"Yes. Of course. But this is Ed, or Cecil?"

"Ed! I told you. It was after one of Cecil's visits."

"OK."

"So..." Victoria rests her elbows on her knees and covers her face with both hands. Speaking through the gaps, her voice all over the place, she continues. "So I closed my eyes, and I put out my hand. And he put his... you know... he put his thing in my hand."

"His *thing*?"

"His dick."

"Ed?"

"Yes."

"Ed put his penis in your hand?" Penny says, unable to believe that she has correctly understood what her sister has said.

"Yes."

358

"When you were seven?"

"Yes."

"Oh *God*! What did you say?"

"I screamed," Victoria says.

"Well, you would."

"Only he covered my mouth with his hand. He was scared Mum would hear."

"But that's horrible," Penny says.

"And then he lay on top of me," Victoria continues, her voice almost inaudible. "He pinned me to the bed. He was much bigger and stronger than me. You remember how sporty he was? Well, he put his hand over my mouth, and he pinned me to the bed."

Suddenly, despite every part of her struggling against it, a perfect vision of Ed, usually so elusive, pops into Penny's mind's eye. It's an unwelcome cinemascope vision of her brother lying on top of her sister. A tiny dollop of acid reflux rises into her throat. "He didn't... *do anything,* did he?" Penny asks.

Victoria shakes her head. "No," she says. "No. He was too young, I think."

"And his dick... was it... oh, never mind. Forget I asked that."

"Yes," Victoria says. "Yes, it was."

"So he wasn't too young, after all?"

"No."

"Oh, God," Penny says, pulling a face of utter disgust and looking away.

"I'm sorry," Victoria says, reaching out to touch her shoulder.

"It's not you," Penny tells her, turning back to face her. "But... I don't know... It's just so..."

"Sordid?" Victoria offers.

"Well, yes. But it's *abuse*," Penny says. "That's what it is."

"Yes, perhaps."

"Poor you," Penny says with feeling. "I had no idea."

"Poor Ed!" Victoria counters. "That boy was *so* fucked up."

Penny stares at her sister for a moment. She shakes her head slowly from side to side as she tries to take it in. Perhaps, she thinks, her sister was right. Perhaps she was better off not knowing.

"You see what I mean?" Victoria says. "It's hardcore, isn't it?"

"Yes," Penny replies. "Yes, I see what you mean. And yes, it's hardcore. But I still want to hug you."

Penny opens her arms now to offer an embrace, but Victoria flinches. "I'm not finished yet," she says ominously.

Penny frowns. *Whatever it is, I'll be fine,* she thinks. *Whatever it is, I'll accept it like the understanding adult I am.*

"So, that Christmas Eve," Victoria says. "After Mum slapped me..."

* * *

Her cheeks still stinging from her mother's slaps, Vicky ran to her room.

She closed the door and locked it. The house had once been a guesthouse so all of the doors had locks, even if they were strictly forbidden to use them. But today, Vicky didn't care. Today, she felt scared – she felt scared of her mother, scared of Ed, and scared, above all, of Cecil. Slimy, lying, frightening Cecil. She threw herself onto her bed, pulled her teddy towards her and cried into his fur at the injustice of it all.

For a while – an hour, perhaps – she listened to the sounds of the house around her. She wondered if Cecil could open her door from the outside the way her mother once had when she had locked herself in the toilet. She hoped not.

She wondered if he would put her over his knee and slap her with his big, manicured hands, or if he would do something worse instead. She wondered if he mightn't punish her by doing to her whatever he had been doing to Ed.

But to her relief, Cecil did not come, and slowly she began to relax until eventually, her nose pressed into the bear's wet fur, she fell asleep.

Lunchtime came and went and no one came to fetch her. She felt hungry but didn't dare go downstairs. She didn't even dare to unlock her door.

The house was silent and all was calm, but in a way it was too calm, it was creepily calm, like a haunted house, like a ghost house, she thought.

She wondered if everyone perhaps had gone to the beach, but that was a silly thought; it was freezing outside.

Watching the movement of the origami mobile Cecil had hung above her bed, she thought again of the way he had lied, the way Ed had lied too, and fresh tears welled up. *It's not fair*, she thought, over and over again. And each time, her mother's voice would appear in her head, saying *Life isn't fair* – Marge's habitual response to any accusations of unfairness. But why? Vicky wondered. Why *couldn't* life be fair? Why couldn't people just tell the truth and be nice to each other? Why would Ed side with horrible Cecil rather than with her, his own sister?

At some point, her little sister knocked on her door, but Vicky was in the midst of a bout of angry tears so she sent her away.

And then, a few minutes later, just as she was feeling lonely and bored, just as she was feeling regretful, Penny knocked again, so she took the risk – she opened the door and pulled her inside. Penny's doll Lucy was hanging from her left hand.

"What's happened?" Penny asked.

Vicky wiped her snotty nose on the back of her hand. "It's nothing," she said. "It's grown-up stuff, that's all."

Penny pulled a face at her. She wanted Vicky to explain, and in truth, Vicky wanted to explain it to her as well, she really did. It's just that she lacked the vocabulary to do so. She lacked the words to describe what had happened even inside her own head, let alone to her five-year-old sister.

"What's happened? Why are you crying?" Penny asked.

"It's nothing," Vicky said. "It's grown-up stuff, that's all."

"Where's Ed?"

"I don't know," Vicky said, blowing her nose on a tatty tissue.

"Why is Cecil leaving?" Penny asked.

Vicky brushed her hair from her eyes, and looked out at her little sister. "Is he?" she asked, as butterflies of hope suddenly fluttered in her chest.

"Yes," Penny said. "On the three-thirty o'clock train. He's busy putting all his things back in his suitcase."

"Good," Vicky told her. "I hate him."

"Why?" Penny asked.

"I can't tell you," Vicky said. And again, it was a problem of vocabulary, not desire, that held her back.

"Why?"

"Look," Vicky continued, "if you want to stay here with me, then you have to stop asking questions, OK?" Penny's questions were making her feel inexplicably queasy.

Penny bit her lip and nodded. "He won't take the presents though, will he?"

"How should I know?" Vicky said angrily. Seeing that Penny was about to cry, she added, "But no, Sis, I doubt it."

"Do you think you'll still get your music player?" Penny asked.

"I had better," Vicky said. "Otherwise..."

"Otherwise what?" Penny asked.

"Nothing," Vicky said. "Otherwise nothing."

Vicky wasn't sure what she would do if Cecil took her cassette player back from under the tree; she wasn't quite sure what she *could* do. But her fear and upset were morphing to anger and she suspected that she would find a way, if, on top of everything else, he ruined her Christmas. Yes, she'd find a way to get her own back somehow. "Where's Mum?" she asked.

"She's drinking the stuff she puts in the cake," Penny said.

"The brandy?"

"Yes."

"Is she drinking lots of it?" Vicky asked. Her mother became relaxed and funny when she drank too much brandy. She also tended to fall asleep in her armchair leaving them free rein to run riot.

"She's drinking it from the bottle, like this," Penny said, mimicking the gesture with one hand.

"Good," Vicky said. "And Cecil's definitely going?"

"Yes. He said on the three-thirty train."

"I wonder what time it is now?"

Penny shrugged. "Do you want me to go and find out?" she asked.

"Yes," Vicky said. "But don't say it's for me, all right? Did you have lunch?"

Penny nodded. "Sandwiches from yesterday," she said. "That yucky fish stuff."

"Can you sneak me one up?" Vicky asked. "I'm starving."

Penny nodded and smiled. She liked it when her sister gave her missions to accomplish. "Can we play a game after?"

Vicky nodded. "If you tell me the time and bring me a sandwich without anyone knowing, we can play a game once Cecil's gone, OK?"

"OK," Penny said, standing up. "Come on Lucy. We've got a secret mission to do."

It was a few minutes before Penny returned with a half-sandwich stuffed up her jumper and good news to share. "It's a quarter-past two o'clock," she announced, precisely, "and Cecil just left."

"Quarter past two?" Vicky repeated, taking the tatty sandwich from her sister's grasp and inspecting it suspiciously before raising it to her mouth. "And he's gone already?" she asked, speaking through a mouthful of bread and fish paste.

"He didn't even say goodbye to Mum," Penny said. "He just walked off up the street. He looked like he was sad."

"Are you sure he's not coming back? Because he's a bit early for the three-thirty. It doesn't take an hour to get to the station."

Penny shook her head. "He took his suitcase and everything," she announced. "But not the presents. I looked under the tree and it's all still there."

"Good," Vicky said. "And Mum?"

"She's asleep in front of the telly."

"Who told you the time, then?" Vicky asked, still suspicious of potential traps and intrigues.

"Ed, of course," Penny said. "He's in the kitchen."

With Cecil gone and their mother in an alcoholic daze, the children's excitement about Christmas rekindled. It was as if the cork holding Christmas in had been released.

Ed, who was feeling both guilty about getting Vicky into trouble and relieved at Cecil's departure, was, for a while, extra-nice to them both.

After creeping into the lounge to check the tree (her cassette player was still there) Vicky silently closed the lounge door on their sleeping mother. The longer she slept, the better, Vicky thought.

They ran to the very top of the house and then Ed, wearing a sheet and making ghost noises, chased them down. They played hide and seek and slides – a game where Ed would drag them around the kitchen floor on towels.

They went out into the back garden after that, and Ed and Vicky took turns at pushing Penny on the old swing until it went so high that she started to cry.

Marge, awoken by the kerfuffle, had rapped on the window pane. "It's too cold out there," she shouted. "Come inside right now!"

As they discreetly passed by the lounge, Marge had stuck her head out. "Play upstairs!" she had ordered. "I can't hear myself think!" And then turning to Vicky, she had added, brutally, "As for you, Dirty Deirdre, I don't want to see your face today. So get out of my sight before I do something I might regret."

They had moved to Ed's big room, and Penny had played with his Action Man, sitting it on the steam train and making choo-choo noises.

At one point, Vicky had gone to the toilet, and on her return, had announced that Mum was "snoring like a pig." They had all giggled at this and Ed had emulated Marge's habitual snoring noises with hilarious accuracy.

"Did you close the door?" Ed asked.

"I didn't open it," Vicky said. "I could hear her from the hallway!"

"We could play bannisters, then," Ed suggested.

"Yes! Bannisters!" Vicky agreed.

"Bannisters!" Penny chimed in hopefully, even though they never let her play bannisters with them.

But Ed had pushed her into her bedroom and shut the door. "You're too little," he said. "You'll only fall and cry and get us into trouble."

Penny quickly became bored in her bedroom, so she sneaked out and headed downstairs past Ed and Vicky to join her mother. If she could accidentally-on-purpose wake her, Marge would hear the noise and stop Ed and Vicky's naughty, exclusive game, she thought.

As she passed by, Ed and Vicky were arguing. They argued a lot. It was nothing unusual.

It was Vicky's turn to slide down the bannisters but she was holding onto the knob at the top and wouldn't let go. "You're a liar," she was saying. "A dirty rotten liar, and you know it."

"It doesn't matter," Ed said, "because Mum will never believe you anyway." Ed then started slapping at Vicky's hands trying to get her to let go. "If you're going to slide, slide," he said, then, "scaredy cat, scaredy cat, Vicky is a scaredy cat."

And so Vicky, who was certainly *not* a scaredy cat, let go of the polished knob and, using her sleeved elbows to guide and slow her descent, let go. But her jumper, which was made of acrylic, gripped the handrail less than she had anticipated, so she reached the end stop with such speed that she bashed her bum against it. Had she not been so determined to prove her bravery, she might have cried.

By the time Vicky had limped back to the landing, Ed was in position. "That was pathetic," he announced.

Vicky shrugged. "You always say that," she said. "You always think you're better at everything, but you're just as useless as everyone else. You're worse, actually."

Ed was sliding back and forth on the bannister like a bobsleigh team preparing to launch. He smiled at Vicky lopsidedly.

"Go on, then," Vicky said. "What are you waiting for?"

"Nothing," Ed said, looking snide.

"What are you doing?" Vicky asked. "Go on!"

Ed half smiled, half sneered at her then. "It's rubbing my willy," he said. "It makes it go all hard like a stick of rock. Cecil's does it too. Do you want to see?"

"Shut up," Vicky said, disgusted even though she didn't quite understand why. "Shut up and slide."

"I might show it to you later on," Ed said, then, in a strange, adult tone of voice she hadn't heard before, he added, "Do you want to lick my stick of rock, Dirty Deirdre?"

Vicky ran at him then, her arms flailing. There was no thought behind her actions, no logic to her moves. She had no apprehension of what might come next. She just wanted Ed to stop saying dirty things to her. She didn't like what he was saying and she needed it to stop, that was all.

"Ah!" Ed laughed, struggling to defend himself against her slaps with one free hand while still holding onto the railing with the other. "Stop! Get off me."

He managed to grab her ponytail, then, and when he yanked at it, it hurt, but as she struggled to twist out of his grasp, his hand came into view, so she bit it. Ed yelped, released her hair, and held his hand up in shock. "You animal!" he said. "You dirty animal!"

And that's when she pushed him. She ran at him with all her might and she pushed him in the chest.

Ed smiled at first. He was falling but he hadn't realised it yet, so he smiled. He thought this was all still funny. And then, as his hands reached for the railings – and missed – his expression changed, so quickly and yet so slowly. He looked amused and then scared, and then as he tipped sideways and, legs kicking, began to fall, as he finally began to vanish from view, he just looked sad.

. . .

"He just looked sad?" Penny repeats.

Victoria, her face wet with tears, nods. "He looked sad. Sort of hopeless. Like he knew. He looked like he knew it was over."

"And you pushed him," Penny says in a monotone voice.

"Yes, I bit his hand and then I pushed him and he fell."

"And then?" Penny asks, even though she doesn't know why she's asking. She's waiting for some thought to manifest but in the meantime it seems that her voice is on autopilot.

"I ran to the landing and I looked down," Victoria whispers. "And when I saw him, I sort of knew he was dead."

"What do you mean you *sort* of knew?"

"There was a lot of blood," Victoria says. "I'm not sure if you remember, but his head hit that knob thing on the end of the bannisters. I'm not sure if I really understood what dead meant back then, but I knew it was over."

"God," Penny says, her voice seemingly still carrying on this conversation of its own accord. "How did that feel?"

"I was horrified," Victoria says. "I was paralysed with the horror of it all. But to be honest, I was glad as well."

"You were *glad*?"

"Yes. I was relieved, I suppose. I was scared of Ed. I had become really very scared of Ed. And I felt glad that it was over, I think."

A shudder works its way through Penny's body as she stares at her sister in silence. Victoria has been crying throughout her story, but until this moment, Penny has been strangely unemotional. But here they come: the emotions are here. Her vision is blurring; her throat is contracting. "So, you pushed him?" she mumbles, uncertainly. "Is that what you're telling me?"

Victoria nods. "Yes," she says. "Yes, I killed him."

Penny's thoughts, so absent just a moment ago, now come all at once, in a rush. So many different, contrasting, at times conflicting thoughts come at once that it feels as if time has slowed down just to fit them all in.

She can sense her inner-self dividing and multiplying like a cell under a microscope, a thousand different Pennys all suddenly present, all thinking different things.

Some of these are professional Pennys. *"No wonder she's so crazy,"* one of them says. *"She's done well, considering what she's been through,"* says another. *"She'll need therapy for the rest of her life,"* says a third. Other voices come from instinctual

Pennys, Pennys who want to leave right now, Pennys who want to run or hide, or hug her sister; Pennys who instead want to slap her hard.

She sits and stares at Victoria's questioning face, and Victoria stares back and waits.

A minute passes and then, yet another different Penny rises up within her, and this one drowns out all of the others. Five-year-old Penny is back, a sweet, uncomprehending little girl who loves her mother, who loves her sister, and who loves her brother, is back, and the sensation of all that love, well, it's heartbreaking.

She's in the lounge, and she can remember everything. The black and white television is there, her mother's knitting has been cast aside. There's a half-empty bottle of sherry and an empty glass on the little table.

Her hand is on the china doorknob, now, and she can feel its cold, shiny surface. Her mother is calling to her, but she's too scared to step out there, she's too frightened to look.

"Go get Cecil!" her mother is crying from the hallway. "Go and get him as fast as you can."

Now she's opening the door, not with urgency, but slowly, with fear, with absolute terror.

Vicky is there looking down at her. She looks cold and waxy, she looks frozen and emotionless. And then she's stepping out into the hallway, turning slowly to look, and now she sees it as she saw it then, because yes, despite what she has told herself ever since, she did see it – she saw everything.

Her mother is there, crouched next to Ed. She is kissing the undamaged side of his face, she is screaming, she is weeping, she is crying, "Ed? Ed, baby? Ed, my baby? Talk to me, Ed? Please, not now, not yet, Ed!"

Her mother is begging them again. She doesn't care who, she says, either she, or Vicky, it doesn't matter, but one of them *must* go quickly to fetch Cecil from the station.

Vicky isn't moving, and her mother is becoming hysterical, so Penny is edging along the hallway, her back pressed to the wall; she's stepping over her mother's feet, she's edging around Ed's splayed arm, she's reaching for the latch on the front door.

And now, with the door before her open, the cold air drifting in, she's turning back to look.

Yes, she remembers it all, now. She remembers the scene perfectly.

It looks like a renaissance oil painting, some still-objective part of Penny's brain thinks. Because there is Vicky in a pink floral dress, a red bobbly jumper, white long socks and shiny black shoes. She's standing halfway up the stairs, one hand delicately placed on the bannister. And there is her mother, lain across the floor, her face tortured like some disciple of Christ, the perfect pleats of her blue Crimplene skirt draped out across the ochre tiles of the hallway. And there is Ed's body, because, no, this is no longer Ed, but his body. She's only five, but she can tell that Ed is no longer present even though she doesn't understand yet quite what that means. His head is at an impossible angle, his body is splayed awkwardly, one side of his face is red and broken, and around him is forming a deep, viscous pool of blood. The quantity, thickness and the deep, dark colour of the liquid surprise her.

And now Marge is looking up at her, shrieking, screaming, "Go! Just go, will you?" And so she turns and steps through the door into the cold sunny daylight where she runs and runs until her lungs smart.

· · ·

Penny turns away from her sister's questioning regard – it has become unbearable to her. She struggles to her feet, wobbles and then finds her balance on the shifting pebbles beneath them.

"Oh God," she says, looking around her now, grasping for an idea of what to do, where to go, what to think.

And now she's running all over again, her feet sinking into the pebbles as she crosses the beach. She's staggering and weeping and running away. She has no destination except *not here*. Anywhere but here.

After thirty yards, she stumbles and, out of breath, falls to her knees where she vomits, unexpectedly, onto the beach.

"How disgusting," a nearby woman on a towel declares, and despite everything else, Penny manages to think, or say (she's not sure if she's thinking or speaking), "You stupid woman!" But then she's on her hands and knees and she's vomiting some more.

Eventually (it must take a while because the woman is gone) she manages to stand. She glances behind her and sees that Victoria is walking towards her slowly, her arms wrapped around herself as if she is cold.

"Don't," Penny tells her, raising one hand in a stop sign. "Just... don't. I need... space."

And now she's running again, just running and running, still farther away from Victoria, still farther away from home, and when eventually she runs out of breath and can run no more, she pauses, her hands on her thighs, and looks back along the vast expanse of beach she has covered. Victoria, she discovers, is nowhere to be seen.

Epilogue

"They're here!" Sander calls out, and Penny, who has just finished preparing the spare room, gives the light-switch a final wipe, then descends one flight of stairs.

On the easel in the bay window, Sander is sketching an outline onto a large canvas. "You're working?" Penny asks. "Today?"

"Not really," Sander says. "I was just doing a bit of prep while we were waiting."

"Right," Penny says, now looking down at the street below where Martin is lifting bags from the back of the BMW. "What's this one going to be of, anyway?"

"A sex-toy party," Sander says. "Women holding vibrators and furry cuffs and stuff."

"Nice," Penny says. "I like it."

Sander puts down his pencil and moves to Penny's side. He slips one arm around her waist. "You *don't* like it," he laughs.

"Oh, don't listen to me," Penny says. "I thought the others sounded horrible, but they're gorgeous, so what do I know?"

"Are you nervous?" Sander asks. "About the reunion?"

"Nah," Penny says. "It'll be fine."

They descend the staircase to find Chloe opening the front door to reveal Martin's beaming face. "Hello people!" he says. Max, in the doorway to the lounge, smiles up at them.

And then Bertie appears, urging Martin forwards, and then behind Bertie, finally, Victoria.

Everyone bustles excitedly into the lounge leaving Penny alone with her on the doorstep. "Hello sister," Victoria says, shyly.

"Hello," Penny replies.

They look into each other's eyes for a moment, then both women sigh simultaneously.

"It's been too long," Penny says, opening her arms for a hug.

"Almost a year," Victoria replies, hugging her rigidly back.

"So, come in," Penny says. "I'll get that kettle on."

The sisters take orders for teas and coffees and cans of Coke and then move to the kitchen to prepare them.

"I don't want to hassle you or anything," Victoria says, once the kettle has been plugged in, "but I was wondering if we could do the ashes thing today? I know that the proper anniversary is tomorrow and everything, but..."

"I had planned to do it tomorrow," Penny confirms, glancing up at her from the line of mugs on the countertop.

"It's just that I'm kind of nervous about it," Victoria says. "So, if we could get it over with, I'd find it easier to relax, I think."

Penny sighs deeply and nods. "There's no reason why not," she says. "It's just you and me anyway, isn't it?"

"I think so," Victoria confirms. "Neither Bertie nor Martin seem overly motivated."

"Then let's have this cuppa and go get it done, yeah?"

"Thanks," Victoria says.

Penny opens the cupboard and reaches in for tea and instant coffee, then returns for a third container, a plastic pot she dumps unceremoniously in front of Victoria. "There you go," she says.

"Um?" Victoria says, reaching out to touch the casket, then freezing. "Oh! That's not her is it?" she asks.

"Yep," Penny says.

"You've been keeping her with the cornflakes?"

Penny shrugs. "We don't have an actual cremains cupboard," she says, "so this seemed as good as anywhere."

The children are excited to see each other after such a long, enforced break. They fill the lounge with noise, and it is Chloe, for once, who seems the most enthusiastic.

But once the two women find themselves alone in Penny's car, the conversation becomes stilted.

Desperate for this reunion to go well, both women are walking on egg shells, and both feel unexpectedly shy in the other's presence.

It's not until they reach the Thanet Way that anyone dares speak. "How long's the drive to Margate?" Victoria asks, more to break the silence than anything. "About an hour?"

"A bit less," Penny says. "But if we're doing this on the jetty we have to drive right into town."

"Maybe we could park up by the old house and walk in?" Victoria suggests.

"Sure," Penny says. "It's a nice enough day for it."

They drive in silence for a few more minutes until Victoria speaks again. "I was so relieved when you contacted me," she says. "I may even have cried a bit when I got your email."

Penny glances across at her and smiles sadly. "I may even have cried a bit when I wrote it," she says.

"Did you?"

Penny nods. "I'm sorry it took so long. But I needed time to sort my head out."

"I know," Victoria says. "I understand. I understood at the time. Even if you had never wanted to speak to me again, I would have understood, you know."

"It wasn't against you. I just had so much stuff to work through," Penny says. "That was the thing."

"Can I have one of these?" Victoria asks, brandishing a packet of mints she has found in the door pocket.

"Sure," Penny says, holding out one hand. "I'll have one too."

Penny sucks her mint for a bit then continues, "I'm not sure if you remember it, but you once told Will that you felt like you were living in a big dark cave."

Victoria nods. "Yes, I remember that," she says. "It was when we were trying to understand what had got into Bertie."

"Right," Penny says. "Well, the thing was, I *didn't* feel like that. I thought all the corners of my life were quite well-lit really. I thought I had it all worked out. I'd done all my processing during my training, and everything seemed tickety-boo."

"Well, it was, wasn't it?"

"Well it *seemed* that way. But then you sort of opened this curtain and all this light shone into the corners and I suddenly realised that I was living in a room full of horrors after all. Does that make any sense?"

"Maybe," Victoria says.

"There were all these things tucked away in the corners, things I thought I'd dealt with and hadn't – like Ed's death – and all these memories I'd completely repressed. And suddenly it was all visible. It was all in the room with me. And the only way to cope with it was to take the time to have a good spring clean to sort it all out."

"Yes, I get that," Victoria says.

"I had to go back over everything," Penny explains, now glancing in the rearview mirror as she indicates to overtake a lorry. "I had to go back into proper therapy, you know."

"I thought you never stopped," Victoria says. "I thought that went with the job."

"Oh, we have supervision, but that's only for work stuff really. No, I had to go to two sessions a week for six months just to work through it all."

"What did your shrink think about your murderous sister?" Victoria asks bravely.

"I wouldn't know, really," Penny says. "He's not the chatty type. But I wouldn't suppose he considered you responsible any more than I do."

"Only, I was."

"You were seven," Penny says.

"Eight."

"OK, you were eight. And he was threatening you. And you pushed him in a game. That's hardly murder in the first degree, is it?"

"I don't know," Victoria says. "I thought of turning myself in at one point. But there didn't seem to be any point. I couldn't see how anyone would gain anything by it."

"The police would have laughed you out of the station," Penny says. "They have way more important things to deal with than you and your guilty conscience."

"I sort of imagined myself getting judged for manslaughter. I used to fantasise about the trial."

"It wouldn't even be manslaughter," Penny says. "It would be accidental death."

"That's kind of you," Victoria says, now turning to look out of the side window. "I thought of going after Cecil too. Of telling the police or something. But I was never quite sure enough of myself. And now it seems a bit late."

Penny can tell from her voice that she is on the verge of tears. "It is a bit, I suppose. I don't know. But you know one of the things *I* had to work on was that I had always thought that *I* was responsible for Ed's death," Penny tells her. "I thought that if only I had brought Cecil back he might have survived."

"But that's crazy," Victoria says.

"Yes. I know. And for you to think you did anything other than give him a silly push is crazy too."

They drive in silence for a few minutes and then Penny asks, "So, what about you? Are you seeing anyone, shrink-wise?"

Victoria smiles and turns back to face her. "I'm seeing four!" she says.

"Four?"

"Yes. I'm still seeing Muller – he's quite good actually. And there's family counselling with Martin and Bertie – that's Wednesday nights. There's a guy at the hospital helping me with my OCD stuff and another one for the Valium. He's more of an addiction specialist really, but he can be quite shrinky too."

"Shrinky," Penny says. "I like that. And it's helping?"

"It is, actually," Victoria says. "I feel much, much better. And I'm almost off the Valium now, so that's good."

"That's great," Penny says.

"The HRT helped masses too," Victoria tells her. "That changed everything, really. I think the menopause thing was quite profound for me, in the end. I wasn't prepared at all and it sent me into a sort of emotional tailspin. I was sleeping about three hours a night at one point, and just that made me feel quite mad."

"Yes, lack of sleep will do that," Penny says. "I've been discussing it with mine. But he's not a big fan of HRT."

"He," Victoria repeats, with meaning.

"Yes, I hear you," Penny says. "But it hasn't been too bad so far. So, I'm OK, really. But if it gets worse, don't worry, I'll be on the phone to your specialist woman in a hot flash."

"She is really good," Victoria says.

"You didn't even see what I did there, did you?"

"I did," Victoria says, smiling wryly. "It just wasn't that funny. Is that really her?"

"Is who really who?"

"Oh, sorry," Victoria says. "I mean, Mum, in there." She points to the plastic urn which Penny has stowed in the drinks carrier of the car. "Do you think it's really her or do they just fill it with a bit of random ash from the whole day's takings?"

"I assume it's her," Penny says. "But I can't say I'm bothered either way."

"No," Victoria says. "No, it's more symbolic really, isn't it?"

They park the car in Garfield Road, right outside their old front door.

"This is weird, isn't it?" Victoria says, leaning back against the car and looking up at the facade. "It still has the same rose bushes in the front garden."

"Yes," Penny agrees. "They haven't even changed the colour of the front door. Do you want to go in? We could knock and ask. They might let us snoop around."

Victoria wrinkles her nose. "No," she says. "No, there's nothing good for me in there. Let's walk."

Penny slips the casket into her handbag and the two women cross Canterbury Road and head down towards the seafront.

It's a warm August day and the breeze is gentle, but both the sky and the sea are a uniform grey colour.

"So, how are your two?" Victoria asks as they descend the steps to the promenade. "Chloe seemed full of beans."

"She did, didn't she?" Penny laughs. "You know, I'll let you in on a secret. I think she's intending to turn Bertie into her gay best friend. She suddenly considers him quite exotic."

"I'm not surprised," Victoria says. "We're all jealous of you and your Will."

"Ah," Penny says. "Yes, I didn't think of that one. Like mother, like daughter, eh? They're getting married, you know."

"Will and Ben? Is he still with Ben?"

"Yes. In October. Will wanted to do it in August, but Ben – you know how that boy likes to dress up – well, he thought they'd all be too hot for a formal do in August, so October it is. Do you want to come? I could try to get you an invite, maybe. It'll be a riot, I expect."

Victoria shakes her head. "Will's lovely," she says. "And he's always been kind to me. He was *great* when all that Bertie stuff was kicking off, too. But no, he's your friend, not mine. I *am* jealous though."

"Well, he's special. They both are."

"And Max is OK?"

"Fine," Penny says. "We're waiting for his GCSE results, and Max is being all dramatic, of course, and saying he's failed everything. But we think he's done fine. He wants to do fashion design, he reckons, so it'll be A-levels next."

"Fashion design? He's not gay as well, is he?"

Penny laughs. "No, he's on his third girlfriend in six months. He just likes clothes. He talks to Ben for hours about it and Ben has started bringing him stuff. He's turning into a right little dandy."

As the promenade rises past the site of the old sun-deck, Margate's only tower block, Arlington House, comes into view. "I had a boyfriend who lived there," Victoria says. "Do you remember?"

"I do," Penny replies. "Wayne something, right?"

"Very good, Pen. Wayne Ellis. Lord, he was chavvy."

"I remember," Penny says. "Imagine if you'd settled down with him. You'd probably still be living there."

"I'd be dead, probably," Victoria says. "He got into heroin or so I heard."

"And how's Martin?" Penny asks.

"Oh, Martin's fine."

"What ever..." Penny starts.

"Yes?"

"Actually, never mind."

"No, go on?"

"It's just, well... is everything all right with you two, now?"

"All right?"

"Yes, you said you had doubts..." Penny says.

"Did I?"

"Yes. Anyway, never mind," Penny says. She looks out to sea and pulls a face. She had forgotten briefly she was supposed to be walking on egg shells.

"I remember that I had doubts," Victoria says. "I'm not denying it. I just don't remember telling you about them, that's all."

"Oh, well, you did."

"Right. Well, it doesn't matter, anyway. There wasn't anything going on in the end."

"Oh, good. That must have been a relief."

"Oh, it was. He was working late, that's the thing. And I couldn't work out where he was. But it turned out that he was doing all this pro bono stuff for some charity. You'd approve. For Syrian refugees and the like. He helps them with their asylum petitions."

"Really?" Penny laughs. "Martin?"

"I know," Victoria says. "No one could be more surprised than I was."

"Gosh. That does surprise me."

"We had this really bizarre conversation when I found out. Because I always thought Martin was really quite right wing," Victoria explains. "And it turns out he isn't at all. I think he voted for Thatcher when she first got in or something, but that's about the end of it."

"That must have led to some pretty heated discussions," Penny says. "I mean, what with you being slightly to the right of Attila The Hun."

"Yes, it did," Victoria says. "I had to talk about it with Muller actually. Because the truth is – and this is a bit embarrassing, so don't tell anyone, OK?"

"Of course not."

"But the truth is that I don't have a political bone in my body. I just try to fit in, really, because I'm too lazy to think about any of it. Actually, it's not even laziness. It's that I don't believe in any of it. I think they're all crooks. But I was just trying to fit in with Martin, I think. Well, I was trying to fit in with what I thought he was. It just seemed easier. But in a way, he was pretending too. He was pretending to agree with me.

So he didn't dare tell me about the pro bono work, because he thought I wouldn't approve. Which is so silly. Anyway, now Martin's all out and proud about being a Labour Party member – he really likes that Corbyn guy actually, but I think he's probably just as bad as all the rest. Or at least, he would be if he ever got into power. But like I said, what do I know?"

"Wow," Penny says. "All those arguments we had."

"I know," Victoria says. "I just keep my mouth shut these days. It's actually quite a relief not feeling like I have to have an opinion on everything. What about yours?"

"Sander?"

"Yeah."

"Oh, he's doing well. He's doing these amazing paintings of these really strange contemporary subjects like shelf-stackers and Tupperware parties. And he developed this incredible technique – it's something to do with working from Photoshop, you'll have to ask him. Anyway, from a distance they look like photos, sort of renaissance photos, if such a thing existed – all dark around the edges and glowy in the middle. And close to, they look completely abstract. He'll show you when we get back. You just have to promise to be positive about them, even if you don't like them. Don't knock him off his stride, because he's hoping for an exhibition next year. I love them, anyway. I think they're stunning, actually."

They have reached the jetty, now, and as they walk past a vast, white hut, Penny says, "The Turner Contemporary. Margate's on the up, you know. Maybe Sander will have an exhibition there one day."

"Is *that* the Turner museum?" Victoria asks. "I thought it was supposed to be some majestuous pebble thing rising from the seabed. I thought it was going to rival Bilbao in Spain."

"It was," Penny says. "But all the money vanished as I recall. So they built a big white shed instead. It's supposed to be good, I think. Sander went, and he liked it. But, well, this is Margate, not Bilbao."

"Right," Victoria says. "Well, of course."

When the women reach the end of the jetty, they stand and look out to sea. It's all still grey, but somehow rather pretty all the same.

"Do you remember when the hovercraft used to come in and land on the beach?" Victoria asks.

Penny nods and smiles tightly. "Yes, it used to blow sand over everything, didn't it?"

"It did," Victoria confirms. "We always used to go and watch it and it always blew sand in our eyes, but we went back all the same."

Penny sighs deeply and reaches inside her handbag. "So, are we doing this?" she asks, pulling out the plastic casket.

"I guess so," Victoria says. "But work out which way the wind is blowing first. Because in films, it's always the cinders that blow back in everyone's faces, isn't it?"

"That's true," Penny says, sucking her finger and holding it up to test the wind's direction. "But I think we're OK. I think it's going that way," she says, pointing out to sea. "Do you want to say any words?"

Victoria shrugs. "I can say them in my head if you want," she says. "I don't want to upset you. I don't want to spoil your moment."

"It's fine," Penny tells her. "It's like... what was it they called it in South Africa? After whats-his-name, Mandela, got out?"

"I have no idea what you're on about, I'm afraid," Victoria says.

"Oh, truth and reconciliation," Penny says. "That's it. So go for it. This is our moment of truth and reconciliation. Or do you want me to go first?"

"No," Victoria says. "No, I'll go first. That way we can end on yours... we can end on a high note."

Penny gestures theatrically towards the horizon. "The stage is yours," she says.

"Um, hi, Mum," Victoria starts, feeling a little silly addressing a seascape. "Oh, do we throw the cinders before or after?" she asks, looking around to check that no one is watching.

"After, I reckon," Penny says.

"OK then, I'll try again."

"It's fine. Just take your time."

"Hi Mum," Victoria says, through a sigh. "It's me. I..." Her voice begins to wobble and her eyes start to tear up as she continues. "I'm really... *angry* with you, Mum. I'm really, really angry with you. I was eight, for God's sake. I was only eight and my dad was dead and you were the only person I could rely upon. Well, *thought* I could rely upon. And what about Ed, Mum? He was eleven! And I came to you, it took all my courage to tell you the truth, but we needed your help, and you didn't believe me. Your own daughter, Mum. And you didn't believe me! I was the most scared I've ever been and the most vulnerable too. And I needed your help, I needed you to protect me. I needed you to protect Ed. And you didn't. You didn't do anything. Because it was easier for you, you chose just not to believe me. And I've hated you my whole life for that. So, I'm not maybe as sad as I should be. Goodbye, Mum."

Victoria pinches her nose, sniffs and turns to face Penny. "That's enough," she says. "I'm done. That covers it."

"Right," Penny says, wide-eying her sister. "So, um, Mum." She clears her throat. "I miss you so much. I'm really angry too as it happens. There are things I didn't know about, things I didn't want to know, perhaps, or things I was too little to understand. But I'm really upset now I know; I'm really angry about what happened to my sister and my brother. It was all, ultimately, uncle Cecil's fault, I suppose. But it was yours a bit, too, Mum. You were, like Vicky said, our only parent. We depended on you. And though, admittedly, you did pretty well with me, I agree you let Ed and Vicky down quite badly."

Penny pulls a face and turns to Victoria. "Is this too much like a court case?" she asks, suddenly self-conscious. "I seem to be sounding more and more like Judge Judy."

Victoria shakes her head. "It's fine. Just get it over with."

"OK," Penny says. "So... what do I want to say? I suppose that, despite all of that, and this is perhaps selfish of me, but despite all of that, those aren't my memories of you, Mum. I remember all the good times, still. I remember baking cakes in that freezing kitchen and stuffing newspapers around the edges of the windows. I remember lighting candles with you during the electricity strike and you teaching me to knit when I was pregnant with Max. And even when you were old and grumpy, even when all you talked about was your bad back or that woman in the housing place that you didn't like, you were still *there*, Mum, and I liked that. Even when I didn't call you, I liked the fact that you were there, on the end of the phone. And now you're not there, are you? And I miss you. I miss you so much. So bye, Mum. This is it."

Penny swipes the tears away from the corners of her eyes and then turns to look at Victoria. "Ready?" she asks.

Victoria nods.

Penny unscrews the lid and steps forwards as she up-ends the casket. The cinders fall in a dusty column and with surprising speed, straight towards the sea below. "Oh! Should I have saved you some?" Penny asks, disconsolately peering inside the empty receptacle.

"No," Victoria laughs, touching her shoulder. "No, it's fine. It's done. Come on."

She slides one arm around her little sister's shoulders and turns her around so they're facing the shore. And then slowly, very slowly, they begin to walk.

Penny finds herself glancing back towards the end of the jetty as if, perhaps, she might catch one last glimpse of her mother in the departure lounge.

"Shall we get an ice cream on the seafront?" Penny asks, after a moment.

"Yes," Victoria says. "Yes, I think I could do with the sugar after that. I feel quite light-headed."

"Do you remember when Mum used to take us for '99' ice creams when she got paid?" Penny asks.

"Yes, I do," Victoria says. "With a chocolate flake sticking out, right?"

"And Dreamland? At the end of the season they used to have a special cheap day and Mum used to take us all?"

"I do," Victoria says. "Ed used to go on the Scenic Railway on his own. He liked to sit at the back where it was most scary, where the train lifted off the tracks. And then I'd go on with Mum while Ed looked after you."

"I was too short, wasn't I?" Penny says. "They had a chart on the wall and you had to be a certain height. I hated that chart."

"That's right. I'd forgotten that."

"But Ed used to buy me candy floss while you were on it which kind of made it all right."

"And I used to hide my face in Mum's chest the whole ride through, because I was too scared to look. 'What's the point?' she used to say. 'What's the point if you're not even going to look.' But I loved being scared. I loved the Scenic Railway."

"Is that why you took Bertie to Blackpool when she died? Were you thinking about when Mum used to take us to Dreamland?"

"I'm not sure," Victoria says. "Not consciously. I'm not sure where that idea came from really. I just wanted to be a long way away from everything and I'd read a thing about that big roller coaster somewhere. But maybe *sub*consciously." She shrugs.

"And what about the cinema on Saturday mornings?" Penny says, nodding towards where the Dreamland cinema used to be. "Do you remember that?"

"Mum used to make us change seats all the time. Anytime there was someone with big hair or a smoker we had to move."

"God, smoking in cinemas!" Penny says. "I'd completely forgotten."

"Unimaginable nowadays. But she was so annoying making us move all the time."

"Yes," Penny says. "I suppose Mum didn't want us breathing in a load of secondhand smoke. I suppose at least she got that right."

Victoria has stopped walking, and Penny now spins around to look back at her. "Vicky?" she says. "What is it?"

"Can I do mine again?" Victoria asks, doubtfully. "Do you think that's possible?"

"Do what?"

"My words."

"Oh, if you want," Penny says, with a shrug. "There are no rules, after all. Do you want to do them here, or do you want to go back?"

"Let's go back," Victoria says. "It'll only take a second, won't it?"

At the end of the jetty Victoria looks out to sea. She takes a deep breath and straightens her posture. A gust of breeze blows her hair across her eyes, so she reaches up and tucks it behind her ears. She looks, Penny thinks, somehow clever and noble and wise. She looks beautiful, in fact. Penny seemed to have forgotten that fact.

"So, Mum," she says. "I don't feel like I was fair to you just now." She glances at Penny beside her who has fresh tears visibly welling up in her eyes. Penny nods gently at her to continue.

"It was true, what I said. I'm not taking anything back," Victoria says. "But I know that if you're there somewhere, then you understand now. And I know that you'll be sorry about all that. And for all that it was bad, and for all that it was true, that wasn't the whole story, was it, Mum? We both know that. So thanks for taking me to Dreamland once a year as well. It must have been really hard for you when Dad died, and as a kid I never thought about that much, I suppose. So yes, thanks for going to work every day, and thanks for feeding us ginger nuts and custard for dinner. Thanks for mending my clothes and thanks for taking us to the cinema even when we didn't have money for the electricity meter. And thanks for not letting me breathe in second-hand cigarette smoke. And thanks, above all, I suppose, for never hunting Cecil down after he left that day, even when things were hard, even when we were broke, even when we were going to lose the house. You let me down, Mum, you really did. But you had your good moments, too. And despite everything that happened, and every insult that got thrown at me, and despite all my pretending otherwise, yes, I did love you, Mum. And amazingly, despite it all, I miss you like crazy as well."

Victoria blows out slowly through pursed lips then turns to face Penny. "Truth and reconciliation," she says. "I'm done."

Penny opens her arms. "Come here," she says, and Victoria steps forward into her embrace.

"I do love you, you know," Penny says. "I don't say it enough, but I do."

"Me too," Victoria replies.

"Let's never fall out again, eh?" Penny says.

Victoria snorts. "Like that's not going to happen."

"OK, then let's never fall out for long, all right?"

"OK," Victoria says. "It's a deal."

Penny opens her bag and removes the plastic casket so that she can reach her tissues below. She hands one to Victoria and uses the other to dab at her own eyes. "I'm so glad I didn't put makeup on," she says.

"Mine's waterproof," Victoria tells her, pointing at her own face. And Penny doesn't dare tell her that it has run all the same, she doesn't dare tell her that she has panda eyes.

"What am I supposed to do with this, do you think?" Penny asks, lifting the plastic casket into view.

"Here," Victoria says, taking it from her and crossing the jetty briskly, then dropping it into a litter bin.

When she gets back, Penny is looking shocked.

"Hey, relax," Victoria says. "It's a plastic, screw-top container. Life goes on."

Penny peers past her at the litter bin and shrugs. "I suppose so," she says doubtfully.

Victoria takes her arm and spins her back towards the shore. "Ice cream, little sister?" she asks, as they start to walk.

"Definitely, big sister," Penny replies. "And mine's a ninety-nine."

"Un quatre-vingt-dix-neuf," Victoria says.

"I'm sorry?"

"Oh, you don't know, do you? I'm learning French."

"No, when did that happen?"

"A few months back. We were talking about how staid our lives have got, and came up with this crazy idea, once Bertie leaves home... Martin thought he might take a year out or something. We thought we might go and live in France for a bit. Well, if we're still allowed to, with all this Brexit nonsense."

"Oh, that would be amazing, Vicky. Where would you go?"

"I don't know yet. Down south, maybe. Somewhere sunny, anyway. But it's something to look forward to, isn't it? We all need something to look forward to. Then maybe you could come and visit *us* for a change?"

"The south of France?" Penny says. "God, I'm already there."

THE END

Also by Nick Alexander

The Other Son

Selected by Amazon as one of the best fiction titles of 2015.

Alice has been lying to herself for years, holding fast to the belief that the needs of her family far outweigh her own.

But her outwardly successful marriage hides dark secrets, and for much of her life, the children were the only reason she stuck around.

These days, though her successful banker son lives nearby, his young wife seems to do everything she can to keep Alice at bay. As for Alice's other son, he has always been something of a stranger and has been traveling for so long that Alice isn't even sure what continent he is on anymore.

Alice can't help but wonder if the effort she expends presenting a united front to the outside world is actually helping anyone and what would happen if she suddenly stopped pretending.

Could life, like the novels she devours, hold surprises in its closing chapters?

And if she did shake everything up by admitting the truth about her marriage, would anyone be on her side? Has the time finally come for Alice to put her own needs first?

For the first time in years, her heart is racing. Can Alice really change her life? Dare she even imagine such a thing?

Also available from Nick Alexander

The Photographer's Wife

A number #1 ebook hit in the UK and France.
Over 200,000 copies sold.

From the author of *The French House*, *The Half-Life of Hannah* and *The Case of The Missing Boyfriend*, Nick Alexander's #1 bestseller, *The Photographer's Wife*, is an epic tale set in two eras, a tale of the secrets one generation has, rightly or wrongly, chosen to hide from the next."

Barbara – a child of the Blitz – has more secrets than she cares to admit. She has protected her children from many of the harsh realities of life and told them little of the poverty of her childhood, nor of the darker side of her marriage to one of Britain's most famous photographers.

With such an incomplete picture of the past, her youngest, Sophie, has struggled to understand who her parents really are, and in turn, Barbara sometimes worries, to build her own identity. When Sophie decides to organise a vast retrospective exhibition of her adored father's work, old photos are pulled from dusty boxes. But with them tumble stories from the past, stories and secrets that will challenge every aspect of how Sophie sees her parents.

Lightning Source UK Ltd.
Milton Keynes UK
UKOW01f2336020117
291259UK00004B/193/P

9 782919 595372